A Keepsake Love

by

Jean Jegel

Published by Emery Press at Kindle Direct Publishing

ISBN: 978-1-7324119-4-4

Copyright © 2019 by Jean Jegel

Discover other titles by Jean Jegel at www.jeanjegel.com

Scripture quotations from The Authorized (King James) Version. Rights in the Authorized Version in the United Kingdom are vested in the Crown. Reproduced by permission of the Crown's patentee, Cambridge University Press Read more at: http://www.cambridge.org/bibles/about/rights-and-permissions/#bxs1vegcPkJMbMpk.99

Cover by Dave Simmons

To Ethan, Jadyn, Olivia and Alexa

With love

Grandchildren are the true joy in life

PART I – 1919

Chapter One

"Don't you find constant supervision rather tedious?" Sumner stared out the window of his father's brand new, red Buick limousine. It was a glorious fall day in Los Angeles, but the mild temperature and warm sunshine did nothing to cheer Sumner Hemmings.

"The pleasure is all mine, Sonny," Merritt Hemmings replied. He reviewed paperwork while the chauffeur wove through traffic.

Sumner frowned. He detested his childhood nickname and repeatedly requested his parents refer to him as Sumner, to no avail. "You haven't been leaving the bank this early. Is there some reason I am deemed especially untrustworthy today?"

"Your recent escapades signal my failure to keep the promise I made your mother. After all, she sent you here so I could encourage mature and responsible behavior."

"If you believe chaining me to the teller position in your bank and keeping me to your ridiculous stipend is going to change my life, I think you and Mother are being rather obtuse. I am a grown man after all."

Merritt chuckled. "It's important you have a thorough knowledge of every aspect of banking operations. Starting your career as a teller not only provides a working knowledge of the bank, it allows you to gain the respect of the employees. You will run the bank at some point. It's my duty to prepare you for that eventuality."

Having listened to endless recitations of his father's plans, Sumner sulked. "I can simply leave, you understand?"

This comment drew a guffaw from his father. "We all know you won't."

"I left before."

"That may be, but you certainly didn't hesitate to take up the good life in New York when you returned from the war. How many of your friends never returned?"

"We've been over this before," Sumner disgustedly replied.

"There will be no repeat of your drunken spree of last Saturday, am I clear? Drinking is illegal in this city. No doubt it will soon be illegal in the entire country. The last thing I desire is to write your mother with news of your incarceration."

Sumner continued to gaze out the window. The multi-storied buildings of downtown gave way to more modest structures. Ever-present palm trees poked above rooflines. The road was no longer jammed with automobiles fighting for space with trolley cars. It was rare to see a horse on the streets of Los Angeles although horses still pulled fire wagons. Familiar olive trees marked the Los Feliz area where Merritt Hemmings made his home.

A sudden longing for the camaraderie of the war washed over Sumner. "You've forgotten, drinking beer and wine in restaurants is completely legal, at least this week." Secret, underground bars in the city flourished since saloons were forced to close last year, a fact Sumner refrained to mention.

"Take this paperwork," Merritt demanded. "We're going next door so you can meet Mrs. Argyle. I recently updated her trust, and I want you to familiarize yourself with our more important customers."

Sumner reluctantly took the paperwork. It meant nothing to him.

"Mrs. Argyle is a wealthy widow who manages her late husband's business. She's a lovely woman. We don't see as much of her as we would like because she often travels for work."

"So, she's a romantic interest?"

"Hardly. I am a married man, after all."

Sumner snorted in derision. "I don't know if I would qualify your relationship as a marriage. You and Mother live on opposite ends of the country. When did you last lay eyes on each other? I'm guessing five years?"

"Your mother and I have different interests. She finds California boorish and pedestrian. My business is here."

"Yes, conveniently located as far from your wife as you could manage. Perhaps you could start a bank in Hawaii and put an ocean between you as well. I actually might like it there. No threat of prohibition, just endless days on pristine beaches and perfect weather. Perhaps I'll start a bank in Honolulu. And by the way, I agree—any city that shuts down all its saloons is quite boorish."

"I hate to tell you, but Hawaii went dry last year. You best find a different location for your bank. Here we are. Alfred, let us out in front of Mrs. Argyle's home. Behave yourself, Sonny, or you'll find your stipend further reduced."

* * *

"Mrs. Argyle, you have guests," announced Dorothy, the downstairs maid.

"Oh dear, who is it?"

"The neighbor, Mr. Hemmings, and a nice-looking young gentleman."

"Show them into the front parlor and serve tea. Let them know I'll be right in."

Sighing deeply, Mary Argyle turned back to the invoices on her writing desk. She intensely disliked being home. Tedious work always waited there. She much preferred traveling, searching for the fine artwork that made her business successful. Circumstances prevented her from living and working in New York—her true regret—but such was the way of life. There was less competition in Los Angeles although she considered it something of a backwater.

As Mary pushed her chair from the desk and headed for the parlor, she considered the burgeoning motion picture business might bring Los Angeles the importance it currently lacked. The newly rich from that industry were easily duped into believing her expensive wares could provide the culture they so obviously lacked.

"Mr. Hemmings," Mary gushed, walking into her tastefully appointed parlor as both men stood. "So good to see you. I assume you finished the work on my trust?"

"Yes. Let me introduce my son, Sumner, who's taken a position at the bank. He's living with me until he becomes established."

Sumner took Mrs. Argyle's hand and displayed his most charming smile. "Lovely to meet you."

"Nice to meet you as well. Have a seat, gentlemen." Mary quickly judged the young man. She had a talent for categorizing men and was quite accurate if she did say so herself. Although she had nothing but respect for the elder Mr. Hemmings—a kind man no doubt married to his work—the younger Mr. Hemmings was definitely trouble. She'd seen his type before—irresponsible and bold almost beyond tolerance. Such was often the case with young men.

An uncharacteristically clumsy Dorothy spilled a bit of cream on the young Mr. Hemmings' hand while offering to flavor his tea. The man calmly used a napkin he was offered to wipe the spill but then stood.

"This is a bit sticky," he noted. "Would you mind if I washed my hands?"

"Straight down the hallway," Mrs. Argyle offered. "Dorothy, would you show him the way?"

"I'm certain I can manage. Thank you."

After Sumner washed his hands and started for the parlor, his attention was taken by movement in the backyard. Stopping to take a closer look through the conservatory window, he gasped in surprise. Beneath the large oak tree that separated his father's property from Mrs. Argyle's sat the most breathtaking woman Sumner had ever seen. Her features seemed beyond perfection. Blond tresses curled on top of her head. Her long, slender neck supported a finely-boned face with flawless skin, crystal blue eyes, a delicate nose and bow mouth. Likely too large for her petite face, she wore a pair of horn-rimmed, round spectacles.

Intent upon a book, the woman primly turned a

page as she sat in the shade, oblivious to her admirer. The lush garden paled in comparison to her beauty.

"Who is the young woman in the garden?" Sumner interrupted as he strode through the parlor doorway.

Merritt scowled at his son's rudeness while Mrs. Argyle explained, "That's my niece, Madeleine Crawford, the subject of the trust you delivered."

Sumner would have to take a better look at the trust. "Oh, of course," he replied, suggesting he understood completely. "Perhaps I should introduce myself."

Mrs. Argyle could not imagine a less agreeable end to her afternoon. "I'm so sorry. Surely, you understand my niece is not well."

"Certainly, but it couldn't hurt if I—"

"It could indeed, hurt. My niece cannot converse. She's not able. It would prove distressing if you appeared in her garden. She is—quite simple-minded," Mrs. Argyle explained with honest regret.

"I see." What a waste of beauty thought Sumner as he made himself busy with his tea. But the glimpse of loveliness in the garden was a significant distraction. It would prove his complete undoing.

* * *

As the days dragged on, Sumner alleviated his boredom with thoughts of Madeleine sitting in her garden. Returning from work each day, he rushed upstairs to his bedroom, which overlooked Mrs. Argyle's yard. After throwing open his window, Sumner stood back to be certain Miss Crawford's curiosity was not aroused, then manned his personal observation post, attempting to catch a peek of his fantasy woman. He realized she was a fantasy albeit one with a face—such a beautiful face.

He imagined how her voice might sound and daydreamed about conversations they could have. Sumner recognized his life had dissolved to an all-time low if his greatest joy was covert observation of a mentally deficient woman. His understanding failed to deter this activity, however.

Almost every afternoon, Madeleine read, did needlework or drew in the garden. Sumner never saw her interact with any other person. He wondered what kind of books she pored over. Were they full of pictures? Something that would interest a child? They did not appear to be. Never able to glimpse her drawings, Sumner contemplated borrowing his father's binoculars to satisfy his curiosity. This activity smacked of impropriety. He wasn't exactly sure why.

Occasionally, Madeleine walked through the garden, clipping flowers. Although he enjoyed the way she moved—she was graceful and petite—this activity signaled her return to the indoors which disappointed him no end. He felt rather pathetic at this realization.

She sometimes sat at a table under the huge live oak. He had the vague idea she painted. His attempts to preview her work on the flat surface met with failure. The leaves and branches were too thick to afford him an adequate view, even from his window near the tree.

Sumner believed Madeleine dressed in the most current designs which seemed something of a waste, although her aunt could certainly afford it. No fashion expert, Sumner's sole, serious interest in women's clothing was how to take it off.

Since fall days were growing short, Sumner raced to balance his work at the bank in order to leave early.

Fortunately, his father took this activity as newfound maturity and devotion to business. Happy to substitute his own work for vigilance of his son, Merritt did not notice when Sonny took advantage.

Sumner left home early on Saturdays, returning well after his father's traditional bedtime. This meant Sumner could frequent his new favorite haunt, The King Eddie Saloon. The original saloon became a respectable piano store while a nearby outside stairwell delivered customers to the basement.

A huge network of tunnels existed beneath Los Angeles, enabling saloons and liquor salesmen to do business out of sight of the general populace. Sumner was a realist and not surprised the police department— subject of countless vice investigations—was complicit in the illegal selling of hard liquor.

Disappointed when congress passed the Volstead Act over President Wilson's veto, Sumner contemplated his current illegal activity was probably the most exciting thing in his life—the most exciting real thing.

Badly hung over one Sunday morning, Sumner dressed and crept to his window to see if the lovely neighbor was ensconced in her yard. Perhaps her perfect features would serve to brighten his day. He hoped she wore her red gingham dress. It was his favorite and showed off Madeleine's modest curves to perfection.

Peering out the window, Sumner believed she did, indeed, have on the red dress. Madeleine was barely visible, seated beneath the tree. Frustrated at the way his head hurt and disappointed at his inability to observe, Sumner decided to crawl out the window onto a tree branch to have a better view. If he was slow and cautious so as not to cause the branch to quaver, he might satisfy his curiosity and discover what Madeleine accomplished at her table.

Gingerly swinging first one leg then the other out his window as he sat on the sill, Sumner grabbed the branch above for support and inched his way toward the trunk of the tree. Looking down in his recently inebriated state, his head began to spin.

When Sumner tried for a firmer grasp, his foot slipped off the limb, and he plummeted toward earth as if in slow motion. Strange thoughts came to his mind. He saw men fall from shattered or burning aircraft during the war and always wondered what they thought, knowing their lives were over. He imagined they prayed, but the trip toward earth must have seemed either inordinately long or much too short. Could one enjoy the ride down while it lasted?

Before he knew it, he was lying on the ground. His beautiful angel appeared above his face. He was certain he could reach up and touch her perfect, creamy cheek if only he could move his arm.

"Sir, are you all right?" spoke the vision.

Try as he might to answer, Sumner's eyes closed as he surrendered consciousness.

* * *

Having eclipsed his father in height at 14 years of age, it seemed especially annoying when Sumner looked up at the man from his prone position in bed and asked, "What did the doctor say?"

"You are incredibly lucky. Nothing appears to be broken."

"I assure you, absolutely everything hurts."

"I can't say I have much sympathy for you. What

the hell were you doing in that tree?"

For this, he had no explanation. Sumner pursed his lips, which also caused pain. He could not conceive of any lie to support a claim of sanity on his part. "Is Miss Crawford quite all right? I saw her in the yard." A change of subject seemed a wise choice.

"No, she is not. You nearly scared her to death when you fell out of the tree at her feet. The doctor placed her on complete bedrest."

"She didn't seem alarmed when she spoke to me."

"What are you saying? The woman can't speak. You hit your head. You were hallucinating."

"No. Before I passed out, she clearly asked if I was all right. Her voice sounded amazingly as I imagined it would. She seemed quite coherent; completely articulate."

"You obviously were not lucid. You are imagining things, Sonny. You can't even work. Your face looks as if you've been in a brawl. The doctor advised you must stay in bed for the next three days and give yourself a chance to heal."

"But I heard her—"

"I will have no more of this, none of it, do you understand? No more climbing trees; no more talk of Miss Crawford. This is your last chance. I am perturbed beyond measure. When you return to work on Thursday, I expect nothing but dignity and attention to every detail of your job." At this, the elder Mr. Hemmings made an abrupt departure.

"Thank heaven," Sumner said aloud. If that was all his father spoke of his escapade, he had gotten off lightly. His mind immediately turned to thoughts of Madeleine Crawford. She seemed normal in every way. Something was terribly wrong. What sort of game was being played next door?

Sumner managed to crawl out of bed in the afternoon to take a look out his window. As his father advised, there was no sign of Madeleine. He picked up a book, but the vision of his neighbor, so close he could touch her perfect face, made it impossible to read. He was certain he hadn't been hallucinating.

If the lovely Miss Crawford was actually able to read, Sumner decided there was no reason he couldn't send a missive next door. If she wasn't able, surely someone would read his note to her. He considered how he might apologize. By Tuesday afternoon, he constructed an acceptable if somewhat improper message:

Dear Miss Crawford,

My sincerest apologies. I am concerned my rash behavior of Sunday morning has caused you distress. Reason abandoned me as I was intent on catching a glimpse of your work. Unfortunately, my boyhood ability to climb trees deserted me in my old age. Imagine my surprise when this reality so quickly became apparent.

Rest assured, I am recovering, having managed not to damage anything of importance except perhaps my pride.

My father informed me my surprise and untimely visit to your garden has proven less than beneficial to your own health. Please accept my genuine regret. If there is anything I can do to ease your troubled spirit, consider me your contrite and willing servant.
Yours,
Sumner Hemmings

He believed the note was too forward. It undoubtedly painted him more an admirer of art than of his neighbor. Certain he'd witnessed a side of Madeleine Crawford he was never intended to see, Sumner bade the butler, James, deliver his message next door.

* * *

Mary Argyle stood back, trying to decide which of the evening frocks displayed across her bed seemed most appropriate to pack for her journey.

"Come in," Mary replied to the knock on her bedroom door. She turned to find her niece's caretaker entering the room. "Jem, which dress do you like more, this maroon or the emerald?"

"Green always looks best on you," noted Jem, who was the senior employee in the household, having worked for Mrs. Argyle since she first arrived in Los Angeles with her baby niece in tow.

Mary nodded in agreement, "You are right, as always. What can I do for you?"

"Miss Madeleine has a note from the neighbor. Their butler brought it by."

"Give it to me." Mary quickly scanned the note then returned it to Jem. "You realize this is entirely inappropriate? Can you imagine the gall of that man? Please destroy it."

"Yes, ma'am. Only, I don't see why Miss Madeleine can't have it herself."

"Jem, you know perfectly well he only wishes to pursue our Madeleine. I certainly don't want to encourage him. I already explained her disabilities."

"Maybe he can see for hisself what you said ain't exactly right."

Mary scowled. The man's proximity posed a problem she never previously encountered. She assumed the elder Mr. Hemmings intended to live alone when he moved in. The fact he had a grown son came as an unpleasant surprise. If only Madeleine was not blessed with beauty, circumstances would be much less complex.

"If he doesn't receive a response, he'll have no reason to doubt my explanation. Perhaps I'll have a word with the senior Mr. Hemmings before I depart."

"Yes, ma'am," agreed Jem as she left the room. But she pocketed the note, having no intention to discard it. Madeleine could not be dearer if she'd been Jem's own flesh-and-blood. The girl had a right to her life, whatever there was of it to be had.

* * *

Sumner scurried back to bed at the knock on his door. There had been no reply to his note. Madeleine hadn't returned to her garden. He felt worse by far than at any time since his fall from the tree. It was as if every bone and muscle in his body were complaining.

"Come in." Expecting a servant with his dinner, Sumner was disturbed when his father entered the room.

"Mrs. Argyle called on me at the bank today."

"That's nice."

"No, it isn't. She had business at the bank and will be leaving soon for her work. You sent a letter of apology to her niece?"

"Yes, I thought it appropriate."

"It might be appropriate if the woman wasn't mentally incompetent. Mrs. Argyle was thoroughly upset. Your note served as a reminder of her niece's deficits. I don't understand your fascination. It seems quite deviant, considering her unfortunate circumstances."

"Have you ever seen her?"

"What does that have to do with anything?"

"She's the most exquisite woman I ever laid eyes on."

Merritt frowned. "You must admit, longing for a woman who is unable to understand your desire is entirely abnormal. What is wrong with you?"

"Nothing is abnormal about Miss Crawford."

"Listen to me. Any further overtures toward the neighbor are unacceptable. There is nowhere left to send you. If you can't control yourself, you will soon be destitute on the street. I understand you don't take me seriously. I assure you, I've never been more sincere in my life." Merritt turned on his heel and strode toward the door. "I will see you at work tomorrow."

Sumner rubbed his hand over his mouth. "Ow!" he complained. He rose from the bed and walked toward the mirror over his dresser to have a look at the bruises on his face. If anything, they were darker than on Sunday after his fall.

Since his father expected him to work, he saw nothing wrong in terrifying the bank's customers. If they were forward enough to ask, he was more than willing to improvise a stirring barroom fight to satisfy their curiosity. Falling from a tree while spying on a neighbor was not an explanation he wished to share.

Standing back from the mirror, he attempted to assess his attributes in as objective a manner as possible. Aside from the bruises and black eye, Sumner believed himself to be a fine-looking man. His black hair was parted slightly right of center. He used only a little pomade to keep it in place and kept his face clean-shaven. His nose was rather finely boned. He had a square chin and blue eyes. At 5'10", he was several inches taller than the average man. Sumner considered his build to be athletic—slim and moderately muscled—although he couldn't recall the last time he participated in anything vaguely athletic. Lifting a glass of whiskey to one's lips hardly counted as exercise. His overall appraisal seemed accurate since women were traditionally eager to share his company, but pilots were a hot commodity.

Sumner learned to fly from fellow affluent students at the university. They impulsively joined the war effort before the States entered the fight. Sumner had only a semester to complete his degree, another source of acrimony with his parents. War quickly took the thrill of flight from him although most of his fellow pilots—the ones who survived—seemed as enamored of airplanes as they were before the war.

The younger Mr. Hemmings had no interests, no serious diversions, no ambition. If his father threw him out, he had no idea how to make a living. Even so, he did not intend to abandon his fascination with Madeleine Crawford.

Annoyed by another knock on his door, Sumner opened it, startling James, dinner tray in hand.

"I'll take that," offered Sumner.

"The note came by way of one of the help next door, sir."

"Thank you." Suddenly hopeful, Sumner tore open the small envelope.

My dear Mr. Hemmings,

I am cheered to realize your interest in my art and enclose a small token of my work to ease your curiosity. Next time I notice you staring at me from your window, I'll be certain to acknowledge your presence.

The doctor has, unfortunately, ordered me to bed until tomorrow at the earliest. While finding your descent from the oak tree quite fascinating, I am relieved you weren't seriously injured.

I can't help but wonder at the fact you did not attempt conversation before your reckless journey through the branches of the tree. I assure you; I don't bite.

However, to prevent my aunt's careful scrutiny— she is overly concerned for my welfare—it might be best to communicate in writing since she is quite opposed to your current methods of exchange. Please address any messages to my maid, Jemimah Doucette.

I look forward to your next missive.
Very truly yours,
Miss Madeleine Crawford

Sumner looked inside the envelope to find an exquisite watercolor botanical of orange pyracantha berries and a leaf. The painting was executed on stiff cardstock measuring about two-by-two inches. It was beautifully initialed in the corner—M C. The woman's writing was elegant and impeccable; her drawing incredibly detailed and technically perfect. She obviously had wit. Why would her aunt label her so unkindly? Unable to help himself, Sumner returned to his window.

He was disappointed but not surprised to find the garden empty. But he managed to garner

Miss Crawford's interest. Nothing prevented him from corresponding further with his beautiful and intelligent vision except the threat of imminent poverty. That was a chance he was more than willing to take.

Returning to work was more difficult than Sumner imagined. His body ached, resulting in a definite lack of patience for customers at his teller window. He quickly grew bored with the shocked reactions to his fictitious injury stories.

There was no response to his latest note to Madeleine, and he failed to catch sight of her in the garden when he arrived home on Thursday or Friday afternoon.

Sumner sat on his bed removing his work shoes as he considered sneaking out to visit the King Eddy. He heard a noise as if a pebble struck his window. Padding across his room in stocking feet, he opened the window to find Miss Crawford standing near the wall between the properties. His heart beat faster at the sight of her. She held her eyeglasses in her hand. Madeleine's blue eyes seemed incredibly large—a window to her soul.

Stealthily, she glanced over her shoulder toward her house, then whispered, "Mr. Hemmings, I accept your invitation. You can come for me at six tomorrow."

Madeleine smiled and walked across the garden, taking a seat near the rose bushes where she normally read. It was obvious she considered herself under some sort of surveillance as she picked up a book.

Sumner raised his hand in agreement and barely made out her nod in reply. Standing back from the window, he continued to discreetly observe and was disappointed when she went indoors. The fading light must have proven too dim for her to read. If Madeleine believed he was still watching, she made no further gestures in his direction.

Somewhat stunned, Sumner returned to sit on his bed. What was he getting himself into? Madeleine's mental condition was not exactly an acceptable dinner topic. If she was truly incapacitated, any number of unpleasant scenarios might result. She could become unhinged with little provocation. What would he do then? She could have some kind of fit or simply become disoriented. She could make unpleasant or undignified accusations against him.

Mrs. Argyle asserted her niece was unable to communicate. What did she mean? Madeleine was clearly able to speak. The longer he sat on the bed with his imagination, the more distressed he became.

By the time Sumner appeared at the Argyle front door at promptly six o'clock on Saturday evening, he had worked himself into considerable anxiety. He was more nervous about taking Madeleine out than he had been with any woman who came before. After knocking hesitantly, he was astonished when, instead of a servant, Miss Crawford swung wide the door and came barreling through.

"Shall we go then?" she inquired.

"Shouldn't I greet your aunt first?"

"Oh, she's gone for the evening."

Sumner offered his arm to lead his companion to the limousine where Alfred stood holding the door.

Madeleine turned her head toward her house. With a sly grin and wide eyes, she spotted Jem in the doorway and shrugged her shoulders as if to convey the message—look at me!

Sumner helped her into the automobile and sat

beside her. For better or worse, he was about to escort this purportedly disabled woman to dinner. He wondered if her beauty would blind him to any deficiencies she might possess and hoped to make it home unscathed.

Jem waved as the limousine pulled from the curb. Considering the repercussions this evening could provoke, she had no regrets. Determined her girl deserved a complete life, Jem was prepared to take any blame that might come her way.

Chapter Two

"I have never ridden in an automobile before," explained Madeleine.

Sumner bit the corner of his mouth. Not wishing to spread gossip by way of Alfred, he put his index finger to his lips then pointed at the chauffeur. "You mean you've never ridden in a limousine before?"

Madeleine shaped her mouth in an "O" of understanding and gave a nod, then proclaimed, "That's what I meant. I've never ridden in a limousine before and certainly not one this grand!" She seemed delighted with her lie. In fact, she seemed a bundle of excitement.

As Alfred turned a corner, Sumner was perplexed and enchanted as his guest grabbed his hand, which rested on the seat between them. Madeleine flashed her dazzling smile. Small, perfect, white teeth gleamed between her slightly parted lips. He could see no flaw in her. Not so much as a freckle marred her skin.

"Why did you never speak to me before?" Madeleine inquired.

"I was given to understand communication might be difficult."

"Whoever gave you that idea?"

"I can't remember. It was offered as common knowledge."

Madeleine frowned uncomprehendingly. "It's just as well you fell out of the tree or we might never have met. Where are we going?"

"I know of a new restaurant in Hollywood called Frank's Café."

Miss Crawford looked down at her clothing and then toward Mr. Hemmings. "Am I dressed appropriately?"

Enamored of her face, Sumner hadn't noticed her attire. She unbuttoned her black velvet coat and displayed a green satin dress with gauze inserts. Beads on the edge of the overskirt glittered in the street lights.

"You look lovely."

"But am I too dressed up for a café?"

"Oh, the name is troubling you. Let me assure you, Frank Toulet hired a French chef to create his menu. The restaurant opened in September and is all the rage." Remembering his manners, Sumner continued, "I wanted to thank you for my tiny piece of artwork. It's exquisite."

Madeleine beamed. "Thank you."

"I've been curious about your art for some time, and now I am a proud owner of a Madeleine Crawford original watercolor. I can only hope this evening proves my gratitude."

It was a short trip from Los Feliz to Hollywood. Before she knew it, Miss Crawford was seated at a table in Frank's Café.

"Would you like me to order for you?"

"Please." Madeleine listened attentively while her escort requested onion soup au gratin, grenadines of beef, Lyonnaise potatoes, creamed spinach and caramel custard for dessert. He conversed briefly with the waiter in French.

"I'm quite impressed."

"That was my intention."

"You mentioned your recent release from the Army Air Corps. You learned to speak French in the war?"

"Yes. I imagine I will quickly lose my skill. I never was much of an expert."

"You sound quite the expert to me, but I'm probably easily impressed. I've never been to a restaurant before!" Her enthusiasm was contagious and completely befuddling to Sumner.

"I find it hard to believe these are all new experiences for you."

"I have led a rather sedate life. My aunt is concerned for my wellbeing."

"So, how did you manage dispensation this evening?"

"Oh, I didn't," Madeleine enthusiastically replied.

Sumner's eyes furrowed. "I can't follow you."

"My aunt went out for a business dinner. She's leaving California shortly and is busily preparing. She doesn't know I left, and Jem will keep her occupied when I return."

"Jem is the woman who saw you off at the door?"

"Yes, she's my maid or nurse—you might call her my guardian."

"Are you certain you should be out?" For the life of him, Sumner could not see any deficit in his neighbor. He was becoming more confused with every word she spoke.

"I am an adult, Mr. Hemmings. But I try to be considerate of my aunt's wishes. I owe her everything, and she is kind to me. My parents passed away when I was a baby. Aunt Mary took me in and has provided for me ever since."

"But there must be some reason you never leave the house?" The waiter placed their soup on the table, and Miss Crawford began to eat. "I'm sorry, I'm being rather nosey."

"Yes, you are," she replied, an impish grin in place. "I will simply tell you; I have a delicate constitution. My doctor is quite strict."

"But I needn't fear you will turn green and faint?"

"Not even a little green. Why are people looking at us? Am I doing something wrong?" Madeleine turned toward an older gentleman who was staring boldly. After she smiled at him, the man immediately focused his attention elsewhere.

"I think you are collecting admirers."

"Why?"

Not quite believing she did not understand her own beauty, Sumner replied, "You are a truly stunning woman, Miss Crawford. Surely you know that?" But he could see by her expression, she did not. "You must have a mirror?" When she did not respond, he continued, "Perhaps it's because we make such a striking couple." Madeleine nodded thoughtfully, seemingly content with this explanation.

Sumner became amazed such a small person could eat so fast and so much. He speculated the aunt did not feed her niece in addition to keeping her prisoner. He supposed there were worse fates.

Madeleine's eyes lit up when the waiter brought dessert. Sumner was surprised at her enthusiasm. She had not left so much as a morsel of food on her plate.

"You're certainly hungry tonight."

"Oh, is that considered rude? Is it more ladylike to push my plate away, claiming my stomach is too small for such a large meal?" Madeleine seemed honestly concerned she made some social blunder.

Sumner laughed. "I imagine it might be more ladylike, but I must admit, I enjoy the fact you've relished our dinner."

"Oh, I have. Are you going to finish your dessert?"

"Why?"

"I don't want it to go to waste." Madeleine confiscated his dish. "Must we go home right away?"

"What time does your aunt return? Will she call the police if she learns I've abducted you?"

"You have hardly abducted me. Are you afraid?" she teased.

"Completely terrified. You and your aunt both scare me half to death."

"Why?"

"I'm not certain, but I intend to enjoy myself anyway."

Madeleine considered her dinner companion. "I believe it's more appropriate for me to be terrified."

"Why should you be?"

"I have never been out with a man before. In fact, I only left my home once before in my life. It wasn't a good experience."

"What happened?"

"About five years ago, I was at a rather rebellious age. After reading *The Adventures of Huckleberry Finn,* I believed there was no reason I couldn't have an adventure myself. I decided to crawl out the parlor window and take on the world."

"And did you?"

"I didn't make it far before I wandered into the street in front of an automobile. I got hit."

"Truly? Was it serious?"

"No, but I recuperated in bed for over a month. My experience led me to believe my aunt's warnings were not unfounded. I was too fragile and ill-equipped to deal with the world on my own terms. I felt afraid to try again."

"So, how is tonight different?"

"Oh, Mr. Hemmings, I have you to watch over me."

This idea both thrilled and terrified Sumner. Miss Crawford was a startling combination of little girl and desirable woman. He was more drawn to her than ever—and genuinely petrified.

* * *

The journey to downtown Los Angeles was not short. Since it was a chilly evening, Sumner draped a blanket over his guest's legs.

"Thank you. Where are we going?"

"You can tell we aren't headed home? I'm impressed at your perceptual acumen."

"That's right. You were under the impression I am somehow debilitated."

"I can see you're not." Sumner needed to be cautious with his subject of conversation since Alfred was once more a party to their discussion. "I thought it might be pleasant to take in a film this evening."

Madeleine's eyes grew wide. "I have never—"

"I imagined so," Sumner interrupted. "I find this Broadway every bit as exciting as the street in New York. They say we have even more lights in our West Coast version. I understand it was a year ago when theater owners fought closure orders due to the influenza epidemic. I imagine you weren't much affected?"

"Not really. However, Aunt Mary was particularly careful about inviting anyone into the house during those months."

"Does she entertain much?"

"Oh, no. I meant delivery people, servants, handymen, people like that. She never has guests."

"I would think she would entertain clients."

"I imagine it's different for a woman to entertain clients at home. It smacks of impropriety. She sees all her clients away from the house."

Sumner noted his companion seemed to think nothing odd about her aunt's behavior.

"Didn't the influenza have an effect on you during the war?"

"It had a profound effect, though not on me, directly. There is a multitude of important people taking credit for ending the war, but the truth is, men got sick and went home. The epidemic is undoubtedly what brought the war to its conclusion."

"I never heard such a thing."

"I was fortunate during the war, but fighting an air war is something new. I had a great deal of privilege, not like those poor bast—men in the trenches. Theirs was a horrific experience. I spoke with soldiers who were cycled out on leave only to slowly make their way back to the front lines, week by week. I had a life of relative leisure.

"We would fly out, complete a mission, then return to a comfortable barracks where there was good food, warmth, fellowship and a cot to sleep in. We never engaged the enemy the way foot soldiers did.

We could never see our victims' faces or the damage and death we caused. I'm sorry. Enough of unpleasant topics. We're here."

Madeleine was awed by the bright lights of Broadway, albeit a copycat Broadway. The street was jammed with motor cars. Alfred managed to pull to the curb in front of the Bradbury Building across from Grauman's Theater—built the year before.

Sumner jumped from the car and helped his guest out, eager to show her the sights. He was surprised when Miss Crawford began her own dialogue.

"This is one of the premier movie palaces built to date!" She tilted her head to take in the 12-story building. "It's done in Churrigueresque—a variation of Spanish Rococo style. See the heroic figures of the arts? Joseph Mora sculpted the symbols of the West. Look! There's the bison head and the longhorn steer skulls. There's an eagle."

"Are you certain you've never been here before?"

"I never thought I'd see this in person, but I do read the papers, Mr. Hemmings."

Read and remember thought Sumner. "I understand there is a complete stage inside. Mr. Grauman is famous for putting on a show before the movie. I think we're in time."

They were indeed, in time. Sumner thought the theater a good idea when he considered plans for the evening, initially doubting they would make it this far.

He observed Miss Crawford's enthusiastic response as they entered the theater. She became completely absorbed with the entertainment. He tried to imagine how he would feel if he led his entire life inside a single dwelling.

As a male singer gave his rendition of the new

Irving Berlin song, *A Pretty Girl is Like a Melody*, Sumner considered the words carefully. His neighbor was as beautiful a woman as he had ever seen. He became enamored of her from the moment he laid eyes on her. Just as in the song, she haunted him day and night. The lyrics about leaving and returning made him uneasy until he decided the words simply referred to the haunting melody and not the pretty girl.

The movie was *The Miracle Man*, a complex tale of crooks who set up shop in a small town and are confronted by a faith healer. Though it was not a new release, it was one of the most popular movies of 1919. But Sumner was too absorbed in admiring Miss Crawford to bother with subtitles.

He could not help but notice Lon Chaney's masterful performance of the monstrous Frog and hoped the film didn't prove too intense for his delicate companion. Sumner thought a movie the best way to entertain Madeleine without the need for conversation, which he believed might cause her difficulty. Instead, it proved the optimal way for him to observe her close up, unabashedly, and without her notice.

When the film ended, Miss Crawford was in no hurry to depart. They sat in the theater while it emptied and spoke about the plot and Mr. Chaney's makeup—for which he was gaining quite a reputation. She seemed completely thrilled by their trip to Grauman's.

Eventually making their way up the aisle, Madeleine took up a new topic.

"Tell me, how is it you came to live in your father's house? Is it your lifelong desire to be a bank teller?"

"How did you know that? I could be a vice-president. Is it your turn to be nosey?"

Madeleine laughed. "My aunt spoke about you in relation to some paperwork you delivered. She said you were a glorified teller, strung to your father's coattails and living off his dime I believe she put it."

"How complimentary of her."

Giggling, Madeleine continued. "You don't seem the teller type to me."

"Because you are such a worldly and well-traveled woman?"

"No, because I believe I see more independence in you than you see in yourself."

It was Sumner's turn to laugh. "I can effectively sum up the reason I live in my father's house and work in his bank in a single word."

"Devotion?"

"Hardly. The word is money. The root of all evil. I am an only child who will one day inherit the sum and total of my parents' belongings and capital."

"I don't believe you should be so frank with a total stranger."

"I believe you have a point there. My honesty puts me in a poor light so let me assure you, fidelity to family is the prime motivator in all I do." Sumner facetiously placed his hand over his heart. "If you ask my father, he will assure you his Sonny is all the offspring he ever desired."

"Sonny?"

"Oh, I shouldn't have let that slip either. It's my parents' nickname for me. It seems when I was small, I couldn't say my name, and Sonny came out instead. They thought that adorable. Despite my sincere desire to leave my babyhood in the past, they can't seem to overcome their habit of calling me the silly, vile name."

"I promise I will only call you Sumner when it becomes appropriate to do so, Mr. Hemmings."

"What's wrong with now?"

Madeleine bit her lip. "All right, Sumner."

"And I will call you Madeleine. Since we're out on the sly anyway, what harm can it do?"

"Oh, I don't want you to call me Madeleine."

"But it's your name. Am I to continue with Miss Crawford, then?"

"Unlike you, I have longed for a nickname. My aunt thought it undignified. I always wished to be called Maddie. I used to imagine a friend who would call me Maddie."

"Then I will be your friend, Maddie. It will be my special name for you." Sumner grinned as he received another of his companion's lovely smiles.

"And I promise never to refer to you as Sonny unless, of course, you make me very angry."

"I will endeavor to never make you that angry," he assured.

Throughout the evening, Sumner strove to remember every gentlemanly rule his mother ever mentioned. For some reason, he felt the need to behave in a courteous and polite manner. He imagined using first names went completely against those rules.

After Alfred held the limousine door for them, Sumner sat quietly and was once again delighted when Maddie placed her hand on his, an improper and forward gesture for a well-bred lady.

He imagined the days of such societal restrictions were coming to an end. The world was changing at an alarming rate. Women won the right to vote in the California state election of 1911. They were entering the workforce as never before.

Women's clothing was more relaxed and comfortable. He was not unfamiliar with the new trends in undergarments: brassieres and the absence of corsets.

Men traditionally found companionship and camaraderie in saloons, which undoubtedly took a toll on home life. The ladies managed to exact their revenge with the recent passage of the Volstead Act.

For the first time ever, birth control was available to women even though the practice currently came with a considerable amount of stigma. Society, no doubt, would soon be turned on end.

As Alfred neared home, Maddie whispered, "Could you have him park at your home? You could walk me to the kitchen door. It would be more discreet. I don't want to get Jem in trouble."

Sumner gladly complied.

"What would you have done tonight if we didn't go out together?" Maddie asked.

"Oh, I would have been a complete wastrel, visiting bars, getting myself into all manner of trouble."

Madeleine considered his reply and a comfortable silence continued until they slipped through the side iron gate of Mrs. Argyle's Spanish revival home and approached the kitchen door. Sumner almost gasped at Maddie's beauty as she made a last comment.

"Thank you! I had such a wonderful time. This has been the best night of my entire life! I feel like Cinderella returned from the ball."

"And did you fall in love with the handsome prince?"

Madeleine grinned, "Don't you wish I did? Don't you just wish?"

At that, she silently disappeared through the kitchen door but not before reaching up to plant a kiss on Sumner's cheek.

* * *

As the week wore on, Sumner became alarmed. He hadn't caught sight of Maddie since Saturday night. It was true, the evenings were chilly, and the sun set early. He could not help but wonder if Aunt Mary learned of their adventure and relegated her niece to the indoors.

He recognized the evening might have been too much for Madeleine, and she could have become ill. She seemed tired though no less enthusiastic when they parted. He sent a note by way of Miss Doucette on Sunday without reply.

Walking from the trolley stop, Sumner was surprised to find Maddie standing on the sidewalk. An eager expression lit her beautiful features.

"Good day, Mr. Hemmings."

"A good day to you, Miss Crawford. It's a delight to see you." He offered his arm and slowed his step as they continued on their way. "What brings you out on this fine afternoon?"

Maddie was full of childish glee as she quietly replied, "I watched to see when you came home. I thought it was your habit to accompany your father in the limousine. I had to pay more attention when I noticed you don't normally travel with him."

"My father stays much too late at the bank for me. There is one true advantage in being a teller. As soon as everything is balanced, I can leave."

"I received your message, but I've been busy this week. Aunt Mary left!"

"I see."

"I accept your invitation for Saturday night."

"Perhaps my calendar filled while I awaited your reply." Sumner could not bear her crestfallen expression. "No, I'm teasing you. We'll start with dinner again then?"

"If it's not too forward, I would like to make a request."

"I believe it is quite forward, but in light of your recent incarceration, I'm more than willing to oblige."

"Are you certain? You won't change your mind?"

"Certainly not. Where are we going?"

"I want you to take me to the drinking establishment where you would normally go. I want to see what it's like."

Sumner was surprised at her request. "It's not a proper place. I think we should do something else."

"But you promised me."

"I did, but you are a gentle person." He refrained from use of the word delicate, although he believed it applied. "I don't want to take you someplace inappropriate. What would your aunt say if she found out?"

"I am not a child," Maddie replied, somewhat childishly. "I am a grown woman. I'm aware of my rights. I'm free to come and go as I choose."

"Maddie, I think you're rather in the same boat as me. Your aunt supports you. You're dependent on her good will."

"She would not approve of anywhere I went. She would not approve of you. What difference does it make if you take me to a barroom?"

"Why would she not approve of me?"

Madeleine considered her reply. She did not wish

to offend, yet wanted to be honest. "Aunt Mary has strict standards when it comes to men. From comments she made, I believe she categorizes you somewhat unfavorably."

"So you mentioned last week. But I come from good family. I have prospects."

"I don't think she considers you ambitious."

Sumner would have to agree with that analysis. "How long is Aunt Mary away?"

A sly grin crossed Maddie's features. "Months. She won't be home until next year."

"I rather imagine we can rack up any number of inappropriate outings before then," Sumner offered.

"Yes, I rather imagine we can."

* * *

Merritt Hemmings was confused at his son's behavior over dinner. For the first time since Sonny joined him in Los Angeles, the boy seemed genuinely cordial. Merritt remained aloof, content to see how the meal unfolded.

Sonny was quiet, withdrawn and pensive since his banishment from New York. From what Evelyn mentioned in her correspondence, the boy had been difficult since his return from the war, often drunk, uncommunicative and sullen. The young man currently seated at his dinner table seemed transformed. Weary of small talk about bank customers, Merritt embarked on his own discussion.

"I've heard from your mother."

"How is she?"

"Well. She has decided to join us for Christmas."

"Has she now? What prompted this reunion? Her desire for a warm family gathering? Has she been to the movies to observe family commitment and decided familial relationships might be nice? Isn't it a bit late for that?"

"There's no need to be offensive. We've been apart for too long. I don't imagine she will stay much past the holidays at any rate." Merritt could not refrain from lecturing his son. "You need to make amends. Do I need to remind you yet again of your reckless and callous disregard for your mother's wellbeing when you left for the war? You shirked your responsibilities to your family and yourself."

Sumner attempted to shake off his momentary lapse. It was his plan to ask a favor. He wouldn't get far if he couldn't assume the role of dutiful and agreeable offspring.

"Very well. I'm certain I can make her feel welcome. It's only for a short while after all."

Merritt was becoming extremely suspicious. "I notice a difference in you, boy. Have you had some change of heart?"

Sumner smiled weakly. Was he so obvious? Honesty, at least relative honesty, seemed his best course. "I suppose I have. Remember, I borrowed the limousine on Saturday last to entertain a customer of the bank?"

"I believe my memory has not deteriorated to the point I would forget so quickly. I rather imagined you simply went carousing."

"That would normally be a fair assessment but untrue in this instance."

"I see. So, you have impressed a client with your banking acumen?"

"Not really. My guest for the evening was a young lady whose family banks with us."

Merritt, impressed by his son's apparent honesty, remained skeptical and thought Sonny's reference to the bank as some mutual enterprise amusing.

"I can assure you our evening could not in any way be qualified as carousing. In fact, I have become cognizant of the opportunity you offer as a result." Sumner realized the money he made as a teller was not going to support his outings with Maddie. "I believe I've mastered the job of teller and am prepared to tackle the next position—with a commensurate raise in pay, of course."

Merritt wiped his mouth, carefully observing his son. "I'm pleased you wish to make the most of your opportunity. This young lady has had a startling effect on you. Who is she?"

"This is a new relationship. It's a bit early for such revelations."

"I'm happy you abandoned your pursuit of the next-door neighbor. Perhaps your fall from the tree served to knock some sense into you."

Sumner smirked in reply.

"I believe any promotion I give will be met by opposition from your fellow workers. After all, you've only worked at the bank a brief time. Others will undoubtedly feel overlooked if you are promoted over them."

"They know I'm your son. I'm certain they expect me to learn your business. It's not as if you made me manager over them upon my arrival."

"I believe it will, without doubt, cause dissention. Are you prepared to deal with that?"

"I am willing and ready. Any position I accept can be explained as a temporary learning experience."

"It will mean longer hours."

"I am prepared."

"Fine. We'll start you as a loan clerk on Monday, but there will be no raise in pay."

"But—"

"That is my final word." Intent to make a man of his son, Merritt watched Sumner seethe without further comment.

Chapter Three

So as not to arouse suspicion, Sumner directed Alfred to park around the corner on Saturday evening. Madeleine was dressed in the same black coat she wore the week before and appeared too excited to stand still.

Sumner leapt out of the Buick almost before it came to a stop. Madeleine ran to him, eagerly taking his arm.

"I can't wait!"

"I think you'll be disappointed. This is not a glamorous locale."

"But we are being so subversive! This is great fun already."

Once Alfred turned the automobile toward downtown, Sumner shared his news.

"My father gave me a new position at the bank. I start on Monday as a loan clerk." He realized this sounded more important than it was.

"You must be doing well to be promoted. Are you taking your employment more seriously?"

"I imagine I am." Feeling the need for honesty, he continued, "I need the money."

"I see. Did you receive a large raise in pay?"

"No. I didn't receive any raise. I believe my father is intent on making my life as difficult as he can manage. It's his way of testing my mettle. My mother is coming from New York for the holidays."

Madeleine laughed. "Does that have something to do with the testing of your mettle as well? Or did your abrupt change of topic fall naturally from your lips?"

"I imagine her visit will provide a test," Sumner replied, light-heartedly. Maddie was a delight.

"Why do your parents not live together?"

"I don't know if I can answer that. I can't recall a time in my life when we were really a family. My mother had her interests, my father, his own. We occasionally ate dinner together. Holidays were about the only time there was an attempt at familial relationships. As you can imagine, those fell rather short of expectations at least as far as I was concerned.

"Once I went away to college, my father moved here to start a new business. Mother came initially, but she didn't stay.

"They both come from wealthy families. For all I know, their marriage was arranged. It evidently never really took. The good thing for me, as I mentioned before, is I will eventually inherit their holdings."

"So, you're willing to bide your time?"

"I believe I am. Few men have this kind of opportunity."

"What if you struck out on your own? Wouldn't you still inherit? Wouldn't your father have more respect for you if you became a self-made man? Isn't that the American way?"

"You are a jumble of questions this evening, Miss Crawford. I don't know where to begin."

"I want your parents to be proud of you."

"Why? You've never even met them. Perhaps they are ghoulish reprobates."

Madeleine laughed at this idea. "I know you. I think your parents are perfectly respectable even if they aren't madly in love."

"You don't know me, Maddie."

"I think I do. I think I've known you all my life."

Blinded by her beauty, Sumner could not argue. The fact he was spending the evening with the charming and gorgeous Madeleine Crawford overpowered his more logical inclinations.

Maddie occasionally engaged Alfred in conversation, which delighted the chauffeur no end. Sumner could see she dazzled the older man whose step grew lighter in her presence. He did not hesitate to agree to Miss Crawford's request his new passenger remain "their" secret.

Sumner had the uncomfortable feeling he needed to compete for Maddie's attention as she began an affable conversation with the driver this evening. But once they reached the King Eddy, he understood the competition was only getting started.

All eyes were drawn to Sumner's sweetheart the moment they descended the staircase and emerged from the hallway to enter the secret barroom. A hush fell over the crowd when Sumner escorted Maddie to a table in the corner. Even he was dumbfounded as he took her coat. She wore a gold beaded dress and could not have appeared more stunning. Though not revealing, the gold of the dress showcased the highlights in her hair. She was a vision, a veritable goddess, and absolutely everyone was paying attention. Sumner swallowed with some difficulty.

"Have I done something inappropriate?"

whispered Maddie.

"No, but perhaps you are a bit dressed up."

"I'm sorry."

"No, no. You are dazzling. Where did you find that dress?"

"Aunt Mary brings me all the latest fashion magazines from France when she travels. I have an eye for detail, and I'm able to copy almost any design I see."

"You made the dress?"

"Yes, especially for tonight. I worked on it all week. The yardage was expensive. Aunt Mary might want to know why I ordered such extravagant fabric on her account at The Broadway, but she won't be back for months! I'll worry about it then."

"You look magnificent."

As the admiring stares faded out of his consciousness, Sumner was overcome with new and unpleasant concerns. An intense possessiveness was impossible to deny. He was the one to find Maddie. He struggled with the idea she must somehow belong to him alone.

Excusing himself, Sumner approached the bar. The bartender confirmed his belief whiskey was the only option. Sumner took two shot glasses to his table to find two men had taken up seats.

"Pardon me, gentlemen." If these men thought they were joining his company, they were sadly mistaken. They slunk away at Sumner's glare. He could be a formidable opponent if necessary; the two smaller men seemed unwilling to take him on. He watched Maddie take a sip of whiskey and wince.

"That's horrible. Why would anyone drink voluntarily?"

Sumner chuckled but kept an eye on the recently departed men who appeared to be conferring at a table near the bar. He recognized how poor a choice he made in agreeing to bring Madeleine here.

"In that case, I think we should find something else to drink—somewhere we can better show off your dress." Before Maddie could object, he took her coat and hurried her out the door.

Relieved when they reached the limousine safely, Sumner made light of their quick exit.

"Take us to the Alexandria Ballroom. Miss Crawford's dress deserves a more appropriate venue." Then he added for effect, "Now."

Alfred got the hint and made a hasty departure.

"We are going to a ballroom? A real ballroom?" Maddie asked.

"A ballroom is a better choice. They likely have cocktails you would enjoy, and we might spot the moviedom elite." Although Sumner was not particularly enamored of the actors and actresses he'd met, Maddie might be impressed. She would undoubtedly cause quite the stir in her gold dress.

"I don't know how to dance," Madeleine admitted.

Resigned to the fact Alfred would soon know all their secrets, Sumner simply replied, "I'll teach you."

* * *

Jem stared at Madeleine's reflection in the mirror as the girl enthusiastically rambled on about her evening. Brushing her charge's golden hair, Jem contemplated her permissiveness might cost her job at some point. She was ready for something new, having saved since Mary Argyle first hired her. She had enough set by to start a business; possibly even enough to travel or retire to some quiet locale and indulge herself. Her devotion to Madeleine would never waiver, however. As long as Jem was allowed to care for her young beauty, she would continue as always.

"Oh, Jem, he is so wonderful, and considerate and caring! I had such a good time."

"Well, that's important, Baby Girl, but you have other matters to consider."

"What are you talking about?"

"Have you discussed your health?"

"No. Why should I?"

"What if he has feelings for you? It's only fair to let him know your limitations."

"I haven't had any limitations while I've been with him. I think I am quite fine. We went to the Alexandria. It was amazing! I don't even think I can describe it. The room was immense. There were huge crystal chandeliers and beautiful soft lighting all along the sides. Sumner told me I looked as if I was born to be there—isn't that romantic?

"A man named Paul Whiteman is the new bandleader. He has a nine-piece orchestra. Everything was completely perfect: the magnificent ballroom, the wonderful music. After we ate a light supper, Sumner taught me to dance—just like that! He taught me to waltz and fox trot. Some people were doing the tango, but it was beyond me so Sumner says we might practice.

"He even procured a drink for me to taste called a Perpetually Rosie—and it's illegal in Los Angeles! It's a cocktail from the book of Hugo Ensslin. I don't know how Sumner obtained the drink. I actually liked it but only took a sip. He drank the rest. Sumner holds my hand all the time now."

"You let him hold your hand so soon?"

"I held his hand first! He's been a perfect gentleman."

"Madeleine, you must behave as a lady. Has he kissed you?"

"Oh no. But I did kiss him on the cheek when he returned me home."

"Tonight?"

"Last week too," Madeleine confessed with total innocence. "Sumner invited me to go to the beach next Saturday if the weather is fine. We'll leave after noon and take in all the pier attractions. I think I must have something new to wear!"

"But you have a closet full of beautiful dresses."

"Sumner has seen all those. This is what I think. Susie at The Broadway is always helpful when I place an order on the telephone. She even offered to send me fabric samples. But I believe Alfred would be willing to drive me downtown so I could shop on Monday."

"Baby Girl, his services belong to the senior Mr. Hemmings. He can't just up and take you riding around the city."

"He's my friend, and I don't think he has much to do during the daytime. I'm certain he would take me if I ask. Mr. Hemmings lets Aunt Mary use his limousine when she's home."

"But you have never been to a mercantile. I don't think you should go by yourself to a huge store."

"I have much more experience in the world than I used to," Madeleine proclaimed. "Besides, we could go together. I'll buy you something—one of those fancy hats you're always longing for."

"Do not tempt me to evil," Jem warned. "Besides,

the doctor comes on Monday. He'll write a report to your aunt. We can hardly tell him you have gone off galivanting."

"I don't need to see the doctor. I'm fine. In fact, I have never felt this wonderful."

Jem watched Madeleine give herself a hug. The girl appeared to be in perfect health. One would never imagine she spent her entire life as an invalid. "I'm done with your hair. You'd best calm down so you can go to sleep."

"I've had another thought," continued Madeleine. "I think there is a way for Sumner to come and visit without anyone reporting to Aunt Mary."

"Baby Girl!"

"Listen, Aunt Mary met him, she told me she did. What if we send a note next door from Aunt Mary, supposedly penned before her departure, requesting his help with something—perhaps a deposit or a creditor?"

"I think you're getting much too wily."

"I wouldn't have to go outside in the cold if he could come here. And if the doctor gives me a clean bill of health tomorrow, we could go to The Broadway on Tuesday. I'll ask Sumner when he comes."

Realizing things were moving much too quickly, Jem felt the need to offer a warning.

"I know you care for Mr. Hemmings, and you think he cares for you, but this is getting out of hand. Your Aunt Mary only wants to protect you. This man could hurt you. You could get into trouble. He could break your heart. What if he has no interest in a woman who is confined to bed—too sick to be a wife to him or run his household?"

"Oh, Jem, I think most men like their wives in bed. Do I need to sit you down and have a talk?"

"Madeleine Crawford!" Jem could not help but laugh.

* * *

Conversation took an interesting turn as Sumner took his place at the Sunday supper table.

"Mrs. Argyle wrote a note to me before she left requesting you come by her house to pick up a deposit."

"She asked me?"

"She didn't wish to take up my valuable time. Mrs. Argyle has always been the most considerate of women. I imagine you can begin your training later in the morning. Since you are involved with a proper young lady, I need not have any fear you will make an inappropriate overture to the disabled girl next door. Or should I?"

"Certainly not. Have no fear in that regard. I am devoted to my new companion. However, there is a topic I need to discuss. I'm not able to make ends meet on my current salary. I can hardly escort the daughter of one of your wealthy clients for hot dogs on the pier every time we meet. I've spent all my funds on outings and am currently penniless. You must agree, it would be wise for me to take her to appropriate and safe locales. It would be a poor reflection on the bank—"

"I get your idea. I don't need to be convinced further. I'll see to it your stipend is increased to a sufficient degree, but I would like to meet your young lady."

"I'll bring her for Christmas Eve supper. She could meet Mother at the same time." Sumner had no apprehension about bringing Maddie to meet his family. Once they saw she was a perfectly normal and healthy woman, all fears could be laid to rest.

* * *

"I think you should stay in bed until the doctor comes," warned Jem.

"There is no reason for me to stay in bed," Madeleine replied as Jem threw open the curtains this glorious, sunny morning.

"Yes, there is. You want him to send your Aunt Mary a good report."

"Or what? She's going to come home and chain me to my bed? Jem, I feel fine. Why shouldn't I tell the doctor of my activities? He may be so impressed, he'll write to Aunt Mary about my good health so she won't worry about me anymore."

Jem had doubts about Madeleine's ideas. "Why not let the doctor write his report as if nothing has changed? He can state your condition as stable. Don't give him any reason to write a bad report."

"I don't see any need—"

"Trust me," requested Jem. "I know your Aunt Mary better than anybody. If you feel fine when she comes home, you can talk to her then. There's no reason to raise questions about your care and activities while you have freedom to come and go. You don't want the doctor to restrict your activities."

Although Madeleine did not fully understand, she replied, "I imagine so. I'll do as you suggest."

Feeling the doctor was sure to notice an improvement in her health, Madeleine was stunned when she was told to stay in bed for several days. She appeared tired and overwrought to Dr. Coolidge.

As she was about to protest, she noticed Jem standing near the dresser, her index finger over her lips.

"Yes, sir," was Madeleine's only comment.

Once Jem showed the doctor on his way, Madeleine bounded out of bed.

"I am *not* staying in bed," she rebelled. "There is nothing wrong with me."

"I tell you what. If you promise to stay abed today, just one day, I'll go with you to the store tomorrow."

"But Sumner is coming today—"

"I'll tell him to come back tomorrow morning."

"I want to see him."

"Do you want me to bring him up here, where he can visit you in bed?"

"No."

"Then it's best if he comes back tomorrow. I'll tell him we couldn't find the deposit, but we'll be sure to have it on Tuesday."

The moment Jem left the room, Madeleine crawled out of bed and went to her window. Although she had a lovely view of the garden, she could only see Sumner's bedroom window if she pressed her face against the glass. She could not escape to the backyard today nor would she be able to answer the door when he arrived.

Using the telephone would alert the Hemmings household to her interest. Sumner seemed more than willing to keep their adventures secret.

Madeleine threw herself across her bed in disgust. Another day of her life would be wasted, and there seemed little she could do about it.

She took up her current novel and attempted to read *Rainbow Valley*, the latest in the Anne of Green Gables series. Seeking inspiration, Madeleine reminded herself of Anne's plucky determination in the face of adversity. She could use some of that.

Hearing a knock at the front door, Madeleine made her way into the hallway where she could hear the sound of Sumner's voice but not what he said. She could imagine. Although it was not her custom to enter her aunt's bedroom, she dashed inside to look out the front-facing window and catch a glimpse of Sumner. She saw him walking down the sidewalk and considered tapping on the glass to get his attention.

When he shoved his hands in his pockets and turned to look back at the Argyle house, he caught sight of Madeleine and stopped in his tracks. Maddie smiled and waved. Sumner shrugged his shoulders and raised his hand in farewell then continued on his way to work, a confused look on his face. She watched until he disappeared down the street.

Disappointed in the way the day was unfolding, Madeleine started for her room only glancing at a box on her aunt's writing desk. The name Madeleine Crawford was carefully penned in the corner.

* * *

Madeleine donned a white cotton dress with narrow black stripes and had her hair done before the sun rose on Tuesday. Jem promised—she was free to do as she liked. She intended to entertain Sumner as long as he could stay this morning and would ask if Alfred might drive them downtown to The Broadway department store. If not, she was willing to call a taxi. Nothing would deter her.

After heading downstairs, Madeleine gave Cook elaborate instructions for morning tea. She felt the lady of the house when Sumner knocked on the front door.

She did not hesitate to shoo Dorothy aside.

"Good morning!"

Sumner was dazed by his neighbor's fresh-faced loveliness. "Good morning," he managed to reply. "I believe you have something for me?"

"I do, indeed. Come in, Mr. Hemmings. Won't you have a seat?" she inquired, taking his arm to escort him into the parlor. Maddie turned and closed the sliding pocket door to Dorothy's great dismay. "Cook prepared tea for us. I hope you haven't eaten?"

"Tea sounds lovely," Sumner agreed as he appraised his hostess who seemed more a little girl playing tea party than the lady of the house. "I'm afraid I can't stay long. I have those new duties at the bank, you remember?"

"I do," Maddie reluctantly replied.

Sumner's heart melted at her disappointment. "I was here yesterday. I had more time since I hadn't begun my new responsibilities."

"I'm sorry. The doctor was here, and I was supposed to stay in bed." Madeleine's eyes flew open at her inadvertent admission.

"Were you not well?" Sumner's concern was evident.

"Oh, I felt fine. The doctor comes by to give my aunt updates on my wellbeing. She is overly cautious about my health, you see."

"No, I don't see." Suddenly, work seemed unimportant. "In fact, I don't understand your aunt at all. She mentioned your ill health and disability when I met her in October. It's difficult for me to reconcile her opinions with the way you act. I can't understand what she was talking about."

"I don't really understand either. I've always been

coddled and protected."

"What is your diagnosis then?" Sumner braced for her reply.

"I don't think I have one," Maddie admitted. "At least, I don't know what it is. Perhaps I should ask since I'm making my own decisions and setting my own course in life. I assure you; nothing is wrong with me."

"There must be some reason for—" Sumner refrained from further inquiry. If Maddie didn't know about her malady, perhaps it was for the best. But he needed to understand. Sumner took Maddie's hand in his. "I would like to meet your doctor. What's his name?"

"Dr. Coolidge, David Coolidge. I imagine I need to ask questions when he comes next time."

"When will he return?"

"He said he would drop by next Wednesday, Christmas Eve morning, to be certain I'm doing well when the holidays commence."

"I'm sure everything is fine." Sumner made small talk appropriate for their tea party but then stood and excused himself. "I wish I didn't have to leave."

"Oh, I so wish you could stay longer. But I have a favor to ask."

"Anything for you."

"Since we're going away on Saturday, I wanted to do some shopping, and I wondered if Alfred would mind driving me downtown? If not, I'll call a taxi."

"No need. If you're ready to go, you can come now. My father went into work early this morning. After Alfred drops me off, he is at your disposal for the rest of the day."

"Truly?" Maddie's eyes glistened with

excitement. "I'll get my coat and collect Jem. Thank you so much."

"My pleasure," Sumner assured. He wished he could do more than supply a chauffeur as Maddie dashed from the parlor.

His breath caught when he considered the fact there might be something seriously wrong with Maddie. He had no right to visit her doctor. The man would undoubtedly refuse to share information. Would he still be interested in his beauty if she were doomed by some wretched malady? Sumner was shocked to realize, although he wanted only the best for her, he did not care what might be wrong. He wanted nothing in life so much as to be in her presence.

Regret for his lack of station pulled at Sumner's thoughts. He was suddenly less than anxious to play the wastrel, waiting for his parents to anoint him with some portion of his inheritance. If only the bank was a better match for his interests. He considered other possibilities.

When Sumner offered the ladies the back seat in the limousine, Maddie quickly took his hand and explained Jem could ride in front. Sumner gave a crooked smile as she sat beside him, clutching his hand as if it were a lifeline.

"You didn't give me the deposit," he remembered.

Madeleine bit her lip and put her hand on his cheek so he would lower his ear. "I lied. There is no deposit," she whispered.

"Thank you, Miss Crawford," Sumner seriously replied. "I'll put this right in my coat pocket for safekeeping." He pretended to place the imaginary paperwork inside his coat. "Be sure to let me know if you find any more deposits." Sumner was touched at Maddie's grin.

"I'll do that."

* * *

Captivated by her charge's enthusiasm, Jem enjoyed Madeleine's reaction as they walked inside The Broadway. It was obvious the girl had never been shopping before as she rushed through the aisles wide-eyed, desperate to take in every detail of her new experience.

Intent on keeping her promise, Madeleine stopped in the hat department. Instead of the gaudy hat she admired in newspaper ads, Jem chose a conservative black hat with ribbon band and millinery flowers.

Never having left the house before, Madeleine's need for hats and shoes was minimal. That was no longer the case. Jem stood speechless as Madeleine selected a bevy of items.

Besides hats and shoes, she purchased a form-fitting, double-breasted, brown wool coat and finished her shopping spree with two dresses; the first a dropped waist, long-sleeved mustard frock with a white collar and pleated skirt. The second dress was pink satin with wide straps over a lace bodice. Satin roses were gathered on the back, left side of a wide sash. All shopping was accomplished by way of Mary Argyle's account at the store.

Jem felt a surge of pride as she attempted to view Madeleine from a neutral perspective. The girl was, without doubt, beautiful, sweet and incredibly naïve. If Jem had any doubts about Mr. Hemmings, she pushed them aside, happy to allow Madeleine her day in the sun.

The ladies admired original artwork covering the walls as they ate lunch at the nearby Pig 'n Whistle restaurant, but then it was time for Alfred to take them home. On their journey, Jem noticed the excitement of the day took a toll on an uncharacteristically silent Madeleine, who welcomed the idea of an afternoon nap.

* * *

Sumner took a stroll after dinner and wandered by Maddie's house to see if she might accompany him. She readily donned her new brown coat and one of her new hats then grabbed tightly to his arm. In this manner, Sumner began a habit of visiting each evening.

Their short outings allowed him to develop an appreciation for Maddie's keen wit. She was well-educated and well-read, easily conversing on topics of the day, books and authors.

"Women are taking over the world," he commented as they meandered away from Maddie's front door one evening.

Smiling, she replied, "You must be referring to Lady Astor. Do you feel personally threatened by a female member of the British Parliament?"

Joking, he answered, "I do, most definitely. The world is changing, Maddie, right before our eyes. Society, entertainment, transportation, even the family relationships we were born with will all disappear."

"I think your predictions rather extreme. Shouldn't we embrace all the wonders in the world?"

"I know you do, but you're an exception. I'm not suggesting we stop progress; I'm only concerned about where it might take us. However did you learn so much, locked away in your aunt's house all these years?"

"I had a tutor, Miss Graham. I spent every morning for as long as I can remember learning all I could. She was a sour old maid with absolutely no sense of humor, but she was a good teacher. I gobbled up every bit of information she offered. She was my link to the world. She taught me how to think."

"What happened to her?"

"When I turned 18, Aunt Mary decided I learned everything necessary. I still have access to all the books I want."

"How much time do you spend with your nose in a romance, Miss Crawford?"

Maddie blushed. "I will admit, I read those, but also history, geography, biographies, everything I can. Before you fell at my feet, escaping in a book was the best part of my day. Of course, I read the newspaper."

"Since we have our walks and our outings on Saturday, you deserted your books? What about your artwork and sewing?"

"I told you I make my clothes although I did buy a readymade dress for our next trip. I'm afraid my art has not been a focus lately."

"Too bad. I appreciate your artistic endeavors."

"Well, I'll just have to throw you over for my love of art, I suppose," she teased.

"I wouldn't go to that extreme."

"You think not?"

"I'm not about to be thrown over, Maddie Crawford. We've only begun, you and I." At his declaration, Maddie stopped in her tracks and gazed up at him.

No one had ever looked at Sumner with such

adoration in his life. What did he do to deserve this devotion? He realized he was the first man to come along and wondered how he might manage to be the last.

Chapter Four

"Madeleine, wait until Mr. Hemmings comes to the door," Jem scolded.

"Why should I wait?" Madeleine breathlessly replied as she hurried outside to meet her beau. "Don't wait up. I'll be home late," she commented over her shoulder, but her focus was on the tall gentleman who offered his arm to escort her to his limousine.

"We only have use of the limousine for a short while. Alfred's driving us to the Red Car station downtown. We'll be on our own today."

Maddie's eyes grew wide once again. "I have never been on a streetcar!"

"I knew you were going to say that. We can go all the way to Venice on the trolley and come back whenever we like."

Always delighted by his companion, Sumner listened as Maddie, thirsty for all the experiences she could have, gave a running commentary on every scene she witnessed through the trolley window.

She was as enthralled with the oil derricks scattered through the city as she was with high rises, the opulent front yards of grand estates and traffic congestion. Maddie about jumped out of her seat when she spotted an airplane. Overcome at her first sight of the beach, Madeleine fell quiet, a stark contrast to her continuous dialogue.

"There aren't many people here today," observed Sumner once they got off the Red Car.

"I want to put my feet in the water. I want to feel the sand between my toes." Maddie walked off the boardwalk toward the shore.

Sumner grabbed her arm. "Wait, Maddie. It's too cold. We're all dressed up. Beachgoing should wait until the weather warms. Even in summer, the water's chilly. See what's on the pier? Let's do rides this visit."

Although it was difficult for her to tear her gaze from the sea, Madeleine soon became enthralled with attractions on the Venice Pier. They experienced the scenic railway, the funhouse and the Whip. They rode the merry-go-round at least five times.

Sumner watched closely for signs of fatigue, but Maddie was too excited for him to gauge her wellbeing. As he escorted his lovely sweetheart around Venice Beach, Sumner felt enormous pride at the looks of admiration they received.

Wearing her new dress and a brown small-brimmed hat, Maddie had eyes only for Sumner, aside from their surroundings. If some bold person spoke to her, she sought the comfort of his presence even more.

They ate hot dogs and cotton candy, more novel experiences.

Maddie was intent to go through Noah's Ark, the newest attraction on the pier. They explored the dark, winding passageways while the boat rocked. Maddie laughed hysterically at the stunts and gags. Sumner was careful to help her balance on the vibrating boards.

To the disappointment of the crowd below, he cautiously steered her around the blast of air from the floor of the top deck, positioned to blow ladies' skirts up.

They tried their hand at bowling, which proved beyond Madeleine's ability. No matter how light the ball, she simply hadn't the strength to throw it down the alley but contently watched Sumner finish her game.

When Maddie spied a beautiful lace-trimmed hankie with her initial embroidered in the corner, Sumner bought it as a remembrance.

He contemplated departing after dinner. "This has been a busy day. I think we ought to head for home." Although Sumner expected resistance to this idea, he was not prepared for Maddie's apparent total heartbreak.

"Couldn't we visit the dance pavilion for a while?"

"Maddie, we probably should save something for our next visit."

"When will we come back?"

Laughing, Sumner paid the bill and directed Maddie onto the boardwalk for a stroll.

"The holidays are fast approaching. My mother arrives next week. My father wants to meet you. I told him I would invite you for Christmas Eve dinner so you could meet them both at one time and get it over with. Can you come?"

"He wants to meet me?"

"Well, he doesn't exactly know it's you he'll be meeting. He believes I'm seeing the daughter of a prominent bank customer." Sumner noted Maddie's consternation. "I need to be honest. My parents don't approve of me, and I admit their reasons are not unfounded. They doubt my ability to court an acceptable sweetheart. But a man needs to find his own way in life, and you are having a profound effect on me."

"I am?"

"Yes, Maddie, you are. I've been thinking about my future, our future. I need to make a better living. I'm no longer willing to wait around for some portion of my inheritance. I guess it's time for me to grow up."

"Sumner?"

"Trace!"

"What are you doing in California?" The tall, blond man wore a loose-fitting, white shirt and Jodhpur pants tucked into knee-high, polished black boots. He pumped Sumner's arm in an enthusiastic greeting as he eyed Madeleine. "You always did have an eye for a beautiful woman. You haven't lost your touch."

When Sumner ended the handshake, he put his arm around Maddie and drew her close against his side. Of all the exciting experiences of the day, this was by far the best. She gazed up at Sumner, unable to utter a word, and tentatively placed her hand on his chest.

"Trace Beggs, this is my neighbor, Madeleine Crawford."

"Miss Crawford, my pleasure." He offered his hand.

Maddie, unhappy at having to move her hand from Sumner's chest, was also upset their interesting conversation had been interrupted. She gave Trace's hand a quick shake and immediately returned hers to its exhilarating prior position.

"Maddie, Trace is an old friend and fellow pilot from the war."

"Very nice to meet you, Mr. Beggs."

"I can't imagine anyone I'd like to see more than you, Sumner, but I can't quite believe my eyes. I thought you were in New York."

"I'm working at my father's bank."

"And I'm certain you're doing a fine job," Trace commented facetiously.

Sumner laughed. "Actually, I don't believe I'm quite up to taking on my father's business."

"Shit, Sumner, I've been working here at Venice Field. Barnstormers have been performing here for years. They even started the first aerial police force. Have you seen the bi-plane? It says 'Venice Aero Police' on the side. I know Mr. Delay personally. I could get you a job, a good job."

"I'm done flying. You know I am."

"Sure, but there's other things you could do. There's a bunch of manufacturing plants at the airport. Delay does movie stunts for all the big studios. You were always good at patching our planes together when the need arose.

"Sumner, you could make a good living here. Tell you what? Here's my telephone number. Ring me up, and we'll get together. I have a bungalow on one of the canals." Trace pulled a pencil from his shirt pocket and jotted down his number on a piece of paper then handed it to Sumner. "You can bring the delightful Miss Crawford if you are so inclined, but fair warning—I'll try to steal her away from you." Trace's joke provoked a glare from Sumner's lady friend. Laughing, he continued, "I'm kidding, Miss. I owe Sumner my life, I would never dream of competing for any sweetheart of his."

Maddie could not resist Mr. Beggs' friendly manner and traded her glare for a timid smile. Trace Beggs quickly bounded out of sight. Sumner stuffed the paper in his pocket.

"Did you really save his life?"

"Who knows? Those were chaotic times."

Maddie had the feeling Sumner was being uncharacteristically modest.

"Will you call him?"

"I imagine so. This could be the opportunity I'm looking for."

"But you would have to move away."

Sumner glanced at Maddie's serious expression. "All my plans have to do with you, Maddie. Don't worry."

When Sumner eventually bade a reluctant goodnight on Madeleine's front doorstep, he offered her first real kiss, which was eagerly received and returned.

* * *

Merritt Hemmings savored his cigar as he waited on the platform of the La Grande Station for his wife's train. He hadn't felt the desire to smoke in several years but was completely immersed in the pleasant activity as he contemplated the upcoming holiday. If nothing else, he would have a fellow tormentor who would focus all her efforts on their son. At least, he hoped he could direct her activities toward that end. It would certainly be more agreeable than having Evelyn aim her attention at him.

Over five years elapsed since his wife packed her bags in a huff and returned to their home in New York.

He could not recall the reason they argued. Fighting with Evelyn was a way of life; one disagreement simply evolved into the next. Living on opposite ends of the continent did wonders for their marriage. Although he was not immune to a pretty face, Merritt was not the type of man to wander.

He doubted if two more divergent personalities had ever wed in the history of the world. If he wanted to go dining and dancing, Evelyn wanted to stay home. If he wished to relax and spend an evening by the fireplace, she decided to go out. In this way, their marriage devolved into endless bickering. No one was ever happy.

When Sonny came along, Merritt hoped his wife's ill temper might develop into maternal graciousness, but motherhood agreed with Evelyn about as well as marriage had. Her son did nothing right, was rude and selfish, although Merritt believed him to be a typical baby. She quickly handed the boy off to a nanny.

Sonny simply became another cause of irritation for his mother, albeit a distant source. He actually felt sorry for the boy, but eventually Merritt grew weary of his wife's constant criticism. In no time, his son fell into a category much like all the other sources of discord in the household.

When the boy returned from war, Merritt believed his wife's current condemnations of their son to be unfounded. He thought her tales of endless drinking binges and wild behavior consistent with her historic complaints—overblown and annoying. After only a month, she shoved Sonny on a train and sent him West. Merritt, likely for the first time ever, found Evelyn's criticisms vaguely accurate. Sonny was unfocussed, content to play the prodigal son. He was unmotivated and sloppy in his work, at least until he met this woman he was seeing. She seemed to have caused some improvement in the boy.

Once he caught sight of the train, Merritt extinguished his cigar. He undoubtedly smoked long enough to affect the odor of his clothing. Evelyn always hated the smell of cigars.

* * *

Evelyn Hemmings stood behind the conductor at the stairs, eager to leave the train. Being cooped up for days did nothing to improve her mood, even though she traveled in the grandest style possible. Her suite took up half a railcar. Surprisingly thrilled at sight of Merritt standing on the platform, she quickly planted a frown on her face. Evelyn stepped down to greet the man with whom she shared her life. At least that was the premise of their relationship.

Turning her face so her husband could apply a kiss to her cheek, she greeted Merritt. "Good evening, husband."

"Good evening. How was your trip?"

"Quite tedious. I don't understand why you found it necessary to plant yourself so far from New York. One would think you could make your place of business somewhat closer and more convenient to our home. Perhaps halfway across the country would have been an appropriate compromise."

"Yes, it would have been infinitely more appropriate. Unfortunately, prairie dogs and antelope don't make good bank customers or I would likely have founded my bank as you suggest."

Evelyn scowled. Evidently, they were to begin as they ended. Her husband was simply a difficult man.

She pressed her lips tightly together to prohibit further unpleasant conversation and took Merritt's arm as he offered to lead her away from the train.

"You look well," Merritt observed, noting his wife was somewhat thicker in the waist than he remembered. "Your hair is turning gray."

"And yours has turned a shocking white."

"But men look distinguished as they age. Women simply look old."

"How is our Sonny doing? Have you managed to straighten him out?" Surely this was a safe topic.

"He's doing much better. I believe, with my guidance, he might actually make a fair bank employee."

"I'm rather astonished. All he wanted to do in New York was carouse with his friends."

"You must understand, Evelyn, Los Angeles is no moral pothole. We have prohibition. Women can vote. This is the progressive capital of the nation. I assumed you were aware of our forward thinking here. The lifestyle you suggest would simply not be possible in Los Angeles."

"Are you telling me Sonny has given up drink?"

Merritt had to think about his reply. He could hardly claim his son adhered to any strict code of abstinence. "I wouldn't say that, but hard liquor is prohibited. One can have a beer or wine in restaurants for now. I believe Sonny might pursue drink on occasion. But he is devoted to his work of late and seems to be settling down. There's a woman."

"Truly? A serious relationship?"

"It may be. She's coming to meet us on Christmas Eve. Perhaps the boy simply needed a calming female influence."

"Are you insinuating my presence in his life is not calming?"

"Exactly right." Merritt smiled as he helped a steaming Evelyn into the limousine. He planned to knock on her door once she retired. Bedroom activities were never a source of discord in their marriage.

* * *

Sumner played innocent bystander to his parents' barbs and insults, happy to let them go at it as long as he was not the object of their comments. As he often had in younger days, he appeared the perfect, quiet son, prepared to extricate himself from any conversation headed in his direction.

It was pathetically easy to provoke an argument between his parents. Even a simple statement such as, "Who was the woman in your office this afternoon?" or, "Why was the delivery man here so long?" was enough to launch a veritable war. He never understood his parents' rush to jealousy when they had so little in common. Only on rare occasions could they carry on a five-minute conversation without quarreling.

Confident his life would become easier once his parents met Maddie and understood his commitment, Sumner both relished and feared the upcoming confrontation. It was impossible for him to think of a gathering with his mother and father in any congenial way.

* * *

When Dr. Coolidge did not appear on time on Christmas Eve morning, Madeleine refused to stay in bed. She had things to do. Her hair needed to be washed and styled. She showed Jem a picture of the design she wanted. Her hair would be swept across her forehead and caught in a pink satin ribbon wound through soft curls piled on her head.

Madeleine was intent upon a facial and obtained the latest in makeup: rouge for her cheeks, eyes and lips and blotting paper to soften her look.

She agreed to walk next door at 2 p.m.—an early Christmas surprise for Sumner's parents. When the couple took their nightly walk on Tuesday, Maddie couldn't tell if she was more or less nervous than Sumner over this plan. She believed he wished for her to dazzle his parents.

Regardless of his encouragement, she felt completely undazzling, never having experienced such an important meeting in her life. She knew Aunt Mary would never approve of Sumner. This did not matter to Madeleine, and she wasn't entirely certain why Sumner felt the need to impress his parents. She realized the simple act of walking next door to dinner would have been beyond her only two months ago.

After lunch, still dressed in her robe and nightgown, Madeleine focused on her makeup. This seemed her biggest challenge, having never used it previously. Her hair was finished; her new pink dress lay across the bed. Recognizing there was ample time, she first applied the eye rouge—a pale blue that matched her eyes. She carefully blotted it with the paper until it blended nicely—not too obvious. Blending the pale pink shade on her cheeks seemed easy in comparison. Madeleine achieved a natural looking result.

Once she applied the red lip rouge, she understood this would take more skill. Although she liked the effect of the red on her lips, they were quite obviously not natural. Maddie turned her head from side to side, considering how much to blot away and flinched at the sound of a knock on the door.

"Come in."

"Miss Crawford, I'm sorry to be late. I had an emergency this morning." Dr. Coolidge stopped in his tracks at sight of his patient sitting at her dressing table, clearly intending to celebrate the holiday in a manner he believed inappropriate. "What have we here? Are we dressing for a quiet dinner at home this evening?"

Normally cowed by the doctor's expert advice, Madeleine was feeling less than cooperative. She did not intend to have her plans spoiled. Her apprehension at meeting Sumner's family evaporated, replaced by a determination she never previously experienced.

Maddie noticed Jem standing in the doorway as she replied, "I'm feeling quite well today, Dr. Coolidge. I plan to go to dinner next door. I see no reason for an examination."

"I'm happy to hear you're doing so well, but perhaps I should use my stethoscope to provide a complete analysis of your condition. It will only take a moment. Have a seat here on the edge of your bed." The doctor placed his bag on the bed and extracted instruments.

Madeleine looked toward Jem for support. The woman nodded her head encouragingly and motioned for Madeleine to do as the doctor requested. Reluctantly, Maddie walked across the room and submitted to a brief examination.

"I'm afraid a celebration tonight would not be beneficial," Dr. Coolidge noted as he returned the stethoscope to his bag. "Perhaps a quiet dinner at home might be acceptable if you nap first."

Madeleine glared at him. "I have no intention of changing my plans. I'm fine."

Dr. Coolidge gave a mocking chuckle. "Miss Crawford, I am the expert here. I have no choice but to confine you to bed."

"I will not stay. There's nothing wrong with me." For the first time in her remembrance, the doctor looked guiltily away. "I'm correct, aren't I? I can see it in your face." She rose from the bed, intending to finish applying her lip rouge. "You are excused," she commanded.

"I'm afraid I can't allow this. Going out tonight will undoubtedly be detrimental to your health. I will have no choice but to report your recalcitrance to your aunt."

"Go right ahead," Madeleine coldly replied.

"Surely, you don't want to upset your aunt? She's such a lovely woman, so concerned about you. Perhaps there's another way." Madeleine would have to admit; she owed her aunt everything. It was not her intention to upset Aunt Mary, only to live her life as she saw fit.

"What is this other way?"

"I have some medicine right here in my bag. It will settle your stomach and your nerves. I can't guarantee it will be as beneficial as rest and homecare, but I'm willing to try it since you are so adamant about your plans for this evening."

Something to settle her nerves did not sound like a bad idea. Madeleine walked toward the doctor who produced a small brown bottle from his bag.

"Sit down on the bed and drink this," he explained.

Jem watched Madeleine down the liquid, a look

of disgust on her face. Soon, Madeleine's focus strayed. She appeared confused and didn't resist when the doctor lowered her onto the bed, sweeping the pink dress to the floor. He lifted her feet and prepared to leave. Jem glared at the man as he bid her good day. She hurried over to see what happened.

"Baby Girl?"

Madeleine's eyes fluttered as she fought for consciousness. "Two o'clock," she mumbled before her head relaxed against the pillow.

* * *

Sumner contemplated his options as the minutes ticked by. Two o'clock came and went. Perhaps Maddie was one of those women who was never ready on time. Perhaps he frightened her with his obvious anxiety over this meeting. Perhaps he told her the wrong time.

What if she was ill? Would she telephone his house? Had he even given her the number? His parents believed she was joining them for an early family supper at four. They were off to a party hosted by his father's business associate at eight. Maddie expressed a desire to attend church, yet another new experience for her.

The Hemmings family dressed formally for supper. Once they gathered in the parlor, Sumner had little choice but to wait until four and see if Maddie appeared.

"Would you like a cognac?" inquired Merritt of his wife and son.

"No, thank you," replied Sumner to his parents' great surprise. When he noticed them staring at him, he innocently continued, "I thought that was illegal."

"It may be illegal, but I wasn't about to throw it

out. In fact, the law states anything already in the home is immune from current law. I made it a point to stock up. I imagine there will be an abundance of liquor flowing through the city tonight what with national prohibition on the horizon. Are you quite certain you don't want a glass?"

"Perhaps Sonny needs to be on his way. Aren't you picking up your guest for supper?" Evelyn inquired.

"No, she's coming on her own." Disapproval of his plan was apparent.

"Is your lady friend some sort of modern, independent woman?" Evelyn asked.

Sumner laughed, "Hardly. I would think you would admire her if so. Aren't you quite an independent woman yourself?"

"I am a properly married woman."

"With unlimited freedom. You should probably include that in your assessment."

"Don't sass your mother," Merritt commanded as he sipped his cognac.

Sumner noted his parents seemed unusually united this afternoon.

"It's almost four o'clock. How long do you propose we wait to be seated for supper?" Evelyn inquired.

At this, they heard a quiet knock at the front door. Sumner waited anxiously for James to deliver his guest to the parlor. He was not prepared for the spectacle standing in the doorway when he turned his head. His jaw dropped in horror.

"Who is this?" a shocked Evelyn questioned.

"Oh, it's the imbecile niece of the woman who lives next door. She must have wandered away from home. James!" he shouted.

"Yes, sir."

"Please accompany Mrs. Argyle's niece back to her own abode."

"No! Wait." Sumner walked toward Maddie who had not spoken so much as a word. She looked dazed. Her lip rouge was smeared across her face. Her hair toppled to the side of her head, covering her ear. She wore her brown coat over what appeared to be a robe and nightgown. Her feet were bare.

Sumner grasped Maddie's shoulders and looked into her eyes, wanting an explanation. She stared back at him, blinking rapidly, confused and disoriented.

Merritt became suspicious at his son's odd reaction. "*Is this the woman to whom you wished to introduce us?*" he roared. "I warned you about this. Are you actually so taken by the woman's looks that you disregard her abhorrent mental state?"

A bewildered Evelyn looked between her husband and son. Evidently, the men of her family had some history with the wretched idiot standing in their parlor. Uncharacteristically, she remained quiet to see if she could gain some understanding.

"She's not an idiot. There's something wrong with her," replied Sumner.

"There *is* something wrong with her. Everyone has told you so. Of all the absurd, ridiculous stunts you ever pulled—"

"No, there's something wrong now. She's a completely normal person, intelligent, witty. You don't know her."

"Sumner, her aunt has always been clear on this and with you I might add. The woman is deficient, mentally. How could you possibly think she would make an appropriate dinner guest much less a romantic prospect? Something is wrong with *you*," but Merritt could only watch in horror as his son lifted the feeble neighbor in his arms and headed toward the front door. He stood, mouth agape, as he heard the door open and close.

Turning to his wife, Merritt was only able to utter, "Our boy has lost his mind."

* * *

As James closed the door behind him, Sumner considered his next move. He couldn't keep Maddie at his home, his parents would never allow it. Her eyes were closed, but he did not feel the weightiness that accompanied unconsciousness. Her arms lightly encircled his neck.

Sumner had no money or legal right to care for her. It seemed he had no choice but to take her next door to her own bed despite his certainty someone there must know about her condition—might even have caused it. Even though Maddie was light to carry, he needed both arms to hold her securely, and so, Sumner kicked at the door rather violently, not caring what damage he caused.

Once the maid answered, he plowed through the doorway, intent someone pay for Maddie's condition.

"Who did this to her?" he bellowed. Curious and leery faces appeared around doorways to see what was going on. The woman Maddie called Jem walked down the hallway toward him.

"What is this?" she asked, obviously concerned. Jem quickly recognized Madeleine must have wandered next door of her own volition. "Follow me," she quietly suggested.

Content to let the woman lead him upstairs, Sumner refrained from further comment until he gently laid Maddie on her bed. He stood back and watched Jem carefully remove her coat and robe.

She got a wash cloth from a nearby basin, tenderly removed the smeared lip rouge from Madeleine's cheek and washed her face, then wiped off her feet. Jem pulled up the covers. Sumner helped himself to a chair he dragged across the room and planted beside Maddie's bed. He didn't intend to leave until he had answers and was assured of Maddie's well-being.

Once her ministrations were complete, Jem stood back and faced the enraged visitor.

"I didn't do this."

"Who did?"

"It's not so simple as you think. Miss Crawford's doctor was late. When he came, he found her preparing for dinner at your house. Once he checked her over, he said she was unfit to leave."

"Why?"

"She has medical problems. She's feeble."

"What kind of medical problems?"

"That's not for me to say."

"Who can tell me? Maddie doesn't even know."

"Her aunt protects her. She gives her a nice, calm life."

Sumner tried to sort out his questions, realizing he was too angry to think clearly. "What did the doctor do to her?"

"He gave her some medicine. She couldn't stay awake then, but she must have got downstairs, took her coat and left without nobody seeing. I thought she was asleep."

"What kind of medicine did he give her?" Sumner leaned forward and pulled Maddie's eyelids up to have a better look. "Did he give her an injection?"

"No, it was in a bottle. He made her drink it. He said it would calm her and settle her stomach."

"Where is the bottle?"

"He dropped it in his bag after Miss Madeleine drank it. Do you know what it was?"

"I have my suspicions. When is the doctor supposed to return?"

"He didn't say. He comes every other week when Mrs. Argyle is away. He sends her reports. I guess he'll be back sooner this time," Jem admitted.

"What would happen if you refused to admit him?"

"He would report to Mrs. Argyle. I could lose my job. It could be bad for Miss Madeleine's health."

"I don't believe it will threaten her health. Does she normally take any type of medicine?"

"No."

"I thought not. Have you ever seen her have any type of spell or fit?"

"No. But she's weak."

"I imagine a life of inactivity would make anyone weak." Sumner glared at Jem who turned her face away.

"Why does Mrs. Argyle tell people Madeleine is mentally incapacitated?"

"I don't know why she does that. Maybe she wants to keep people away—men."

"I'm not leaving until I know Maddie is all right."

"Fine by me."

"I don't want you to let the doctor in unless I'm present."

"I'm sorry, sir, but you don't have rights here. I can't simply—"

"Who does have authority when Mrs. Argyle is away?"

"Dr. Coolidge is in charge when Mrs. Argyle is gone. He has a paper."

Sumner bit his lip, trying to formulate a plan. "Does Mrs. Argyle know I've been taking Maddie out?"

"No."

"Do you plan to tell her?"

"No."

This was like pulling teeth. "Why not?"

"I love Madeleine as if she was my own. You make her happy. I don't know much about her health, but I think she deserves some happiness in her life, however short it might be."

Sumner took this comment more seriously. "I'm not leaving until I can speak to Maddie, but I need you to promise you won't let the doctor give her any more medicine if I'm not here."

"The doctor can take Miss Madeleine away, out of the house. He has control of her."

"She's an adult."

"But there are papers."

Sumner had nowhere to turn. He would have to come up with some plan while Maddie slept.

Chapter Five

The crash of waves on the shore was barely audible through the open window. Sumner listened intently to the relaxing sound as he observed the sliver of moon shining through the same window. He smiled as Maddie, sound asleep, snuggled against him. No matter how right this moment felt, Sumner was disappointed in himself yet again.

Without question, he rescued Maddie from a potentially dangerous situation. His disappointment lay in the fact his solution was temporary at best. The events of the past 24 hours made that wholly apparent.

In some ways, his plan could not have played out any better had he prepared for months. The fact Maddie fell instantly to sleep, content to leave their worries to her new husband, made him all the more desperate to concoct a plan for their future.

When Maddie awoke late on Christmas Eve night, Sumner knelt beside her bed and proposed. Grasping at some logical motive for his impetuous query, he knew beyond a doubt he loved his bride. He was stumped as to why she was eager to marry him, despite her fervent proclamations of love. Sumner knew he was simply her first beau. The fact Maddie could take her pick of suitors was not lost on him.

At his instruction, Maddie wrote a note and left it on her pillow, informing Jem she was taking a house at the beach for a few days. She did not mention their plan to marry or any involvement with Sumner. They stuffed some of Maddie's clothes in a pillowslip and snuck out of her house. Since his parents hadn't returned from their party, Sumner grabbed a few of his belongings.

He had no income of his own aside from his modest pay from the bank. He had no home or plan for his future. He couldn't afford a wedding ring, not that one could be purchased on Christmas Day.

It was easy enough to find a preacher willing to marry them between Christmas services. Fortunately, they caught Trace at his bungalow just as he was leaving to spend the holiday with his sister's family in San Diego. He offered them a free and private place to honeymoon.

On some level, Sumner imagined his parents would be as taken with Madeleine Crawford as he was. This situation would have lent itself to their full support—familial and financial. After her appearance at supper, their marriage would be a hard sell. Although he no longer wished to be beholden to his parents, he saw no way around this for the time being.

If Sumner contemplated the idea they could simply begin a life together on his paycheck, a poor couple making their way in the world together, Maddie's own shortcomings came immediately to light.

When Sumner happily suggested Maddie could start their marriage off right by cooking Christmas dinner, she burst into tears. He was speechless at her admission she never cooked a thing in her life. She didn't know how to clean house or do laundry either.

"I thought you said you could sew?"

"I can sew," she sniffed between sobs, "but that doesn't mean I can do these other things. I don't even know how to start a stove or boil water!"

In short, she was as unprepared for their modestly funded marriage as was he. He still considered her the most perfect woman he ever met.

Sumner was no cook, but he knew how to scramble eggs. Maddie patiently watched him, trying to take in all the information he offered. Their Christmas feast and first meal as husband and wife was a plateful of eggs scrambled a bit too hard. But he knew Maddie would learn her wifely duties; this was a less daunting obstacle than his financial one.

He imagined Jem would presume he had some part in Maddie's plan. As he contemplated their limited choices, Sumner realized he needed to add some authenticity to the note Maddie left.

* * *

If Sumner thought he was disappointing his bride when he left early Friday morning for work, he would have been surprised to observe the new Mrs. Hemmings as she gleefully walked along the canal toward Venice Beach. Her beauty was always apparent, but she literally glowed with happiness as she took careful note of her surroundings, intent to find her way back to Trace's house without assistance and without being run over. She was free to do as she liked and go where she pleased for literally the first time in her life.

As Maddie considered her new role as Sumner's bride, she determined to be the wife he deserved. Her cheeks turned pink as she recalled Sumner's gentle way with her, the thrill of touching and being touched so intimately.

She began today's adventure without a goal in mind. Once she spotted a small market, Maddie settled on a practical plan to prove herself a valuable marital asset.

Mr. Thomas felt befuddled by his new customer. He could not recall having served such a beautiful woman nor one in need of so much aid. Overwhelmed with the woman's questions as he stood at his meat counter, he finally retrieved his wife from the back of the store.

Hilda Thomas was not a patient woman, especially when it came to young housekeepers. But even her heart melted at this young woman's plight. Hilda finally raised her hand to quiet the girl's inquiries.

"Let me see if I understand. You don't know how to cook, not at all?"

"Correct," the beauty admitted. "But I want to surprise my new husband when he comes home from work. You see, we had scrambled eggs for dinner last night, and I want to make a real dinner tonight—to prove I will make a good wife."

Hilda imagined the husband could care less about his wife's abilities in the kitchen. A man would be a fool to let such a gorgeous woman slip through his fingers because she couldn't cook. Still, she admired the girl's gumption. She was a charmer, all right.

"I need to make simple food that tastes good. I need to know how to do something basic. The grocer recommended a roast, but I don't know what he's talking about. I looked at this cookbook, but I don't know how to do any of these things—"

"Hold on there a minute. I think a roast is a good choice. You can put it in a Dutch oven, add some peeled potatoes and carrots and make gravy. It's probably the easiest meal you could make, and your husband will be impressed." Hilda noted her customer's crestfallen face. "What's the matter?"

"What is a Dutch oven? How do you make gravy? How do you peel vegetables? I don't know what supplies are in the kitchen where we're staying."

"How much money do you have?"

"My husband left this on the dresser when he went to work, but I don't think he intended me to spend it." Madeleine pulled the modest funds from her handbag.

"It will do. He'll have to understand, if you're going to set up housekeeping, you need supplies. A great many meals can be prepared in a Dutch oven." It took Hilda 30 minutes to give instructions and gather the ingredients for a roast beef dinner, the oven and a whisk. She only hoped there was more than a frying pan in the kitchen of their house. Hilda was enchanted by the intense gratitude her customer bestowed while furiously shaking her hand.

"Thank you so much. I'll bring all my future business to you. You've been such a help!"

"Wait!" Hilda stopped the girl before she hurried out the door. "Take this."

Madeleine gave her benefactress a curious look. "Oh, I don't have any money for the cookbook, and you've already been so generous."

"Consider it a wedding gift," Hilda smiled. "You seem like a bright girl. The instructions will make more sense once you have some experience. Feel free to come by any time." Hilda turned to see her husband's amused expression. "What's got into you?"

"Oh, nothing. I'm surprised you were so nice to that girl. Patience has never been your strong suit."

"Shows what you know," Hilda angrily replied. But she would have to admit that was the sweetest girl she had met in a long while.

* * *

As Sumner walked past Maddie's home, he stopped in his tracks as if he suddenly remembered his need to pay a call. He strode to the front door. When the maid answered, he inquired after Miss Crawford. Sumner tried to gauge the maid's curious stare as she asked him to wait. He remained on the porch until the door reopened.

"Come in, Mr. Hemmings," bade a serious Jem.

"Isn't Madeleine well?" Sumner asked as he entered the parlor, certain to convey a proper amount of alarm.

"Don't you know where she is?"

"Where she is? She was in bed asleep when I left on Christmas Eve."

"You didn't talk to her then?"

"She woke up for a moment. I told her I would come by today after work. I was checking to see if she might like to walk after dinner." It was all too obvious Jem believed Madeleine had gone with him.

"She's not here."

"You didn't let the doctor take her, surely?"

"No, the doctor came this morning. I showed him a note Miss Madeleine left for me."

"What note?"

"It said she was going to take a place by the

beach. She plans to return in a few days."

Mr. Hemmings seemed surprised. "What did the doctor say?"

"He was so mad, he called the police."

"The police?"

"Yes. He's in charge of Madeleine, after all. She's not prepared to go out in the world by herself."

"Yes, everyone has made quite sure of that. What did the police do?"

"Nothing. She left a note, and she's an adult. They said to call if she doesn't turn up. Dr. Coolidge tried to explain his duties as her guardian, but they weren't too interested. They said if she could write a note and she was over 18, we had to be patient and see if she comes home."

"I imagine the good doctor was quite unhappy."

"He surely was." Jem studied Mr. Hemmings' face carefully as she continued, "I thought she went with you."

"I can see why you would think so. If she tries to contact me, I'll let you know. I'll go on home now and see if she left word for me."

"Thank you," replied Jem, but she wasn't certain Mr. Hemmings was being entirely honest. She watched the man hurry next door.

"Mother!" Sumner yelled as he entered.

"I'm in the parlor. For heaven's sake, what is wrong?"

"I wanted to let you know I'm leaving for a few days. I won't be back until after the New Year."

"Where have you been? Did you tell your father?"

"I returned Madeleine home and stayed to be certain she was well. And no, I was hoping to leave that to you."

"Well, it depends. Are you off on some bender, intent to enjoy the vice of drink as long as possible?"

"No. I actually ran across an old buddy from the war. I'm considering changing jobs, but I'm not prepared to give up my position at the bank yet."

"Your father will be cross."

"Then perhaps we shouldn't tell him. It can be our secret."

"Are you trying to charm me?" asked Evelyn.

"Yes I am. Have I lost my touch?"

"Not entirely," she thoughtfully replied. "Why exactly should I support you in this?"

"Well, you always enjoyed making your husband unhappy. But I will admit I've been a derelict and disappointing member of our family, and I believe a change is in the air."

"I assume it must have something to do with the pretty little imbecile next door."

"I don't expect you to believe me in light of what happened on Christmas Eve, but I promise you, Maddie is no imbecile. I will prove this to you in time, but the plans for my future employment are another issue entirely. Have I your support in this? You never imagined I would make a good banker, did you?"

"True. I don't believe you were cut out to be a banker. It will devastate your father when you tell him. I want to be there to watch."

"You have my word."

"I see a change in you although I'm not certain what it is. Do you need money?"

Sumner desperately needed money—he had been able to scrape up very little. He replied with a convincing, "No. I'm all right."

"Well, since you spent Christmas Day next door,

you didn't open your gift from me." Evelyn reached into the branches of the Christmas tree standing in the front parlor window and pulled out a small, exquisitely wrapped gift. "You'd best take this along on your expedition."

"Thank you, Mother." Much to her surprise, Sumner applied a kiss to his mother's cheek as he dropped her gift in his inside jacket pocket.

Once he was seated on the Red Car with a valise full of clothing, Sumner unwrapped the gift. Grinning, he realized he owed his mother much more than a kiss on the cheek. The box contained cash—500 dollars— more than enough to finance a honeymoon and serve as seed money for their future.

* * *

"What is that aroma?" Sumner inquired as he entered Trace's front door and dropped his valise on the floor. Before Maddie could reply as she walked from the kitchen, he scooped her into his arms and planted a thorough and possessive kiss. Continuing his embrace, Sumner observed his bride's lovely face and waited for a reply.

Maddie was too distracted by her husband's kiss and his pleasant mood to remember the question.

Sumner prompted, "The smell? Have you prepared dinner?"

"Oh, yes! It's a good thing you're late. It took me much longer than I dreamed it would."

"And here I thought I would whisk you away to a restaurant. What are we having?"

"It's a surprise! Wash up and come have a seat. I set the kitchen table for us."

Maddie's enthusiasm was obvious. Although

Sumner wondered what he was in for, he was determined to appear a true enthusiast for his wife's first attempt at cooking. His fears were quickly laid to rest. The roast was tender and flavorful, the vegetables thoroughly cooked. He applied lavish and well-earned praise.

"The gravy isn't right," moaned Maddie. "I tried my best."

"I think sauces take experience," Sumner consoled. "But it has great taste."

"It's too thin and lumpy."

"Madeleine Hemmings," he scolded. It was the first time Sumner thought to use her new name, and it delighted her. "Last night, I made us scrambled eggs for Christmas dinner. If you can so drastically improve our menu after only one day of marriage, I'm afraid I'm doomed to become a fat old man. Come here and sit with me."

Maddie put her arms around her husband's neck as she sat on his lap.

"I'm afraid we have to talk about some serious things." He kissed her then she laid her head on his shoulder.

"Must we, really? Can't we enjoy our evening together? You've been gone all day."

"I have been gone, but the good news is, I don't have to leave you again. We can have a proper honeymoon, and I will attempt to find another job once Trace returns."

"Then we're going to stay in Venice?" Maddie kissed her groom's neck.

Although Sumner was distracted, he needed to focus on their future for a few moments. "That's what I need to talk to you about." He took Maddie's shoulders and held her away to look in her eyes. "My mother gave me some money when I stopped at home."

"For our wedding?"

"No. It was my Christmas gift."

"You did tell her we were married though?"

Sumner's expression grew serious. "No, Maddie, I didn't. Do you remember what happened on Christmas Eve?"

"Dr. Coolidge came. He gave me some medicine, but I knew I had to be at your house at two. I came as soon as I could. I remember being sleepy."

"Well, your appearance reinforced something my father believes. You see, he thinks you are backward—that you have some mental deficiency."

"Why would he think such a thing?"

"Your Aunt Mary told him so."

"She would never do that."

"She would, Maddie. She told me the same thing the day I first came to your house. I saw you sitting in the garden, and I wanted to meet you. I'm convinced the doctor drugged you to prevent you from leaving. You didn't appear yourself."

"So, your father believes there is something wrong with me, and he wouldn't approve of our marriage?"

"Yes, but it's not the real problem. With time, we can change his opinion. When I took you home on Christmas Eve, Jem informed me your aunt has paperwork giving her control of you. It gives Dr. Coolidge control when she's gone. Do you know anything about this paper?"

"She's my guardian. That's all I know."

"Why do you need a guardian? You're an adult."

"I don't know. I don't know anything about a

paper."

"I didn't tell anyone about our marriage. Only Trace knows. I think we must find out about this paper for one thing."

"Why, what else is wrong?"

Sumner took a deep breath. "I want to be married to you more than anything I ever wanted in my life. I need you to believe me. But the truth is, I'm not in a position to support you. I hate my job at the bank. I never cared before, but I want to be a good husband—a good provider. I have to find a better job and need to make some money. We have nothing."

"We have a Dutch oven, a whisk and a cookbook. We don't need anything else."

"We definitely need a bed and a place to put it," Sumner teased as he kissed her cheek. "But we do need more, Maddie. I'm not prepared financially to be a husband, and you need to work on your domestic skills. If dinner tonight is any indication, you'll be an expert quite soon.

"I think we should keep our marriage a secret for now. You'll have your holiday at the beach and go back to your aunt's house temporarily. I need you to find out about this paper she has. And I'll probably end up at the bank, at least for a while."

"It isn't honest to let our families support us when we're married," Maddie asserted.

Sumner took a deep breath. "It's only for a short time. I'm certain I can get a good-paying job here at the airport. We can rent a bungalow somewhere nearby. If we're lucky, we can be back here together in a matter of weeks."

"But I want to be with you—live with you."

"I want that too. I think we have to be practical."

Despite good intentions, Sumner's newfound practical side would have lasting repercussions.

* * *

Maddie's first attempt at oatmeal proved a shocking failure, completely inedible. Sumner teased her outrageously.

"I always wanted to know how they made baseballs," he commented, knowing his wife was persistent, and clever and would soon master cooking.

Deciding she deserved a real honeymoon, Sumner relocated his bride to the Cadillac Hotel right on the beach. He purchased a modest gold wedding band, which Maddie adored as if it were an extravagant and rare piece of fine jewelry. Unable to refrain from gazing at her hand, she understood the need to hide the ring once they went home. Sumner found it necessary to supplement Maddie's wardrobe since she brought so few belongings in the pillow slip.

They enjoyed rides and attractions on the pier including the two roller coasters, Maddie's favorites. They frequently rode the Race Through the Clouds and the smaller but wilder Big Dipper. Sumner noted his bride was as enthusiastic and excited on their tenth ride as she had been on their first.

The boisterous honky-tonk atmosphere on the piers was exhilarating and contagious. Developer Abbot Kinney's desire to provide a cultural and educational destination had long been overruled by the public's desire for the thrilling and sensational.

The Hemmings visited the freak show although Maddie seemed disturbed by the display. Sumner tried to console her by claiming the "freaks" made a good living and undoubtedly appreciated their patronage.

They went dancing on two occasions, and Maddie, begging endlessly, convinced her husband to take her roller skating. Sumner nervously attached the ball-bearing roller skates to his wife's shoes. Never did Maddie seem more vulnerable than when she urged him to let her skate alone. With a worried frown, Sumner skated beside her finally persuading her to skate as a couple as other pairs on the rink were doing. Once he had firm hold of her, Sumner relaxed, reluctantly admitting he enjoyed the experience.

They appreciated quieter moments: walking on the beach, watching the sunset and even picnicking on the shore one fine afternoon. Both were ever eager to return to their honeymoon suite.

Sumner came to understand it was more than Maddie's looks that intrigued him. She was fun and happy, always a joy. She was clever and rather opinionated.

It became apparent Maddie was never exposed to the feminine warnings and societal restrictions imposed on proper girls. Since no one anticipated her involvement with a man, she was unprepared for that eventuality. Her naiveté quickly led to an intimate and all-encompassing marital relationship. Maddie had no inhibitions or self-conscious physical boundaries.

Sumner understood how gullible she was. Maddie's innocence and complete trust had an odd effect. Where he traditionally sought to take advantage of women, he felt responsible and uncharacteristically honest, wanting only to protect and cherish his wife. Sumner wished more than anything to deserve her trust. He considered himself a model husband, careful to answer Maddie's questions and introduce her to a fulfilling physical relationship. If only he could prove himself such a spectacular model of husbandly responsibility out of the bedroom. Having their own bedroom would certainly be a step in the right direction.

* * *

Trace returned home and found Sumner's note then phoned the Cadillac Hotel to explain his efforts on his friend's behalf. He took Sumner away from his honeymoon to introduce him to contacts at the air field. There was little activity due to the holidays and the gloomy winter weather, but Sumner remained hopeful he might have a job within weeks. Greatly appreciating his friend's help and hospitality, Sumner treated Trace to lunch.

Finding herself seated at the table alone with Trace when Sumner left to make a phone call to a prospective employer, Madeleine started a conversation.

"I have to thank you for your help. You were so kind to let us stay at your home and now helping Sumner find a job."

"I told you when I met you, I owe him my life. This is really the least I could do. Did Sumner tell you about our adventures during the war?"

"He doesn't discuss that."

"Well, I'm not surprised. I'm the one who talked Sumner into joining up. We both liked to fly before the war. It became apparent Sumner did not care to be part of the action. He always was the smarter one," Trace admitted, smiling.

"He got into the habit of having a shot of booze before we flew. He said it helped him get into the cockpit when his legs wouldn't let him."

"He was drunk?"

"You have to understand; medicinal brandy was the antidote to any difficult flight. Sumner simply took his earlier than most. Taking off had a sobering effect on him. He was the steadiest flyer in our squadron, always alert, always in the right place at the right time.

"My plane got shot up, and I was limping back to base when an enemy squad caught sight of me. I was pretty sure I was a dead man. I could barely keep the plane in the sky. I lost speed and most of my ability to maneuver.

"Sumner kept an eye on me, and when I came under attack, he took on the enemy single-handedly. He gave me enough room to get back to base. When he didn't follow, I was certain he sacrificed his life for mine, but I was wrong, thank God. He won a Silver Citation Star. His parents must be proud of him."

"I'm not sure they know."

"Yeah, that sounds like Sumner."

Chapter Six

The honeymooners dined at an elegant restaurant on New Year's Eve and shared a glass of wine—the last legal glass they would have on the holiday most connected with drink. Prohibition was set to begin on January 17 at midnight.

Sumner was amused at the degree of inebriation his wife displayed after only one glass. It was no wonder the drug the doctor gave her had such an extreme effect. He smiled indulgently as he escorted Maddie back to their room while she crooned *I'm Forever Blowing Bubbles* for all to hear. Beauty though she was, her singing voice left something to be desired. Everyone they passed along the way seemed entertained by the gorgeous woman loudly singing, even if she was about as off-key as she could get. If Madeleine weren't so drunk, she would have been embarrassed.

"Sing with me, Sumner—you can do it," she encouraged.

Sumner only laughed and guided his bride into the elevator. As it started to ascend, Maddie lurched toward him. "Look, Sumner, I'm flying like the bubbles!" At this she threw her arms wide and almost fell. Alone save for the operator, Sumner scooped her into his arms.

"Whatever would your husband say about this, Mrs. Hemmings?"

"Why he'd say, 'you better kiss that girl right now!'" and so he did, much to the disapproval of the elevator operator.

Backing out the door of their floor, Sumner explained, "Don't mind us, we're newlyweds." He laughed when Maddie blew the man a kiss and continued her aria.

It was time to go home before they knew it. Sumner slept later than he intended and awoke to find his bride at the window, staring toward the ocean, tears streaming down her face.

"What's wrong?"

"I don't want to go home! I want to be with you. How can you ask me to give you up?"

"I don't want you to give me up. I certainly don't intend to give you up."

"But we won't live together; we won't sleep together."

"I knew it was my lovemaking you would miss the most," Sumner teased. "I should have realized you only married me for intimate adventures." He watched Maddie's cheeks turn a brilliant red as he took her hand and pulled her back into bed. "It's only for a few weeks, my darling. Don't cry."

They may only have been married a short while, but Sumner had a more thorough understanding of Maddie's health. She showed no sign of frailty although she tired easily.

It was incredibly refreshing and exhilarating to see the world through her eyes. He was saddened to observe her despair on this last day of their honeymoon.

Maddie remained so emotional, Sumner almost gave in to her anguish. Certain his plan provided their best course, he stood on the corner and watched Maddie enter her aunt's house. Her eyes were red as she turned toward him and attempted a smile. He did not imagine after-dinner walks would serve their needs and desires any longer. Sumner needed to find a way to see his wife in private during the weeks they lived apart and yet so very near.

* * *

Once Sumner returned home from work on Monday, he made a beeline for Maddie's house. Jem answered the door, a stern expression in place.

"Miss Crawford cannot walk with you this evening."

"All right, but I'd like to see her."

"I'm afraid it's not possible."

"Why?" Sumner's jubilant mood quickly vanished. He looked forward to this moment all day.

"Dr. Coolidge was unhappy when he came. He confined Miss Madeleine to bed because she's overwrought."

At that moment, a determined Maddie pushed her way out the door after grabbing her coat and hat. She handed the coat to Sumner and commented, "That will be all, Jem."

"But the doctor warned you—"

"I explained my position to Dr. Coolidge. I do not need to stay in bed. I will go for my nightly walk just as I have been."

"Madeleine, this is bad for you. The doctor

warned—"

"Yes, the doctor is good at warnings," Maddie continued as she slid her arms into the coat Sumner held. "I'll be back in an hour or so. If you feel the need to call the police again, you can have them wait in the parlor until I return."

Sumner's eyes grew wide at his wife's firm speech. He had never seen her so determined. He couldn't resist grinning at the dour Jem as he offered his arm and escorted Maddie down the walkway and out the front gate.

"I think I'm afraid," Sumner admitted as he gazed at his wife's lovely smile.

"Afraid? Of what?"

"You! I feel the definite need to toe the line. What happened when you got home?"

"My home is with you. When I got to Aunt Mary's house, Jem called the doctor right away. I don't trust her, Sumner. I don't feel safe."

"I'm right next door. But what did the doctor tell you?"

"He said I wasn't well. I'm supposed to stay in bed for two weeks."

"And what did you say?"

"I said there was nothing wrong with me. I asked him for my diagnosis. He said it was not to be a concern of mine. I could ask Aunt Mary about it when she returns. He threatened me!"

"How so?"

"He told me quite specifically if I don't adhere to his advice, he will have no choice but to take more stringent action."

"What does that mean?"

"I don't know. But I have no intention of staying

in bed. I don't understand this, any of it. I was always led to believe I was an invalid and would forfeit my life if I didn't adhere to doctor's orders. I can't remember living any other way. Yet, when I'm with you, I feel wonderful! If they are lying to me, then why? If they are telling me the truth, why don't I feel ill?"

"I want to take you to a doctor, Maddie, a different doctor."

"No! We need to save our money for our future. I don't want to waste it."

"But we need answers. I can't tell you how flattering it is to think you would risk your life to be with me, but I'm concerned about you. I want us to grow very, very old together. Have you thought about where to find the papers Jem referenced? Could you ask her about them?"

"I can't ask her. She told me she wished she never let me go with you. I don't know if she's worried about her job or if she's afraid of Aunt Mary. When I tried to talk to her, she clammed right up. And the more I think about it, I'm certain I've seen a box with my name on it. But I can't remember where."

Since Madeleine appeared perturbed, Sumner changed the subject. He talked about his day at the bank then asked his wife if she acquired any new housekeeping information.

"I did! I told Dorothy I wanted to learn how she keeps the house. I explained someday I might need to hire a housekeeper, and I need a working knowledge of what should be done. She proved a wealth of information. I even jotted down notes so I will have a reference. I'm going to be the best housekeeper you ever saw!"

A Keepsake Love

* * *

Once Sumner deposited her at Aunt Mary's front door, Madeleine decided to confront Jem. Having never argued with anyone in her life, she found the experience unsettling. Jem dodged her questions, obviously uncomfortable with her young mistress's newly formulated ideas and opinions.

But Jem's own fears became obvious as the quarrel reached its climax. Madeleine found this the most troubling aspect of the entire exchange. The woman was clearly concerned Madeleine's recent excursions caused some irreparable damage, not to her health, but to her freedom in the household. Madeleine would admit, she had almost no freedom in any case. But Jem cried hysterically, urging Madeleine to stay in bed as the doctor ordered. Jem apologized profusely for looking the other way when Sumner came calling. Her regret seemed sincere.

Although Jem felt some dire consequence was about to occur, she honestly seemed not to know what might happen. Madeleine felt ill at ease, and Sumner's assurances he was right next door did nothing to console her.

Sitting cross-legged on her bed in the midst of her reverie, Madeleine heard a tap on her window much like when a bird flew into a pane of glass. But it was dark, and the tap quickly recurred. She climbed out of bed and opened her curtain to find Sumner balanced on the decorative iron rail that wrapped around the bottom of the window, a nervous expression on his face. Maddie quickly threw open the window and grabbed his hand as if she were strong enough to hold him in case of another fall.

"What are you doing?" she hissed.

Feeling much steadier once his feet were firmly planted on Maddie's bedroom floor, Sumner quietly replied, "I've come to find my wife. Do you know where she might be?" At this, he embraced Madeleine and kissed her soundly.

"I don't think I've seen her," Maddie responded. "Why don't we lie down and wait to see if she comes?"

"My thoughts exactly!"

In this way, the young Hemmings couple began their marriage. Sumner called each evening to walk with his wife. He found a short step stool in the garden shed and propped it against the back corner of the wall behind the shed. Once Maddie's bedroom light went out—which occurred earlier each night—Sumner climbed over the wall and up the iron railing on the side of the house.

Initially concerned there was no lock on Maddie's door, he placed a chair beneath the knob to keep out any possible intruder. This practice fell by the wayside as nights went by and no one bothered them, just as Maddie claimed.

Maddie felt safe at night with her husband by her side. After more amorous activities, they often whispered together for hours before falling asleep.

Consoled by the hope they would soon have a place of their own, Sumner crawled out of bed each morning before sunrise and scurried to his parents' house.

Maddie's endless questions about the bank, Sumner's co-workers and customers caused him to pay attention at work. Knowing Maddie hungered for information about life "on the outside," he was more than happy to appease her curiosity. His former disinterested and rushed demeanor faded away, replaced by seemingly genuine interest in people at the bank.

Unexpectedly, his fellow workers were sources of information. They happily responded to Mr. Hemmings' questions about their lives, families, even how they traveled. The customers Sumner helped were full of praise for the bank's personal interest and kind attention.

Sumner reported to Madeleine on the events of his day. When seen through her eyes, his workday held endless opportunities and fantastic experiences.

No one noticed this behavior more than Merritt Hemmings. His son's sudden interest in work became obvious although he rarely saw the boy or spoke to him. Merritt believed the feeble woman from next door had somehow inspired his son's mature and responsible performance at work. If true, he found Sonny's interest in an imbecile, no matter how beautiful, completely unsatisfactory. Considering his options as far as his son was concerned, Merritt lit his cigar as he leaned against the headboard.

"You are not seriously going to smoke a cigar in my bed!" commented Evelyn.

"It does look as if I am."

"Take that nasty thing outside this instant."

It was too dark to see well. Merritt used the glow of his cigar to look at his wife's stern expression. She appeared as serious as she sounded.

"I might remind you, this is my house."

"And I might remind you, this is my bed."

"Does this make you want to leave California?"

"What is that supposed to mean?"

"When are you leaving? I think I have a right to

know. Your abrupt departure last time was quite rude. The holidays are over."

"Are you trying to get rid of me?" Evelyn was incredulous. Merritt was easier to tolerate of late. She had no imminent plans for departure.

"Not exactly. I only want to understand your intentions. I've enjoyed our time together, here in your room. I desire to know how much longer I can expect our relationship to continue."

"Not long at all if you smoke."

Thoughtfully, Merritt took one last puff and carefully put the cigar out in the ashtray on the bedside table, intent on finishing his smoke in the morning. "So, when are you leaving?"

"If you're asking me to stay, you're not being kind."

"It was never my intention to be kind. Aren't we well past that stage of marriage?"

"Why must we be? Kindness is simply an aspect of love."

"Love! Have you gone mad, woman?"

"I think Sumner is in love."

"I sincerely hope not."

"Haven't you noticed the change in him? He's like a new man."

"His work at the bank has certainly improved. For the first time, I feel he could make a success of himself. But falling in love with an idiot is hardly cause for our support. I took away his stipend."

"Everett! You did not!"

"I certainly did. He can make do on his salary. We can't support his infatuation."

"He says she is quite normal."

"Sonny has been blinded by her beauty since the

day he first saw her. Would you want your grandchildren born simpletons? I am surprised you, of all people, would be taken in by this."

"Why? Am I so terribly cold?"

"In a word, yes."

"I think you best go sleep in your own bed," Evelyn suggested.

* * *

In an effort to appease the anxious Jem, Madeleine donned her nightgown and crawled into bed when Dr. Coolidge returned.

"So, you are taking my advice and staying abed?"

Madeleine, feeling entirely uncooperative, managed, "Yes, sir."

"Well, you're doing splendidly. I'm happy you decided to take care of yourself."

Madeleine managed only a weak smile, which served to frame her disabilities more in her favor than intended. For Jem's sake, she continued, "I'll do exactly as you suggest."

"Wonderful! I'll be back next Monday. Your aunt should be returning shortly. I am bound to report your errant behavior, you understand? My reports have been quite specific. Perhaps my assertion you returned to your normally cooperative self will have a soothing effect on her."

"Yes, perhaps so," but Madeleine would be the first to admit she did not understand the doctor's rhetoric.

Later that night, Sumner eagerly regaled his bride with the description of a lovely widow who brought her daughter into the bank and secured a loan for her late husband's haberdashery business. Maddie then offered her own account of Dr. Coolidge's visit.

"I'm surprised you decided to appear the cooperative patient."

"Jem was immensely relieved. I'm worried."

"I told you not to worry," admonished Sumner. "Soon, we'll reveal our marriage, and off we'll go."

"Have you heard any more about a job at Venice Field?"

"Not much. I plan to go there soon. But I've been thinking. If that doesn't pan out, perhaps we could take a room at a boarding house. We might get by on my salary at the bank, but it wouldn't be ideal. We couldn't save much money."

"What if I took a job?"

"You? What on earth would you do?"

"I don't know. But I'm going to look in the newspaper for a position," Maddie determinedly stated. "If you told your parents about our marriage, don't you think we could live with them for a while?"

"It's an option I've considered, but my father is extremely opposed to our relationship."

"He wouldn't be if he met me."

"The thing about my father is, if he has a bad opinion, it takes a lot to change his mind. I think the boarding house is the better avenue. If I don't have a job by the end of the month, we can look further into finding a place. Something near Pershing Square might be nice. You could go there to draw during the day. How is your housekeeping going?"

"I made thorough notes about cleaning, including what is done on a monthly and yearly basis. I can't exactly practice, but I did make lunch! Cook, although confused by my efforts, has been a real help. I feel I can follow almost any recipe, but I need more experience."

"Have you located the box with your name?"

"No, and I've looked everywhere in the house. I used my interest in housekeeping to thoroughly inspect the cupboards and drawers. The only place it could be is in my aunt's bedroom. I almost never go in there."

"That's enough discussion for tonight," Sumner suggested as he took his wife in his arms.

* * *

Jem lay in bed listening to the sound of rain falling. Remembering she'd seen Madeleine's window ajar when she was in the bedroom, Jem decided to close it. With the wind blowing, the rain might soak the curtains and cause a mess. Madeleine could catch a chill.

She quietly opened the door and peered inside to make certain her dearest girl was soundly asleep so as not to startle her, but it was Jem who was startled instead. A man's body was clearly visible in the bed, his broad shoulders and bare back faced the door, Madeleine's sheet was drawn up near his waist. Jem's first inclination was to set up a hue and cry until Madeleine slipped her arm around the man's waist and embraced him. A stunned Jem quickly withdrew but stood in the hallway staring at the closed door. She had no doubt as to the identity of the man.

After collecting herself, Jem returned to her bedroom. Admonishingly, she thought herself a fool to believe Mr. Hemmings' intentions regarding Madeleine could be good. The man was reprehensible and took advantage of her darling girl who had no worldly experience nor religious upbringing. She likely hadn't any idea she was behaving in an immoral manner. Jem attempted to instill ethical behavior in her charge. Her efforts obviously fell short. She had only herself to blame.

With sudden clarity, Jem understood her role in Madeleine's life was coming to an end. She allowed the girl unprecedented freedom that would prove both their undoing. Sleep evaded Jem as she dreaded the return of Mary Argyle.

* * *

Sumner knocked on the front door, eager to share news of his impending trip to Venice Field. Maddie made a point of coming to the door herself, but tonight, a dour Jem peeked through the cracked doorway.

"I've come to take Miss Crawford for our walk."

"She's not at home." Jem started to close the door.

"Where is she?" an alarmed Sumner inquired as he pressed his hand against the door.

"I don't believe it's any of your business, Mr. Hemmings."

"We had a prearranged meeting. Did she leave a note for me?" He saw hesitation in the woman's expression and pressed, "I can see she did. Can I have it?" Jem seemed almost a coconspirator on Christmas Eve when Dr. Coolidge gave Maddie the drugs. The woman was completely hostile now. She reluctantly handed him a small envelope and left Mr. Hemmings standing on the porch.

The envelope was sealed, Sumner did not imagine Jem had pried.

My dearest husband,
I took the opportunity of this lovely day to go into

the city and see if I could secure some form of employment to supplement our savings. Wish me luck! I'll tell you all about it tonight.
M

Sumner scowled as he walked next door. He did not want his wife working. No matter how strong and independent she thought herself to be, he doubted her actual endurance was adequate to any form of employment. He considered her a delicate if not sickly woman, accustomed to sitting in her garden all day. Maddie was used to living a sheltered and protected life. He believed she would be disappointed when she could not find anything she was able to do.

His life certainly changed since he met Maddie. Sumner's first and only objective when he arrived in Los Angeles was to see how quickly and how often he could manage to get drunk. Now his concern was all for his wife, how to provide for her and give her a life of ease.

Heaving a sigh, Sumner knew his mother, at least, would be pleased he was home for dinner. Having no illusions his parents repaired prior damage to their marriage, it was clear a truce developed over the holidays. Now, their familiar and ceaseless bickering returned in full force. Sumner often found it difficult to refrain from laughter at their snide comments. He knew beyond question, he wanted something better for his marriage. If he didn't have a guide to good marriage, he certainly understood what to avoid.

* * *

Madeleine smiled warmly at Jem, who met her at the front door. Her cheery greeting was met with a scowl.

The fact Jem did not approve of anything she did was clear.

Walking to the kitchen, Madeleine was intent on helping herself to leftovers. Determined no one would ruin her delightful day, she hummed a silly tune, *Sahara, Now We're Dry Like You*, as she retrieved dinner from the ice box and set about rewarming it. She was surprised when Jem made her own appearance in the kitchen.

"What on earth are you doing?"

"I'm warming up my dinner."

"Isn't this Cook's job? Did you ask her to get your food?"

"It's not necessary. I can do it myself."

"Where've you been all day?"

"I took the Red Car downtown and walked around the city."

"It's not a safe thing to do. I forbid you to go again."

"Now Jem, I don't work for you. I'm an adult, and you can't control me."

"I only try to keep you safe."

"I know and appreciate it. But this is my life, and I intend to live it to the fullest."

"Promise me you won't go out tomorrow."

"I can't. The world is an exciting place, especially when a person has been cooped up their whole life."

"What if you get lost?"

"I find people are extremely helpful and kind."

"Maybe they're just tryin' to help theirselves to things you might not want to give them."

"What is that supposed to mean?"

"It means folks might try and take advantage of you, like Mr. Hemmings."

"What makes you think Mr. Hemmings might take advantage of me?"

"I have eyes. I don't think he's a righteous man."

"Let me assure you, Mr. Hemmings has my best interest at heart. There's no need for you to worry where he is concerned." Madeleine sat at the kitchen table, curiously observing Jem. The woman was behaving strangely.

"Your aunt wrote to me."

"How unusual. What did she have to say?"

"She's worried about the doctor's reports. She wants me to make sure you follow his orders."

"Well, assure away. Whatever it takes to put her mind at ease."

"She won't put up with your antics once she comes home."

"Jem, even Aunt Mary must realize I was bound to grow up someday."

Jem shook her head in disgust. Madeleine simply didn't understand the complexities of life. Aside from playing informant to Dr. Coolidge, there was little she could do to control the girl. Jem's uncomfortable apprehension returned in full force as she watched Madeleine finish her plate of food. Lost in thought, Jem was not prepared for Madeleine's question.

"Why did you change your mind?

"About what?"

"You initially supported my friendship with Mr. Hemmings. When did you change your mind?"

"On Christmas Eve."

"When Dr. Coolidge was here? What did he say? Has my condition deteriorated?"

"No." Jem was torn. This was an opportunity to impress Madeleine with her concerns, but how much could she tell the girl? "I thought it would do you good to get out in the world, but when the doctor drugged you to keep you home, I started to think I made a mistake by letting you go out. You should do what the doctor says, Baby Girl."

"I have my own life, now," was Madeleine's only comment.

* * *

Maddie lay in bed wrapped in her husband's embrace. He was breathing deeply, having finally drifted off to sleep. They shared and enjoyed each other completely, both physically and conversationally.

Sumner, concerned at her disappearance, didn't hesitate to state his opinions of married women who work. He made broad assumptions. Their husbands were derelicts and drunks. Women were forced against their will to support their families in a harsh and cruel world. The war was over, and women belonged at home.

Madeleine had nothing but enthusiasm for her day despite her husband's negative ideas and clearly defined commands. Listening to stories about his workday served to embolden her to seek similar experiences. Any trepidation was quickly overcome. They certainly could use the money.

Sumner had his own employment news to share. Trace called about a job. Sumner planned to head for Venice early Friday morning and return on Saturday.

His scheme could not have better conformed to Madeleine's. She applied at a restaurant with a help wanted sign in the window. Once she turned to leave, a female customer tapped her on the shoulder.

"Have a seat, miss. I heared you ask about a job,

and I think I know somethin' could be of profit to you." The woman was elegantly dressed, obviously affluent. Her speech was uneven and uncultured.

"You have a job for me? You don't even know if I'm qualified."

"Oh, you're qualified; there's no doubt of it. Here's my card." The woman handed Madeleine a business card engraved with "Conquest Connor, Sutter's Dance Studio."

"You have a dancing school? What could I do there?"

"Honey, you just need to show up. Men want to dance. They line dance halls waiting for a turn. Of course, we don't have no liquor in dance halls now. My business partner, Ruben, and me got this idea from back East. Men go to dancing schools and pay for the chance to practice. They ain't enough women to go around here. Why, men will line up right proper to dance with a looker like you. We charge ten cents for each dance. You get to keep a nickel. Think how much you can make in a single night. You look to be a bright girl."

Madeleine stared apprehensively at Conquest.

"I see you doubt me. Rest assured, this is on the up-and-up. The men are gentlemen or they get throwed out. It's not like the dance halls where they used to serve booze. Besides, I think you just might be our best attraction so far."

"How? I can barely even dance."

Conquest chuckled. "You'll see. You can come and go as you like, just look for me the first time you show up. If you try it and don't like it, you don't have to come back. But any of the girls will tell you, it's an easy way to make a buck."

Now, Sumner would be away on Friday night. Madeleine decided to pay a visit to Sutter's Dance Studio.

* * *

Sumner stared down at his trembling hands. Trace supplied him with a jigger of brandy when he climbed into the cockpit. Even though he hadn't been drinking lately, the belt of booze didn't last.

He needed another drink. Sumner jumped from the biplane and got his bearings. There were no restrictions on drinking in Venice. He could buy whiskey until midnight tonight, when prohibition kicked in. As he strode off the runway, an excited Trace attempted to keep up.

"Wait, Sumner! I've got your money."

Sumner stopped in his tracks. After all, improved finances were the goal of this experiment. He turned toward his friend and took the bills, counting them before shoving them in his pocket. The tidy sum could finance quite a bender. Closing his eyes, Sumner shook his head to clear his thoughts. He flew today for Maddie, to give them a boost for their savings. He decided to have one drink and head for home.

"So, Sumner, Eddie really liked your work. Experienced pilots are hard to come by. He said he'd pay you twice what you made today if you stick around and fly tomorrow. They want to film a big scene—lots of planes and a mock dog fight."

"No. I need a drink, then I'm going home."

"Look, Sumner, I know you need the money. Let me see if I can get you more."

"No. I tried this once, and I don't like it."

"Did you ever think that's what makes you such a

good pilot? You're conscientious, careful and meticulous."

"I'm just a drunk when I fly. I came here in hopes of getting a steady job so I can get a place and support my wife. I didn't come to fly."

"But Sumner, the movie industry is growing like crazy. Flying could get you in on the ground floor."

"Except for the fact I don't want anything to do with flying, you have a great idea. Show me the way to the closest bar. I don't even want to stay at your house tonight."

The pair arrived at The Shady Lady Saloon to find the wildest party they ever witnessed. Intent on making the evening as memorable as possible, customers were mourning the murder of booze. Several men danced around tables carrying a coffin as the piano player performed jazzy dirges. The building was crammed so full, Sumner found it difficult to get the bartender's attention. He finally managed to buy a bottle of whiskey to share with Trace. The two men enjoyed the wild abandon of the night right up until the stroke of midnight when the revelers somberly exited their favorite haunt for the last time.

Before Sumner staggered into his room at Trace's house and collapsed across the bed, he agreed to fly on Saturday.

Chapter Seven

Weekends had been spent in modest pursuits since the young Hemmings couple was on a budget. They took long street car rides, which emboldened Madeleine to take her solitary rides downtown.

They strolled through parks where the new bride fantasized aloud about her desire to take up tennis, bicycling, croquet and even horseback riding. Sumner's dubious looks were accompanied by vague promises alluding to a time when the weather warmed and they had more money.

Madeleine could see her husband considered her an invalid, an opinion she wished to dispel. She always thought of herself as an invalid, but no more. Perhaps, she reasoned, all it took was determination to be and do all one could achieve. For the first time in her life, Maddie felt entirely able.

To avoid complications, the former Miss Crawford stayed in bed each morning Dr. Coolidge paid his call. Upon Maddie's return from her honeymoon, the visits occurred frequently. She appeared the model patient, agreeable and willing to comply with suggested medical management. Her subservient demeanor resulted in less frequent visits.

Maddie's foray into the world of taxi dancing proved to be a fun, physical, and social experiment she intended to repeat. She made over a dollar before she reached the end of her stamina. The other girls assured she would gain strength as time went on.

Conquest was proven correct in her assertion Madeleine would have no trouble acquiring dance partners. Some men eagerly taught her dance steps. Some were quiet and nervous; others were eloquent. They had wildly differing degrees of ability. All were polite and well-behaved. Madeleine believed she met and spoke with more people in 15 minutes on the dance floor than she had in her entire life. She found the experience exhilarating.

When Sumner did not come home on Saturday, Madeleine decided to return to the dance studio. As on Friday, her lack of vigor became an issue early on.

Maddie was concerned when Sumner failed to appear at Aunt Mary's by the time she got home. Lying in her lonely bed, Mrs. Hemmings wondered what became of her husband and what she might do about it.

The sound of Sumner's voice as he clumsily climbed the iron trellis became much too apparent. Madeleine dashed across her bedroom and threw open the window.

"Hush! You're making too much noise," she hissed.

"Hello there darlin'," Sumner enthusiastically replied.

"Shhhhhhh!"

"What's wrong? You're not glad to see me?" Sumner slurred.

"Get in here!" Madeleine shushed as she grabbed

Sumner's arm. Had he slipped and fallen, she would have fallen as well, so firmly did she take hold. Maddie quickly shut the window and put the chair under the door knob as Sumner, who collapsed upon his entrance through the window, crawled across the floor toward the bed.

"What is wrong with you?"

"Nothin'. Why? Do I look funny?" Sumner rubbed his hand across his face.

Noting the obvious odor of alcohol, Maddie accused, "You've been drinking!"

"Yes, I have. It's illegal now—probably a federal offense. I'm quite the sinner."

"What about your job?"

"Well, it didn't exactly pan out." Sumner, now seated on the floor against the bed, fumbled in his pocket and managed to retrieve several bills. "But I got this for us."

"How?" Madeleine noted her husband could barely keep his eyes open and wondered at the fact he found his way home. She urged him to stand and get in bed, but he seemed unable to part ways with the floor. She was certainly not strong enough to move him.

"I flew. I'm famous now. I'm in a movie. I'll make enough to support you, as a proper husband should." At this, Sumner slumped to the side and began to snore.

Incredulous, Madeleine could do nothing but ponder Sumner's trip to Venice as she gathered his money from the floor. Between them, they managed to put aside a substantial sum in two days. Finally deciding she could do nothing for her husband but let him sleep it off, she climbed into bed alone.

Maddie believed if they continued in this manner

for a few more weeks, they might supplement Sumner's Christmas gift and have enough to purchase a small bungalow, even if they couldn't completely furnish it. She watched the papers and found ads for homes requiring only a modest payment, as low as $400. There were weekly payments like rent until the home was paid in full.

She better understood Sumner's initial plan of keeping their marriage secret. She also realized flying did not agree with her husband and further—admission of her newfound employment opportunity would doubtless have serious repercussions.

* * *

Although Maddie tried to wake Sumner when the sun came up, her efforts proved fruitless. Madeleine lay in bed listening as Sumner finally stirred. She peeked over the edge of the bed to find him awake, looking around the room in obvious confusion.

"Good morning, sunshine! I haven't woken up with you since we came home from our honeymoon. How are you feeling this beautiful morning?"

"Like shit," muttered Sumner, briefly amused by Maddie's shock at his profanity. "Oh crap, it's already light out." He sat up, then groaned and laid flat on the hard floor. Every muscle in his body ached; his head was splitting. It was all he could do to keep from vomiting.

"Looks like you will be my captive prisoner all this fine day," tormented Maddie. "Too bad you're sick or we might start the day as we did in Venice. You do remember how we started those days? Marriage hasn't aged you to the point you have forgotten, surely?" She suggestively unbuttoned the top few buttons on her nightie, content with Sumner's look of regret.

He continued to stare at her face until she abruptly laid back on her bed, out of his sight.

"Don't go," he urged as her nightie hit him in the face. He groaned as Madeleine giggled on the bed.

Unable to resist such temptation, Sumner quickly developed a plan for their day. Temporarily donning her discarded nightgown, Maddie kept watch as her husband used the bathroom down the hall. When Jem knocked on the door, Maddie retrieved the money she left on the end of the bed and stuffed it in her dresser drawer as Sumner hid. Jem was informed Miss Crawford intended to spend the day abed, reading. Madeleine ordered up a hearty breakfast, which she forced on her husband. Hungry herself, she picked at his eggs, bacon, grapefruit and muffin while he ate.

If Jem thought it odd when Madeleine ordered coffee, she said not a word. Maddie wondered if Jem knew what was going on and had heard Sumner's noisy arrival the night before. Somewhat surprised her lifelong caretaker was quiet while her ward committed all manner of supposed sin, Madeleine made herself blush as she lay in bed next to her husband.

"Why are you blushing?" inquired Sumner as he rested his head on his bent elbow and stared at his wife.

"I'll tell you for a quarter."

"Well, I am a poverty-stricken new groom. I can only afford a penny."

"I see. I will tell you this much. I think Jem may be on to us."

"How so?"

"You made a rather noisy entrance last night. Maybe even your parents know you're here."

"Of course not. I'm always discreet."

Madeleine shook her head. "Why did you drink so much?"

Sumner laid back on the pillow, staring at the ceiling. "Trace didn't have a job at the airport for me after all, but he's been flying planes for movies. The money is good. He managed to get me a job on Friday. It was easy money. I flew a bit where they told me, I landed, I was done. But I don't like to fly, Maddie, I don't care if I ever fly a plane for the rest of my life."

"Why?"

"War is ugly. I hated being there once I arrived. I was lucky to come out of it unscathed. I can't get in a plane without remembering what it was like, the sounds, the sights and smells, the fear."

"Then why didn't you just come home to me?"

"I had a chance to make some money, good money. I got drunk and flew on Saturday as well."

"How can you fly when you're drunk?"

"Whiskey gets me in the cockpit, and it relieves the tension when I get out. I had a fine plane, no flying bathtub for the movies. I knew I was safer than I have ever been in the air. They even provided a parachute, but that didn't help."

"You never used a parachute during the war?"

"No. They thought it would motivate pilots to abandon their aircraft needlessly. The Germans had them."

"Maybe you're not so unscathed by the war as you think."

"What do you mean?"

"Sumner, if you have to get drunk to fly, I don't

think you should go again."

"If I take on jobs like this one, we can get our own place." He turned to Maddie and rubbed his thumb over her cheek. "There's no reason why we can't go now. Pack your things. We could start our life together."

"What kind of life would it be with you drunk all the time? Besides, it's illegal now. I don't want a jailbird for a husband."

"It isn't illegal to drink, only to make and sell liquor. I'm still working on getting another job at Venice Field. Flying would tide us over until then. There are a lot of jobs for pilots at the beach. I can do stunts over the ocean or real estate promotions. I can give rides. The police department in Venice uses planes to patrol. Maybe I could get a job there. We can stay at Trace's for a night or two while we find a home."

"No, Sumner. I think you were right about saving up for a while. I don't want you to take a job that makes you sick. We can save for a couple more weeks. Whatever we have by the end of February, we'll make do, even if we have to live in a shack on the beach.

"I will make us fine dinners in our Dutch oven, and you can find a real job, one you like. I won't go with you today." She could see the disappointment her words caused but believed they could manage to live apart for a while longer. Maddie would quietly supplement whatever Sumner managed to make plus his bank salary. Perhaps they could even move out before Aunt Mary came home. Jem's nervous warnings were having an effect.

* * *

Despite Madeleine's pleas, Sumner would not resist the opportunity to improve their financial condition. He informed his father he would be absent from work on Thursday and Friday to pursue other employment. The ensuing argument was concise only because Sumner walked out.

Although he longed to take his wife to Venice, Sumner realized this would cause further acrimony. He agreed on one point—he shouldn't need to drink in order to fly. He was anxious to prove this, not to Madeleine but to himself. Once he overcame this obstacle, Sumner could ask Maddie to accompany him to Venice by the Sea in good conscience.

He studied her face as he prepared to climb out the window on Thursday morning. The sun was coming up. It was light enough to clearly see her features. Sumner was as appreciative of Maddie's looks as he had ever been—her delicate chin, rosebud mouth, milky complexion and tousled blond hair. Unfortunately, as was usually the case when he left, her big blue eyes were closed. He could not believe she belonged to him.

Sumner planned to look at bungalows in the Venice area, having listened intently when Maddie recited her research from the newspaper. He knew many of the ads were come-ons intended to get prospective buyers into real estate offices. Even so, he hoped to find something close to the beach they might afford. He had no intention of waiting weeks to share a home with his wife. Admittedly confused by her change of heart, Sumner assumed she would jump at the chance to live together when he offered the opportunity.

He dared to touch Maddie's lips before he left.

She stirred, smiled and settled into her pillow. It was this vision of his wife Sumner would carry in his heart for years to come.

* * *

Knowing there was about to be trouble, Trace landed his plane, hardly waiting for it to stop before hurdling out of the cockpit. He ran toward Sumner and grabbed his arm as he strode purposefully across the tarmac. Trace was not surprised when Sumner threw him off.

"What the hell do you think you were doing up there?" Sumner growled at the smiling boy being congratulated by his eager friends.

Boldly, the boy replied, "I was flying, what the hell were you doing old man?"

At this, Sumner landed a punch in the boy's jaw, which sent him sprawling. Both Trace and another experienced pilot grabbed Sumner's arms.

"You stupid idiot. This is not some absurd game. You almost got me killed."

"Maybe you're too old to react," the boy taunted as he wiped blood from his mouth with the back of his hand.

"Well, if I'm so old, come and get a piece of me. I'll wait until you haul your ass off the ground."

"No, Sumner. He's just a foolish kid," urged Trace. "Let's go get a drink."

"That kid tumbled out of the sky right in front of my plane!"

"I know, and it was a stupid stunt. If you were any less a pilot, you'd both be dead now."

"And what about your movie people?"

"It made for great cinema. I don't think they care. Nothing came of it but good film in the can."

Sumner shook off Trace's arm again and stormed off the field. The "old man" was all of 24 years old.

* * *

Sumner rode a street car to the city. He made a tidy sum for his work on Thursday and Friday but hadn't found a place to rent or buy. Too much of his time was taken by the movie shoot.

He had a lead on a job at Venice Field, a management position where he would make a good wage and have regular hours.

Sumner knew after today, he would never fly again. Proud of himself, not even the stunt this afternoon drove him to take a drink. The fact he needed one aside, Sumner tried to push his anger and fear away, intent on thinking about his lovely wife.

Certain he could talk her into packing her things and coming with him now, Sumner decided it was time to reintroduce Maddie to his parents. He was ready to come clean about his marriage and plans for the future. What could possibly go wrong this time? He would go next door and take her from Aunt Mary's house forever.

The man in the seat across from him began to speak. Sumner let the man prattle on, hoping he would stop talking. Unexpectedly, the conversation became interesting.

"I think I'm in love. You ever been in love?"

Sumner smiled weakly and did not reply.

"I went to this dancing school. It's hard to meet a lady here in Los Angeles unless you go to church. I'm not exactly the church-going type. I know it's not normal in this city. It seems everyone here is off to church on Sunday morning. Don't get me wrong, I've considered it as a last resort but then a friend of mine got me to go to this dancing school.

"I thought, why not? At least I'd get to dance with a woman—talk to her. At most, I might find a swell girl so I went last week. Lo and behold, I met this humdinger of a woman, a real beauty. Of course, every man there wants to dance with her."

Sumner gave another weak smile.

"So, she was there again last night. I spent 30 cents. I danced three times, and I stood in long lines to do it. She's real refined, mind you. A delicate beauty; blond hair, the biggest blue eyes I ever seen. She ain't a real good dancer, but why would anybody care?"

The man's description intrigued Sumner. "Does your lady friend have a name?"

"Oh, she's got a swell name, Madeleine. Did you ever hear such a beautiful name? Everything about her is handsome. I'm going to ask her out tonight. She promised she'd be there."

"Where is this fine dancing school? I might invest in such an establishment," Sumner asked as the anger of the day welled again in his throat.

"Sutter's Dance Studio."

* * *

Believing it unlikely the Madeleine at the dance school was his wife, Sumner found it necessary to reassure himself. He exited the trolley at the stop after his eager fellow passenger departed and walked back along the route until he came to a sign that read Sutter's Dance Studio. Taking a deep breath, Sumner wondered about his need to delay his trip home over such nonsense.

He quickly swept his gaze across the dance floor and was dumbfounded to find his wife in the arms of another man. She was apparently having a fine time although her partner was no dancer and only sloughed from one foot to the other as he talked. The man might not be getting much of a dance lesson, but he was obviously getting his ten cents worth of entertainment.

A fury unlike anything Sumner had ever known washed over him as he stood transfixed. To think, he risked his life today for his ungrateful wife. She completely disregarded his position on women working. If he were thinking clearly, Sumner might have realized his assertion working women had drunks for husbands hit a little too close to home.

Recent events overwhelmed him: his desperation to prove he could fly without drinking, the stupid antics of the reckless boy pilot and his so-far unfulfilled desire to be a competent bread-winner. Now, he was ashamed to find his wife selling dances to supplement their income and furious she allowed other men to touch her.

Madeleine undoubtedly turned down his offer to move immediately to Venice by the Sea so she could sell herself in this immoral manner. At least it seemed immoral to the indignant Mr. Hemmings. The idea he much preferred her shut up in her aunt's house briefly dawned on Sumner as he walked purposefully across the dance floor.

Maddie did not see her husband until he grabbed her partner by the scruff of the neck, turned him around and slugged him in the gut. She was befuddled by Sumner's look of sheer hatred before he turned and walked out the door of the dance studio.

She knelt down to inquire if her unlucky partner was all right. The man, gasping for air, smiled and nodded his head affirmatively, intent on appearing as virile as possible from his prone position on the floor.

Glancing at the shocked faces all around, Maddie leapt to her feet and, grabbing her coat from the rack near the door, followed Sumner outside. Catching a glimpse of his back, she first yelled his name then hurried after him, quickly realizing she would never catch him as he strode down the street, ignoring her calls.

Standing in the middle of the sidewalk, Madeleine felt an uncharacteristic guilt. Her intention was only to earn a bit of money they could use to set up housekeeping. She enjoyed the companionship, freedom and exercise—which she was certain served to make her stronger—and considered these pleasant byproducts of her employment.

For the first time, she understood the deceit of never having mentioned her employment to her husband. She knew it would upset him. Somehow, she needed to find a way to make this up to Sumner.

Madeleine doubted she would ever have the opportunity to do so as the weekend progressed. Sumner did not come to sleep on Friday night; he did not come calling on Saturday or Sunday morning.

Maddie considered the possibility she might call on him. His parents would be shocked at her appearance, but this could give her the opportunity to prove herself a competent daughter-in-law. Perhaps she might appease Sumner's anger enough to have a conversation.

After all, she had no commitment to her job. She didn't even have to quit. If Sumner still wanted to leave immediately for their new life in Venice, she would pack her bags and go. But then, she had no bags to pack.

A Keepsake Love

In anticipation of her trip next door and her new life as the public Mrs. Hemmings, Madeleine remembered Aunt Mary recently purchased new luggage. She decided to forego pillowslips and borrow a piece or two of the old luggage. Maddie could pack while she contemplated her bold venture. After all, if she appeared, bag in hand, how could Sumner turn her away?

Walking down the landing to her aunt's room, Madeleine found two valises behind the corner chair, which she pulled into the middle of the room to have a better look. She glanced toward the window and went to open the curtains, suddenly remembering where she saw the box with her name. It was on Aunt Mary's desk and must still be there unless someone in the household moved it.

And there it was, as she remembered. Curious to see what was inside, Madeleine untied the string securing the box and carefully removed the lid. The box was full of paperwork and newspaper articles.

Madeleine surmised Aunt Mary must have interest in the influential man who was the subject of the articles, clipped from Eastern newspapers. She could not fathom why such information would be kept in a box with her name.

The contents seemed to be in date order, oldest at the bottom. The newspaper article on top was dated before Aunt Mary left on her trip. Her aunt must have forgotten to put the box away after adding the last article.

She quickly grew bored by the clippings, which focused on business, politics and social events. She turned them face-down on the desktop and focused her attention on the other contents.

The words Medical Report were scrawled across sealed and dated envelopes. A small stack of letters was tied with string. Although Madeleine had a definite interest in these, she needed time to read and reseal the report envelopes so she added them to the pile of clippings.

She next came across a legal document granting Aunt Mary full custody and control of her niece. Madeleine was not particularly interested in the paper and doubted she could understand the legalese it contained. Laying it crosswise on the pile, she would examine it to ascertain if Dr. Coolidge had control over her and to what age. After all, she was 20, considered an adult by any means.

As she neared the bottom of the box, a document caused her knees to give way. Madeleine sank to her aunt's bed to avoid collapsing on the floor, unable to comprehend the information on her birth certificate. The mother was listed as Mary Crawford and the father listed was the influential subject of the clipped articles. She read and reread her name on the document, certain it must be an error. If this was accurate, Aunt Mary was not her aunt at all but her own mother. And her father—how could this possibly be?

Her head spinning, Madeleine picked up the last item in the box, an old picture of a woman severely dressed in black mourning clothes. The woman had an uncanny resemblance to Madeleine, eerily so. If she did not know better, she would swear she posed for the photograph herself. Madeleine turned the picture over to find it was inscribed with a message, "Dearest Mary—Best wishes in your new life. Feel free to contact me if you need anything."

"Surely we're not planning a trip?" came a voice from the doorway. Then Mary Argyle looked beyond her old valises sitting in the middle of the bedroom floor. "Oh, Madeleine, you should not be looking in that box. Now there's nothing to do but call Dr. Coolidge upstairs. He thoughtfully picked me up from the train station. What an unfortunate circumstance—for you."

Chapter Eight

Sumner stood fuming on his neighbor's front porch. True, he was furious at Madeleine Friday last, but he was prepared to make amends when he returned from work on Monday. After all, they couldn't repair their marriage if they didn't speak.

Admittedly, he missed the comfort of his wife at night. Lying alone in his own bed proved an atoning experience, more than he imagined possible after such a short time as a married man. Armed with a litany of grievances, he was not surprised when told Maddie was not available.

He purposely stayed away on Tuesday, hoping some extra time apart would calm Maddie. Surely, she missed him as much as he missed her. But his attempts to see her on Wednesday, Thursday and Friday were met with equally disappointing results.

How angry could one tiny woman be? He realized in his mother's case, anger could last a very long while indeed, months, even years—well beyond a time when the original injustice could be recalled.

He found it difficult to devise any plan, short of climbing up to her bedroom window. If Maddie was still angry, she could simply keep the window locked and deny him entry.

Sumner wished to spend this pleasant Saturday with his beloved. There was so much to talk about; so much to plan. He found it impossible to turn and walk away after the maid delivered the standard message, "Miss Crawford is not available."

Shoving his hands in his pockets, Sumner finally turned toward home when the front door of Madeleine's house opened, and Jem waved furtively for him to return to the porch.

"Be at the corner in ten minutes," Jem urged then closed the door in his face.

"What the hell?" Sumner uttered aloud, but he turned right when he reached the sidewalk and waited on the corner as instructed. It was unlike Madeleine to be dramatic. Then again, she might be having difficulty getting out of the house. It was his understanding her aunt had returned, or that was what his father suggested.

As the ten minutes dragged on, Sumner constructed the dialogue he wished to have. Tired of their secretive marriage, he would insist Maddie move out of her aunt's house at once. He was not about to put up with her current endeavors to enhance their savings. Sumner planned to put his foot down as was his right as a husband. There would be no further discussion on these topics.

Disappointed when he saw, not his wife, but a distraught Jem hurrying down the sidewalk, Sumner asked, "What's wrong? Where is Madeleine? If she's still angry at me—"

"Listen closely. I can't stay here and talk to you. I don't know who in the house might be watching."

Sumner's befuddled expression might have been

funny if the situation was not so dire. "Where is Madeleine?"

"Mrs. Argyle come home last Sunday. She took Madeleine, I don't know where. When I asked about her, she told me Madeleine would not be coming back. She told me I need to find a place to live, my services here are no longer required. After almost 20 years, I'll be out on the street at the end of the month."

"Can't you find out where she went?"

"Mrs. Argyle won't tell me nothin' about Madeleine, not where she went, not why. You think she was mad at you? Could it be why she left?"

"I was the one who was angry. I don't even know if Madeleine was irate. I imagined she was when she wouldn't see me. What should I do?"

"These here things must have been Madeleine's dearest belongings. I found them hid in her room."

Jem reached in her pocket and pulled out the handkerchief Sumner bought Maddie on their first trip to the Venice Pier. Sumner placed it under his nose to find it held Madeleine's scent.

Next, Jem handed him Madeleine's gold wedding band and gazed at him with understanding. He took the ring uncomprehendingly and looked squarely at Jem.

"What does this mean?"

"She didn't take anything along, not even clothes. All her things are in her room where they belong."

"Is Mrs. Argyle at home?"

"She stays at her store from early morning 'til late. She don't come home to sleep most nights."

"I need to talk to her. If I give you my telephone number, can you call me when she comes in?" Sumner scrawled his number on the back of a business card and handed it to Jem. Clutching the handkerchief and

Maddie's ring tightly in his hand, Sumner went home.

A dark fear took root. If Maddie was angry and left of her own accord, she would have taken her things. If Mary Argyle somehow learned of their marriage and disapproved, Maddie would still need clothes. This made no sense.

Sumner bounded up the stairs and hurried to his bedroom window to stare into Maddie's backyard. Scenarios, all improbable, crowded his thoughts. He paced nervously around his bedroom.

The telephone did not ring that night nor the next day. This was not unusual as his parents were reluctant to use the modern convenience and preferred to communicate in more traditional ways. Only occasionally did his father get phone calls about banking business. Sumner sat at the dinner table on Monday when the phone finally rang. He bounded away to answer it.

"She's here," were the only words he heard before the phone went dead.

After abruptly excusing himself, Sumner walked purposefully to his neighbor's house and pounded on the door. As usual, the maid answered and informed him, "Miss Crawford is not available."

"I've come to see Mrs. Argyle. I have business with her."

"Mrs. Argyle is not available."

Sumner was not about to be put off. He pushed his way past the maid, catching sight of Mary Argyle seated on the davenport, thumbing through mail.

"I was wondering when you might turn up," Mrs. Argyle calmly commented, a smug expression on her face.

"I need to see Madeleine."

"I'm sure you do. Perhaps she does not wish to see you."

"Why wouldn't she?"

"I don't know. She's not a normal girl. I understand you took her for walks. You could have said or done anything to set her off. You don't understand her as well as you believe. Perhaps you're the one who encouraged her to leave this household in my absence. You've been a bad influence on my niece so let me make this clear. I forbid you to see her."

"Madeleine is an adult. I think she can decide these things for herself. I want to see her."

"She may be an adult in age, but mentally, she is completely dependent on me. I have paperwork to prove it."

"I know there's nothing wrong with her. She's a completely normal woman. Why do you lie about her?"

Mary chuckled, amused by the young man's intensity. "I could ask you questions as well. How can you consider her normal? Why do you defend her? I understand you are taken by her looks, but you can't make her into something she's not."

The woman was so convincing, it made Sumner doubt himself. Defensively, he continued, "I know Madeleine better than anyone. Better than you. I have my own paperwork."

"Really? And what paperwork might you have? Something to refute doctor's reports dating back to Madeleine's childhood? Did you have some quack examine her?"

"No, I have other paperwork. I want to see her. Where is she, upstairs?"

"I forbid it."

This command set Sumner in motion. He turned and hurried up the staircase. "Madeleine," he yelled, hoping against all reason she would answer. He walked along the landing toward her room. The door was open; the room exactly as he last saw it. Her brush and comb were on the dresser top. Her coat lay across the back of the chair they used to secure the door. "Where is she?" he growled as Mary Argyle entered the room behind him.

"It's none of your concern. She's obviously gone. You need to leave as well."

"What have you done with her?" Sumner realized he was close to violence but saw he did not intimidate Mrs. Argyle in the least.

"She's in safe hands, recovering from her recent ordeal with you."

"With me?"

"You expected too much of her. She had a breakdown. She's recovering."

"Where?"

"I'm afraid I can't tell you. Seeing you would only worsen her condition."

"I don't believe you. You're lying. Everything you say is a lie."

Mary chuckled. "Too bad you have no proof. If you don't leave of your own accord, I'll call the police and have you removed. You have no rights here; you have no rights as far as Madeleine is concerned. Her welfare is my concern and mine alone. You need to go."

"I do have rights."

"Please leave, Mr. Hemmings. I'm going to call the police."

"I *do* have rights. Madeleine is my wife."

This, at least, caused Mary Argyle to hesitate as she walked toward the stairs. "What did you say?"

"Madeleine is my wife. I have every right to know where she is. I insist you tell me immediately."

The woman paused as she contemplated Sumner's admission. "I'm sorry, Mr. Hemmings, you have no rights. Leave now. It's your last chance."

"You don't believe we're married? I can prove it."

"I'm certain you can. You seem such a terribly sincere husband. You simply must realize, it doesn't matter to me at all."

"*What do you mean, it doesn't matter?*" Sumner yelled at Mary's retreating figure. There was no further reply.

When the police came, they took Sumner to the station and listened to his frantic pleas with a modicum of sympathy. The man seemed somewhat deranged. When he tried to file a missing person's report, insisting he was only attempting to find his wife, the legal entanglements became more than the arresting officers could sort through. They decided to leave the matter to a judge.

Sumner was charged with breaking and entering. Disgusted that Sonny remained bewitched by the unfortunate girl next door, even to her detriment, Merritt Hemmings sent an attorney to pay his son's bail.

The trial was continued due to the accuser's important business trip. Sumner seethed in silence.

Tired of his father's constant criticism, Sumner worked at the bank by day but at night, visited the speakeasies around the city. Sumner attempted his usual solace, in a bottle of whiskey. He knew people were dying of poison passed off as illegal liquor. Often, wood alcohol was the culprit. Desperate for a drink, victims first went blind then died within hours. This did not deter Sumner from his favorite habit.

He learned too late of Maddie's disappearance and realized she could be almost anywhere. He obtained Jem's new address and promised to contact her if he had any news of Madeleine. She did the same.

Sumner used their household savings to hire a Pinkerton man. His money was quickly returned. Mary Argyle refused to talk to them after asserting her niece was not missing. No one in her household had any concrete information. The interesting allegations Jem made were discounted. Since she was fired, there was likelihood she held a grudge and was eager to cast aspersions on her former employer. Dr. Coolidge, who Sumner only imagined might have information, also refused to be interviewed. There simply were no leads to follow. Sumner got the impression the agency did not wish to be associated with any type of deviant behavior. Aunt Mary's lies served her well.

Determined to have his day in court, Sumner believed he could convince the judge to force Mary Argyle into revealing Maddie's location. Certain his marriage certificate was valid, he sought constant reassurance from his attorney of his rights as a husband. The elderly Mr. Johnstone was only interested in defending his client from the charges of breaking and entering. He was prepared to embellish upon Sumner's fine war record, heroism, and family connections and throw his client on the mercy of the court.

Months went by as the court continued the trial two additional times to accommodate the lovely

Mrs. Argyle. It was May when Sumner finally took his place beside his attorney in the courtroom.

Testimony came from arresting police officers and the Argyle maid who attested Sumner forced his way into the house and refused to leave.

Finally, Mary Argyle took the stand. Sumner could barely restrain himself as he listened to her testify. After rudimentary questions, Sumner became still as the trial took a turn in what he assumed was a favorable direction.

"Mrs. Argyle, do you have any idea why the plaintiff broke into your house?"

"He claims to be married to my niece."

"I assume he can prove this to the court's satisfaction?" the Judge asked. The prosecutor stared at his rival, seated next to Sumner.

"We can. Your honor, we have evidence to submit. I will be glad to enter it now. It's the marriage certificate of Mr. Hemmings and Miss Madeleine Crawford." Mr. Johnstone approached the bench with the document in question.

"This appears to be in order."

"This has nothing to do with the charges at issue," complained the prosecuting attorney.

"If you'd give me the opportunity to explain, I'm certain we can clear this up," Mary Argyle offered as she presented a stack of documents to the judge.

"Those were never submitted into evidence," complained Mr. Johnstone.

"Hold on there, Horace, all in good time," answered the judge as he stared over his glasses at the documents.

"You see, Your Honor, my niece is incapacitated. She has been a burden her entire life. I took responsibility for her when my sister and her husband were killed in an accident. She was an infant. Her disabilities became apparent quite early on as you can see from the medical reports. Mr. Hemmings was taken with Madeleine's beauty."

"You're a liar," shouted Sumner as he rose from behind the table. "There's nothing wrong with her. She's perfectly normal."

The judge slammed his gavel on the bench. "Control your client," he commanded.

Urging Mr. Hemmings to be seated, Mr. Johnstone comforted him. "I promise you'll have a chance to speak."

"Mr. Hemmings was a bad influence on my niece. He upset her and behaved inappropriately. In short, he took advantage of her weak mind. She was distraught when I returned from a recent trip abroad. I had no choice but to institutionalize her. It was for her own good. She's improving. One can only wonder at a man who would take advantage of a feeble-minded girl." Mrs. Argyle peered disgustedly at Sumner.

She stepped from the witness box after a few more questions. Madeleine Crawford's medical reports were entered into evidence. Despite Sumner's fervent and sincere testimony, which included his love and commitment to his wife, the judge had few options but to find him guilty of breaking and entering.

Sumner did not care about the charges or his possible sentence. When the judge asked him if he had anything further to say, Sumner's only request was to know where his wife was being kept.

"Your Honor, might I have another word?" requested Mary Argyle. "We can all see Mr. Hemmings, despite his deviant tendencies, has concern for my niece. Although I can't in good conscience allow him to upset her further, I would be willing to drop the charges if you would be so kind as to annul the marriage. I would have this done in any case. This will save me further legal obligations. It is my duty as her guardian to protect her interests. She simply isn't capable of making this kind of decision as you can see from her records."

Sumner sat, completely spent and shocked at this request. "You can't do this, your honor," he begged. "I'm telling you, my wife is perfectly fit, completely able to make her own choices. You have to believe me."

Once court was adjourned, a stunned Sumner found it impossible to stand. Not only had he failed to obtain Maddie's location, they were no longer married. It didn't matter if the charges against him were dropped. He lost everything.

"Come home, Sonny," urged his mother, who attended against her son's wishes. Helpless, he allowed her to take his arm and guide him from the courtroom.

The trial proved the start of a new and novel relationship between mother and son.

* * *

"Get up Sumner."

"What? What are you doing in here?" A blurry eyed and hungover Sumner struggled to focus as his mother stood in front of his bedroom window after throwing open the curtains.

"Get up and get dressed. I'll be waiting downstairs."

"Why?"

"It's Sunday. I went to court. You can come with

me to church."

Sumner snorted in derision. "Since when do you go to church?"

"Since today, and you're coming too. Don't try going back to sleep. I'll be back in ten minutes with a pan of ice water, which I will not hesitate to throw on you if you are still abed."

"And since when did you carry pans of ice water?"

"I will have James do it," she threatened, before departing the bedroom.

Sumner found himself in a church pew beside his mother in short order. It was not as if he had never been inside a church before. As with most boys, he was a reluctant Sunday school attendee. He struggled to appear interested today in order to appease his mother who was acting strangely. Relieved when the service ended, he shook hands with the minister and escorted his mother to the limousine.

"Will you tell me what this is about?"

"This may be difficult to understand, but I do love you, and you are my only child."

"I understand less now than before I made my query."

Evelyn frowned. She was no model parent. Watching her son struggle in the courtroom caused her to experience rather frightening maternal compulsions. In short, Evelyn Hemmings felt the need to mother her only son.

Certain she could put him on a better path, she decided to start by attending church. People always told her it was the way to peace and inner fulfilment. The fact she never believed them did not quell her desire to appear a competent mother. It was never too late to start.

"I realize your father considers you a pervert because of your attraction to Miss Crawford. You truly seem to love her, despite her apparent shortcomings. I want to believe in you. I wish I had the opportunity to know your Madeleine and judge for myself. Since that's not possible, at least for now, I am inclined to support you—my duty as a mother."

"I never knew you thought much about being a mother."

Only rarely did Evelyn attempt to avoid confrontation. She had no intention of being drawn into an argument now. "Jest if you will, it does not deter me. I am taking charge of you until you come to your senses. We may only be going through the motions of being a family at first, but I believe it will become natural with effort."

"So, you're staying in Los Angeles?"

"Absolutely. I am married to your father after all. Further, nothing will stop me from caring for you, not even your father's nonsense. I know exactly what you need to do."

Amused at his mother's assertion, Sumner could not help but smile. "And what is that?"

"You need to make yourself into the man your Madeleine deserves—the best man you can be. Mark my words, if you do, she will be yours forever. I don't know how; I only know this to be true."

Sumner suddenly recalled Maddie's desire for his parents to be proud of him. Knowing his mother's intentions were good, he made an effort to appear an appropriate son, albeit a cynical one.

He could not walk by Maddie's house without feeling her loss. Sumner lay awake at night wondering where she was, what she was doing and if she would ever come back to him.

He regretted not taking her to a doctor as he intended. If they made their marriage known earlier, Mary Argyle would simply have annulled it that much sooner. Sumner could not fathom the woman's motives or behavior. Her smug look as she stared at him from her seat in the courthouse haunted him. He considered methods to force Mary Argyle into revealing Maddie's location.

Evelyn and Sumner returned home from church one Sunday to find Merritt unconscious on the library floor. The doctor was called immediately. His diagnosis was apoplexy—hemorrhage of the brain. The elder Mr. Hemmings was not expected to recover.

* * *

Initially, it was important to allege Merritt Hemmings was temporarily incapacitated to avoid a run on the bank. The recently irritable young Mr. Hemmings appeared at the bank on Monday, returned to his formerly affable self. He relied heavily on his favorable experiences with customers and coworkers from the time he provided workday information to Maddie. If bank employees thought his sudden change of heart odd, they seemed content to enjoy it while it lasted since it did not last previously.

Ensconced in his father's office, determined to appear competent and in charge, Sumner bluffed his way through the week while learning as much as possible. If his questions sounded incredibly stupid to bank officers, he smiled affably at their shocked replies and asserted he was only confirming his own ideas or testing them on their knowledge. Thankfully, by

Friday, his father tried to speak. Understanding him was a talent in itself.

Trapped in a body that no longer complied with his commands, Merritt's sole concern was his business. If he were at all thankful his son managed to guide the bank through the week unscathed, his gratitude was not in any way apparent.

Frustrated by his limited ability to communicate, Merritt spent every possible moment attempting to provide information about the bank to his son. If his anger caused his speech to worsen, it also served to provoke him into movement, limited though it was. He first moved his fingers then his hands. Despite these improvements, the doctor indicated a complete recovery was unlikely.

* * *

Convinced a drink would help him get through the day, Sumner continued his favorite activity. During periods of inebriation, his anger dissipated and Sumner became thoughtful. If what Mary said in court was true, Madeleine was in some sort of institution. This would explain why she left her clothing behind. But what kind of facility would accept a patient who was so obviously healthy—mentally and physically?

He often wondered at his own sanity. Was Mary Argyle right, and he was somehow deluded?

Sumner understood the need to play it smart. Mrs. Argyle was a serious opponent. The woman obviously knew what she wanted and how to get it although her motives and goals remained a mystery to Sumner. He had regrets. He might have understood Maddie was missing if he hadn't let his anger get the best of him.

Tormented by longing for his beautiful wife, Sumner closed his eyes each night and thought only of Madeleine's big blue eyes, her smile and her enthusiastic wit. He intentionally brought to mind her features on the morning he left her asleep in her bed, choosing to ignore the last time he actually saw her—dancing with another man.

It was difficult to search for a person without so much as a photograph. He decided to increase his own efforts to find his wife and visited the County Farm in nearby Hondo where the mentally ill were housed in the most modern of facilities. Here, the infirm gardened, farmed and made handicrafts.

Sumner understood his predicament made him sound a bit cracked and so, refined a tale he invented. He was attempting to find his younger sister. An aunt admitted her to an unknown facility and refused to divulge her location due to family issues. He only wished to ensure his sister's wellbeing.

Sumner spent one Saturday travelling to the Southern California State Asylum for the Insane and Inebriates in San Bernardino County. The idea Maddie might be trapped in some similar, vile asylum caused him to redouble his efforts.

There were many facilities located in Northern California, too far for him to visit. He believed Mary had time to secrete her niece at a distant location so he started a letter-writing campaign in spare moments at the bank. Helpful hospital workers also suggested various private facilities where the wealthy housed debilitated family members. Sumner wrote to them as well.

His most direct method of locating Maddie remained forcing Mary Argyle's confession. When

Sumner received negative responses to his inquiries, his mind turned toward ways to make the woman talk.

* * *

Sunday was Independence Day. After attending church with his mother in an effort to get her out of the house, Sumner planned to reward himself with a cold beer. His farcical pose as responsible bank manager was grueling, and another week of deception was about to begin.

"Sumner, I know your father seems only angry, but I want to thank you for what you're doing at the bank. It's important to give the impression of control. People get nervous about their money. We rely on your father's income, and I have no desire to die a poor old lady."

"We always counted on Father to be the breadwinner. I'm as guilty of that as you. You could sell the bank."

"It's a possibility. If you fill in for another week or two until we see how he does, it might prove our best way forward."

"You do understand what the doctor says? He doesn't think Father will ever fully recover."

"He is improving, though. I want to see if he continues. His speech seems better each day. I see how hard he tries, poor dear. He's very frustrated. It does appear his mind is intact; I mean as far as intelligence. How odd."

"What is odd?"

"You and I. We have so much in common. We have lost our partners. I am counting on you as never before in my life. I know you won't disappoint me."

Sumner briefly considered his upcoming

confrontation with Mary Argyle. This would almost certainly land him back in jail.

"I will do my best," was his only comment.

Chapter Nine

Knowing her sanity could easily slip away, Madeleine was determined to resist her increasingly dark moods. She endeavored to think of her circumstances as a sort of game. Aunt Mary was winning at the moment, but in the end, Madeleine would remain the rational woman she had always been.

Against her better judgement, memories of the way she arrived in her present difficulty replayed almost constantly in her mind.

"Explain this to me," Madeleine demanded.

"Don't be stupid. It's quite simple. I had an affair with an affluent man. I was a child really; he took advantage," began Aunt Mary. "When I told him about your impending appearance, I was ecstatic, thinking he would throw over his new wife for me. I was a fool, at least initially. I quickly realized you were my meal ticket.

"Quite naturally, I hoped for a boy. It's difficult for a man to resist a male child, especially since there was a probability his wife would not give him an heir—a useful secret I became privy to. Your paternal grandmother, the woman in the picture you're holding, was quite fond of me, and she disliked Wally's wife with an intensity I came to appreciate. She provided encouragement and aid when I was in need. Unfortunately, she died not long after she sent me that picture. When you so disappointedly turned out to be female, I considered the best way to profit from my circumstances. Wally was eager to pay my way—get me out of the city. I fully intended to make his generosity a permanent fixture so I developed my plan."

"What plan?"

Mary smiled condescendingly. "I felt I could convince him to support me, or us, in fine style so we would keep our little secret. I imagined ways to extract maximum benefit. Wally was rich and well positioned. He was only considering a public life then. What could be more undesirable and embarrassing than a mistress and a bastard child? Of course, I thought to myself, a congenitally defective child, a driveling idiot girl who could make such an interesting picture in the newspaper. How better to put his very character and heritage at my mercy?

"When I conveyed the tragic news of his daughter's disability, Wally, quite naturally, wanted nothing whatever to do with you. To be honest, I doubt he ever did. All my desires, my wildest requests were instantly granted. Even the paperwork I needed to start a new life was instantly prepared.

"I was a young widow with all the proper credentials including a marriage license, guardianship documents, and death certificate for my pretend spouse. I started the business of my dreams and became the independent worldly woman I longed to be.

"Unlimited travel, shopping and access to

fabulous venues were at my fingertips, all provided by you. And then, I was not really cut out for motherhood. But my appeal as the beneficent aunt proved such an advantage, especially when your disabilities were mentioned. I appeared quite angelic to perfect strangers.

"I quickly understood my initial desire you be a boy was foolhardy. Boys are too independent. You were so simple, so easily cajoled into the role of invalid. There were a few doctors before Dr. Coolidge who were more than happy to write any report I dictated for a fee. Dr. Coolidge is a true find. He did exactly what I wanted for little more than an occasional tryst in his office. I believe he considers himself in love, the fool.

"Of necessity, this part of our game is now over. I can hardly have you running around spouting off about what you saw in the box. I really only kept you around for emergencies—the unlikely possibility your father might request evidence of your existence. He occasionally asks about your health." Mary looked up to see Dr. Coolidge standing in the doorway. "Ah, the good doctor has joined us. It seems our Madeleine has been up to no good."

Before Maddie knew what happened, the doctor walked behind her and placed an odorous cloth across her nose. She had no choice but to breathe in the vile fumes and awoke sometime later in her current cell, at least she thought of it as a cell.

Knowing she'd been drugged from her previous experience, Madeleine couldn't determine how many days had gone by and so refrained from trying to keep any type of record.

Her basement room had a small barred window at

ground level, high above her head. There was a cot, a small table and stool, and a bathroom with a sink and toilet. The floor was dirt.

Maddie wore a simple, loose-fitting gray dress. She sat in stunned silence when her arms were tied and her hair was cut close to her scalp. The haircut was qualified as an attempt to combat vermin. Maddie mourned the loss of her hair not for any vain reason but because she would be so easily identified were she able to escape.

No proclamations of sanity made the least impact on anyone she saw. Her attempts to converse were met with icy silence. Thinking she might procure her sanity with reading material, Madeleine was thrilled when a Bible was left in her cell.

Although she could hear other patients outside her window, no one else shared the basement. She learned to listen for the latch on the stairwell door, secure in the knowledge she was otherwise alone.

She spoke out loud to herself, telling stories or recalling pleasant experiences. Deciding she needed exercise, Maddie walked relentlessly around the perimeter of her cell, ten circles in one direction, ten circles in the other. Then she would start over, determined to be strong enough to escape when an opportunity arose.

Madeleine began each day by uttering the assurance, "Sumner will come for me today." She desperately clung to this belief then proceeded to think about pre-planned topics she scheduled throughout her day.

She recalled every moment spent with her husband from the day he fell at her feet. Maddie replicated their conversations and recalled in detail the fantastic times they shared. She described the contents of her closet and categorized every piece of clothing she could recall Sumner ever wearing. Bringing to mind all the ads she clipped of furniture sales and homes, Maddie decorated their dream house in her mind, placing it a block from Venice Beach.

Then she would talk about the day she planned once she was free—visiting the grocery store, cooking and cleaning as a proper wife should.

Her last thought of the day was, "Sumner will come for me tomorrow."

Her suspicions were confirmed when she felt the baby kick. Determined no one would know, she sat on her cot facing the corner whenever food was placed inside the door.

Madeleine needed to escape as never before. She resolved to be with Sumner when their baby came and fantasized about his reaction when he learned of his impending fatherhood.

The thought she might be able to dig a short tunnel under her cot occurred. But there was no covering on the floor, nothing she could use to hide an excavation. Her silverware was carefully counted.

Seemingly remote and well-behaved as she sat in her corner, Madeleine knew the staff took her apathy for granted. An older, stout woman with red curly hair seemed especially lax, often leaving the door ajar when she checked the bathroom or left clean sheets on the table.

Madeleine started to pray at mealtime, an activity she read about in books. Her prayers always ended with a simple request that Sumner would come and take her home—the new home of her imagining.

Although Madeleine thought herself fit and

understood she was never disabled, she also realized she was no match for any of the workers who came to her cell. She was a small woman unlikely to overcome an adversary, even a female one.

She started keeping track of days, more for her baby's sake than her own.

The little table proved high enough for her to see out the window when she climbed on top. Madeleine caught sight of some boys setting off firecrackers in a nearby field. Thinking it must be close to Independence Day, Maddie knew her baby could come in as soon as two months.

She wrapped her arms around her middle, hugging her unborn child and promised aloud, "Your daddy will come for us tomorrow."

Believing her location was near the beach, she caught the scent of sea air when the wind direction was right. There were frequent foggy days; gulls were often present.

Opportunity for escape occurred so unexpectedly, Madeleine almost let it slip from her grasp.

Hearing the muffled noise of distant fireworks one night, Madeleine formed the opinion it was actually the 4th of July. Balancing on the table, she peered out her window to have a better look then smelled smoke. She caught sight of the boys who lit firecrackers in the field in recent days running away. Evidently their furtive celebration caught a tree on fire.

The sound of the stairway latch caused her to scramble to her usual position—facing the corner as she sat on her cot. She recognized the lumbering gait of the red-haired matron.

"Do I smell smoke?" asked the woman of no one in particular. Madeleine, unable to encourage conversation initially, never responded to these random comments. A flare of light came through the window.

"My God, it is a fire!" yelled the matron as she hurried from the cell.

Although Madeleine knew the latch on the door didn't click, she was too stunned to move. Sudden realization this was the chance she'd waited for caused an uncomfortable thrill of excitement. Spurred to action, Madeleine walked to the door and pushed to be sure it would give way. It did. For no logical reason, she peered back toward the cell as if to burn its memory into her brain before making her way to the stairs. A doorway to the outside was located at the top of the staircase. Madeleine carefully turned the knob and let herself out.

So excited she could barely breathe, Maddie determinedly strode toward the street. The sound of people yelling, "*Fire!*" rang in her ears. She could hear a distant fire bell. Having planned to walk west toward the ocean should she ever have the opportunity, Maddie decided to head east—away from the fiery field. When a man hurried toward her on his way to the fire, she turned her head as if to take in the excitement.

Stealing a scarf from a laundry line provided a way to hide her hair. After walking for some time, Madeleine found herself in a small town. Whatever celebration was taking place, the drama of the nearby fire served to draw the townspeople's attention.

Glare from the ever-expanding blaze lit the sky. The road she chose took her steadily upward toward the hills.

A subtle pain Madeleine experienced through the day grew in intensity. Even the excitement of her escape could not quell her discomfort. The pain started in her back and now radiated to her legs. Determined to make her escape, she was making little progress. The pain became so sharp, Maddie nearly cried out but understood the need to put as much distance between her and the cell as she could manage.

The idea she could walk off the road into the brush and lie down became appealing, but she spotted a better alternative. Illuminated for the holiday, a church steeple could be seen in the distance. Madeleine knew criminals historically took sanctuary in churches. Surely that could work for her.

It seemed an interminable length of time before she finally stood at the church door. Wanting to scream in pain, she opened the door and collapsed on the floor.

The last thing she saw was the kindly face of a man gazing down at her. He had warm brown eyes and graying temples. As he put his hand on her forehead, Madeleine mumbled the only word that mattered, "Sanctuary."

Chapter Ten

It had been a period of interesting accomplishments. Due to his father's relentless badgering, Sumner was doing an adequate job at the bank. He began to understand and respect his father's business acumen. The bank was heavily invested in oil and real estate.

Sumner doubted he would ever be brave enough to make the decisions his father made. He reviewed huge loans Merritt Hemmings approved for obscure businessmen, which paid off handsomely.

Sumner envisioned other opportunities. Los Angeles was a strange city. Normally, some industry or resource caused a town to develop at a strategic location. In Los Angeles, people had simply come and continued to come in record numbers. Industries sprouted up due to the ever-expanding population.

He considered the importance of building in the ever-growing city. Sumner had tentative ties to the movie and aviation industries. There was so much potential.

Midwesterners who relocated to Los Angeles usually brought their entire life savings. Appealing to new arrivals would undoubtedly cause the bank's assets to grow, if not in one large chunk, steadily over time.

Sumner had an advantage his father did not. Although an older, stable male figure as head of a bank was a comforting symbol to the public, Los Angeles was a city of young men, novel ideas and risk-takers. Sumner had a kinship with these young entrepreneurs his father could never develop. The opportunities he envisioned excited him. As enthusiasm for his father's bank grew, Sumner's drinking subsided.

* * *

The Sunday sermon was devoted to the sanctity of marriage, a topic interesting to Sumner. Despite the hasty annulment, he felt no less married to Madeleine Crawford. The sermon intensified this belief. For the first time, he sought out the pastor after the service and asked for a private word.

A talkative Sumner unburdened himself to Pastor Klinger. He gave a thorough account of his failures—what he considered his cowardice during the war, his disappointing parental relationships and his belief he was the worst of husbands. A hopefulness Sumner only rarely experienced in his life took root. The Pastor proved a more than adequate confessor.

His words, "What God hath joined together, let no man put asunder," rang in Sumner's ears as he left the church office.

"What was that all about?" inquired Evelyn.

"I needed some clarity on my marital state."

"Did you find it?"

"I believe so."

"We need to talk about selling the bank."

Sumner considered his reply. "I need to take care

of some business. Let's wait another week or two to decide."

"What will be different then? It's quite clear your father won't be returning to the bank."

"Trust me," urged Sumner. "I might be interested in running the bank, but I have some hurdles to eliminate before I decide."

Intrigued by her son's fervor, Evelyn hoped, despite the recent tragedy in their lives, things were on the uptake.

* * *

Evelyn felt the need to take charge of her husband's household. Merritt always ran their life the way he ran the bank. The fact his wife was less than eager to cooperate was the real stumbling block in their marriage. He never found a way to effectively control her.

Since Merritt was not himself, Evelyn believed the staff was taking advantage. It was her careful inspection of the gardener's work in the front yard that caused her accidental introduction to Mary Argyle.

As she stooped to confirm the weeds under the bushes between the properties had been pulled, she noticed Mrs. Argyle descend from an automobile in front of her house.

"Hello," Evelyn offered as she stood straight and smiled warmly.

"Oh, hello," offered the neighbor, slightly disoriented at having been addressed by anyone in the Hemmings household. She quickly recovered. "You must be Mrs. Hemmings. So nice to meet you, finally." Mary realized she had nothing to fear. She was the devoted aunt after all, simply shouldering the burden of her sister's child. "I understand Mr. Hemmings is ill. My sincerest condolences. Servants do talk, you understand."

Evelyn chuckled. "Of course, they do, but don't we all? Let me take the opportunity to allay any trepidation you might feel. My husband is in complete charge of the bank. There is no need for concern."

"Yes, I telephoned the bank when I learned of his illness. They attempted to connect me with your son. I managed to speak to another bank officer. He put my fears to rest."

"Sumner is doing his part at the bank, mostly relaying his father's wishes. Since Merritt is not engaged in the everyday workings right now, he is busily preparing some new investments. I think the bank will soon grow as never before. We're quite proud of our son's efforts." Evelyn watched to see Mrs. Argyle's reaction to her comments.

The woman was lovely, about 40, Evelyn guessed. She appeared worldly, not the type to devote herself to a disabled relative. Evelyn noted the slightly evil smile appearing on Mrs. Argyle's enchanting features as she haughtily tipped her head.

"Well, it was lovely to meet you. I must be going."

"One more thing," Evelyn ventured. "I wondered if you've visited dear Madeleine lately? How is she doing?"

"I wasn't aware you knew Madeleine."

"Oh, I know her quite well. Sumner brought her over on several occasions. I didn't know about the marriage, however. It's difficult for me to understand her condition. She seemed completely normal in every respect." Although Evelyn had no motive in her rambling lies, she was instantly rewarded by Mary's response.

The arrogant Mrs. Argyle seemed uncomfortable as she struggled to reply. "I see," she muttered, having no idea any credible witness existed to verify Madeleine's apparent health. She immediately attempted recovery. "It's unfortunate. Madeleine can appear normal to anyone who doesn't understand her deeply disturbed mind. Then your son's physical demands proved both inappropriate and overwhelming. She's such a delicate little thing. Rest makes a world of difference. Madeleine is recovering, however slowly. She was bodily and emotionally depleted. I was extremely unhappy with the care her doctor provided in my absence. I can assure you, matters would not have gotten so out of hand if I were home. But thank you for your concern. Good day, then."

"So, Madeleine will be returning home?" Evelyn carefully hid her anger. Mary Argyle was not the only one with clandestine social skills.

"I would love nothing more," replied Mrs. Argyle, unable to hide her true feelings. It was evident having her niece at home was not an option she considered.

Evelyn believed in her son as never before.

* * *

Mary slammed her basket, hat and handbag on the parlor settee. This was the most abysmal day in her memory, possibly the worst since she arrived in Los Angeles with that mewling brat, Madeleine. The unwelcome conversation with the neighbor seemed a fitting end to this horrid day.

She walked to the mahogany sideboard in the dining room and helped herself to a shot of brandy, which she downed in a single swig. As Mary set the glass on a beautifully polished silver tray, she glanced in the mirror and gave herself a coy smile. She was still a beautiful woman, a gracious and lovely companion—when she wished to be. But for now, she needed to keep her wits about her and rejected her desire for another drink.

She sat alone at dinner, an unusual occurrence. Normally, Mary sought male companionship. Dr. Coolidge was always a last resort. But he disappointed her, and now these idiots at The Home completely ruined all her carefully laid plans. She should have known better than to trust those fools. Decisions had to be made and made quickly.

Mulling over her options, Mary recalled today's unpleasant conversation. She imagined this a waste of time but wondered if the telephone call held some option she hadn't considered so she wallowed in the opportunity to replay it in her mind.

"Mrs. Argyle? This is Dr. Thomason at The Home. I hope you're doing well today?"

"Fine, thank you. Is there a problem?"

"I'm afraid so. You see, your niece took ill with the influenza. We weren't concerned initially, but this morning, she showed signs of pneumonia. I'm so sorry to tell you, she passed only hours ago." A fuming Mary kept her silence, afraid she might say something she would later regret. "Mrs. Argyle, are you there?"

"How did this happen?"

"I explained to you, Madeleine became ill suddenly. She was such a frail girl, there was nothing we could do. Due to the nature of her illness, it was necessary for us to inter her as quickly as possible. I'm certain you'll approve our choices regarding her burial.

I wanted to let you know there will be an invoice for these services, which were above and beyond our normal costs."

Mary seethed as she stared at the telephone. "Just send me the bill," she commanded and slammed down the receiver.

She took a deep breath. There were no clues to help her make a decision.

One option was to pretend this hadn't happened, and Madeleine was still alive. Mary could continue on her present course until some distant time when the need to prove Madeleine's health or well-being might become an issue. If history were an indicator, that would never occur.

The other obvious choice was to tell dearest Wally his sadly defective daughter had died. She was certain it would be a relief to him. Mary could request a large payment for her dutiful service through the years and suggest unfortunate facts might be released to the press if there was any failure on his part to please her.

She never considered her monthly payment as any sort of blackmail; it was simply her due as the mother of Wally's bastard child. Even though his bounteous donations through the years enabled Mary to build a successful and lucrative business, she depended on his monthly contribution to her income. Could she be happy with a single large endowment and no further supplements?

The nosy neighbors must be considered as well. Could she manage to keep Madeleine's death a secret from them forever? The boy, Sumner, was easily manipulated. If his mother became a player in their little game, things might not go as smoothly.

Trying to fathom a more acceptable choice, Mary disinterestedly picked at her food. She considered the possibility life would be easier if she simply moved her household. While visiting clients, she'd seen some interesting new properties in the Hollywood Hills.

It was late when Mary, doubting she would be able to fall asleep, finally made her way to her bedroom.

Turning off the light, Mary reclined on her pillow. Her eyes flew wide when the hand covered her mouth. Her vision had not adjusted to the darkness, and it took a few moments to make out the smiling face of Sumner Hemmings.

Sumner watched Mary's expression turn from shock to anger. When she tried to strike him, he gripped her arms and pinned them above her head, then moved his hand to her neck, forcing her into the bed. She struggled for breath. When her fear became obvious, Sumner loosened his grip.

"Would you care to talk?"

"What do you think you're doing? I will have you arrested! Let go."

"I assure you, I have an airtight alibi. It will be your word against mine, that is, if you survive our little chat." Sumner found he enjoyed making Mary Argyle nervous. "It would be friendly of you to answer my questions."

"I have no interest in being friendly. Let me go."

Sumner slowly pressed his hand against her neck.

"Wrong answer. Perhaps we should start over." Panic set in. Mary's eyes darted around the room. Sumner released his grip slightly, and she gasped for breath. "I want you to tell me what you did with Madeleine. Where is she?"

Mary silently considered her options now that Madeleine was dead. Perhaps Sumner Hemmings made her mind up for her. She would hit dear Wally up for a final payment. The house in the Hollywood Hills could become a reality.

"I'll be happy to tell you. You should have asked before. She's at a place called The Home in Santa Paula. I'm assuming even you will be able to locate the facility with that information. Or I can find the address if you let me up."

"No, it's all the information I need. Why so cooperative?"

Mary glared at him. "It won't do you any good, this information. There isn't any way you can be with Madeleine now."

"We'll see," Sumner bluffed. He had no plan beyond finding Maddie. His current strategy worked much better than he imagined. He entangled Mary in the sheets and hurried out her bedroom door. Sumner watched from Maddie's bedroom as her aunt ran down the stairs in an attempt to apprehend him. He casually departed the house in his usual manner, through Maddie's bedroom window and across her backyard to his own. If dear Aunt Mary dared call the police, he was prepared.

* * *

"I decided to deal with the Crawford woman's disappearance," admitted Dr. Thomason as he removed his slippers and crawled into bed beside his wife.

"You telephoned her aunt and explained her escape?"

"No, I went the same route we did when the Duggan boy escaped. I told her Miss Crawford became ill and died unexpectedly."

"But the Duggan boy really did die."

"Yes, but that was when he got hit by the train, well after he escaped. If this Crawford girl is as smart as she seemed, she left as fast as she could and went as far as she was able." His wife's look of confusion confirmed her ignorance of the nefarious and lucrative side of his business.

The doctor believed the girl meant nothing to her aunt. He would continue to assume the death of any of his patients was a relief to their long-suffering families.

"No need to worry, Martha. The boy has a fine grave and a beautiful headstone. No one need know his body is actually buried in an unmarked grave in potter's field. I don't think it makes a difference to God.

"You should see the lovely marker I chose for Miss Crawford. I still have to respond to her brother's correspondence. I'll write tomorrow, and our efforts on Miss Crawford's behalf will be at an end."

Too bad that, thought Dr. Thomason. Mrs. Argyle paid top dollar for her niece's care; a tidy bit of income gone for good. Such low overhead, too.

* * *

Sumner waited only an hour to see if the police arrived. Since they did not, he gave Alfred the next day off and planned to use the limousine.

Making his way on mostly dirt roads north across the San Fernando Valley, Sumner traveled through the Newhall Tunnel then west to Santa Paula. The Home proved more difficult to locate than he imagined. On the outskirts of town at the edge of the Santa Clara Valley floor, the house sat alone. No one would imagine it was a facility for the mentally incompetent.

An hour after his arrival, Sumner stood in the graveyard where his wife was interred. A curious Dr. Thomason peered across the grave at the man who claimed to be the husband of Madeleine Crawford.

"I can't say I understand why Mrs. Argyle would let you come here when she knew Miss Crawford was dead." Dr. Thomason considered himself a sophisticated man, unaffected by displays of emotion. This young man's apparent distress was unsettling even to him. Mr. Hemmings appeared dazed, and distraught and was completely unresponsive. "I'll just be going then." When there was no reply, the doctor turned and headed toward the cemetery entrance.

He rode with the youthful Mr. Hemmings in his fine limousine, but it was only a little over a mile to The Home. He felt comfortable walking back. Hearing a strange noise, Dr. Thomason looked back to see the young man had dropped to his knees at the grave, shaking visibly and sobbing hysterically. The doctor shook his head and continued his short journey, relieved he needn't deal with the man further.

* * *

"I'm going to kill her," stated a seriously intent Sumner.

"Don't say that, Sumner. Don't even think it," urged his mother. "You couldn't do such a thing."

Sumner grunted. "Why would you think so? I was in the war, remember? I've killed many men. What did you think I was doing, having tea parties?"

Evelyn was shocked at her son's cold demeanor. She hurried after him when he first barged through the front door and was staggered at the unemotional explanation of his trip to Santa Paula and Madeleine's death.

"She let me go there knowing Maddie was dead, knowing some stranger would tell me, knowing how happy I was to be able to see her. I am going to kill her, Mother."

"You can't say things like that. You have to get control of yourself." Evelyn was becoming frantic. "They'll know you did it." There had to be some way to forestall his plan, if only temporarily.

"It's fine by me. I don't care."

Tears fell down Evelyn's cheeks; she never felt more desperate in her life. "Don't do this Sumner, I'm begging you." She would say anything to appeal to her son's better nature. "I need you so desperately. Your father needs you. Please don't do this. At least wait. See if you feel differently after a time. I can't stand this, Sumner. Promise me you won't do anything. You might regret it, and your father and I simply can't get by on our own."

Sumner glanced toward his mother. He had never seen her upset, angry certainly. She was hysterical. He fought the urge to comfort her, but eventually walked across the room and hugged her.

"All right, Mother. For now, you can count on me."

"Give me your word!"

"You have my word, for now."

* * *

Sumner took it upon himself to stop at Jem's house and relay the bad news. He was surprised at the depth of feeling the woman displayed. She appeared on the verge of collapse when Sumner guided her toward a chair on the porch of her modest home. He leaned against the porch rail as she attempted to compose herself, pulling a hankie from her pocket and loudly blowing her nose as she continued to sob.

"Are you all right?"

"Sweet Jesus, I'll never be all right again. This is my fault. I knew better than to let Madeleine out of my sight. I should never have let her go with you. It put ideas in her head. I spent my life keeping such things out of her head."

"What do you mean? Do you know why her Aunt Mary sent her away?"

"Not for certain. But I been trying to protect that girl almost since she was born."

"Protecting her from her aunt?" This idea made no sense to Sumner, although he realized Maddie was not close to her only relative, not even as close as Sumner managed to be with his parents. His hatred of Mary Argyle caused him to press further. "Why did Madeleine need protection?"

Sniffling loudly, Jem replied, "I went to work for Mrs. Argyle and mind you, I was glad for a job. She paid real good, I mean real good. But money was never why I stayed.

"There are a bunch of folks who say chil'ren should be seen and not heard, but Mrs. Argyle, she thought they shouldn't be seen neither. It was clear from the start that woman wanted nothin' to do with her niece. Here, Madeleine was such a pretty baby, you can just imagine. She was the prettiest baby I ever laid eyes on, and sweet and even-tempered too. But every baby fusses sometimes.

"One night she was havin' the colic, and I went to the kitchen to warm some milk. You could hear her fussin' in her bed. When I come back to her room, there stood Mrs. Argyle. Her back was to me, mind you, but I swear she had a pillow over the baby's face. When she heard me come in the room, she moved the pillow under Madeleine's head and turned and smiled at me. Right sweet, she was. 'Poor dear, I was trying to make her comfortable.' Then she skedaddled out of there.

"One other time she got mad because Madeleine was runnin' around in her room making noise. She told me if I couldn't keep the baby still, she was goin' to tie her to the bed. Now people can get mad and say things they don't mean, but I swear to you by all that's holy, she meant them words, and she would do it.

"It was why I stayed. I was bound to protect my Madeleine. We made quiet games; we played in her room. Sometimes the doctor said she was sick and needed to stay in bed so I kept her there. You could see as the months went by how weak it made her. No child wants to lie abed, even if they are sick.

"Mrs. Argyle wouldn't never let me take her out. I heard her say on more than one time Madeleine was a dim-witted baby. I know it wasn't true. It was the reason why she wouldn't let the girl outside, because she knew folks would make over such a pretty child, and they would see there was nothin' wrong with her mind.

"I tried to make stayin' in her room and playin' quiet as much fun as I could. As years went by, she got used to that, I guess. It seemed normal to her, the way life was supposed to be. I did believe the doctors when they told me she was sick. I thought it might be her heart, but still, I thought she should enjoy her life as much as she could.

"It was me what talked Mrs. Argyle into letting the tutor come. I made her think about how it would occupy Madeleine's mind and keep her quiet and out of the way.

"It was me what got Mrs. Argyle to let Madeleine go out in the backyard so she could draw and read. That girl was so excited about being out-of-doors every day." Jem turned her attention to her guest. "Do you think she wasn't sick at all?"

Sumner could see Jem's distress. He felt a desire to comfort her.

"Jem, I think you did all you could. Madeleine would have had an awful life; she might not have lived at all if not for you." Mustering what little strength he could, Sumner continued, "I need to thank you, Jem. If not for you, I would never have known Madeleine, never could have taken her for my wife. I know those months will always be the most precious of my life. I can never repay you for what you did for her."

"Thank you, Mr. Sumner. I appreciate you sayin' so. It will ease my mind."

If only Sumner could find some way to ease his own.

* * *

It was after Thanksgiving when Evelyn awoke to find the neighborhood crawling with police. Something happened next door. In an attempt to steady her nerves, she closed her eyes and took a deep breath. Dressing quickly, Evelyn anticipated a knock on the door.

She checked on Merritt, who was still asleep. He made an amazing recovery over the last months. He spoke clearly and had complete functionality in his hands, arms and upper torso. It was unlikely he would ever walk again. He even went to the bank a few days a week, albeit in his wheelchair. Officially, he was still the president.

Although Merritt fought tooth and nail against Sumner's ideas initially, the two formed a true partnership. The bank was prospering as a result. Both men seemed content, even delighted in their work.

Evelyn started to think this particular moment would never come, and yet here she was, braced for the knock on the door resulting in Sumner's forever absence.

No one was more surprised than Evelyn when Sumner was not charged with Mary Argyle's murder. His alibi, a holiday with his friend, Trace Beggs, held up to police inquiry.

As it turned out, there was an almost unending list of suspects. Evidently, Mrs. Argyle led a duplicitous life. She made a multitude of enemies including wives of clients and jilted business partners. Even a Dr. Coolidge was the subject of investigation. Hints of blackmail both of and by Mrs. Argyle made for drama newspapermen could not resist.

It was determined the next-door neighbor had been smothered by her own pillow. There was no sign of forced entry.

Someone, either Mrs. Argyle before her death or her murderer, spent considerable time burning documents in the bedroom fireplace. A few edges of incinerated newspaper articles were all that remained of the contents from a box left near the hearth.

It took a number of weeks for the sensational news stories to die down. People still drove by the Argyle home, pausing and pointing at the now infamous woman's murder site. The house, which was for sale before the murder, remained unoccupied.

Sumner indulged his mother's questions when she tried to talk to him about Mrs. Argyle's murder. Her death freed him in a way Evelyn thought suspicious. Drinking heavily after his return from Santa Paula, Sumner seemed lighter of heart once the holidays were over. He put all his energy into Merritt's bank.

Intent on closing the window, Evelyn wandered into his bedroom one afternoon when Sonny left his door ajar. Stopping at her son's dresser, her curiosity was aroused as she picked up an old photograph of a beautiful woman in mourning clothes. Why would such a thing be in her son's possession?

PART II – 1925

Chapter Eleven

Sumner beamed as he held the door for Ann at a shop in Ventura. Life was good, it was a beautiful day, and Ann, as usual, was her calm and pleasant self. Trace and his lady friend of the hour, Edra something-or-other, followed behind. Sumner politely held the door for a departing shopper before making his way to Ann's side.

The tiny establishment catered to seaside tourists. Intent this side trip should not cost him time nor money, Sumner attempted to hurry Ann through the store.

"It's very close in here," he commented.

"You can wait outside for me," suggested Ann, smiling slyly. She felt she understood Sumner as well as any woman could understand a man. His intention to rush her shopping was obvious. She glanced at the floor to find Sumner tapping his foot in irritation. As she was about to relent, Ann caught sight of something that might serve as a reminder of their day at the seashore. "Look at this!"

"Ann, we have to go," urged Sumner, ignoring her find. "I know you ladies love to shop, but we need to get to dinner. We have to be back at the plane before it gets dark."

The two couples made a day of it, flying out of the Glendale Municipal Airport, landing at a field outside Ventura and enjoying the beach before a planned supper at The Pierpont Inn.

"No, really, aren't these swell?"

Rolling his eyes in disgust, Sumner beheld Ann's treasure, tiny watercolors of beach flora and fauna. She held one picture of a shell and handed another of a starfish to her escort. The images were exquisite, finely detailed.

Naturally, the price was extraordinary as well, a whopping 50 cents each. Sumner almost gasped when he caught sight of initials in the lower corner—M H. Remembering Maddie's long-ago gift of the pyracantha berry water color, he realized the M on this diminutive painting appeared very like the initial on his own. M H, Madeleine Hemmings—why were his thoughts so easily captured by his late wife after all these years?

Sumner offered, "Which one do you like? I'll buy it for you."

"Only one? How about two?"

"Very well." Ann selected the starfish and a botanical portrait of a single brilliant poppy. Each work of art was only about three inches square, slightly larger than the watercolor Maddie made for him. "I'll get this and meet you outside," Sumner offered.

After paying, he tucked the small brown bag in his jacket pocket. On impulse, Sumner stopped before putting his wallet away. Instead, he carefully opened the compartment where he kept his bills and pulled Maddie's painting from its hiding place.

As Sumner assumed, the M was similar to those on the new pictures. He should have known without looking, having endlessly studied every remembrance of his life with Madeleine, few though they were. The unwelcome idea today's activities were a horrible mistake began to pulse through his thoughts.

"Excuse me," Sumner interrupted the clerk who was helping his next customer. "Can you tell me who painted these?"

"That would be the Widow Hall. You held the door for her when you came in."

Sumner nodded. "Thank you." He struggled to recall the woman who walked through the door as he held it. She was short, dressed in black and wore a hat with a gathered crape veil. Traditions changed since the war. It was unusual to find a woman dressed in deep mourning in these modern times.

He knew without doubt Maddie was dead. She certainly would not walk by without acknowledging him. His obsession was not as diminished as he assumed.

Understanding he was letting an initial ruin his day, Sumner tried to divert his attention to other matters. If Ann noticed his forced eagerness to please, she didn't say a word.

* * *

"Can you come back here for a second, Sumner?" Trace stuck his head around his pride and joy, a four-passenger Junkers F-13 monoplane.

After helping the ladies aboard, Sumner found his friend well to the rear of the tail of the plane. "Is there some problem?"

"I want to know what happened. Did Ann tell you no?"

"I didn't ask."

"What the hell? I thought that's what today was all about."

"Are you trying to get me married off? I find that rather odd in light of your recent string of beauties."

"I'm not the marrying sort. You are."

"Really? What makes you say so?"

"Look, Sumner. You were never so happy as when you had Madeleine. You're better off than you've been since she died. Ann's good for you."

"Maybe you're just trying to eliminate the competition."

"I'm not joking around. I owe you everything. I want what's best for you. Don't be such an ass."

"You don't owe me anything, Trace. Whatever debt you thought you owed me has been paid in full."

"How?"

"All your help after I married Maddie."

"You know that was nothing."

"San Francisco then."

"I didn't do anything."

"You know better. You saved my bacon. If not for you, I'd probably be dead."

Trace shook his head. "That doesn't make up for the fact you saved my life."

Slapping Trace on the shoulder, Sumner replied, "That was just fate, my friend, nothing more. You better fly us out of here. I'm not about to do it."

"And what happens with Ann?"

"What are you, some kind of gossip monger?"

"You might be a banker, Sumner, but you let things slide in your personal life. Don't let Ann get away."

"I'm not. Today wasn't the right day."

"When will it be? You sure had everything

planned out."

"Soon, Trace. Very soon."

* * *

It was difficult to compete with a ghost, even more so with an angel. Ann Girard gladly took on this contest, in fact, she welcomed it. From the first time Ann laid eyes on Sumner Hemmings, she wanted nothing more in life than to share his.

She took some things for granted. Sumner's descriptions of his late wife had to be exaggerated. Ann doubted any woman could possibly live up to Sumner's narratives of his bride's beauty, joy or grace.

The trouble was, the brief Hemmings marriage left no room for reality to set in. There was no time to catalog irritating habits or character deficits. The tragedy of their parting scarred Sumner deeply.

Ann was happy to befriend him initially, knowing he didn't think of her in any romantic way. When Sumner opened up about his past, his marriage, the love and commitment he could not abandon, she listened sympathetically. If anyone apprehended Sumner's deepest feelings and concerns, it was her. Ann listened intently, without jealousy, simply happy to hear Sumner's voice and be in his presence. Always a realist, Ann knew if she were ever to capture Sumner's heart herself, she needed to understand.

When he proved a good listener, Ann shared her own life story although it certainly was not as dramatic as Sumner's.

He always told the truth, a trait Ann found all too rare in men. She wanted the truth even if it hurt him, even if it hurt her. She believed it was the only way forward for them.

Ann first caught sight of Sumner at church over two years ago. She liked to sit in the back pew despite disruptions from new mothers who frequented the rear of the church.

Sumner attended regularly, always accompanying his mother. He seemed a calm and composed person, and Ann set her mind to conversing with the handsome man. She "accidentally" ran into him after church one Sunday as she left her pew. It was enough exposure that Sumner acknowledged her on Sundays. They began to chat after the service. When Ann mentioned she was looking for a job, Sumner gave her his card and suggested she visit him at work.

Ann made a fine teller, the first woman to hold the position at Sumner's bank. She had a good head on her shoulders if she did say so herself. Somewhat taller than the average female, slender and fashionable, the dependable Miss Girard managed to walk the fine line between employee and friend with tact and grace.

It took months to develop her friendship with the bank manager, longer before he unburdened himself to her. It took well over a year before he looked at her as a woman. Things between them were going well over the last several months—so well, Ann assumed she would soon receive a proposal of marriage. In fact, she believed their trip to Ventura might lead to the question she most wanted to hear.

Something happened today, something she couldn't quite put her finger on. As had always been her way, except the day she literally ran into Sumner at church, Ann intended to be honest, even brutally so.

Having returned to L.A. in Trace's plane after their opulent dinner, Sumner crawled into the driver's seat of his new Rolls Royce Silver Ghost. By all

A Keepsake Love

accounts, Ann was treated like a queen the entire day, and she delighted in Sumner's attention. He was always courteous, always thoughtful, always considerate even if he didn't want to spend money on souvenirs.

It was late by the time Sumner stopped his car in front of Ann's house. Whenever he took her home, it was their custom to talk together. He threw his arm over the back of the elegant two-seater.

"This was fun," Sumner began. "Did you have a nice time?"

"I don't know," teased Ann. "You picked me up in your luxurious new automobile and whisked me away by airplane to a lovely seaside day, ending with a sophisticated and sumptuous dinner with dear friends. How could I possibly manage to have a nice time?"

Sumner smirked and gazed out the front window. "I think you should set the agenda for our next outing so I can give you a hard time. Where would we spend our day if you could choose?"

"Hmm," pondered Ann as she planted her finger thoughtfully on her cheek. "Let me think. I rather supposed your romantic destination today might include a proposal. My mother assured me I should be prepared for that eventuality. I guess I would like to go somewhere you might pop the question. The beach was a lovely idea, but now I think I would like a public place—maybe a restaurant? Somewhere you might have to make a fool of yourself to win my favor."

Taking a deep breath, Sumner slumped in the driver's seat. "You know me all too well, Ann. It actually was my plan for today. I'm not as sneaky as I imagined."

"So, what stopped you?"

He turned his head and admired Ann. She was a lovely woman, a true friend. Sumner knew she would make a wonderful life partner. Ann was supportive and understanding, everything he could want in a wife. "I love you."

"I know you do. I love you too. I would imagine that should make a proposal imminent."

"Not now. Not yet."

"Why? Something happened today. You became distracted somewhere along the line."

"I did. It was my usual, unfortunate distraction."

"Madeleine?"

"Yes. I haven't been thinking about her as much, but today, something inconsequential brought her to mind. I realized I'm not ready to move on."

"I told you I don't mind sharing you with her. She was a part of your life, an important part. Did it ever occur to you, one of the things I love most about you is your devotion to the people you love? You are a wonderful and caring son, an unusually thoughtful employer, a kind and generous man. I'm not jealous of Madeleine. I never will be. Now if she were a living, breathing rival, I can assure you that wouldn't be the case. You are dearer to me because you still care for her."

"But it's not fair to you. You deserve a husband who will put you first, above all else. I'm not certain I can. This is my deficiency. Why should you suffer for my obsession?"

"It's not an obsession, just memories—happy memories. But we can make happy memories too. We already are. We can set up a household; make a family. We can build a life together. You can't live in the past, Sumner. Life is for the living, like they say."

Ann was frustrated by her beau's lack of passion. He was always a proper gentleman, never seeming to desire a more physical relationship. This made her feel safe and treasured, but she welcomed the idea of a sensual bond. Sumner never got angry or lost his temper, always holding himself in check. Ann wondered what would happen if he ever let go and allowed his emotions to prevail.

"Kiss me."

Sumner stared at her, surprised by her request. He leaned forward and took her tentatively in his arms. His gentle kiss soon became unrestrained. Ann responded in kind, shocked at the passion in Sumner's kiss and in her own reaction. Understanding how quickly this might get out of hand, Ann pressed against Sumner's shoulder to end the kiss.

"I'm sorry, that wasn't proper," admitted Sumner.

"It certainly was not," added Ann. "I liked it." She pulled on the hem of her jacket to straighten her clothing. Although Ann never pressured Sumner in any way, she felt confident to say, "I won't wait forever, Sumner. I love you, but I want a family. I want a family with you. I have no doubts about this. Nothing you say will shake my certainty about us. I know all there is to know about you, and Madeleine will never come between us."

"Everything you see, everything I've achieved is due to her."

"So you say, but you're the one who made yourself into the man I love. You never acknowledge your accomplishments or your character. I thank Madeleine for any hand she had in shaping your present self, but you need to take credit, too."

Sumner still believed his temper and poor

decisions likely ended Maddie's life. "I know God forgives me, but I have a hard time forgiving myself. I've done awful things."

"So you keep telling me, but being impetuous and unthoughtful is the way of youth. Don't be hard on yourself. I adore you, Sumner Hemmings. Don't throw that away."

With her subtle warning, Ann exited the Rolls Royce and hurried to her porch, turning and waving to Sumner before she disappeared through her parents' front door.

Before he started the engine, Sumner sat alone in his car, pondering his choices. He loved Ann. She was perfect for him. Why was he unable to leave the past where it belonged?

* * *

Sumner parked outside the graveyard. The year 1925 was proving extremely difficult. For the first time in years, he needed a drink. Resting his elbow on the steering wheel, Sumner watched the yellowed leaves of nearby aspen trees flutter in the breeze.

Maddie loved fall. She enjoyed painting the autumn colors and shared her favorite watercolors— dramatically toned fall leaves. It seemed a shame they never shared this season as man and wife.

His mind raced over events of the past several months. Sumner returned home after his trip to Ventura to find his father in dire circumstances. Everett Hemmings enjoyed only a brief recovery after his initial illness. The intervening years were filled with small, debilitating spells that caused his health to steadily deteriorate. He lingered on for only a few weeks after this last episode, always fighting against the inevitable.

Sumner closed, then rubbed his eyes. At least he managed to make his father proud in the end.

The women in his life amazed him. Sumner never imagined his mother would prove such a devoted wife. He knew Ann was anxious to wed all the time she patiently stood by his side through his father's final illness, death and burial. He could not have asked more of her, understanding her frustration all the while.

Now they were forced to wait an acceptable mourning period before he asked for her hand. He intended to be prepared when the time came. But this nod to social convention was not the only thing keeping Sumner from proposing.

Knowing he needed release from his past, Sumner drove to Santa Paula to visit Maddie's grave. He had not made this pilgrimage since the day he came to find her dead. Admittedly, today's journey seemed unlikely to solve his dilemma, but Sumner was unable to imagine any other method to advance the stalemate that was his future. Something about coming here felt right to him.

With a heavy heart, Sumner crawled from the car and carrying a lavish bouquet, walked directly to the grave. It seemed as if he was here only moments ago. Lost in time, he remembered exactly where his Madeleine rested.

* * *

The Reverend Neelson sat on a tree stump, smoking one of his cherished cigarettes. His wife detested this habit even though it was considered quite fashionable, or so he'd been told.

Whenever he performed a burial, it was his

custom to stay until the gravediggers completed their duties. It was his way of handing his parishioners off to God. Further, he found the cemetery a peaceful and calming place.

He was always dumbfounded by the ridiculous assertions graveyards were horrifying areas where ghosts and demons tormented the living. One only needed to visit a cemetery at night to feel the incredible and overwhelming peace abiding there.

Having observed a solitary man visiting a grave during the service, the Reverend noticed the man lingering there.

The thought of visiting the Smith home was unappealing. There were whole families who simply could not cook, and the Smith women were particularly deficient. Perhaps if he chatted with the stranger for a time, he might miss the buffet completely.

As Reverend Neelson approached the man, he offered a greeting, "Might I be of service?"

Sumner turned from his contemplation of the flowers he placed on Madeleine's grave.

"Thank you, Reverend, but I rather doubt it." It was easy to see the man's occupation. He wore a clerical collar and carried a Bible.

"Was she someone dear to you?"

"The name on the headstone reads Madeleine Crawford, but her name was Madeleine Hemmings. She was my wife."

"How tragic." The Reverend struggled to remember this particular grave, knowing it was him who performed a basic funeral. If he recalled correctly, no family member or friend was in attendance. "The marker says she died in 1920. Do you visit often?"

Santa Paula was a small town; this man was an obvious outsider.

"I came once when I found she died. I've never been back."

"What brings you here today?" Reverend Neelson was startled at the bleak expression crossing the younger man's face.

"I came for forgiveness, release, perhaps atonement. I don't seem to feel any differently now than when I arrived. This was a stupid idea."

"Maybe not. Why don't you tell me about your wife?"

"She was beautiful, spirited, rather childish, actually. We were married briefly when she was taken away from me. I can't seem to get over her, get on with my life. I foolishly thought coming here might provide a way forward for me.

"I'll tell you something I've never told another living soul. I traveled to Venice on Christmas Day, the year my wife passed away. We were married on Christmas Day and spent our honeymoon at Venice by the Sea. I tried to numb myself with alcohol since her death. I'd even considered suicide as a way to end the pain. I decided it might be best to make myself hurt as much as I could and get over it if I could manage.

"I went by the church where we were married and walked by the hotel where we stayed. Memories came flooding into my head, but when I came to the pier where we shared so many happy times, I was devastated to find it burned down days before. I stared at the pier, or what was left of it—burned timbers, disaster, black ash and debris on the beach. It was like looking at my heart.

"The only attraction to survive the fire was

Madeleine's favorite roller coaster, The Big Dipper. I dropped on my knees and bawled like a baby on that cold winter day. The pain kept washing over me, and when I finally managed to pull myself together, I found it hadn't helped a bit. I thought coming here might prove cathartic, but I can't say it has."

"Do you have any of your wife's belongings?" The Reverend was interested in this man's sad tale and wanted to allow him the opportunity to express his sorrow.

"I have little of her, actually. I brought a few things today, thinking I might leave them here along with my pain. Her handkerchief is in my pocket." Sumner pulled the small piece of linen he bought Maddie at the pier from his inside jacket pocket. "I keep a painting she made in my wallet," but Sumner did not present the tiny watercolor, the cause of his current distress.

"What do you have there?" inquired the Reverend when he saw what looked like a photograph enclosed in the handkerchief.

"Oh this. It's a picture of one of Madeleine's relatives." He offered the picture to the Reverend. "I don't have a picture of my wife, but she looked very much like this."

"Dear God!" Reverend Neelson could not hide his shock.

"What's wrong?"

"Nothing, nothing. Don't abandon your remembrances quite yet. I think I know someone who might be able to tell you about your wife. I'm expected at a gathering, but let me give you directions." The Reverend pulled out the notes from his eulogy and drew a map on the back with street names clearly marked.

"You follow this road in front of the cemetery. When you come to 10th Street, turn toward the left where the sign marks the way to Ojai, up in the hills. Turn here and when you come to the second curve, there will be a small shed. Park and walk on the trail behind. It goes off into the canyon but not far. There's a small house, yellow with green trim. The woman who lives there might be able to help you. You'll be glad you went," he added cryptically.

After the two men exchanged business cards, the befuddled preacher tipped his hat and hurried away.

* * *

As directed, Sumner parked his car alongside the shed. The Reverend proved to be good at maps. Sumner glanced in the window of the shed to find a flivver parked inside. Good. Evidently the woman he was here to see was home.

Sumner walked along the path wondering what on earth he was doing. What did the reverend's reaction to his picture mean? Against every bit of logic in his being, the idea he might find Maddie excited him. But his attention was soon taken by the beautiful surroundings. Aspen trees, sporting their grandest fall color, stood against the canyon walls. Hints of red were undoubtedly poison oak or poison ivy turned scarlet for the season.

Sumner spotted the modest house and stepped onto the porch. No one answered his knock so he decided to explore. Walking around the side, he discovered an immaculate little garden. A white picket fence surrounded late season flowers including mums and asters. Neat rows of vegetables occupied the center of the plot. It looked as if a winter crop had been started.

Having heard the sound of water since he left his car, Sumner walked behind the garden and looked down a slope toward a picture-perfect creek tumbling over rocks about ten feet below.

Since no one was home, Sumner parked himself on the porch. A thrill of excitement pulsed through his veins. He came this far and had no intention of leaving without meeting the lady of the house. If all she had was information about Madeleine's last days, Sumner knew he would be disappointed. He hoped there was, at least, some shred of information to ease his troubled spirit and allow him to say goodbye to Maddie forever.

A swing took up one side of the porch, a rocker the other. Sumner noted a pleasant arrangement of pumpkins near the door as he chose the rocker, which afforded a view of the fall color. The afternoon light faded, casting a golden radiance on the aspen trees. The canyon seemed to glow as Sumner caught sight of someone in the distance.

He stood and watched a woman head his way. Her hair was as golden as the trees. She wore a yellow gingham dress and carried a small basket over her arm. The woman paid no attention to the stranger on her porch.

Sumner gasped and grabbed the railing. Maddie. His heart raced as she approached. He watched as she spotted him and stopped in her tracks. She finally continued, not running to meet him, simply walking with conviction. Stopping at the bottom of the porch stairs, she looked up into Sumner's eyes.

"Maddie? Are you real?" he whispered.

In response, Madeleine climbed the stairs and put

her arms around his waist.

Crazy ideas rushed through Sumner's mind. Had he died? Was this heaven? If it was a dream, he never wanted to wake up. He placed his hands on Maddie's shoulders and bent to kiss her, passionately, then wantonly. He picked her up and carried her into the house. A bedroom door was ajar, and he hurried through. She said not a word as he placed her lovingly on the small bed and joined her there.

* * *

Panicking as he awoke, Sumner knew something was missing. Maddie—he shared Maddie's bed, but she was gone. With his heart pounding frantically in his chest, Sumner tried to get his bearings.

He caught the aroma of food cooking. Sunlight streamed through lacy white curtains. It was morning. Maddie must be making breakfast.

Swinging his legs off the bed, any notion he died and this was heaven quickly dissolved. There was no pain in heaven. After years of abstinence, his conduct of last night had clearly come home to roost. He briefly wondered if he might not be able to walk.

Sumner remembered last night as being completely romantic, sensual and virtually silent. Every time Maddie tried to speak, he kissed her. If this night was all he would ever have of her, he meant to demonstrate how much he loved his wife, how he cherished and missed her. Words were no substitute for the intense passion he felt, and he didn't want any sound to awaken him if this was only a dream.

Attempting a standing position, Sumner took in his feminine surroundings. A subtle flowered wallpaper decorated the walls. The furniture in the room was not new, but everything was clean and decorative. Frilly doilies covered every surface. A rag rug occupied the center of the floor. He had a vague memory of the charmingly dressed bed. A pink flowered quilt lay in a heap on the floor. He noticed the pillow cases were trimmed in lace and beautifully embroidered.

After pulling on a minimum of clothing, Sumner gingerly walked through the small parlor, finding the same attention to detail and immaculate housekeeping he noticed in the bedroom.

His goal was the kitchen where he hoped to find his wife yet feared he would not. What if his desire led him to believe the owner of this house was Maddie when it was someone else? Though slender, this woman had a fuller bosom and rounder hips than he remembered Maddie having.

Sumner's fears were laid to rest as he walked through the kitchen door, and Maddie turned to greet him.

"Good morning."

"Good morning," he tentatively replied. "Aren't you tired? We barely got any sleep."

"Sit down, your breakfast is ready." Madeleine placed a beautiful plate of food in front of her confused husband.

The table was arranged with a large crocheted square over a yellow cloth. Mismatched dishes had only the color pink in common. A tiny bouquet of flowers was carefully arranged in the center of the table. Sumner took his place and sampled a bite of the eggs benedict. It was perfection, including the rich hollandaise sauce. He stared at Maddie as she poured him a cup of coffee and sat down across the table.

"I didn't hurt you last night?" he carefully inquired.

"No, of course not. I see by the way you walked in here you did more than a little damage to yourself though," she teased.

"Am I dreaming?" Sumner asked, seriously.

"I don't understand," replied Madeleine.

"I can't believe I'm here with you. It's a dream come true." Sumner watched his wife's expression, cognizant of the fact she was not the effervescent girl of his memories. Maddie had not smiled at him even once although she seemed as happy to see him as was he to find her—at least that was his impression.

Afraid of the course his thoughts were taking, Sumner continued, "This is wonderful. You've become a fine cook and from what I see, an impeccable and imaginative housekeeper. I saw your garden. Did you make it by yourself?"

"I'm quite independent. I make my own living. I can drive. I bought this house and my Model T. And you? Have you accomplished all your goals?" Maddie put a forkful of breakfast in her mouth and considered Sumner from across the table. Still trim, he was no longer a wiry young man. He seemed solid and self-assured. With age and added weight, his face filled out. He was a handsome man.

"If you mean can I support myself, my answer would have to be yes. I manage the bank now."

"Your father must be proud."

"He was proud, actually. He was ill these last years and passed away recently. We grew close."

Maddie clenched her jaw, then inquired, "I imagine he was happy when you abandoned your interest in me."

"Maddie, I never abandoned you."

Not wanting to argue, Maddie raised her glass of milk. "Here's to us, then. We accomplished everything we set out to do."

"What do you mean?"

"We couldn't be together because you weren't a proper husband, and I wasn't a proper wife. We seem to have rectified our deficiencies however dearly that cost us."

"I think we need to talk."

"It's probably the last thing we need to do. I find silence much more soothing. That's why I live here. It's what I'm used to. I have created Aunt Mary's house on my terms except I don't have to put up with anyone, and I can do as I please."

"What happened to you, Maddie? Why didn't you come to me?"

"I could hardly show up at your house. Aunt Mary lives right next door. She's the one who took me away in the first place or have you forgotten?"

"Things have changed. A lot happened. Your Aunt Mary is dead." He could see she was surprised. "I know you weren't close. There's more."

Sumner took a sip of his coffee, stalling to collect his thoughts. Maddie rose from the table, abruptly interested in the view from the kitchen window. She crossed her arms and in a flat voice asked, "What else?"

"She was murdered in her house."

"Who killed her?"

"They never charged anyone with her murder. There wasn't enough evidence. I was briefly considered a suspect."

"Why would you be?"

"Because of you. Why didn't you let me know you were alive?"

Staring curiously, Maddie turned to appraise Sumner. "I saw you."

"When?"

"A few months ago. You were with Trace and two women. One of them appeared quite attached to you. I watched through the shop window."

"Ventura. You were the woman wearing the veil."

"Very good."

"Those were your watercolors. I didn't see how it was possible, but I knew."

"Where is your lady friend now? Won't she be disappointed when you tell her you've come across your wife? Or did you only come to be free of me?"

"You're not making any sense, Madeleine. I came for you. I love you."

"You came for me now, but you're too late."

"What are you talking about?"

"I sat in that awful place Aunt Mary put me, and the only thing keeping me from going insane was the knowledge you would come for me. I told myself every morning, 'Sumner will come today.' Every night I said, 'Sumner will come for me tomorrow.' But you never came. No one came. I fought each day to keep the sanity no one believed I had. You were all I cared about, the only person I trusted. But you left me there to rot. You didn't care."

"You don't understand. I did try to find you. I was desperate to find you."

"Not desperate enough."

"I love you, Maddie, you're my wi—"

"What are you saying? Why did you stop?" She turned back to the table. It was clear Sumner ventured onto a topic he hadn't meant to discuss.

"I was going to say you are my wife, but in all honesty, I can't."

"Why?"

"Our marriage was annulled, but I never considered you anything but my wife."

"And yet you have a sweetheart. You came here and made love to me knowing we weren't married. How could you, Sumner?" His admission hit her like a physical blow.

"I thought you were dead."

"I don't believe you."

"It's true. When I finally got your Aunt Mary to tell me where you were, you were already dead. They took me to your grave. That was five years ago. I've never stopped loving you. You have to believe me."

"This is not so easy as it seemed last night, is it?"

"It can be easy. We can work through this."

"I think you need to go."

"No. I won't leave you here alone."

"You have nothing to say about it. We aren't married. I have my friends, William and Morgan. They see to my welfare."

Jealousy, the likes of which Sumner had not felt since Maddie's disappearance, swelled inside him. Who were these men? Was Madeleine as apt to jump in bed with them as she was with him? "You're telling me you don't want me?"

All the loss and pain Maddie experienced took sudden and unexpected possession of her tongue. The fact Sumner annulled their marriage to be with another woman made her reckless in her agony.

"Oh, you're finally starting to understand. I don't want you, and I don't need you or anyone else. I have my own life. I came to understand how disappointing you were. I was a fool to ever believe in you. You let me think we were married last night. I can't tell you how relieved I am to find I'm not beholden to you."

As she arrogantly tipped her head to the side, Sumner was reminded of Mary Argyle. "How could you be so cold? Why would you let me think you were dead all these years? Do you understand how I suffered? You could have written if you were afraid to come in person. I assume you're still able to write? Or were the things your Aunt Mary said about you true after all?"

Madeleine threw her glass of milk in Sumner's face.

Slamming his hands against the table, Sumner pushed himself away, grabbed his clothes and hurried out the door.

* * *

"I simply cannot believe you did this!"

"I didn't do anything," defended the Reverend Neelson.

"You certainly did! How could you send a strange man to our Madeleine's house? What if she doesn't want to see him? What if he is of poor character? What have you done?"

"Why, what would you have done, Teresa?"

"I would have taken the man's card and sent him on his way. We could have told Madeleine about him and let her make up her own mind about what to do."

"You simply don't want her to leave. She's like a daughter to you. We always knew she must have people."

Teresa heaved a heavy sigh and poured her

husband a cup of coffee as they sat at the breakfast table. They bickered ever since the reverend came home last night.

"She's like a daughter to you as well, you know she is, Hiram. You don't want her to leave either."

"You didn't meet this man. After five years, he is completely devastated by his wife's death."

"What if our Madeleine is not his wife?"

"You didn't see the picture, Teresa."

"I don't understand why you never made the connection between Madeleine and that grave."

"Madeleine came to us on Independence Day. It was weeks later when Dr. Thomason asked me to preside over his patient's interment. How could I have made a connection? Is everyone named Madeleine supposed to be the same person?"

Teresa became thoughtful as she calmed down. Something was wrong with this entire scenario. "If Madeleine Crawford is our Madeleine, who is in her grave?"

"I never thought of that."

"Finally, you're being honest. You haven't been thinking at all. Shouldn't we go to the Sheriff? I never liked Dr. Thomason and his strange house."

"He and his wife are gone now, probably four years already. Remember, they disappeared one night, left their house and patients, never paying their staff what they were owed."

"I know what happened, Hiram."

"I don't know what the Sheriff can do about this."

"Why, I believe they will have to dig up that grave."

"You're getting carried away, Teresa."

"I don't think I am at all. I'm being realistic. I

want you to go to Madeleine's house this morning and make sure she's all right. She may never speak to you, now you've interfered in her life."

"Mark my words, Teresa, God's hand is in this. If the Smiths weren't such wretched cooks, I would never have stopped to talk to that boy."

Teresa rolled her eyes. To hear her husband talk, God made the Smiths poor cooks just so a man could find his wife. Where had this Mr. Hemmings been all these years, anyway? Why would he wait five years and turn up now? Men could be such imbeciles.

Chapter Twelve

Sumner stopped his automobile short of the Newhall Tunnel and turned off the engine. Surprised he managed to get this far without being stopped for speeding on his wild ride from Ojai, he heaved a sigh. Pushing the palms of his hands into his temples, Sumner wished he could press some sense into his head. What happened?

Purposefully controlling deep breaths, he calmed down. What was it about Madeleine that caused such extremes of emotion? No one thrilled him as she did. He desired no other woman as he did her. He felt as if he died when she did.

Admittedly, Maddie never did anything to provoke his jealous reactions, which even he considered excessive. The last place he wanted to be was sitting here in his car. She was alive, a fantasy made reality. What was he doing?

Maddie was right, things were not so simple. It was obvious they were both changed since their brief marriage. Embarrassed, Sumner recognized Ann never entered his thoughts. She became completely irrelevant, so obsessed was he with Madeleine.

He failed to ask questions or get answers to the ones he thought to ask. How did Maddie come to live in Ojai? What were the widow's weeds about? Why did she never contact him once she had the opportunity? Maddie didn't seem particularly shocked by her aunt's violent death. He was stunned at the thought she was living happily, letting him believe she was dead all these years. She seemed genuinely surprised at the idea he thought her dead.

Staring toward the tunnel, Sumner needed to make a choice. Madeleine was on this side—simple and beautiful, full of delight. At least, those were his memories of her. On the other side lay the road home. It represented the life he'd been living.

Before he found himself at Maddie's grave yesterday, Sumner's fondest desire was to put her in the past. Ann meant the world to him. She was his best friend. He was anxious to make a future, commit without reservation. He allowed himself to become involved, eventually responding to Ann's friendly and patient overtures.

Further, he knew he would never have chosen his current occupation if not for his father's ill health. Yet, as he gained knowledge and confidence, he found work at the bank to be challenging, even exciting.

Sumner made a few personal and risky investments, although he did careful research beforehand. So far, they were paying off handsomely. It was thrilling, not unlike gambling.

Feeling a complete fraud, he realized he let others make his choices. Ann pursued him or he would never have been interested. He fell into his father's plans for his future and even let Trace talk him into going off to war.

He'd grown to love Los Angeles with all its complexity and diversity. The moralistic Protestant community, the wild abandon of the movie industry, the constant new arrivals, opportunity, and rapidly expanding development all served to make a dynamic place to live. Times were good. Current music, unparalleled prosperity and prohibition leant an exciting background to the whole wild melee.

The only choice he made of his own accord was Madeleine. Although he never understood her reasons, she once loved him unconditionally. But she distanced herself from him. She was cold today, even angry, and disappointed in his failure to come to her rescue. Ironically, he was the one who brought about these changes beginning with his fall from the tree.

It was several years since he felt a failure. The feeling was unwelcomed now.

Sumner started the Rolls Royce and drove into the tunnel.

* * *

A lovely Ann sat across the dinner table at the Tam O'Shanter in Hollywood, which both she and Sumner considered "their" restaurant. The building appeared transplanted from Scotland, complete with thatched roof.

Los Angeles was a patchwork of architecture. It was as if every person who came had their own vision of what a building should be and didn't hesitate to build it. There were structures shaped like binoculars and owls and homes so extravagant, they were substituted for exotic locales in movies. It was this eclecticism the rest of the world poked fun at. But there were also beautiful buildings to be found, designed by the finest architects in the world.

Normally, the pair came to the Tam O'Shanter on Sundays for their famous country-style chicken dinners. Tonight, Sumner felt this location where they shared so many happy memories was the perfect place for a proposal. It was too soon after his father's death to become engaged, but they already waited a long time. He saw no harm in making his promise even if they kept it to themselves for a while.

"Are you tired?"

"No, why? Do I look tired?" inquired Ann.

"You look beautiful, but we took a long drive on Mulholland Highway. We're eating rather late."

"It's fine. I enjoyed the ride. We should have gone sooner. The highway has been open since last year." Ann felt a thrill of excitement. She imagined this would be the night she finally became the future Mrs. Sumner Hemmings.

"Did you enjoy the weekend with your cousin?"

"Very much. Nola and I were close growing up."

"Sometimes relationships spoil as time goes by."

"Not with us. We picked up right where we left off. But then, we correspond regularly. We had a delightful visit. I think Nola might move here."

"It would be nice for you if she did."

Ann smiled becomingly. "Yes, it would. Did you manage to keep yourself entertained in my absence?"

"Yes, it's what I need to talk to you about. The car was a bit noisy for conversation." Sumner looked up as the waiter approached with their food.

"As you well know, I wanted to clear my plate as it were, about Madeleine."

Ann could tell this was going well. Sumner seemed relaxed and self-assured. She tried to make her breathing even as she stared into his eyes. Too excited for food, her fork remained on the table.

Taking a deep breath, Sumner first smiled to reassure both Ann and himself. Somehow, proposing seemed easier than the account that would necessarily precede his invitation to join her life to his forever.

"I decided to go to Santa Paula and visit Maddie's grave," he began. "I hoped I could find some peace, some release from my bond to her."

"And did you?"

"Not in the way you might imagine. You see, I found Madeleine instead."

Ann could not help but feel alarm at this admission. She felt the color drain from her face.

"Are you all right?" Sumner asked, visibly concerned.

"I need you to explain."

"I know this must not sound advantageous, but I don't know how else to start. Listen to me for a few minutes. I think you'll be surprised.

"There was a man at the cemetery, a reverend. He came over to chat. He thought he could help and directed me up a mountain road to a town named Ojai. When I arrived at the house he mapped out, Madeleine was there. You can imagine my surprise, shock, really."

"I don't understand."

"I didn't either. It was as if I was living some kind of dream. She was there, alive, exactly as I remembered her. But it quickly became apparent she is not the same person. She wouldn't answer most of my questions, but she clearly blames me for not coming to rescue her when she was in need."

"That doesn't make sense. You did all you could,

above and beyond. Did you tell her you hired the Pinkerton men? Did you tell her how you visited asylums and corresponded with every facility you could find?"

"No, I never got around to specifics. I remembered Maddie as a sweet, innocent and happy girl. All those traits are gone."

"How long has she been free?" Ann asked suspiciously.

"I'm not certain, but evidently for years."

"Why did she not tell you? How could she let you think she was dead all this time?" Ann's dislike of Madeleine was growing rapidly.

"To be fair, I don't think she knew anyone thought her dead. She's made a success of herself. She bought a house and a Model T. She made it clear there is no room for me in her life. Evidently, there are other men."

"Oh, Sumner, I'm so sorry. This must have come as a terrible shock to you," but Ann realized it was certainly a boon to her.

"I don't want you to think you are a second choice. You certainly are not. For the first time, I feel release from my obligation and my bond to Madeleine. Actually, I can't imagine how this could have turned out any better. You should eat some of your dinner before it gets cold," Sumner suggested.

Too excited to consider food, Ann politely picked at her meal. She began to think out loud. "So, she thought you were still married or did she already know you weren't?"

"She didn't know about the annulment. She said it made things easier. I had no say in her life, and she wanted it that way." Ann's look of delight could not have been more obvious. She fairly glowed with happiness. "There is something more I have to tell you though, Ann, about what happened when I first found Madeleine."

Ann was too excited to notice the change in tone of Sumner's recital. She urged him on with a wave of her fork and took a dainty bite of potatoes.

"I don't know if I can make you understand this, but I was sitting on the porch waiting for whoever owned the house to show up. I saw Madeleine walking in the distance. I was stunned and thought perhaps I was dreaming. It felt like a dream, that night did." Sumner paused and watched as Ann's countenance fell visibly.

"You didn't—"

"I spent the night with her, Ann. I felt married to her. For those few hours, it was as if we went back in time, and none of the bad things happened. In retrospect, I think it was our farewell to each other." Sumner was not prepared when the water from Ann's glass came flying at his face.

* * *

Evelyn sat in back of the church, having difficulty concentrating on the sermon. Perhaps God would take her wandering thoughts as a prayer. The longer she considered this, the more fervently she ignored the service.

She sat alone this Sunday, reflecting on the fact life was basically a solitary ride. Considering she might be approaching an age when people contemplated their mark in the world and what they would leave behind, Evelyn never imagined she might be substantially past that age already.

There were highs and lows along her journey. The more she thought about her marriage to Merritt, the more fondly she remembered him. According to Sumner, she rewrote all the memories of her suddenly saintly husband.

One thing she knew for certain, she and Sumner had become incredibly close. Evelyn would go so far as to say her relationship with her son was her one true personal success. She respected Sumner and the way he saved their finances. He grew to manhood at exactly the right moment. Any sooner and he might have already made his own life; any later and all would have been lost.

When Ann came into his life, Evelyn could not have been more pleased. The woman was level-headed, sensible, quite lovely and a fine, steadying influence.

Sumner explained his plan to propose. For propriety's sake, they would keep it quiet for an acceptable time. Evelyn imagined the couple would announce their engagement sometime in January if they could wait that long. She felt privileged her son let her in on his secret. Evelyn considered Ann the daughter she never had.

Then something went terribly awry. She thought it odd when Sumner explained he found his Madeleine alive and well yet appeared so unemotional. It was obvious he and Ann had some serious falling out. Wedding plans, secret or not, were placed on the back burner.

Having planned a holiday visit in New York with her sister's family, Evelyn contemplated the idea her son likely needed her. She felt he was at some important crossroads.

Although her own experiences with men and marriage were admittedly less than satisfying—on the rare occasions when honesty prevailed—she believed herself a caring mother during her time in Los Angeles. Surely, this made up for any prior shortcomings. To be on the safe side, Evelyn prayed for forgiveness for past maternal failings and asked God for some sign she was supposed to cancel her trip. No sign was forthcoming.

* * *

Sumner smiled warmly when Ann knocked then entered his office at the bank. She managed to avoid him since their disastrous dinner at the Tam O'Shanter. Ann said not a word as she crossed the room to deliver an envelope to the bank manager.

"What is this?"

"My resignation."

"Ann, don't do this. I'm sorry. I want to make this up to you." In desperation he added, "You need this job. Don't make yourself suffer for my shortcomings." He hoped he sounded sincere. He truly did not understand why Ann was so unforgiving. She, above all, understood how he pined away for Madeleine. He had no way of knowing the woman he loved was gone forever, changed into someone he barely recognized. Anyone could make that mistake. "I love you. Take this back." Sumner reached out to return the envelope.

"Do you even know what that means?" Ann asked. "First Madeleine showered you with affection, thought you invincible and perfect so you thought you loved her. Then I did the same in my own way. I made our relationship easy on you. I did all the work; I made all the compromises. I was the one to wait patiently."

Cynically she added, "I was the one who adored you. When Madeleine no longer considered you her knight in shining armor, you threw her away. You thought so little of me, you expected me to run into your arms after you told me you had sex with someone else.

"I think I know you better than anyone, Sumner, and I am completely disgusted. Love isn't about what you get, it's about what you give. I assure you, when I marry, it will be to a man who wants to give me love, not someone who is so needy all he can do is take." At this, she turned abruptly and strode out the door.

Sumner clenched his teeth and threw the resignation on his desk. How could Ann be right? And yet, he seemed a miserable failure with women. Ann's assertion he was needy particularly rankled. Sumner braced his elbow on the arm of his chair and nervously rubbed his fingers across his mouth. He became still as his old longing for a stiff drink flared then subsided.

In recent days, he thought almost continuously of only two things. Although he missed Ann's friendship, it was nothing like his longing for Maddie when he thought her dead. The second was the golden vision of his Madeleine walking toward him through the glorious autumn afternoon.

Work was what he needed. Lots of work, brain-numbing, intense, 20-hour-a-day work. The fact he might be turning into his father never occurred to him.

* * *

"Now Sumner, if you should need me, all you have to do is call long distance. I left Aunt Goody's information right inside the cover of the book in the telephone table." Evelyn hadn't ceased her restless banter since they left the house. "I still think I should stay here. Are you certain Ann won't come for Christmas? Have you begged her forgiveness for whatever you did?"

"I will be fine, Mother. I don't think Ann is ready to forgive and forget. I ruined our relationship. I truly didn't mean to, but I have. Only time will tell if she will come back."

Evelyn had not been able to discover what exactly came between her son and Ann no matter how she tried. Their problem seemed much more than a lover's spat, much worse than anything in her own relationship with Merritt. Even though she and Merritt lived apart for years, they were never truly mad at each other. It was simply a little game they played.

"And what about your Madeleine?" Evelyn watched as Sumner smirked.

"I seriously doubt I have any future with my former wife. But perhaps when you return, I'll manage to provide a new prospective daughter-in-law. Stranger things have happened."

"Sonny," she rarely used her pet name, knowing how her son disliked it, but it slipped out. "I have prayed for a sign, and God seems to be telling me to visit Aunt Goody."

"Mother, I know you came late to religion, but I don't think your newfound devotion necessarily puts you on speaking terms with God." Why was it the later in life one found religion, the more fervent they were to impress and convert everybody in sight? The same could be said of reformed drunks and sobriety. "Let me assure you, I'll be fine. Go and have a good time with your sister and her family."

Sumner kissed his mother on the cheek and helped her up the steps of the train. Waving farewell, he turned to walk down the platform. A strange phone call yesterday served to supply Mr. Hemmings with a definite destination.

* * *

Having parked at the cemetery in Santa Paula twice before with life-changing results, Sumner wondered what this day might have in store. Although he could not envision any outcome to rival his previous dramatic visits, today would prove the most disturbing and remarkable of Sumner's life to date.

Cold from his drive on the crisp December day, he stuck his hands in his pockets and sauntered over to the site of Madeleine's grave only to find the headstone removed. Sumner glanced around curiously, certain he came to the right spot. Soon Reverend Neelson approached from behind a structure near the entrance to the graveyard.

The engaging man of the cloth held his hand out and applied a friendly handshake. "I'm so glad you could join me here today. Thank you for coming."

"How could I resist? You sounded so mysterious on the telephone."

Reverend Neelson chuckled. "I'm sorry. I couldn't locate your card at first, and I wanted to have a talk about Madeleine."

"I see. She's well, of course?"

"Oh, certainly, don't have any worry about her health."

"I see her marker is gone."

The Reverend bit his lip, "Yes, we wondered who was in the grave once I realized Madeleine Crawford was really our Madeleine and very much alive."

"We wondered?" Sumner also did not understand

how Madeleine became theirs.

"Yes, my wife and I. Well, to be honest, it was my wife who had the powers of deduction, or curiosity or nosiness—however you'd like to qualify her idea."

It was Sumner's turn to chuckle.

"I couldn't think of another place for us to meet. My church is up the road. The parsonage is right next door, but it's a bit difficult to describe over the telephone."

"It's all right. I don't mind being here."

"Well, this is as good a place as any to begin my story. You see, we ended up talking to the sheriff about this grave. They came out and exhumed the body."

"And who did they find?" Sumner acknowledged his own curiosity.

"They found no body at all, only some bricks sewn into a piece of canvas, weighted like a body might be. There was a brief investigation regarding Dr. Thomason. He was the man who ran The Home where Madeleine was admitted. You see, there were three other people buried here from The Home. All had death certificates signed by Dr. Thomason. Two of the graves seemed authentic when they were dug up, but another was empty, just as Madeleine's was."

"So why was the investigation brief? Did the doctor admit to some wrongdoing?"

"Actually, the doctor and his wife ran off years ago. No one knows where they are. They left their patients and their business.

"The mystery of the other empty grave will undoubtedly remain a mystery. That young man's family was quite distraught. Why don't you walk with me? It's a good way to stretch your legs after your long drive. My wife will have our lunch ready by the time we get home."

Sumner strolled beside the older man. "This is all very interesting, but I don't understand what it has to do with me."

"It has to do with Madeleine. I don't think she was particularly honest when you found her last October. From what she told me, I don't think you were particularly honest either."

Sumner considered his reply. Was this pastor referencing his less than honorable activities? "I considered Madeleine my wife in every way. I didn't think of my love for her as shameful."

"She told me of the annulment, your current lady friend, even that she saw you with this woman. I have other concerns."

"You're making it sound like I had the marriage annulled to be with someone else. Are you telling me she believes I got our marriage annulled when her aunt committed her?"

"Isn't that the case?"

"Certainly not! Besides, I didn't need an annulment, I believed my wife was dead. It's been years. Madeleine could have contacted me at any time since she was released. Did she think I would sit on my hands and wait to die of loneliness?" Sumner was becoming quite perturbed. All the anger he felt at Maddie's accusations came roaring back.

"Now, now, this is why I asked you to come. There are matters to be straightened out. So, there is an annulment? You did tell Madeleine your marriage was annulled?"

"Yes," Sumner managed a modicum of control. "Madeleine's aunt had the marriage annulled against my wishes. Yes, I do—I did have a sweetheart, and evidently Madeleine saw her while she was masquerading as a widow on the streets of Ventura. It's been five years since she died or since I was led to believe she was dead."

Sumner quickened his pace in his anger. The Reverend was having difficulty keeping up. The conversation unexpectedly seemed cathartic to Sumner.

"Maddie did not hesitate to blame me for things her aunt did. Her aunt is the one who put her in The Home. I got put in jail trying to get her aunt to tell me where she was. I hired Pinkerton men, I wrote letters to godforsaken places and visited asylums attempting to find her.

"When I finally managed to get her aunt to tell me where she was, I found only a grave. For all my efforts, Maddie blames me for not coming to rescue her. She has the nerve to set up housekeeping in her canyon and let me believe her dead all these years. Did you ever hear anything so absurd? She wouldn't even let me explain!" Sumner stopped in his tracks. The Reverend was now several feet behind.

"I think we need to walk back to the cemetery. There's something there you need to see. I was going to wait to explain, but I think it's best to show you now."

Frowning, Sumner trailed behind Reverend Neelson as he turned and walked back the way they'd come.

"You see, Madeleine came to us in rather bad shape. They did not release her, she escaped one night when there was a fire. She walked into my church and collapsed."

"Why? What was wrong with her?"

"She'd been imprisoned in the basement for months. They never let her outside. She wasn't allowed to speak to anyone. They cut her hair short because of vermin. She believed she was kept alone in the basement for protection. I think you can imagine what happens to women in places like that. Evidently her aunt did not want any harm to come to her, physical harm at least, and I learned she paid a tidy sum for Madeleine to stay there. Madeleine nearly died, you see." They were back at the Santa Paula Cemetery. The Reverend walked toward a grave covered in flowers. Sumner read the name on the tiny headstone—Baby Girl Hall, July 5, 1920.

"What is this? What are you saying?"

"Madeleine went by the name of Hall. The baby came much too early. It was a miracle Madeleine survived. Both mother and infant usually pass on in that circumstance. It makes you wonder how strong Madeleine is, despite her delicate appearance. When I saw the picture during your last visit to the cemetery, I knew for certain you were her husband. I imagined Madeleine would tell you about this."

"No, she didn't say a word." Sumner could not stop looking at his daughter's grave. "Didn't they know about this at The Home? How could they not?"

"You must understand, it's quite normal for the mentally deficient to be sterilized. I'm certain they would believe it to be the case for Madeleine. She also told me she hid away in the corner when her food was delivered. They had no way of knowing. It probably wouldn't have mattered if they did.

"I've seen mothers grieve for their babies and children all through my career. It is truly the most heartbreaking aspect of my profession. They have wildly differing ways of coping with their loss, everything from complete and unrelenting hysteria to an inability to ever bond with another child.

"I have never seen a mother grieve to the extent Madeleine did. She felt she lost everything when her baby was stillborn. Although the physical experience did not kill her, I imagined her grief might.

"You can see for yourself the way she keeps the baby's grave. She could never dress her or hold her so she brings fresh flowers at least every week, more often if it rains or is windy."

The Reverend watched a tear slide down Mr. Hemmings' cheek.

"But Madeleine's despair proved an opportunity for my wife and I, well, especially for Teresa. You see, all our children live some distance; we rarely see them. Madeleine became a daughter to us when she appeared in the church and asked for sanctuary.

"First Teresa nursed her back to health. Madeleine evidently never attended church before. She took to church like no one I'd ever seen. I don't know if she needed to believe her baby was happy and loved somewhere or whether she needed to find some peace for herself after her wretched experiences. You could always find that girl sitting in a pew when she wasn't to be found elsewhere. She read or sewed in the church. It seemed to give her serenity.

"Madeleine helped my wife around the house. She wanted to learn to be a good cook, and she begged to clean. As months went by, her physical condition improved.

"We told people my niece came from back east for health reasons. So many people come to Southern California for respiratory problems, no one thought a thing of it.

"Madeleine told me she went to a freak show once and felt people looked at her as if she was a freak. I didn't understand at first, but I came to realize how people stared at her. She is an incredible beauty. She told me the only reason her husband loved her was because of the way she looked."

"That is not true!"

Hiram raised his hand to quiet Sumner so he could continue his story. "She hated people staring. This is why she dressed in widow's weeds. She wore black to mourn the baby but donned the heavy veil for privacy. I never approved but soon understood it made her feel protected.

"At the same time, Madeleine developed an independent streak. She started painting and decided to sell some of her work. She developed a business and made a good income.

"The first thing Madeleine purchased was this headstone for her baby. Eventually, she earned enough to buy her house and the Model T. We were sad to see her go, but her work and accomplishments proved incredibly beneficial.

"She comes for church and Sunday dinner every week and stops by whenever she brings flowers. I always hoped to see a day when the tiny grave ceased to be covered in flowers. I believed it would mark the day Madeleine moved on, but as you can see—"

"Didn't she ever talk about her husband? Didn't you wonder where I was?"

"She rarely spoke of you. In light of all you've been through, I know this doesn't seem fair. I'm quite certain she believes if you came for her, the baby would be alive. I tried to reason with her and explained her baby girl was not meant to live. God has taken her to heaven. Somehow this is all for the best even though it is difficult to accept, but she does not want to hear that." Reverend Neelson took Sumner's arm and urged him toward the road. "People who endure harrowing circumstances don't always react typically—as we would expect them to. Certainly not as we hope they might. Madeleine's veil, lonely lifestyle, her devotion to her dead child and her reluctance to return to her former life indicate a desire to barricade herself from further suffering. I truly believe Madeleine is doing the best she can.

"My wife was angry when I sent you to find Madeleine. I believed you had a right to know where she was. I don't know who was correct, but I see God's hand in what has happened."

"How so?"

"I went to see Madeleine the day you went home. She didn't seem particularly sorry you left. We had a lengthy conversation. She, of course, did not tell me about your indiscretion. I realized her anger toward you seemed unfounded, and if anyone is on her side, it would be me. I tried to make her understand. Forgiveness doesn't only benefit a wrongdoer. Holding a grudge is unhealthy for the wronged. Madeleine has certainly been wronged, but I can't understand her belief you are the one to blame. I suspect if the baby lived, she would have welcomed you into her life. And so, here is where God has stepped in. You see, Madeleine is expecting."

Sumner stopped walking, too stunned to move. "What did you say?"

"You will be a father. I know this must come as quite an extreme shock, first to find you have a daughter who passed on, now this."

"Does Madeleine know I've come?"

"She wanted me to tell you. Actually, Madeleine didn't believe you would show up. This demonstrates how deeply discouraged she is with you. I know this is a difficult situation. I will help in any way possible."

"Is Maddie having lunch with us?"

"No, she didn't know you were coming today, only that I planned to contact you. Here we are. Mr. Hemmings, this is my wife."

Before lunch was over, the trio was on a first-name basis. Sumner had never appreciated anyone's courtesy and kindness so much as he did this day, and it was only getting started.

"Did you want us to arrange a meeting with Madeleine?" offered Teresa.

"No. I believe I'll drive up and try to talk to her today."

"Please understand, if you need our help, we are here for you."

The Neelsons stood on their porch waving farewell as Sumner walked toward the cemetery and his Rolls. Teresa asked, "Do you think he'll do the right thing?"

"He seems an honest and reputable man. Our Madeleine would not marry someone who was not. I'm certain he'll marry her again."

"But will Madeleine marry him?" This answer proved more difficult to predict.

Chapter Thirteen

While Sumner drove through the mountains, he attempted to strategize. Unfortunately, Hiram Neelson's words kept crowding his thoughts. By the time he parked his car next to the shed, Sumner's sole plan was to refrain from saying anything he might later regret.

No sooner did he start down the path to Maddie's little house than two boys of about eight walked toward him.

"Is this your car, mister?"

"Yes, it is." It was obvious the boys were in awe of Sumner's Rolls.

"You must be rich," commented the taller of the two tow-headed admirers.

Sumner laughed. "I don't know about that. What's your name?"

The taller boy replied, "I'm Willie. This here's Moogie."

"It's a pleasure, gentlemen, but I must be on my way."

"Are you gonna see the Widow Hall?"

"Why, yes. Do you know her?"

"She ain't a witch," offered Moogie.

"That's good to know. Does someone claim she is?"

"It's just—folks don't know her. But she's a real nice lady," Willie declared.

"Kids at school say she's a witch, though, I guess because she hides her face and lives alone."

"She makes us cookies! She's a real purty lady."

"Yes, she is," agreed Sumner.

"She's got cookies today," shared Moogie.

"I'll have to ask her for one. Thanks for the information." Sumner turned and continued on his way when he had a sudden thought. He turned and shouted, "Moogie, what's your real name?"

"Aw, it's Morgan. Don't be callin' me that now."

"I promise I won't." William and Morgan, Maddie's sweethearts. Sumner felt a complete fool as he continued on his way.

Taking the four porch stairs in two strides, Sumner politely knocked at the door. The curious look on Maddie's face when she answered quickly became a frown. She hesitantly grasped the edge of the door, trying to decide if she wanted to open it or slam it in his face.

Finally opening the door wide, Maddie uttered a formal, "Come in. Have a seat."

Sumner said not a word but took a place on the sofa.

Madeleine folded her arms and looked down at him. "So, you know, then?"

"I accepted an invitation to Reverend Neelson's house for lunch. He was quite informative. Much more than you were."

"What did he tell you, exactly?"

"Everything, I think. I hope he did; I don't believe I can take much more in one day. He told me about your escape, your illness, our daughter." Sumner watched Maddie's expression carefully. She stood completely still with no apparent reaction to his words. "I told him about my sincere efforts to find you and my mourning for you all these years."

"Yes, you must have mourned a long time before you annulled our marriage and found another love."

Sumner took a deep breath, determined not to be drawn into any argument. "I need to better articulate what happened. It was not me who annulled our marriage. It was your Aunt Mary, much against my wishes. I had a difficult enough time trying to claim you when we were married. It became quite hopeless once we were not.

"I did all I could to find you, and when I finally did, all that was left of you was a grave. It was only in the last several months I became seriously involved with someone else."

"What's her name?"

"Ann Girard. I met her at church years ago and gave her a job in the bank as a teller. We became friends."

"Do you love her?"

"I think we need to be honest if we're to make a new relationship. Yes, I love her, and she loves me. I was planning to propose. It's sheer luck I haven't married before this."

"It would have been better if you were already married."

"In light of your present condition, I believe a marriage would only complicate matters more than they already are." A brilliant blush lit Maddie's face.

"Yes, the Reverend explained. It's why I'm here."

"I don't think there's any need to rush into anything," Maddie offered. "I wasn't able to carry our baby to term before. There's a substantial likelihood I will fail again. Then you'd be free to marry the woman you love. There's nothing between us now."

Sumner was shocked at her flat and emotionless suggestion. "You were not so cold when I first showed up here. I have some understanding of your anger at me thanks to Hiram. I don't believe you have any basis for your feelings, but I imagine I can't talk you out of them."

"Then you've come to fall on your sword? Make an honest woman of me? Really, Sumner. I thought you were more sophisticated than that."

"Make fun if you like. I'm here to ask you to marry me again."

"What if I say no?"

"If you have our baby's best interest at heart, and I believe you do, you will say yes. There is a terrible stigma to being born a bastard. If you care as much as you assert, you won't make our baby suffer such an indignity." Sumner could see Maddie was torn about her decision.

"You can divorce me after the baby comes. Then you can marry your Ann."

"Believe it or not, I have gotten some religion since our parting. I believe God intends for marriage to be permanent. I always felt married to you despite what your aunt did. Another ceremony is of little consequence to me. We are married in the sight of God as far as I'm concerned. But for our child's sake, I think we ought to make it official."

"So that's all there is to this? You want to do the

honorable thing even if it ruins your life and mine as well?"

"I tell you what. I'll drive us back to Santa Paula. We can visit the Reverend and his wife, and maybe he can convince you this is the right thing to do."

"I'll be outnumbered then."

Surprised at Madeleine's assertion, Sumner laughed. "Well, you are certainly free to make your case. No one can force you into this, Maddie. I listened to what the Reverend had to say. We should seek his counsel together. Do you have something else to wear?" Sumner appraised Maddie's dress. Black and plain with tight buttoned sleeves and a dropped waist, the severe color only made Madeleine appear more delicate.

"I always wear black."

"Not the day I found you here."

"I had on a housedress. I can't wear that into town."

"Very well," Sumner rose and offered his arm. Maddie turned and walked alone out the front door. The ride down the mountainside was quite frosty and not from the cool afternoon.

* * *

If Madeleine bought herself time by agreeing to ride to Santa Paula, she felt completely cornered now.

"I don't want to marry him," she bluntly admitted.

"We have been through this before, Madeleine," explained Reverend Neelson. "You were married, and now there is a baby to consider. This is the right thing to do. You of all people should realize your baby needs and deserves a father."

"He loves someone else."

"You are making excuses. He agreed to marry you and recognizes the import of what you two have done."

"But he deceived me."

"We need to address current problems," the Reverend patiently continued. Madeleine clearly dug in her heels. "Your loss is difficult to understand, but it is God's will. He knows best. You are not smarter than He is. You cannot change His plan and neither can Sumner. You must accept this and move forward, Madeleine. Your baby cannot grow up in isolation while you play the part of crazy widow. We agreed on the best course of action."

Sumner was more than surprised at the blunt conversation he was witnessing and was grateful the good Reverend was not so harsh with him.

"Sumner, do you have something to ask this young lady?" Hiram asked.

"Madeleine, will you marry me?" recited Sumner on cue.

Maddie looked from one face to the next. Dear Teresa looked about to cry. She was undoubtedly a sucker for any wedding, even a forced one. A stern Reverend Neelson glared at her expectantly. And then there was Sumner, who looked about as taken with her as she was with him, which was not at all. Putting her hand to her waist, she knew what was best for her baby, the only person that really mattered.

"I will," she said, frowning.

Sumner pursed his lips then inquired, "When shall we tie the knot?"

"There's no time like the present," gushed the Reverend.

Madeleine's face turned pale, "We can't possibly

marry now."

"Why ever not?" inquired Teresa.

"I need to go home. I should get my things."

Realizing the need to accomplish the ceremony before Madeleine might decide to flee, Sumner offered, "We can buy you new clothes in Los Angeles. I think this is a fine idea."

Before Madeleine could achieve an escape, she found herself standing in front of the altar reciting vows. Although equally spontaneous, this was serious business not at all resembling their first impassioned wedding.

Madeleine found it almost impossible to form the words "I do." The idea she owed this man, this virtual stranger, her obedience rankled beyond belief.

She was surprised when Sumner produced her wedding ring, which was attached to his watch chain. She thought his devotion to that remembrance overly dramatic. Perhaps it was a ploy to attract women. What foolish girl could resist a good-looking man enamored of a dead wife?

Much too quickly, the Reverend jubilantly spoke the final words of the ceremony. "You may now kiss the bride!"

Madeleine braced herself for Sumner's kiss. As she feared, Sumner's effect on her was unchanged from October. His touch was irresistible, and from the shocked look on his face, Sumner was no less moved.

* * *

"I don't see why I can't go and get my own things. At least I should lock my house up tight. Why can't we go there tonight?" Madeleine whined.

"It's already late, and we have a long drive ahead

of us. I took today off, but I have to be at work in the morning. It will take another 90 minutes to drive to your house and make it back here. Besides, all women like new clothes. I insist on one thing though."

"What?"

"No black, Madeleine. Absolutely no black."

Madeleine glared at her new husband while the Neelsons looked on.

Sumner held his wife's arm and helped her into the car.

"Thank you so much, *Sonny*." No single word could so completely define the animosity Madeleine felt. No single word could so infuriate the groom.

Teresa smiled and waved as the newlyweds sped away in their grand car.

"Hiram, you have made a terrible mistake here. I'm as certain as I have ever been of anything in my life."

"What are you saying?"

"I don't see how they can possibly make a go of this. I have never seen a couple so diametrically opposed to each other. They will never survive intact."

"As usual, Teresa, you fail to see God's hand in this."

Theresa rolled her eyes. "That's because God's hand isn't in this—yours is."

* * *

The longer the pair rode in uncomfortable silence, the more Sumner believed he made the biggest mistake of his life.

"Don't you have anything to say?" he ventured.

"What are you going to tell your precious Ann when you see her? Sorry, darling, I've up and married someone else. You're on your own."

"I never noticed what a sarcastic and cruel person you were when we were married, Madeleine. Maybe I was simply too smitten to notice.

"There's something I need to say. After you died, or rather, when I thought you were dead, I begged God to let me stop feeling. I wanted the pain to go away. I just wanted to be numb. It took me a long time to fall in love again. After I was with you, when we fought the next day and you blamed me for everything, it was as if my prayer was finally answered. I have felt numb ever since.

"I went home and planned my proposal to Ann—my original intention. She turned me down. I should simply have let her believe you were still dead.

"But I've always been honest, and I didn't think my single night with you would prove my undoing. If I thought time might serve to mend that relationship, it's off the table because here you are. For some reason, Ann's rejection did not bother me. I got over my love for you—finally. I feel nothing, absolutely nothing. Maybe I never will again.

"I tried to find you; I don't understand why you never tried to find me. Just a word, a phone call, a letter would have completely changed my life, no—our lives. There would be no Ann to contend with if you did that one simple thing. If you don't understand me, I can assure you, I don't understand you. How could you be so cruel?"

"Stop the car!"

"What?"

"*Stop the car!*"

Sumner swerved to the side of the road and slammed on the brakes. If Madeleine planned to exit the car and walk back home, let her.

Much to his surprise, she walked off the side of the road and retched behind a bush. What was he supposed to do now?

Sumner assumed this bore similarity to the way he felt when he drank too much. Men never thought over-imbibing a cause for sympathy—only relentless mocking.

He tried to envision some supportive response. What would he have appreciated when he was hung over? Having few options, Sumner exited the car and used the canteen he kept in the trunk to wet his handkerchief. He gingerly approached Madeleine who was sitting on the ground bent forward on her hands.

"Here," was all he said as he handed the handkerchief to her. She took it and placed it on her lap.

"Is this supposed to be some sort of cure?" she sarcastically responded.

Angrily, Sumner grabbed the handkerchief and wiped her face and mouth. He watched as she closed her eyes and relaxed. He sat down beside her and let her lean against him.

"We can stay here until you can continue," he offered, but looking up at the darkening sky, he realized it was already late. "If you think it will help, we can stop up ahead. There's a roadhouse café I've visited before. We can get something to settle your stomach."

Maddie only nodded in reply. He helped her up and settled her back in the car. She turned toward the door and drew her knees up under her chin, remaining quiet until Sumner parked the Rolls in front of a café in Newhall.

Madeleine first drank a cup of tea then tried a cup of broth and crackers while Sumner got a sandwich for himself. He noted the color returned to her cheeks. He was not prepared for Maddie's next comment.

"So, you love her very much."

"I love her, but it's not the kind of love I had for you. It never was. She's my dearest friend. I think it's what I miss the most."

Maddie responded, "In answer to your comments, I was first too ill to do anything. As the weeks went by, I considered what happened was for the best—you and I were simply children playing at love, never two serious adults. We didn't even manage to live under the same roof. I don't think we knew each other.

"I couldn't face returning to Los Angeles. I was afraid of what Aunt Mary might do next. She's my relative after all, maybe I share some of her characteristics. It might be best I was not a mother."

Sumner found these comments disturbing. "Are you telling me because Mary was your aunt you are somehow destined to be like her?"

"She is my mother's sister. Maybe my mother was like her."

"I'm certain your parents were wonderful people."

"Why, because they're dead? I'm sure they were as full of faults as anyone else, maybe more so."

"No, because you were the sweetest girl I ever met—before all this mess happened. Your parents must have been wonderful people to have such a lovely child. The apple never falls far from the tree."

Madeleine cringed at his comment. "Where do you live now?"

"The same place I always lived, next door to you,

er, next to your Aunt Mary's house." He felt Madeleine's eyes bore into him. "I worked closely with my father when he became ill, and then I tried to be a help to my mother. I simply never moved out."

"You're telling me you took on your father's job, you live in the same house, work at the same business, and enjoy it as he did. Now you're unhappily married to me, just as your parents were unhappily married. You are reliving your father's life. But I cannot possibly be like my aunt?"

"That's beside the point, Madeleine. If you didn't want to be married, you should at least have let me know you were alive. What if I had other children who would suffer for this? When did you start thinking only of yourself?"

"When did you think of anyone but yourself? Wasn't that night about your desire, your longing? You didn't stop to think about me or even let me talk. You definitely weren't thinking about your lover back home."

"She was never my lover. I would never disrespect her."

"But you didn't have a problem disrespecting me, knowing we weren't married."

Sumner gritted his teeth, not wanting to fight. At least she made him angry, perhaps that was a start. Silence prevailed for the balance of their journey.

He glanced out the corner of his eye when they drove past Madeleine's childhood home. She protectively drew her arms around her middle, staring intently out the window. The simple reaction made the curious and confused Sumner begin to think.

"It's probably best you take a guest room for yourself. I'll have the maid settle you in and get you some night clothes."

"Won't your mother be disappointed when you turn up married and didn't invite her?"

"She's on her way East, visiting a sister. I took her to the train station this morning. I imagine she will be delighted when we tell her she is to be a grandmother. Although my mother never cared about children before, she's been badgering me to propose— I mean, she seems anxious for me to provide the next generation of Hemmings. She's under the impression she will make a loving grandmother although I can't see it myself." His disparaging remarks about his mother went unanswered. At least he found a topic Madeleine did not argue about.

* * *

Despite exhaustion from the emotional havoc of her second wedding day, Madeleine lay awake most of the night in the strange bed. By the time she pulled on a borrowed robe and made her way to the breakfast table, she was surprised to find her husband still seated.

Sumner considered Maddie's frail and fatigued appearance and was curious when she flinched at the clamor from outside.

"What is that noise?"

"Your aunt's house remained empty for years after her death. There's a certain stigma attached to a house when a murder occurs, especially an unsolved murder. A young family finally made a low offer. They seem happy with their purchase. There are three children, I think. They're all quite small. They seem to thoroughly enjoy your old backyard."

"But why do they make so much noise?"

"I think it's pretty normal," Sumner replied. "Maybe you're tired." He watched Maddie approach the window, knowing the wall was too high for her to see. "You can go in my room upstairs. It has a historic view of the yard if you recall.

"I made arrangements for you to put anything you like on account at The Broadway. If I remember correctly, you used to enjoy shopping there." Sumner reached in his pocket and withdrew some bills from his wallet. "This should take care of any other activities you might plan for today." He folded the newspaper and excused himself, leaving a lost and befuddled Madeleine to fend for herself.

Madeleine ate a light breakfast. She had not been bothered much with morning sickness but Sumner's unfocussed driving managed to upset her stomach.

In recent years, she developed a weekly schedule, which she enjoyed. There were days for cleaning, laundry, ironing, sewing—including new projects and mending—and gardening, although her schedule was not immune to spontaneity. At first, she considered cleaning house to be drudgery, but as she beautified her home, the weekly cleaning became an opportunity to admire her things and make improvements. She spent at least some time each day sketching and painting.

Maddie sold small tourist pieces at gift shops in Ventura, Ojai and Carpinteria. Larger works went to an art gallery in Santa Barbara.

She enjoyed driving her little flivver. Pride of ownership when one earned her own living was quite addictive. Then, there was church and her visit to the cemetery every Sunday, more often if her thoughts turned to her baby. Somehow decorating the tiny grave gave Madeleine a connection to the hereafter where she knew without doubt, she would eventually be reunited with her own baby girl.

Her notion the baby would miss her mother's attention she knew to be both unhealthy and illogical. She quickly pushed it out of her thoughts.

When Maddie first recovered, she had an undeniable longing for Sumner. She frequently dreamed about his strong arms, his engaging smile and the fun they shared. But fond remembrances were always washed away by her disappointment and mourning. If she became bitter through the years, there was seldom anyone from whom to hide it. Madeleine consoled herself with the fact she was lucky enough to afford exactly the life she wanted.

She was curious when Moogie and Willie showed up one day, intent to find her practicing witchcraft. They were shocked to see her without a veil, one of the few times in Maddie's life she was thankful for her good looks. Had she appeared an ogre, her infamy would undoubtedly have spread.

She enjoyed watching the boys jumping on rocks in the creek, playing tag and climbing trees—all activities she envisioned boys doing. They were blossoming entrepreneurs who brought her fish in exchange for cookies.

The two boys never engaged in any behavior vaguely approaching the pandemonium she observed through Sumner's bedroom window. These neighbor children were much smaller than her two young gentlemen. Having no experience with children, Madeleine could not even begin to guess their ages. The two older girls pushed, and fell and didn't hesitate to scream at the top of their lungs. She only caught sight of the baby, a boy, for a few seconds. There were frequent tears, yelling and arguing. After staring out the window long enough to make her head ache, Madeleine felt overwhelmed by the virtually endless activity.

Having no choice but to wear the clothing she wore yesterday, Madeleine prepared for a shopping excursion. If Sumner would not let her have her own things, she intended to make him pay dearly for new ones.

The highlight of her day was Alfred's warm greeting. Thrilled someone was happy to see her, Madeleine had to fight back tears when she took her place in the limousine.

Her shopping extravaganza proved extremely fruitful. She purchased 8 pairs of shoes, 15 dresses, 5 suits, 2 coats, several skirts, blouses and sweaters before she finished off her spree with 12 hats and boxes full of luxurious satin and lace undergarments and night clothes. She even found an evening gown she liked, realizing there was little probability she would have occasion to wear it. The dress was completely black and elegantly beaded.

Modern fashion being what it was, Maddie imagined she could continue to wear the loose-fitting clothing for several months. The stylish dropped waists and full skirts would undoubtedly serve to hide her expectant condition.

Deciding to finish her day by strolling through the multitude of book shops on 6th Street, Madeleine made several purchases including a picture book for the children next door.

She came to a sudden halt on her return to the limousine. Sumner sat with a woman in the window of a delicatessen. He seemed intent on their conversation. The woman looked happy as she chattered merrily away.

She recognized Sumner's Ann, who was more attractive than Madeleine remembered from her glimpse through the window of the shop in Ventura. No doubt, she would have made a loving and giving wife. From the jubilant expression on her face, perhaps Sumner suggested some agreeable way forward. Madeleine would not stand in their way.

* * *

"When I asked you to meet me for lunch, I had no idea you would surprise me with this kind of news," Sumner frowned.

"You have your news, and I have mine. I'm happy for you. Madeleine is who you always longed for. In fact, you are quite the success: accomplished businessman, husband to a stunning wife. You have a luxurious home and an opulent automobile. In short, you are living every man's dream."

"You know that's not the case. You know better than anyone my life is not what it appears. I think you're making a terrible mistake, Ann. This is all my fault."

"Don't be such a martyr. I cared for Prescott in the past. When he proposed, I could not have been happier."

"Do you love him?"

"Of course, I do. I wouldn't marry him if I didn't."

"Do you love him as much as you love me?"

"I didn't know there were degrees of love. But to be honest, I doubt I will ever love anyone the way I did you."

"Did?"

"Yes. You are the past; Prescott is the future."

"You're marrying him to get back at me."

"He is a kind and loving man who cared for me for years. He's successful and puts me first. I have no doubt he will make me happy. And I will do all I can to live up to his expectations."

"This sounds more like a business venture than a romance."

"I can assure you, it is quite natural. I didn't have to listen endlessly to his emotional longings for some other woman. I didn't have to hold his hand to get him through the rough patches in his life. I didn't have to lend emotional support at the expense of my own feelings. He's a grownup, and we will have a happy and prosperous union. I have no doubts at all. I do have a favor to ask."

Sumner scowled, wondering how many lives Madeleine's secrets were bound to ruin. "What?"

"I want you to come to my wedding. Naturally, I want Evelyn to come. She's been like a second mother to me. I want you to bring Madeleine."

"No."

"Listen, Sumner, you owe me this much. I have a right to meet Madeleine, and I need to allay any doubts Prescott has about my past. Every person who has been important in my life is going to be there for me. It's the least you can do. Give me your word."

Sumner hesitated as long as he could before answering. "Fine. We'll be there. When is it?"

"Valentine's Day. It's a Sunday afternoon. I'll send you an invitation."

* * *

It was with extreme trepidation that Madeleine went next door on Thursday morning. She baked Christmas cookies and wrapped the beautifully illustrated children's book. It was her intention to simply drop off her neighborly gifts and introduce herself. She felt Christmas Eve was ideal timing since everyone was busily preparing for the holiday. The last thing she wished to do was go inside.

Madeleine smiled warmly when a woman about her own age answered the door, the little boy in her arms.

"I don't want to bother you on this busy day, but I brought a book for the children and some cookies. I'm Mrs. Hemmings, the next-door neighbor."

Madeleine was completely taken off guard at the sound of a crash somewhere down the hall. The lady of the house quickly pushed her toddler into Madeleine's arms and with a quick, "Hold him!" hurried off to see what catastrophe had occurred.

Wide-eyed, Madeleine awkwardly attempted to secure the serious looking boy in her arms and walked inside to keep him out of the cold, clumsily setting her gift and plate on the entryway table. She stared at the house, virtually unchanged since the day she left. Startled when the young mistress returned, Maddie attempted composure.

"Nothing broke!" she happily observed. "I'm so sorry, Mrs. Hemmings. Here, let me take him. I'm Mrs. Graydon and this is our young Oscar. Won't you come in? It's so lovely of you to bring the children a gift. Girls, say hello to Mrs. Hemmings."

The two girls, dressed in identical green velvet dresses, stopped their wild abandon long enough to greet Madeleine with a polite, "Good morning, Mrs. Hemmings."

This excellent behavior vanished in short order as the girls begged for a cookie. Their mother relented, giving each child their pick from the beautifully decorated cookies Madeleine baked.

"This is Claire. She's three. And this is June who is five. Won't you come in and have tea?"

"Oh, I don't want to be a bother." The idea little June was five was most intriguing to Madeleine. Her own baby would be five now. This was how a five-year-old looked, talked and acted. Madeleine was entranced.

"It's no bother at all. I was about to have a cup myself. Would you mind terribly coming into the kitchen? It's so much easier to keep an eye on Oscar in there."

"I wouldn't mind at all." Madeleine could not help but gawk as she walked down the hallway. She lived virtually her entire life within these walls. They seemed to close in around her as memories came flooding back.

The women chatted for several minutes while Madeleine kept an eye on all the children but June especially. Thoughts of her room upstairs and nights spent with Sumner overwhelmed her. Standing, she offered apologies about a forgotten errand and hurried toward the front door.

"I'm sorry, I hope you aren't upset by the house. I imagine you know its history."

"I truly have to take care of something."

"People stay away. They're afraid. But this is a perfectly lovely home, much nicer than anything we could have afforded. To think, it came completely furnished. I assure you," she whispered, "there are no ghosts."

"Ghosts?"

"You do understand, there was a murder here? It won't keep you from coming back will it?" Mrs. Graydon sounded desperate for company.

"Certainly not. I knew about the murder. It doesn't bother me in the least," Madeleine assured. "Would you like to come for tea one afternoon next week?" she offered. "Your children might enjoy playing in my backyard. How does Tuesday sound?" Although Madeleine had no intention of beginning a neighborly relationship when she walked next door, the delighted expression on Mrs. Graydon's face seemed to indicate a friendship was brewing.

* * *

Christmas came and went without fanfare. Madeleine failed to draw Sumner's wrath with her lavish purchases. Her gift to him was a history of California. His was a pair of kid gloves—polite gifts for strangers.

They attended church and had a quiet Christmas dinner alone. Neither attempted conversation. Sumner retired early with a brandy and some banking business.

It was not as if Madeleine would have enjoyed an opulent Christmas at the Neelsons, but their home was always full of warmth and friends, even if the friends were not her own. Neither Madeleine nor Sumner uttered a word about that first Christmas, their wedding day, when their only disappointment was scrambled eggs for dinner.

Chapter Fourteen

Once Sumner left for work on Monday morning, Madeleine, anxious to observe little June, took her cup of tea and proceeded to look out his bedroom window.

Although the day was brisk, the two sisters were outside. Quieter than usual, the girls watched something in the dirt beneath the rose bushes. The garden was not as glorious as it was under Madeleine's watchful eye but seemed to be recovering nicely from the ill effects of abandonment.

Madeleine nearly spilled her tea at June's panicked scream when her sister tossed a bug at her. Evidently, Claire was immune to the girlish horrors of creepy crawly things, having picked up the bug to chase her sister about the yard. Madeleine's smile turned to a frown as she considered her own girlhood. If Aunt Mary's ghost occupied her old home, it must be quite cross at the riotous goings on.

It was the house that haunted Madeleine now. Mary claimed it was ridiculously easy to control her by way of her imaginary critical illness. Madeleine had no memory of wild activity the likes of which the Graydon children enjoyed. She believed her confinement was to ensure her health when all the while it was simply a ploy to keep her quiet and out of Mary's way.

Madeleine dared not consider the fact Mary was her mother. The fears she mentioned to Sumner about familial tendencies were true concerns. Mary kept her own daughter a virtual prisoner to control and use her. Madeleine felt herself completely stupid, having never realized what was happening. She was merely confused at her good health when Sumner took her out in the world.

There were times even now when Maddie felt inclined to limit her activities due to her health, a lifelong habit she found difficult to break. How cruel to make a child think she was in imminent danger of death every waking hour of her day. How brutal to keep her imprisoned, friendless and alone. How vicious to present her as a half-witted invalid to keep others away. It was Mary who was likely deranged. What if these tendencies were inherited? How would she manage to be a good mother when her own childhood was so bereft and her own mother such a poor example?

Suddenly, the joyful play of next door seemed too much to bear. Turning to leave, Madeleine saw the drawer to the small bureau next to Sumner's bed was open. Reaching down to close it, she noticed an expensive velvet jewelry box. Undoubtedly, this must hold Ann's engagement ring—the box was the right size.

Unable to restrain her curiosity, Madeleine picked the package up and popped open the lid. The ring was exquisite, a large round diamond set with smaller but substantial diamonds all around.

She glanced at the plain gold band on her own

hand. It meant as much to her as if it were the most opulent ring ever made when Sumner first gave it to her.

Snapping the lid closed, Maddie carefully placed the box back in the drawer when she noticed another item. An old photograph occupied the bottom of the drawer. She pulled it out and stared at the picture of her grandmother, the one from her box at Aunt Mary's house. How could Sumner possibly have this picture? Unhappy with her reflections of the morning, Madeleine returned the picture to the drawer and closed it, unable to contemplate one more ugly thought.

* * *

By the time Tuesday tea rolled around, Madeleine had a severe case of home sickness. With little to do in the well-staffed household, she reminisced about her own home full of doilies, flowers, mismatched china, quilts and sunshine. Although she appreciated the Hemmings home's craftsman style, the large, paneled rooms were dark on the brightest day.

After a more careful inspection of her new home, Madeleine moved to a corner bedroom with uncharacteristic bright wallpaper and a large covered sleeping porch, which unfortunately prevented sunshine from entering the room. She would be happier when the weather warmed so she could spend her days outside.

Maddie picked up a few art supplies as she made her way through the book shops on 6th Street before Christmas. These remained untouched. She had trouble focusing on any book she purchased. It seemed too early to prepare for the baby, and she had no idea how to accomplish that in any event. Despite reluctance to play hostess to her neighbor, at least Maddie found an activity that served to refocus her attention.

She gave careful instructions to the cook, going so far as to select recipes for the items on her list, much to the cook's dismay. Madeleine enjoyed cutting the last of the roses and the few remaining flowers in the winter garden for an arrangement she supplemented with a variety of greenery. There was always greenery at hand in Los Angeles.

On impulse, she picked a few pansies for the cook to glaze, thinking they would make a welcome and bright addition to the elegant tea plates. It was obvious the cook did not appreciate her thoughtfulness.

Once her guests arrived, Madeleine provided quiet activities for the girls. If anyone was expert at quiet activities, it was the former Madeleine Crawford. A somewhat sleepy Oscar seemed content enough in his mother's arms as the women shared their elaborate afternoon tea.

"I don't mean to be nosey, but I realize you weren't living here until recently. Are you and Mr. Hemmings newlyweds?" inquired Mrs. Graydon.

Unprepared but understanding she should have planned for such questions, Madeleine slowly replaced her teacup on its saucer. "No, we're not newlyweds. We lived apart for some time."

"So, you've reunited, how wonderful!" Mrs. Graydon gushed, although if she were honest, she would have to admit having frequently seen Mr. Hemmings with another woman.

Madeleine quickly nibbled on a cookie. "I have my own nosey question."

"How delightful, although I don't think anything

in my life is quite as exciting as a true love."

It was plain to see Mrs. Graydon was fond of sensationalism and romance. "You mentioned you bought your house intact. Did the sale include the personal items of the woman who lived there?"

"There were a lot of items left in the house. At first it was rather like a shopping trip, inspecting everything to decide what I wanted to keep and what to discard. I was rather repulsed at the idea of going through the dead woman's clothing and personal items. Actually, my husband took on clearing out her things. We thought it best to donate those. It was the one room we completely changed—her bedroom was where the murder occurred.

"My husband was not thrilled at the idea of purchasing new furniture, but I put my foot down. I can appreciate the value we enjoy because we're willing to live in a notorious home, but I refused to sleep in a bed where a woman was murdered. If those walls could only talk, but they're different walls now," she added brightly. "I hope this is not too extreme a topic for you, Mrs. Hemmings?"

Madeleine relied heavily on the fact few people saw her when she lived next door. That was years ago, at any rate. She doubted anyone would give her away to Mrs. Graydon. "No, no. I can't imagine the difficulty of moving to a new home and having to clear away the previous owner's things before settling in. There must have been a lot to discard: paperwork, books, any manner of household items. Did you donate those as well?"

"The police must have taken a number of things for evidence, which I imagine they keep. Having been repeatedly searched, the house was not tidy at all. We discarded a lot of paperwork and anything broken or useless. There were some lovely clothes we packed away in the attic although they will likely be out-of-date by the time the girls could use them.

"Someone in the house was an artist, and we boxed up quite a number of watercolors. Actually, by the time we were ready to move in, we put aside quite a few things, intending to weed through them. With three little ones, there simply isn't time."

"If you should ever need help, I'd be glad to volunteer," offered Madeleine, hoping she didn't sound too eager. "Mr. Hemmings' mother runs this household quite effectively. I'm a bit at a loss as to how to fill my days even now while she's away."

"Funny you should ask," Mrs. Graydon commented. "There is something you might do."

Madeleine tried to keep her eagerness at bay and so replied less enthusiastically than she felt. "What might that be?"

"It's my mother-in-law's 50th birthday next weekend. We're taking the children up to Sacramento on the train—they are so excited! My maid comes twice a week. She will be here Friday, but I was wondering if you might check on our cat over the weekend? I'm worried about her water dish, which she always upends. I know this sounds quite unhygienic. Our cat prefers to drink water as it falls from the faucet, and I fear she might become dehydrated."

"Oh, I'd be delighted. She stays in the house then?"

"Yes. The girls named her Princess. I imagine if you turn the faucet on, she'll come running. Just allow the water to dribble into the sink until she finishes. We can hardly go off and leave the water on. I'd so appreciate your help. I'll bring a key before we leave."

"No problem at all. I'd be glad to help." Madeleine relaxed in her chair. She long since abandoned any ties to her old things, her clothes or paintings. It was the box she was interested in, the one with her name. Perhaps if it was neatly tied, the Graydons simply placed it in the attic to consider at some future time.

* * *

"I understand you had guests today," commented Sumner across the dinner table. Since their angry trip to Los Angeles, the pair shared little in the way of conversation. It seemed silence was preferable to any comment that might cause dispute.

"Does your staff spy on me and report to you on a daily basis?"

Sumner pressed his lips tightly together to prevent an angry retort. "I was simply trying to make small talk, Madeleine. We do live in the same house.

"I need to explain something to you. You are a banker's wife now, and there are social obligations." He glanced toward her to gauge the effect of his words. She resembled a deer caught in the headlights of an automobile. The reaction served to empower him. "First of all, we're invited to a New Year's ball at the Biltmore on Thursday night. It's a wonderful opportunity to socialize with prospective clients. I expect you to play your part."

"What part is that?"

"Gracious and lovely wife. I don't expect you to promote the bank. You will be window dressing. No experience required nor even any effort need be expended in your case. You are a natural beauty.

Appropriate formal attire is required. I understand the need for another shopping excursion. You need a fur. I will provide jewelry. This is a fantastic opportunity. The Hollywood elite will be in attendance, authors, artists, the cream of Los Angeles society, such as it is."

"You haven't given me much time to prepare. You know I dislike being stared at."

"How vain of you. The most gorgeous movie people in the world will be there. Do you expect to outshine them?" Sumner could not resist the barb, knowing full well Madeleine's beauty might easily eclipse anyone in attendance. He drew a glare in response.

"Further, I've spoken to Ann. She agreed to marry an old beau of hers and invited us to her wedding in February. I gave her my word we would attend. I'd appreciate if you could select a wedding gift on your trip to the store. Something opulent. You have an artist's eye. I'm certain you can find an appropriate present. But I'd like to see it before you send it off." He watched Maddie's mouth form a small "O" of disbelief. Sumner was a bit stunned at his own audaciousness.

"She must not have been as upset as you imagined when you told her you were married." Madeleine considered he waited a week to mention his meeting with Ann unless he continued to see her.

"She had her own good news to share," was his only reply.

The rest of the meal was spent in familiar silence.

* * *

Curious to see how his wife prepared for the New Year's Eve festivities, Sumner waited patiently near the front door to get the full effect as Madeleine walked down the staircase, exactly on time. He was disappointed she was wearing her fur.

The coat undoubtedly set him back a pretty penny. It looked to be mink and had a plush fur collar and hem—probably sable, but he was no expert. It closed on the side with a single button, which appeared to be covered in rhinestones but could have been a cluster of diamonds for all Sumner knew. Maddie did her hair in soft side rolls. Her makeup was subtle, except for exceedingly red lips. She looked quite the modern woman. The coat served to frame her beautiful face. Sumner surmised nothing could detract from that.

"Are you ready?" Madeleine noticed her husband cut quite a fine figure in his black tuxedo.

"I am. There's one more thing," Sumner noted as he reached into his pocket and pulled out a long string of pearls. "No flapper would be caught dead without these," he explained as he carefully placed them over Madeleine's head. He watched her drop them beneath her coat. "There's nothing to be ashamed of. They're quite real."

"I'm certainly not ashamed. They don't go over my coat. Thank you, Sumner. I hope I live up to your idea of a proper banker's wife after all this expense."

"I haven't seen your dress."

"You're right," Madeleine noted as she walked toward the door, having no intention of revealing the dress at this juncture.

The couple traveled to the Biltmore Hotel in silence. Sumner recalled their early rides together in the limousine when Madeleine improperly clutched at his hand and arm in her naiveté. She never hesitated to demonstrate her need for him in those days. No such need was evident now. Apparently, years of living alone and supporting herself fostered her independence. Maddie appeared a fine example of the modern, accomplished woman. Sumner yearned for the gullible, excited and childish girl he married.

Despite her attempt at composure and sophistication, Sumner managed to catch a glimpse of the younger Madeleine Crawford once the limousine stopped to let them off at the Tiffany Room. She seemed awed at the opulence of the open corridor where guests entered the hotel through several doorways.

Sumner gasped when he removed Maddie's fur to check it. Her jet-black beaded dress was sleeveless and had a V-neck and deeply V-shaped back. The gown was form-fitting with a dropped gathered tulle skirt. Madeleine doubled the pristine white pearls so they fell at differing lengths then looked up to see his expression. She was not disappointed in her husband's admiring gaze.

"I take it you approve?" she offered nonchalantly.

"Very much. You chose an exquisite gown." Sumner's own attempt at indifference was proving futile.

"It's black," taunted Madeleine. "I believe you forbade that particular color."

"Your ensemble hardly resembles widow's weeds. I think you get a pass," he noted as he offered his arm to lead her toward the Crystal Ballroom. He was amused as Maddie gaped at the 12-foot wide Austrian crystal chandeliers and the sumptuous frescoes by Italian artist Giovanni Smeraldi.

"This artist worked in both the Vatican and the White House," Sumner noted as Madeleine strained her neck to take in the Greek and Roman gods, angels, cupids and mythological creatures adorning the ceiling.

"You come here often?"

Sumner laughed. "Hardly. I'm a small-time banker. But this is an irresistible opportunity for me."

A five-course sit-down dinner began the evening. Sumner seemed familiar with the businessmen at their table of eight. Madeleine listened, intent to refrain from conversation as much as she was able. She found people who valued her looks often treated her as the mentally deficient person Aunt Mary claimed her to be. Maddie did not appreciate the judgmental nature of comments offered to her, as if she needed additional clarification. When an older man sitting on her right offered an explanation for interest earned at a bank, Madeleine had quite enough.

"I assure you, Mr. Greenham, I have a general grasp of banking. No further explanation on your part is necessary or welcome."

Sumner hid his smile. Greenham was condescending in general. It was probably time someone put him in his place. He noted Greenham's stunned expression.

"I assure you, madam, it was not my intention to insult you. I was merely trying to explain."

"Yes, surely no woman could possibly understand something as complex as earning interest at a bank."

"It's simply that women do not have a grasp of business."

"Now you are becoming quite rude, Mr. Greenham," Madeleine continued. "I am an artist. I supported myself for many years, running my own business and selling my own wares. I purchased my own house and automobile. I assure you, most women have far more knowledge than you are willing to credit them. In rare instances when they may not have a grasp of business, it's likely because people like you never gave them the opportunity to learn. Women are not stupid, Mr. Greenham."

Sumner could see Greenham was dazzled by Madeleine's beauty. Unprepared for her tirade, the man seemed unable to form a response.

"I'm certain Mr. Greenham did not mean to offend, Madeleine." Sumner decided to rescue the older man. "You simply don't understand your effect on the opposite sex. We all tend to become tongue-tied and fatuous in your presence."

Mr. Greenham chuckled nervously. Sumner imagined the man might not appreciate being characterized so harshly but certainly welcomed the opportunity to make amends.

"Look, the dancing has begun. Would you care to join me on the dance floor?" Sumner politely suggested. He needed a word with his wife and didn't give her the opportunity to object as he rose and pulled her chair from the table. "Do you know how to Charleston?"

"Of course, Sumner. I spend all my Saturday nights dancing in the garden."

He chose to ignore her sarcasm and grasped her hands. "Watch, I'll show you. When I put my foot forward, put yours back." He demonstrated. "Then when I put a foot back, put yours forward. When you place your foot, swivel your heel inwards. There are straps on your shoes, that's good. They won't fall off." Shortly, Madeleine grasped the simple dance. Sumner glimpsed her delighted smile as she stared at his feet.

"Now look up at me. We'll take up dance position

so I can lead. You don't have to watch my feet."
Maddie did not appear embarrassed to learn to dance in
front of more accomplished couples on the floor. She
was always a quick study, but she didn't hesitate to
take a job at the dance studio when she knew almost
nothing about dancing. Intent his final remembrances
of Madeleine be favorable, Sumner usually pushed
memories of the dance studio from his mind.

They clapped when the song ended. Sumner took
Maddie's arm as they returned to the table.

"You never taught me to tango," Madeleine
commented. "You promised me that long ago."

"So, I did. You mean no one at the dance studio
tried to teach you?" Maddie pursed her lips to refrain
from a harsh reply. "Go easy on Greenham. I'm trying
to persuade him to deposit some of his vast fortune in
my bank. He is clearly taken with you. You might be
gentler."

"Beguile him into making an investment as a
proper banker's wife should?"

"Only ones who look like you," Sumner coldly
stated. He watched Madeleine take her seat and place
her hand on Greenham's arm. She offered a lively
account of the Charleston and even took the older man
out on the dance floor to teach him the steps she just
learned.

Sumner stared at them over a glass of bathtub gin
he obtained from the nightclub down the hall. He
entertained the uncomfortable feeling he pimped his
wife out for the evening and felt rather ashamed.
Maddie did seem to be enjoying herself despite
apparent dislike of her partner. Perhaps it wasn't an
issue for her in light of past experience as a taxi
dancer.

Sumner took the opportunity to promote his bank, the real purpose of the evening as far as he was concerned. There were a few additional trips down the main galleria with prospective clients for a taste of the forbidden gin. Each time Sumner returned to the ballroom, he found his wife dancing with a different man including several actors in attendance.

Her current partner escorted Madeleine through the archway to the adjoining Tiffany Room. Before Sumner could storm after the couple, the man returned alone to the party. Sumner, with apparent nonchalance, headed for the Tiffany Room himself, only to find his wife exiting the ladies' lounge.

"You are quite the triumph tonight," goaded Sumner.

"I'm simply making business for the bank. Isn't that the idea?"

"Do you know who that man was—the one you just danced with?"

"No, but he said his wife was here. He said he wanted to put me in motion pictures—rather bold for a man accompanied by his wife."

"It certainly is. But I'm sure he was serious."

"Why do you think so?"

"That was Douglas Fairbanks."

"Who is he?"

"You can't be serious."

"Sumner, I only ever went to the movies with you. I have no idea who Hollywood people are."

"He has the ability to put you in movies. He has his own studio. I hear he forbids his wife to dance with other men. He likely had her consent to dance with you. It was your chance to be famous."

"I have no interest in fame. Besides," she

commented as she placed her hand below her waist, "I'm sure he wouldn't be interested if he knew I was expecting."

"It's probably for the best. The Hollywood crowd, despite their opulent lives of wealth and what I would call infamy, do not seem particularly happy." As they reached their table, Sumner pulled Madeleine's chair out then bent down to whisper in her ear. "Do you see the woman in the corner?"

Madeleine nodded.

"That's Barbara La Marr, the movie actress. She is known as 'The Most Beautiful Girl in the World,' but I doubt the term is completely applicable. She collapsed on the set recently. She's been married five times. Evidently the fast life is not agreeing with her. Her beauty is fading at the ripe old age of 29. She doesn't look well, does she?"

"No, she doesn't."

"She doesn't hold a candle to you, Maddie, but she never did."

This drew a scowl from his wife. A countdown to the New Year began. Sumner downed his glass of gin and stood to embrace his wife. At the stroke of midnight, he took her in his arms for a kiss, more a public display of marital harmony than anything romantic. Sumner was stunned at the emotion he felt as Madeleine relaxed against his body and kissed him in return. Regretfully ending the kiss, he looked into her eyes. He could not tell whether her reaction was sincere or simply amusement at his passion.

* * *

Madeleine walked through the door of her childhood home as the afternoon light started to fade. She first made her way to the kitchen and turning on the faucet, found a thirsty, small, gray cat.

"Hello, Princess," Madeleine uttered the words aloud. They echoed softly in the kitchen. She noted the empty dish on the floor and used a towel to blot up the water Princess dumped. "Silly cat," Maddie commented as she started toward the hallway staircase, leaving Princess to quench her thirst.

Realizing she never set foot in the attic, Madeleine nonetheless understood how to get there. She stopped briefly at the doorway of her bedroom to peer inside. It was Oscar's nursery, although her furniture remained in the room. No doubt, Oscar would soon grow out of the crib sitting against the far wall.

Sumner's decision to take his Rolls to get air for the tires provided the opportunity Madeleine waited for all day. If history were an indicator, he would take a drive before returning, and she could escape his house unnoticed.

Her time in the Graydon household would be necessarily short. She hurried up to the attic only to find an incredible mess covered the entire width and length of the ample space. Madeleine had only enough time to make a superficial observation.

Flipping on the hanging bulb light, Madeleine walked up and down pathways that allowed access to stacks of myriad items, not all of which belonged to Aunt Mary. There were piles of baby clothes, crates of unfamiliar dishes and housewares piled atop what must be the original contents of the attic.

Her heart beat hard in her chest when she thought she heard a noise. That must have been the cat, Maddie thought to herself as she returned to her hasty observation.

As she neared the back wall of the attic, she discovered some of her old dresses neatly folded on a shelf. Her sudden desire to touch them proved irresistible, and she ran her thumb along the edge of the clothes, retrieving the memory of each garment in turn. Fingering clothing she made—the red dress Sumner so loved, the dress she wore for their wedding and for their first trip to the Venice Pier—Maddie was unprepared when a hand closed around her arm.

Screaming at the top of her lungs, she turned to find her husband, who quickly placed his hand over her mouth. He removed it once she stopped struggling.

"Sumner! What are you doing here? You scared me to death."

"What are you doing here?"

"I came to give the cat her water as Mrs. Graydon requested."

"So, the cat lives in the attic?" Sumner facetiously inquired.

"No, well, I wanted to look in the attic for something."

"Your things are here? You have a longing for your things? The Graydons might notice if you take your clothes."

"I'm not going to take anything. What are you doing here?"

"I told Mr. Graydon I would keep an eye on his house. When I saw the light was on, I thought I better check to see if there was a robber. Now I see there is."

"I'm not a robber. How did you get in?"

"How did you get in?"

"I have a key." Madeleine produced the key from her pocket and waited for Sumner's response.

"I came in using my traditional method," Sumner

confessed. "Are you quite finished?"

"No, I want something here. Help me look."

"What am I looking for? We really can't stay, Madeleine. Some nosey neighbor might call the police. How would it look if they found us here?"

"We have an excuse."

"You used to live here. You are the niece of the victim, and I was a suspect in her murder."

"I'm looking for a white box approximately this high." Madeleine spread her hands about eight inches apart. "It was tied with string. It's the box with my name on it."

Sumner took his wife's arm to lead her toward the stairs. "You won't find it here."

"How do you know?"

"Because they found your box when Mary was murdered. It was on her floor, open and empty."

Madeleine stopped in place. "Where were the contents?"

"Someone burned them in the fireplace. All that remained were the charred edges of newspaper articles. No one will ever know what was in the box."

Madeleine allowed Sumner to lead the way downstairs.

"Why is this box so important to you now?"

"It held the answers to the questions of my life. What if all the contents weren't burned? Someone might still have control over me. Who inherited Aunt Mary's things, her business, her home, and her money?"

"Your trust did."

"If I never claim my trust, no one will know I'm alive, unless someone in the neighborhood suspects your new wife is your old one."

"It doesn't matter, Maddie. You were dead. The trust went to the executor."

"Who was that?"

"Dr. Coolidge. He was also a suspect, but I believe eventually, he managed to take control of everything in the trust. There was no one to contest his claim. The reason for the trust was placed as evidence at my hearing. He had no reason to burn the papers," Sumner commented as they approached the front door.

"Wait! I have to turn off the water," Madeleine explained as she hurried toward the kitchen. Someone did know what was in the box and one of the contents occupied his bedroom bureau drawer.

Chapter Fifteen

Evelyn bounded through the front door. "I'm home!" she boldly announced, dropping her purse on the hallway table and removing her gloves. Spotting James, she inquired, "Is my son here?"

"No, ma'am. But Mrs. Hemmings is in the dining room."

"Mrs. Hemmings?" Evelyn was incredulous. What had Sonny gone and done in her absence? She excitedly headed for the dining room door and turning the corner, began, "Ann! My darling Ann!" but stopped dead in her tracks at sight of a different woman sitting at the table.

Embarrassed at her assumption, Evelyn noted the young woman only stared at her, unsurprised at her blunder. "You are Madeleine, aren't you?" She almost whispered the words.

Madeleine looked toward the ceiling as she thought. "Oh, that's right. We met that Christmas Eve. I couldn't imagine how you might know who I was."

"Who else could you be?"

Madeleine rose from the table, offering her hand in greeting as she walked toward Evelyn. "It's nice to really meet you, at last." She offered a warm smile. Whatever her problems with Sumner, they were not his mother's fault. She would never admit Evelyn's gaffe hurt her feelings.

"You're very gracious. I imagine my faux paus would have embarrassed most newlyweds."

"I suppose I don't consider myself a newlywed. I was just finishing lunch. You must be hungry after your long trip."

"Oh, no. I met a gentleman on the train, and we shared lunch before I came home. Where is Sumner?"

"I'm right here, Mother." Having heard her voice as he entered the front door, Sumner strode into the dining room and gave his mother a warm embrace. "You surprise me. I thought you wouldn't be home for another week."

"The weather back East is abysmal. My old bones couldn't adjust. It's wonderful to be in the sun again. And now you have this surprise for me!" Evelyn felt herself a fraud. The last thing she wanted was to make small talk. What exactly was going on here? What happened to Ann? "You never thought to notify me of your marriage?"

"I thought it would be best if I told—we told you in person."

"I see and so you shall give me all the details. I am rather tired," Evelyn lied. "Sonny, would you mind bringing my bag upstairs? I think I could use a short rest before we all sit down to have our talk."

Madeleine looked on as Sumner escorted his mother out of the dining room. She attempted to decipher their conversation as they climbed the stairs. Although she could not hear the words, the tone changed dramatically as the pair walked across the upstairs landing. It was apparent Evelyn Hemmings was quite disappointed. Their little chat never did occur.

* * *

Sumner was surprised when his assistant directed Reverend Neelson into his office. "What brings you here, Hiram?" he inquired as he stood and shook the man's hand.

"My favorite almost daughter, of course. I thought I'd see how things were going. I'm here for a short conference and wished to make good use of my time."

"Please have a seat," Sumner offered.

"I have to tell you; we recently received a letter from Madeleine. I didn't know what to make of it. I'm fairly certain she did not intend to reveal some of the things we noticed but then again, perhaps it might have been something of a cry for help."

"What do you mean?"

"We were able to read between the lines. Please tell me if my ideas lack substance. For instance, we have the impression another woman has come between you, that you and Madeleine are not trying to make a go of your marriage, and she is uncomfortable living next door to her aunt's house. I have a point to this, please don't think I'm here to admonish you. Madeleine, I'm certain, has done her share to provoke your marriage to this unfortunate circumstance. But please, if I'm wrong, feel free to correct me."

Sumner threw his pencil on the desk. "I didn't know Madeleine was uncomfortable in the house, at least not before my mother returned from her trip. The rest is true enough. The other woman, the one Maddie saw me with in Ventura, is a thing of the past. I was in love with her. She decided to marry someone else when I told her Madeleine was alive. I admit I miss her. She was my dearest friend, and we built our relationship over several years. Madeleine and I fought most of the way home, and we haven't spoken much since."

"I'm sorry to hear about your difficulties. But there's really no reason for you to continue as you are."

Shaking his head, Sumner replied, "I doubt there is any other way to continue."

"Since you married in December, what's the best time you had together?" A joyous expression lit Sumner's face, exactly what Hiram hoped for.

"Without a doubt, New Year's Eve."

"What happened then?"

"I took Madeleine to a party. She didn't want to go. I knew she wouldn't. It's not as though we were exactly cordial, but we were together. It was extravagant and exciting. I taught her to Charleston. It was a memorable evening."

"And the next day?"

"We returned to silence and solitude."

"Why do you suppose that happened?"

"There's been too many bad things. I blame her; she blames me. We can't seem to let go of our disappointment. I don't think we can start over."

"I don't think you should start over. Do you remember the obstacles you encountered when you were first married? Didn't those seem overwhelming? I know you weren't together for long when Madeleine was taken away. Perhaps you never saw any of your obstacles overcome? But I imagine as you look back, most of those problems seem insignificant."

"You're right. They were."

"Perhaps as years go on, the obstacles you face now will seem less important. I know you've each been through unfortunate circumstances. If you can manage to conquer this, you both might find the partner in life you're looking for."

"I don't even know where to start."

Hiram grinned. "Well, it's my job to help you. The Lord has given us guidelines for every important aspect of our lives."

"So, you're going to quote the Bible to me?"

"No, I don't need to. Being faithful doesn't mean you show up in church on Sunday and know you are saved. It means you apply biblical principles to your life. Then you not only make a good life for yourself but a good example for others.

"I'm certain you've heard Ephesians 5 quoted in church. It's the part where women are told to be subject to their husbands. Unfortunately, most men stop paying attention after that. A man is supposed to be the head of his household not dominate his wife and demand her obedience.

"Obedience on the woman's part is a voluntary submission out of respect for her husband. Women are to be revered. A wife is man's gift from God. A husband is supposed to treat his wife with as much care and concern as he does himself. He should be her protector and vitally interested in her welfare; make sure she understands completely how much she is valued, loved and respected.

"Then, you need to put your money where your mouth is. Show her how much you love her by sacrificing your interests and even your welfare for hers. Do you know what Madeleine wants? Do you know what she needs? Do you even understand her interests much less encourage them? In a very real way, being the head of your family means being a servant to them.

"I assure you, if you start doing what is best for Madeleine—not merely provide her with a place to live and money to spend—she will respond in kind. I think you'll be amazed at the difference you can make."

Sumner listened intently. "I know you're trying to help, but I wouldn't even know where to start. I've been honest with Madeleine. We haven't pulled any punches. I can't undo what has been said."

"I don't think that can be undone. I'm suggesting a way to a happy future. I will speak to Madeleine before my return home. She is a bit too clever and stubborn for her own good. Think about what I've said. Perhaps you can begin by listening."

"If I can get her to talk."

"Oh, if you start listening, I assure you'll get an earful. Try to be good-natured, and see if you can separate the fear from the facts."

"Fear? Madeleine is not afraid of anything as far as I can tell. She doesn't seem to need or want a thing from me."

"Just listen. You'll be surprised."

* * *

As far as Sumner could figure, the Reverend's advice translated into two simple words—pay attention. He was prepared to attempt a better home life when he walked through his front door that night. He was the man of the house after all.

Since his mother descended on the household,

unhappiness had given way to almost complete despair. He rarely caught even a glimpse of Madeleine so intent was she to hide away from all unpleasantness. She even took supper in her room. He briefly contemplated his wife was made a prisoner all her life, and he was currently playing the part of jailer.

Deciding to start with his most formidable opponent, Sumner walked into the library where his mother was ensconced with her knitting.

"Good evening, Mother. I believe we need to have a talk." His cheery greeting was met with a scowl.

"You're in a fine mood."

"Yes I am. You see, I've decided we need a happier home." As Evelyn disgustedly dropped her knitting in her lap and turned to address him, Sumner raised his hand to halt her reply. "I understand you're disappointed in the personal choices I recently made. I've listened to your incessant disdain for letting Ann 'get away' as you put it. I know you were intent on bringing her into the family, but you've had time to come to grips with this. Frankly, I have no more patience for it. My life is as I have made it. Madeleine is my wife."

"You didn't have to marry her again. You were a free man thanks to Mary Argyle."

"No more, Mother. We have other concerns. You will be a grandmother. I believe we should all focus on this new member of our family."

Evelyn tipped her head and stared at her son in disbelief. "So, this is what prompted your marriage?"

"I didn't say that."

"I can see the guilt clearly written on your face. No wonder Ann was furious. It all seems so clear now."

"I'm not going to talk to you about the past. I expect a welcoming demeanor as far as Madeleine is concerned. No more snide comments. No more exasperation over Ann's wedding next weekend. If it upsets you, I'm sure she'll understand if you are not well on Sunday."

"I wouldn't miss it for the world! You more than anyone realize how dear Ann is to me."

"Then I expect you to behave. I'm going to see if I can persuade Madeleine to sit down to dinner tonight."

Sumner sat alone at the dinner table within five minutes, the two most important women in his life having fled. His mother's congratulations directed at her daughter-in-law turned quickly into a general rant about immorality in today's younger generation directed at her son. He smiled graciously and tried to change the subject.

Noticing the same protective reaction Madeleine displayed when he first drove her past Aunt Mary's house, Sumner recognized his wife would not stay in this hostile environment forever. She tasted her first real freedom after her recovery in Santa Paula. Even if Madeleine wouldn't talk, he knew she wished to return home—perhaps more than she wanted to give her baby a father.

Sumner hoped once Ann's wedding was accomplished, the new grandmother might accept current circumstances, at least he wished she would. His own home was a tiny slice of hell on earth. No one in their right mind would voluntarily occupy the Hemmings household.

Before Sumner retired for the evening, he stopped in front of Madeleine's door. His intention was simply to speak to her if only to ask after her welfare. Once he raised his fist to tap on the door, he paused when he discerned the whirring sound of the new electric sewing machine.

As intent as she was to spend his money, Sumner hadn't found any of his wife's purchases extreme. She stared defiantly at him when he mentioned this most recent purchase only to confirm the accuracy of his invoice. Even in her anger, Maddie was incredibly beautiful. He was willing to spend all he had if it would make her happy. Uncomfortable at this surprising idea, he lowered his hand and walked away.

* * *

Sumner surmised if he were a fly on the ceiling, his current predicament might be entirely amusing. Living through this day could prove the greatest achievement of his life. Being a veteran of the Great War, that was saying something.

He was grateful to God, so much so he actually said a quiet prayer when his mother and wife managed to make the trip to church in complete silence. Although Madeleine coped with her mother-in-law by avoidance, he never imagined this would continue indefinitely. If anyone understood Maddie's sharp tongue, it was him. One of the more unpleasant scenarios he imagined for today was Madeleine and his mother coming to verbal blows in the middle of the ceremony.

Sumner escorted his wife into the church behind the usher who took the elder Mrs. Hemmings' arm, much against her will. It seemed her intention was to foist the usher off on her daughter-in-law so she could be accompanied by her son. Sumner deliberately took his seat between the two ladies.

When Madeleine stood to remove her coat, Sumner helped and for the first time, noticed her delicate condition was apparent.

At this particular juncture, his mother found it necessary to lean forward and have a better look. This obviously embarrassed Madeleine who stared red-faced toward the front of the church as she again took her seat.

Sumner glanced at Maddie's pink frock spread across the pew near his leg. It was by the slimmest of odds they were together now. If not for the unlikely meeting with a stranger at the cemetery, she would still be in Ojai, and he, very likely, would be the one waiting at the altar for Ann. If Sumner had concerns about his own feelings at Ann's wedding, there wasn't time to dwell on them as his mother started bawling conspicuously.

Lost in thought, he did not notice the bridal procession begin and was late to stand when the bride appeared. He considered Maddie's attire more carefully. Her dress was tailored, without a ribbon, bow, ruffle or frill in evidence. The dress had a pleated skirt and elongated pointed white collar ending above the dropped waist. The long sleeves were gathered at white, buttoned cuffs. It was the beautiful shade of pink that exuded femininity and leant the appearance of delicacy. He knew Maddie was not fragile. She was an intelligent and self-sufficient survivor with incredible inner strength.

Sumner felt a pang of regret. He failed to be her hero when she so desperately needed him. Maddie was no longer the naïve and needy girl he fell in love with. She was right, things were more complicated than he imagined when he found her.

A modest reception was held in the church meeting hall. Sumner found himself seated at a small table with his wife as she picked at her slice of wedding cake.

"We can leave as soon as Mother finishes visiting. From the way she's behaving, one would think she was the groom's mother."

"It was her intention. She no doubt feels slighted today," was Madeleine's flat-toned response.

Curiosity tainted Sumner's next question. "Why do you remain silent when she's rude to you?"

"What good could I do? You argue constantly. It doesn't encourage her to be polite."

"She's having a difficult time. She's never been an easy person to get along with."

"But you mentioned how well you've been getting along."

"I think she felt we were companions facing the world together after my father grew ill. Then she made a warm relationship with Ann."

"And I came along and ruined everything. You have a wife she doesn't like, and her relationship with Ann will undoubtedly fade as time goes on."

Sumner felt it best to change the subject. "What did we give the happy couple? Ann literally gushed her thanks. What did you buy?"

"I showed you. A set of fine china."

"It seems a proper enough gift. It must have been expensive?"

"Extremely. Didn't you see the bill? It seemed a fitting gift for such a dear friend."

"Yes, a friend," Sumner mumbled as he caught sight of the bride.

Madeleine turned her head to consider her escort. Ann assumed her almost-husband took the time to select the gift himself. She had undoubtedly been touched by the subtle message the dishes conveyed. Softly painted forget-me-nots rimmed the edges of every piece.

"They seem happy," commented Sumner nonchalantly. "You look lovely today. You outshine the bride."

"That was not my intent. This is her day."

"I imagine you could have worn a feed bag; you would still outshine her. Ann never took my comments about your beauty seriously. I think she was shocked to see you in the flesh." Sumner admittedly took some delight in the brief episode although he never cared if Ann did not compare favorably with her predecessor as far as looks.

If Ann's desire to have him attend the wedding was an effort to wound him in some way or cause acrimony in his own marriage, she failed. To be honest, the acrimony existed without any help.

"I don't care for your comments. I dislike being paraded about like some trophy. Appearance is a shallow way to judge people. I truly don't understand why your Ann would go out of her way to assure my presence. I don't even understand why you would come or why you felt it necessary to mollify her. Doesn't this bother you? You should be the groom after all. This should be your lovely and memorable Valentine's Day wedding, nothing like our rushed and spontaneous trips to the altar."

Sumner was surprised at his own lack of feeling. As difficult as his mother made the day, watching Ann marry another man had not proved disturbing at all. He likened it to watching a sister marry. Perhaps it was his lingering emotional incapacity that made the ceremony so painless.

"This seems to bother you. I'll round up my mother, and we can be off," Sumner suggested, considering himself quite the caring spouse.

* * *

Madeleine sat in the middle of her bed in the dark. Normally, a lightning storm would intrigue and delight her. Unusual weather was always noteworthy in Southern California. Tonight, it only served to grate on her frazzled nerves.

Having managed to overcome so many horrible circumstances in life, Maddie made it her custom to attempt gratitude at the end of every day. Try as she might, her unpleasant current predicament pounded through her thoughts like some buffalo herd, impossible to ignore.

She considered ways to avoid the wedding today. Her brief visit with Reverend Neelson brought an end to her fantasies. She couldn't defend her current role as wife to Sumner Hemmings. The Reverend scolded her relentlessly with her own vows and did not hesitate to expound the biblical principles of being a helpmate.

Maddie admitted she made herself as difficult to live with as she could. She had not hesitated to turn a cold shoulder to her husband and was shocked when the proper Reverend gave her a stern lecture about the importance of intimacy in marriage. Even though she believed her friend only meant the best for her, the idea all men stuck together brought an undeniable bitterness to her memory of the conversation.

In the darkest days of her life, Madeleine never

felt so lost. She currently lived in a house with people who despised her and felt her inadequate to fill the shoes of the precious Ann. Sumner loved another and was stuck with her and a baby that ruined his life. The house next door loomed over her, a bitter remembrance of her unnatural childhood and lifelong incarceration. Thoughts of her parents, their horrible and corrupt relationship and her solitary childhood made her hesitant about her own maternal abilities.

There were times when she looked at Sumner and longed for the life they had six years ago. Discouraged at the thought they could never be close again, Madeleine was unable to stop the tears she held back for so long. Her fear Sumner murdered Aunt Mary and might yet be punished by the authorities was never far from her thoughts. How would his crime affect her baby? How could a child understand his father was a murderer?

Today was another in the string of awful days since she and Sumner were reunited. How she managed to appear steady and calm while feeling unsure of herself could only have been an answer to prayer. Maddie had not felt so alone since she lived in the basement of the asylum where Aunt Mary banished her. Trying her best not to seem cold at the wedding, she imagined there were those who thought her the victor in a war for Sumner Hemmings—an attractive and prosperous man. There were undoubtedly those who thought her supposed tactics devious. Try as she might, the stares and hidden comments behind gloved hands could not be ignored.

Longing for home came over her in waves as she began to sob. Maddie would never be good with people, having lived such an isolated life. It was only when she and Sumner were close that she felt protected and comfortable in society. Bored beyond belief in the Hemmings household, Maddie longed for the hard workdays at her house in Ojai. She craved the anonymity of her widow's veil.

More than anything, she wanted a healthy baby. Her desire to hold her child in her arms was almost unbearable. How could she want something so desperately when she didn't have any idea what it was to be a mother? Maddie would gladly go through any ordeal, even one worse than last time, to see her baby's face and hold its tiny hand. If something happened again, she doubted she would ever recover. Despite her tendency to blame Sumner for their daughter's still birth, she was certain it was her own shortcoming. Maddie wondered how she might be able to succeed now.

Her entire body jerked at the explosion of thunder from a nearby lightning strike. A dull pain settled in her back. Panic set in as Madeleine remembered how her premature labor started with subtle back pain on that long ago 4th of July.

* * *

Sumner lay in bed, unable to sleep due to the storm. He listened as rain pelted his bedroom window. Amused, he recalled Ann's befuddled look when he expressed his heartfelt hope this was the start of a wonderful and happy life for her. He believed her to be the most innocent victim in the mess that was his life. Ann had every right to be angry. He led her on, believing Maddie was dead. He would have made a good husband and believed without doubt, they could have built a happy marriage. For the first time, Sumner speculated they were all victims of Mary Argyle, to one degree or another.

Surprised, Sumner realized how easily he forfeited his life with Ann. If she married in an attempt to bring him to his senses, perhaps she succeeded only not in the way she intended. He hoped her marriage was sincere. If it was accomplished with the intent to make him jealous, Ann likely ruined her life for naught.

Sumner considered the manner in which he drifted through life, reacting to events around him, barely planning for himself. Even when he took over his father's role at the bank, it was never his dream or intention. His decision to propose to Ann now seemed merely a natural result of their long friendship. The kind of passion he felt for Maddie was never a factor in his relationship with Ann.

Why were women always telling him he was self-centered? If anything, he was simply a leaf in the wind, being blown and tossed about by other's desires and whims. The only choice he made in his life remained Madeleine. He always gave her credit for making him into the man he became. If not for her influence—the fact he changed himself into someone she could respect—he would likely have drunk himself to death by now. His parents were on the verge of tossing him out on his ear when he met her. Ann would never have considered the young Sumner a candidate for marriage. Yet, Maddie saw something in him he never saw in himself. Were the allegations he was self-centered true?

When he first wanted to kill Mary Argyle, it was not Madeleine's death sparking his anger. Sumner originally didn't make the connection between the asylum and the illness that took Maddie's life. He believed it was Mary's cruelty in letting him travel to Santa Paula for a presumed reunion that so infuriated him. In retrospect, he might have been more willing to address his anger than to face the crushing blow of Maddie's death.

He remembered the day still, so clearly it might have been yesterday. Euphoric with anticipation of seeing her, touching her and sharing his life with her served to whip him into something of a frenzy. Having all his hopes and dreams dashed so purposefully was the worst thing he ever suffered. Even knowing how Maddie suffered, he still felt slighted by her withdrawal from the world and from him. Her allegation he was to blame deeply offended him. He thought only of his feelings, his pain, since their parting in October. Until today, he was so focused on what he lost, he remained blind to what he actually found.

Although intellectually, Sumner understood his child was steadily growing in Maddie's womb, he was astonished at the fact she was showing. He saw so little of her since New Year's, the reality of his impending fatherhood proved rather stunning. But more than her silhouette affected him today. He was as proud of Maddie as he ever was, as attracted to her as he had ever been. She was the one who aroused his passion, his protective nature. Ann's marriage no longer mattered to him if it ever truly did.

Now the question remained, how was he going to win Madeleine back? How could he free her from the past to join him in a future together? Sumner considered ways to fulfill Maddie's needs and desires and make himself indispensable, never realizing this was exactly the course Hiram Neelson suggested.

No sooner had this idea begun to form than he heard a soft knock at his bedroom door. Rising to answer, Sumner was stunned to find the subject of his thoughts within arm's reach.

"How might I be of service?" he asked, jovially.

"I'm afraid."

"Of the thunder? Surely you have lightning and thunder in Ojai, or is that not permitted in your private wonderland?" But as he took a closer look in the dimness of the hallway, he saw Maddie was trembling. Sumner reached out to touch her arm and found his belief confirmed. "Come in here," he suggested and pulled her into his room, closing the door behind her. "What's wrong?"

"Can I stay here? I don't want to be alone. Can I lie down here with you?"

He directed Maddie to his bed and sat her on the edge then lifted her feet onto the bed and covered her with his blankets. He went to the other side and crawled in beside her, taking her in his arms.

"Are you cold?"

"No. Just hold me."

"Maddie, something is wrong or you wouldn't be here. Tell me what's troubling you. Is it the baby?" He didn't know where that idea came from, but he felt her tense beside him and assumed his guess was correct. "Do I need to get the doctor?" Sumner's alarm was apparent.

"No. I don't know."

"Tell me what's wrong." No sooner did he finish his sentence than the bedroom flashed with another close lightning strike. Madeleine jerked when the thunder boomed.

"It's just, before our baby was born, I had a lot of pain in my back, and I'm having pain now."

"Severe pain?"

"No."

Sumner needed to get his wits about him. Knowing their baby was more important than anything to his wife, he regretted forcing her attendance at Ann's wedding and the stress it undoubtedly caused. Feeling the definite urge to panic, he purposely calmed his voice in order to calm Madeleine.

"Relax, Maddie. You're all wound up. Maybe you pulled a muscle when you reacted to the thunder. Let me rub your back. How does this feel?"

"It's lower."

Sumner repositioned his hand and tried to keep his tone of voice warm and soothing. "I'm sure this will help. Relax and let me warm you up. This is nothing to be concerned about." If only his sincere desire to make everything right could be made fact with words.

"I'm sorry," offered Madeleine.

"It's all right, I wasn't asleep."

"No, I'm sorry you didn't get to be the one to marry Ann today. I can imagine how devastated you must be. You were brave to put on such a cheerful front. That must have been difficult."

If Sumner was not so concerned about his wife, he might have laughed at her disquiet. "Did it seem to you I was unhappy today?"

"No, you were truly valiant."

"I would hate to take credit for something I didn't do. I think you're misjudging me."

"How so?"

"Maddie, I seemed unconcerned about the

wedding because I was unconcerned. Now relax and close your eyes. I'm here, everything is fine." He held her close and continued to knead her back with the palm of his hand.

Thinking it seemed rather unwise to crawl into bed with the man who murdered her mother, Madeleine could not resist the comfort of Sumner's body and quickly dozed off despite the drama of the weather outside.

* * *

After bounding down the staircase whistling *If You Knew Suzie*, Sumner gave his mother a peck on the cheek and joined her at the breakfast table.

"You're late for work."

"Yes, I am. But I'm the boss, and that's my privilege. You're looking dour and unhappy this morning, Mother."

"Your father was never late for work. I believe my expression is an accurate reflection of my feelings, Sonny. I was overcome with emotion at the wedding yesterday. In light of the fact Ann is lost to you, I should imagine your mood would be more pensive."

"You make it sound as if Ann died. I don't believe things are quite so dire, and it seems my attitude this morning reflects my feelings as well. Please take a breakfast tray to Mrs. Hemmings and a pot of the rose petal tea she likes," Sumner directed the maid. "You'll find her in my bedroom."

It was difficult to hide his smile as his mother gawked at Sumner in disbelief. He quickly hid behind his cup of coffee and took a sip. If she believed he was having intimate relations with his wife, Sumner would only encourage that idea even though he had done nothing but comfort Maddie and sleep in the same bed. He would like to repeat the occurrence tonight but doubted the weather would cooperate. If she didn't come to him, he contemplated the possibility of joining Maddie in the guest bedroom. He was content to bide his time and pursue his plans of indispensability.

"Something wrong, Mother?"

Evelyn pursed her lips then responded, "I suppose no red-blooded man could resist that woman's wiles. She is every bit as easy on the eye as you always claimed."

Deciding to ignore the back-handed compliment, Sumner inquired, "What are your plans for the day?"

"I haven't any. I believe I need to recover."

"Very well, then. Have a nice recovery on this beautiful, crisp and clear day, and I'll let you know if we'll be joining you for dinner tonight."

"Why? Where are you going?"

"I have plans to spring my wife from her prison."

"What is that supposed to mean?"

"It means you've missed your calling, Mother. I believe if they put you in charge of the penitentiary system in California, no one would dare attempt escape. Your acid tongue would keep them firmly behind bars."

"You are being silly this morning. I believe I'll take my tea in the library."

"Yes, you do that," Sumner sipped his coffee. "I need you to understand something before you go. I'm tired of fighting. I'm sorry our relationship has deteriorated to this degree. I rather enjoyed it when we got along. Madeleine has been left to her own devices since I brought her here. My intention is to make her feel welcomed.

"I know you're unhappy having her for your daughter-in-law, but I want to be honest. I am making a go of this marriage. In fact, I'm so determined, nothing will stand in my way. If you wish to have a relationship with your grandchild, I suggest you find a way to accept my wife."

Sumner watched his mother turn her back and exit the dining room. Maddie was right, it did no good to argue with Evelyn Hemmings.

Plans to woo Madeleine flooded his thoughts. He could give his ideas more attention with his mother stewing in the library instead of across the breakfast table.

Chapter Sixteen

Sumner gazed at his wife, bundled up beside him in the limousine. He could tell she was apprehensive when he telephoned to invite her out to dinner and to see the popular new film, *Ben-Hur*, at the Million Dollar Theater. It was billed as the movie every Christian should see, and it ran to rave reviews since December.

"Did you enjoy the film?" he asked.

"Very much, didn't you?"

"Yes, but I must admit it had more than entertainment value to me. I'm afraid I was looking at it from a business perspective."

"Why?"

"Because I have a few investments in the motion picture industry."

"You have a stake in *Ben-Hur*?"

"Not directly. I think this particular studio shows a great deal of promise, though. You have to admit, the visual effects and action sequences were almost beyond belief."

"Aren't movie studios risky investments?"

"Certainly, but that's the trick—balancing a few risky ventures with more stable projects. My father was actually good at that. I use his strategies in my work. I started personal investing once I made a good salary. I've been doing well, my point being, I think we need to change a few things."

"What kind of things?"

"If you could go anywhere, where would I take you?"

"I'd like to visit the baby's grave," Madeleine replied without hesitation.

Sumner nodded thoughtfully. "What if I take next Friday off and we head to Santa Paula, weather permitting?"

"Oh, Sumner, I would like that very much!"

"We'll plan on it then," but Sumner had plans far exceeding a trip to the cemetery. "I have a surprise for you. I've planned a luncheon."

"What kind of surprise?" Madeleine hesitantly inquired.

"Don't worry, I guarantee you'll enjoy yourself. I'll pick you up at 11:30 tomorrow. I have a favor to ask." Sumner whispered in Madeleine's ear to see if she would sleep in his bed again tonight. He was delighted when she looked into his eyes and nodded assent.

* * *

"Whose house is this?" Madeleine inquired as Sumner opened the door of his Rolls and took her hand. They were in a lovely neighborhood, a relatively new development, but almost everything in Los Angeles was relatively new.

"I told you, it's a surprise." Sumner guided Maddie onto the front porch and rapped on the door. Eager to watch the homeowner's reaction, he realized his surprise might prove too extreme as he watched Jemimah Doucette's face pale to a shocking degree. It was certainly never his intent to kill the woman.

"My gracious. Baby Girl, is that truly you or have I died and gone to heaven?"

Sumner took the woman's arm and led her to a nearby chair. "Are you all right?"

"Let me see! Let me see her."

A stupefied Madeleine followed behind and bent down in front of Jem's chair. "It's me Jem. I'm alive."

Sumner stood back to watch the reunion he constructed.

Initially too overcome to speak, Jem finally managed, "When I called Mr. Sumner up and told him I come back from Washington with my cousin, he told me he had a surprise. It was just too cold there for me. I told Isla we are going back to California like it or not. I was so glad I didn't sell my house when I left to take care of her. Here I thought Mr. Sumner up and married his Ann. I never dreamed in a million years he found you. Where have you been? Oh Lord, let me hug you. I can't let you go ever again. And what's this? Are you with child?"

Sumner almost laughed at Madeleine's shock as Jem boldly placed her hand on his wife's abdomen. Oblivious to her own tears, Jem held Madeleine's cheeks to wipe hers away. Thinking it best to leave the two women alone, Sumner walked out on the porch and took a seat, content to wait until lunch was served, however long that might take.

* * *

Madeleine was quiet as Sumner drove leisurely toward home. Impatiently, Sumner prompted, "I hope it wasn't too much for you. You're feeling fine?"

"It was a lovely surprise but probably too much for Jem."

"I'm sorry about that. I guess I didn't understand what a shock it would be. She promised to send me her new address in Washington when she left. I would have let her know about you before if I were able. We made something of a friendship when you were gone. I didn't have anyone else to talk to—about you."

"She aged since I saw her last. I never noticed how old she was. Jem told me she would come and take care of me and the baby. I didn't know what to say to her. I don't need anyone to take care of me. I want to take care of my own baby," Maddie added, almost defensively.

"You mean our own baby."

"Yes, our baby. Isla is nearly blind. She needs Jem's help now."

"Well, you can see her as much as you like. Alfred can drive you over or you can have Jem and her cousin to our house. That will no doubt infuriate my mother. It might serve to drive her away for a day here and there."

"I like your idea, I don't mind admitting. Thank you, Sumner. This was thoughtful of you even if it did prove a little too shocking."

* * *

They began to converse more easily. Sumner had no intention of pressuring Madeleine into a physical relationship. Content to lie in bed and talk, he managed to give an account of his relationship with Ann in an effort to clear the air. Somehow, he was able to explain without offending Maddie, at least he thought that to be the case. Sumner attempted to clarify his despair having found her grave. He offered stories about his rise to proficiency at the bank and the way he used his connections to the motion picture and aircraft industries to bring a diversity of investment.

Maddie explained her lengthy convalescence and despondency, the security she felt in anonymity and her pride in being able to make her own way in the world. If their relationship was not exactly warm it was definitely cordial.

Madeleine purposely avoided her mother-in-law, which wasn't anything new. She didn't know if her success caused her lighter heart or if it was merely an enhancement. Maddie knew Sumner made a difference. She had no idea where his new devotion was headed or if it would last but was content to see what might happen next. As Madeleine stood at the front window watching for Sumner to return from a meeting at the bank, she turned to see Evelyn approach.

"You must be waiting for Sonny. I wanted to have a word before you left."

Madeleine only stared in response.

"I realize I have been difficult. I would like to call a truce."

"I don't believe I've done any disservice to you. Why would you feel a truce was in order?" Madeleine boldly replied.

Evelyn expected a meeker reply. She saw Madeleine as a mousy, delicate and subservient wife, determined to use her beauty to blind Sonny to her various faults. Somewhat nonplussed, she continued, "Well, I simply mean I would like to propose a friendlier relationship. As a mother, I do keep my son's best interest at heart, and you are his wife."

"I've been his wife for some time now. This seems a rather striking contrast to your attitude since returning from New York." Madeleine had no intention of being gracious at this juncture.

Evelyn babbled somewhat mindlessly, "It's just that ever since you disappeared, I've seen how hard this has been on Sonny. You simply don't understand how devastated he was. I begged him not to kill your aunt. He was determined to avenge you."

This last comment drew Madeleine's attention. "How did you manage to change his mind?"

"I explained how much we needed him, how he might come to regret his actions. I said anything I could think of. I'm certain you can understand my desperation. I made him promise he wouldn't kill her. He only agreed to refrain temporarily. Just when I was certain he'd come to his senses, the police came to question him after your aunt's murder. I was certain they would take Sonny away. No one was as amazed as me when he had such an air tight alibi."

"You were his alibi?"

"No, no. He was with his friend, that Trace young man, the flier. I've counted down the years since Mrs. Argyle's death."

"Why would you?"

"The statute of limitations, of course. Seven years and there's no need to worry."

Madeleine considered her reply, all the while Trace's words rang in her ears. "I would do anything for Sumner," he said. "I owe him my life."

"I hate to tell you this, Evelyn. There is no statute of limitations on murder."

"Are you quite certain?"

"Entirely. There's Sumner now. I'll be going."

"Think about what I said," encouraged Evelyn as Madeleine walked through the front door. She had the sinking feeling what Sonny said was true. There wasn't much hope for a relationship with her grandchild if she couldn't find a way to make amends. And she knew beyond doubt she dug herself a substantial hole.

* * *

Sumner parked beside the Santa Paula Cemetery and grabbed Madeleine's hand before she could exit the car.

"I need to tell you something. I replaced the headstone."

"Why?"

"Because the baby's name is Hemmings not Hall."

Madeleine carefully considered this turn of events, surprised Sumner even cared about such a thing.

"It's the same stone you picked. Everything looks the same except the name."

"When did you have this done?"

"Right after Christmas." Defensively, Sumner added, "She is my daughter. She should have my name."

Without further comment, Madeleine opened the car door and walked toward her daughter's grave.

Full of trepidation, Sumner followed. Prior events in this cemetery proved earth-shattering. He was developing a definite aversion to it.

The thing Sumner least understood about Maddie was her refusal to come home or send word once she was able. True, if her aunt found out she was alive,

Maddie would likely have wound up in another asylum. Even so, this was the one issue Sumner could not get past.

As he observed his wife at the grave of their child, he grasped the depth of her connection to the baby. While arranging flowers on the plot, Maddie talked to the headstone much as if she were speaking to a baby in a cradle. At first, he found her behavior rather shocking and looked nervously about to make certain no one else could see. He was stunned at her apology for having been gone so long and smiled weakly when she introduced the baby to her daddy.

He felt awkward and unsure when Madeleine stood and blew a kiss toward the grave before she took his arm to go back to the car. She seemed light of heart and oblivious to his discomfort as Sumner started the engine and drove away.

"You're turning the wrong way, Sumner. The road we came on is to the right."

"We don't have to go back yet. I thought we'd take a ride."

They drove along in silence for a time. Madeleine hummed as she watched the scenery. Sumner's discomfort at the cemetery was obvious. It was Madeleine who finally broke the silence.

"I know the baby isn't there, Sumner, if you're stewing about my sanity."

"I didn't say anything."

"Only because you don't know what to say. I understand you don't feel as if you lost a child. You didn't know about her. I imagine her grave means nothing to you. I'm surprised you bothered to change the headstone."

Sumner calculated their child had been dead

almost six years. "What does it mean to you?"

"Our baby is in heaven where there is no pain, no sorrow or grief. Someday we'll see her there. But when I lost her, she was everything to me. My very own family, my child to love, my secret companion at the asylum. I never got to hold her or see her smile. I never touched her soft skin or fed her. She never took a breath, Sumner. It seemed so unfair.

"The only thing I could do to soothe my pain was spend time at the cemetery, talking to her. I felt this was all my fault. My weakness caused her death. Had I done something differently, she would have lived. Reverend Neelson repeatedly explained this was God's will, and even if I couldn't see any good in it, I was certainly not as smart as God. When I tried to blame you, he told me you weren't smarter than God either. He even defended Aunt Mary, although to be honest, I never discussed much about her. It wouldn't have changed his mind.

"He thought when I moved to Ojai, I would stop visiting the cemetery. I can't tell you how frustrated he was when I continued to come. The only reason I left here was because there is a new baby to consider." She turned to stare at Sumner and continued, "My child is here, this is where I belonged."

Sumner put his hand over his mouth and pulled his fingers toward his chin, having no idea what to say. Finally, he managed, "This is difficult for me to understand. How could a grave be more important to you than I was?"

"I guess something died in me when the baby died. I didn't care about anyone, not even myself. I only cared for her. I imagine I spent too much time wallowing in my grief. I knew it wasn't healthy, but I couldn't seem to stop."

"And when you saw me in Ventura, you could so easily have come to me."

"You were with someone else. You seemed happy. I thought that was for the best."

Another awkward silence ensued until a suspicious Madeleine inquired, "Sumner, where are we going?"

"I thought you might enjoy spending the weekend at your house. I brought a box of paperwork from the bank to keep me busy while you do your housekeeping or whatever you do there." He was not prepared for Maddie's jubilant reaction.

"Oh, truly! Sumner, nothing could make me happier!" She had difficulty sitting still until Sumner parked his car next to the shed.

First looking through the window to ensure her flivver was parked inside, Maddie dashed down the path out of sight.

Taking a deep breath, Sumner had more doubt about a life with Madeleine than at any time since making his Valentine's Day resolutions. Wondering what he was getting himself into, Sumner grabbed his box and small valise and headed toward his future.

By the time Sumner walked through the front door, his wife shared her hastily-made plans. A flurry of activity was about to commence. Teresa Neelson thoughtfully removed all the perishables from the kitchen. They needed food. She would quickly make a list and they could drive into Ojai, which was not far away. But first, Maddie needed to wash the bed linens. After their shopping excursion, she would put dinner on. Believing she might be able to clean the entire house before supper, she knew the kitchen and bathroom were top priorities. Regretting there wasn't time to work in the garden today, she planned to tackle it tomorrow.

Maddie chattered on about wildflowers on the way to Ojai then directed Sumner toward the dry goods store, showing him the best place to park. It was as if Madeleine was asleep and awakened to find the world completely to her liking.

Sumner was reminded of the girl he married years ago who was thrilled to simply walk out her front door. The trip to the cemetery definitely knocked the wind out of his own sails. But as their shopping trip progressed, Sumner found himself swept up in Maddie's excitement. She didn't even notice when people stared.

"I imagined you have everything you need as far as clothing, but if I'm wrong, you better shop while we're in town," Sumner offered.

"Oh, I don't think I need anything. If we go by the butcher's, we'll be done. It's right here," she commented, making a sudden turn through a doorway.

As she ordered, Maddie was interrupted by a boy sitting near the window. "Mrs. Hall, is it you?"

"Oh, Willie, so nice to see you. But it's Mrs. Hemmings now."

Willie observed her companion, the man with the handsome car he met right before Mrs. Hall disappeared.

"You don't wear your veil no more."

"You're right. We're only here for the weekend, but if you and Moogie come by tomorrow, there will be cookies." Madeleine smiled her most dazzling smile.

"I sure will tell him!" Willie replied as he dashed

out the door of his father's shop.

"I'm sorry I didn't recognize you, Mrs. Hall," the man behind the counter commented.

"Oh, why would you?" Madeleine graciously responded. "But it's Mrs. Hemmings now. This is my husband."

Sumner felt inordinately proud as Maddie took his arm. He was certain gossip about the crazy Widow Hall would spread like wildfire through the community. Perhaps formerly crazy was a better descriptor, at least he hoped so.

* * *

Sumner sat on the porch with his paperwork in an attempt to stay out of the way. His hands were busy trying to keep his work from blowing in the breeze when Maddie came outside to shake a throw rug.

"What's wrong?"

"There's too much wind. I can't stay out here and work. Are you done in the parlor?"

Maddie stooped down and picked up a rock from the flower bed then walked up the porch stairs. Wiping the dirt from the rock on her apron, she plopped it on the stack of papers.

"Now you can work until supper. It's almost ready. This is called a paperweight just like the cavemen used."

"What a creative solution. I'll have to bring some rocks back to the bank," he teased.

"Yes, you do that. It's the Madeleine Hemmings solution to all your problems."

"Are you the solution to all my problems?" Sumner inquired, more seriously.

Maddie walked around the small table where

Sumner was working and to his surprise, sat on his lap and put her arms around his neck, still grasping the throw rug in one hand.

She pressed her cheek next to his and responded, "I believe we always had the solutions to our problems, we simply never implemented them." She planted a quick kiss on Sumner's forehead and bounded away before he could say a word.

If Sumner felt any irritation at the tiny house, the irksome breeze, the cold weather or the fact Madeleine might be as crazy as her aunt claimed, he was quickly mollified by the delicious dinner his wife concocted. There was a tasty beef stew and freshly baked biscuits dripping in butter. Dessert was a small apple tart, which they shared.

"Why do you have a coffee pot when you don't drink coffee?" Sumner asked suspiciously.

"I have recipes that call for coffee, mostly desserts, so I bought one. And aren't you glad I did?"

"Very. There's nothing like a cup of coffee after a good meal."

"Oh, you like my cooking?"

"I do, indeed. We may have to come back here sooner than later so you can fatten me up." Sumner was surprised when his innocent comment drew a frown. "What did I say?"

"I don't want to talk about leaving. We just got here."

"You want to pretend we're here forever? Then you'll be happy?"

"Yes."

"Well, I think I can pretend for the weekend. What are your plans for tomorrow?"

"I want to do more cooking and give the front

porch a thorough cleaning. It seems unproductive to do much in the garden, but I could clean up a bit."

"Maddie, isn't this too much for you? Aren't you tired? Maybe you should take it easy. I can help you tomorrow."

"I feel fine."

"Your back hasn't been hurting?"

"No, I want to work. I think it's good for me. This is such fresh air. It's so beautiful here. The wildflowers are popping out. The sweet peas have gone wild in the garden. But I would like it if you helped me."

"I'll sleep on the sofa tonight so you can get a good night's rest."

Madeleine took his hand across the table. "No, Sumner, I like sleeping with you. Please come in the bedroom. You'll keep me warm."

"Well, it is going to be a cold night."

"Yes, we do need to be practical, after all."

* * *

The effects of breakfast wore off quickly as Sumner found himself in the garden at Maddie's beck and call. He was not used to physical labor. Working in the bank made him soft. He wondered aloud at his ability to last until lunchtime, which Maddie assured him would prove an ample reward for his efforts. He noticed her struggle to pull a root out of the flowerbed under the bedroom window.

"Here, let me help you," he offered. "Don't you have something better to use than a trowel?"

"I've almost got it."

Sumner took hold of the trowel as the root gave way. Dirt flew off the tool into his face. He sat back brushing dirt from his eyes. His distress amused

Madeleine who laughed the pleasant, tinkling laughter he so well remembered.

"You think this is funny, huh?"

Maddie adopted a serious demeanor as she answered, "I do."

"Well, maybe you should have a little dirt on your face," he teased. Wiping his mouth on his shirtsleeve, he leaned forward to give his wife a kiss. Withdrawing to look in Maddie's eyes, the brief kiss seemed lacking, and he pulled her into his embrace to kiss her fervently.

Sumner ended the kiss and drew Maddie beside him as he lay back in the newly weeded dirt, cradling her head against his shoulder.

"I love you. I've always loved you, Maddie. I think it's why I never committed to An—to any other woman. Deep inside, I must have known you were still alive. That seems irrational, and yet I ought to have paid attention to my feelings. I should have found you. I never protected you as I should have. I'm sorry."

His apology meant more to Madeleine than she could express.

"I'm sorry, too. I should have tried to tell you where I was. I was selfish. I do love you, Sumner."

With imperfect timing, Willie's call from the front of the house broke the spell.

"Mrs. Hall, are you home? Me and Moogie's here. I mean, Mrs. Hemmings!"

Sumner scrambled to his feet, helping Madeleine off the ground.

"Oh!"

"Is something wrong? Did I hurt you?"

"No, I felt the baby move." She took Sumner's hand and placed it near her hip. "Can you feel that?"

Sumner shook his head, "No, I don't feel anything."

"You will in time," she assured.

An unapproved morning cookie respite followed. After Mr. and Mrs. Hemmings' young guests departed, gardening was abandoned. They agreed their bed seemed an appropriate place to languish away the chilly afternoon.

Mutual apologies would serve as a new beginning. Their words were good and right. But it would take more than words to mend the fissures in the Hemmings marriage.

* * *

Madeleine quickly understood it was easier to cook without Sumner kissing the back of her neck or attempting to embrace her. She thoughtfully put her knuckles to her cheek and tried to recall if any ingredients in her French chicken dish with rice had been forgotten. It smelled as it should. Although she tried to pay attention to the recipe card, the distraction Sumner provided was difficult to overcome. Maddie was relieved when a delighted expression lit her husband's face.

"It's delicious!"

"Well, if I didn't make it correctly, at least it's edible," Maddie replied as she took her seat. Between gardening and their entertaining afternoon in bed, an exhausted Maddie fell asleep for a time before preparing supper.

"I thought we might stop at Reverend Neelson's church in the morning." Due to their newly revitalized marital relations, Sumner was surprised to see Maddie's serious frown in response to his suggestion.

"Why can't we stay here, Sumner? I don't want to go back."

"I know you don't, and I don't blame you. I understand how difficult it is for you to live in my parents' house. Will you trust me enough to come home? I don't want to leave you here alone. I don't want to let you out of my sight. I promise we will make changes. My goal is to make you happy." Sumner took her hand across the table. "Will you come back and give me some time to work things out—new things? Please say you will."

"Will you bring me back here when I want to come?"

"I give you my word. But we have to get a bigger bed. My feet hang off the end of yours."

"But it's where we consummated our marriage."

Sumner tilted his head and replied, "I seriously doubt anyone is going to wonder at the validity of our marriage. It's rather apparent we will soon be parents. What's wrong? What did I say?"

"I'm sorry. You didn't say anything. I never would have thought our first marriage was in jeopardy either when things went so terribly wrong."

"Well, there's no one to stand in the way of our marriage now. Your m—your Aunt Mary is gone. There's nothing to worry about.

"What were you going to say?"

"When?"

"You started to say something else before you said Aunt Mary."

"No, that was what I was going to say."

Madeleine let it drop, but she was certain Sumner started to say your mother. "Whatever happened to our Dutch oven? Do you know?"

"I have no idea. Maybe it's in the neighbor's attic. Look, I do have something of yours I always keep with me." Sumner grabbed his wallet off the sitting room table and opened it to retrieve the pyracantha painting Maddie gave him after his fall from the tree. His sentimentality touched her.

"I'm certain Hiram and Teresa will be thrilled to see you tomorrow." Sumner was not prepared for yet another frown. "Aren't you excited to see them?"

"My last conversation with the Reverend was not especially amicable," Maddie admitted. "He redressed me quite soundly on my deficiencies as a wife."

"I see." Sumner noticed Hiram seemed rather heavy-handed with Madeleine on previous occasions. He likely treated her more as a daughter than a parishioner. "I'm prepared to be your knight in shining armor. After all, you are my perfect wife, and I will not be shy about expressing my devotion to you. You can consider this my first true test."

"Are you prepared to discuss your bedroom activities in detail?"

Sumner spluttered on his coffee. "You are not serious?"

"I believe your friend, Hiram, feels it necessary to supervise our marriage. I think he is out to prove to his wife what a good idea this is," Maddie explained.

"Well, it was a good idea after all. I'll be certain to shield you from any indelicate inquiries."

But there was no need for probative questions. It was obvious the young Hemmings couple was much in love when they visited Reverend Neelson's church on Sunday morning. They soon commenced their journey to Los Angeles, he with a lunatic, she with a murderer. But that was fine by them.

Chapter Seventeen

"Have a seat, Lt. Corbett," Sumner offered as he sat down behind his desk. "What can I do for you today?"

"I was hoping you might fill in some details regarding an investigation I'm conducting," the Lieutenant began.

Sumner appraised the man, who was several years his elder. Short and stocky with dark hair, the man exuded confidence.

"I'd be glad to help in any way possible. Does this involve some patron of the bank?"

"No. It actually has to do with your neighbor, Mrs. Argyle."

Curious, Sumner held up his hand at a quiet knock on the office door.

"Yes."

Peering around the corner of the door, his secretary quietly stated, "Your wife is here, Mr. Hemmings."

"Please ask her to take a seat. I won't be long." Sumner looked at the officer for confirmation. "I won't be long, will I?"

"Likely not," was Lt. Len Corbett's vague reply.

As the door closed, he continued, "You have quite a successful life, Mr. Hemmings. First a member of the Lafayette Air Corps then the 103rd Aero Squadron during the war. You were only one kill short of being an ace. You're quite the hero. Now the manager and half owner of this bank."

The comment served to anger Sumner. In truth, he had more than enough kills to qualify as an ace. Keeping score as if he were in some sporting event disturbed him. He never hesitated to give other pilots credit for his work. He was no glory seeker. It was men's lives he'd taken: fathers, brothers, sons and husbands. The fact it was kill or be killed never soothed his guilt. Satisfying the officer's curiosity suddenly held less appeal. His displeasure served to lend an unfriendly crispness to his responses. "You come well prepared, Lieutenant. I'm beginning to think you've been investigating me. What has this to do with my deceased neighbor?"

"I found an interesting link between Mrs. Argyle and two bodies that were recently discovered in the hills above Santa Barbara. I was hoping you might be able to help me understand their association. You see, a Santa Paula doctor ran a home for disabled relatives of wealthy patrons. You know of this place?"

"Yes, it was called The Home."

"You visited there in the past?"

"I was looking for my wife, Mrs. Argyle's niece. She told me I could find her there."

"And you went to visit?"

"I went there to retrieve her, but I was too late."

"How so?"

"I was informed by Dr. Thomason of her death from pneumonia, a complication of influenza."

"When?"

"September of 1920."

"Did you see Dr. Thomason since?"

"No. It's the only time I ever saw him."

"But you did see Mrs. Argyle after September of 1920? Let's see. She was murdered in December of that year, I believe."

"Correct."

"And you were a suspect?"

"Briefly, yes. I had an airtight alibi, and others were quickly added to the list of suspects, many others." Sumner believed the Lieutenant already knew the answers to all these questions. "What has any of this to do with the bodies you found?"

"The bodies were of the doctor and his wife. They've been dead for a long time, years. They were identified from personal effects found nearby. Dr. and Mrs. Thomason disappeared from Santa Paula after the death of Mrs. Argyle. It's not possible to tell how long they lived after their sudden departure."

"Was there some sort of accident?"

"They were murdered. It seems an extreme coincidence for murders of people who were both associated with the late Madeleine Crawford to have happened so close in time or at all for that matter. You say you were married to Miss Crawford?"

"We were married, yes. Her aunt had the marriage annulled." Sumner was getting the same look of disdain from Lt. Corbett he received from his father when his attraction to a backward woman became a topic of conversation.

"You were accused of breaking and entering Mrs. Argyle's home."

"I was trying to find out what she did with my

wife. Those charges were dropped."

"Did you ever return to Santa Paula after your initial visit to The Home?"

"I did but only recently. I went to visit my wife's grave. Am I under some sort of suspicion?"

"I'm simply trying to determine if there is some link between these murders. You, for instance, had a motive in Mrs. Argyle's death, but you have an alibi. It would be difficult for you to provide an alibi for these subsequent murders since we can only guess when they occurred. You have a motive, after all."

"I've never set eyes on Mrs. Thomason. Dr. Thomason was kind enough when he explained my wife's illness and death. What motive could I have?"

"They were supposed to be caring for Miss Crawford. Perhaps she would be alive if not for them."

"That's something of a stretch, isn't it?"

"I'm simply trying to determine if there are any ties, Mr. Hemmings. There's no need for concern."

But Sumner believed the good Lieutenant was fishing around for someone on whom to pin the homicides, which would no doubt be a feather in his cap. It was rare when crimes of this type were solved. He asserted Sumner had both motive and opportunity. Sumner wondered how the Thomasons were murdered.

"How did you find the connection between Mrs. Argyle and the Thomasons?"

"The doctor and his wife evidently left town in a great hurry. All the paperwork from their business has been sitting in a box at the sheriff's office. Once the bodies were discovered, the paperwork was reviewed in depth. I was brought into the case when Mrs. Argyle's name showed up on the ledger as a client. Her death was sensationalized in the papers. It was a high-profile case, nothing like the missing Thomasons. Still, there is a definite link."

And I am that link thought Sumner.

The officer left his card and affably excused himself, requesting Sumner contact him if he thought of any pertinent information. Walking through the door of the bank manager's office, he spied an unusually beautiful woman, evidently the new Mrs. Hemmings waiting for her husband. A grim determination took root in Corbett's brain. Coming from a poor family, he always took special delight in applying justice to the privileged. He was just the man to bring this banker to his knees.

* * *

"I don't understand, Sumner. Why didn't you tell him I was alive?"

"I think it's best to keep you out of this. I don't want him harassing you. Let's leave the past in the past."

"It sounds to me like he's trying to uncover information to use against you. What happens if he finds out I am Madeleine Crawford and quite alive?"

"He will question you."

"But won't that cast even more suspicion on you? Why wouldn't you have told him?"

"I answered all his questions accurately." Sumner turned and looked at Maddie as he drove toward the beach and honestly stated, "I didn't kill the Thomasons."

Maddie believed him but noted he had not said the same about Aunt Mary.

"This is probably some bizarre coincidence. I

doubt I ever hear another word from Lt. Corbett. Look, we're here!" For someone who was just questioned about murdered people, Sumner seemed extremely light of heart.

"What is this place?"

Sumner helped his wife out of the Rolls. "With your approval, this is our new home." All thoughts of the morbid morning conversation instantly vanished as Sumner used a key to open the front door of the cottage, set right on the edge of the beach in Santa Monica.

Maddie walked through the rooms in wonder. There was a sitting room, dining room, kitchen, bathroom and office on the bottom floor; three bedrooms and a bathroom upstairs. A balcony extended from the master bedroom, which faced the sea. There was room for a modest garden and Madeleine envisioned a play area for the baby in the fenced backyard.

"Oh, Sumner! This is perfect. It's not too large and the rooms are manageable."

"Not too large for what?"

"For me to keep the house myself."

"But you don't have—"

"I want us to be alone here. This is our home. I don't want a house like your parents or Aunt Mary. This is perfect! This is ours?"

"Well, not yet. But I do know this banker—"

"Oh, you're the banker, Sumner. Don't tease me."

He was startled when Maddie grabbed his hand and placed it below her waist.

"What is that?"

"The baby, you can feel it?"

"I can. Doesn't it hurt?"

Madeleine shook her head and fell into Sumner's embrace. Frowning, Sumner considered the view of the ocean through the window. Their baby seemed so real. He would be a father before long. Sumner could only pray he would do a better job than his father managed.

"When can we move in?" asked Madeleine.

"How about next weekend? We need a lot of furniture, though."

"I know what we need. I can shop through the week and have it all delivered on Friday. I did set up housekeeping for myself after all."

"I thought we only needed one thing."

Madeleine's expression grew instantly serious. "Only one thing?"

"Yes, you once assured me we only needed a Dutch oven to set up our household. How quickly we forget." Sumner laughed as Maddie threw her arms around his neck once more. Certain they would be happy here, he just didn't want to see the bills.

* * *

Madeleine planned her week in detail and included shopping excursions for at least part of each day. She was determined to have one last visit with Mrs. Graydon and the children and invited them for a "farewell" tea on Wednesday afternoon when she knew Evelyn would be out of the house. Since Evelyn's return, the two younger women met at the Graydons' on their occasional visits.

"I'm sorry we're late," Mrs. Graydon breathlessly exclaimed as she removed the children's sweaters on the cool day. "Oscar didn't wake from his nap at his usual time."

"No problem at all. Please have a seat."

Madeleine thoughtfully purchased each of the children a gift to entertain them while the grown-ups enjoyed their tea. The girls unwrapped their own bone china doll tea sets and commenced a miniature tea party on the ottoman with diminutive food Madeleine instructed the cook to prepare, much against her will. Baby Oscar unwrapped a brown teddy bear and seemed content to watch his sisters, especially when they offered the bear his own tea. Madeleine was thrilled with Mrs. Graydon's baby gift—a beautifully knitted blanket.

"I couldn't resist the opportunity to make something for the new baby," Mrs. Graydon admitted. "I love to knit! I hope you don't mind."

"It's perfect! Thank you so much. Whenever did you have time?"

"You have been so generous. We're all going to miss you. It must be exciting to have a brand-new house."

It was at this moment Evelyn, having returned early from her ladies' club function, made a grand entrance.

"So sorry, am I interrupting?" Evelyn noticed the crestfallen expression on her daughter-in-law's face.

"Certainly not. Please join us," offered Madeleine who quickly made introductions.

"I met Mrs. Graydon when she first moved in," Evelyn remembered. "I didn't realize you ladies were friends. What an odd situation."

"How so?" inquired Mrs. Graydon.

"Why, the fact Madeleine lived in your house all her life. It must be strange for her to return as a guest."

Evelyn could see the neighbor had no idea who Madeleine was. The woman seemed shocked to the core and glared at Madeleine in disbelief. Evelyn was not at all surprised when Mrs. Graydon quickly made an excuse to leave and bundled her children out the door. Madeleine sat shocked and alone, still holding her teacup on her lap.

"I'm sorry," offered Evelyn disingenuously, "I thought you would have told her."

"Obviously, I didn't," replied Madeleine as Evelyn smiled a cold smile.

"I'll check on supper then." Evelyn scrambled out the door intent on avoiding what might become an unpleasant scene.

A disappointed Madeleine contemplated this was her own fault for not having been honest with Mrs. Graydon. The woman was her first friend. What must she think now? Did she know Mary Argyle's niece was purportedly an invalid, a lunatic, feeble-minded or dead? She would undoubtedly wonder why Madeleine never divulged her true identity and could only speculate about her motives.

Madeleine bit her lip and reached over to finger the meticulously knitted, sunny yellow baby blanket. Perhaps it didn't matter. She would never be good with people, and she was about to move away.

* * *

Try as she might, Madeleine could not see any difference in the cheaper glassware. Fishing her spectacles out of her bag to have a better look, she pondered which set to purchase. When she noticed a gentleman standing at her elbow, Maddie turned and gasped in surprise. Ann's groom smiled warmly, all his attention directed toward her. Madeleine struggled to remember the man's name, even a first name. She had intentionally put as much of the wedding out of her mind as she was able.

"Mrs. Hemmings?"

"I'm sorry. I can't remember your name. I know you married Ann Girard. I'm so embarrassed."

The tall, blond, bespectacled gentleman chuckled. "No need for embarrassment. I completely understand. Although my wedding day was the most memorable of my life, it must have been difficult for you. Thornwell, Prescott Thornwell is the name."

"Oh, I do recall now you mention it. Is there something I can do for you?"

"I wondered if you might help me with a purchase."

"Of course. I feel so badly I couldn't remember your name."

"You see, I found these two vases, and I can't decide which Ann would like most." Prescott was amused by the startled expression on Mrs. Hemming's face. "Let me explain. I have long supposed the beautiful dishes were your selection not Sumner's. My wife will never believe me. When I saw you today, I imagined you could help me select an equally memorable gift for my wife. I promise she'll never know you helped."

Madeleine eyed the two vases Mr. Thornwell was considering then walked toward a display case against the wall.

"I don't know how much you intend to spend today, but I like these. I think Mrs. Thornwell might feel the same if she appreciates the dishes as much as you say. You see, the colors in these Wedgwood vases compliment your dishes so they would make a wonderful addition to the dining table. They also make excellent display pieces on their own. The vases you found are lovely but possibly a bit less timeless."

"You're politely telling me they're too trendy?"

"Perhaps so. Egyptian motifs are all the rage though. The colors in those vases are striking."

"Maybe too striking for the elegant dishes?"

"Maybe so." Madeleine smiled. The man seemed so willing to accept her opinion.

"The Wedgwood pieces it is then. Thank you for your help. I wonder if I might repay you?"

"It's not necessary. It was my pleasure."

"And it would be mine to take you to tea. Isn't this what shoppers do, spend a lot of money and recover over a cup of tea, a few sweets and savories?"

"Well, shopping experiences throughout my life have been quite limited, but I believe I could use a respite. I'm attempting to furnish an entire house in a week, and I seem to be having more and more trouble making decisions. Perhaps a cup of tea is just the thing." Madeleine had the impression Mr. Thornwell's mind was set on something more than tea and frivolous conversation.

She settled on the more expensive set of glasses. If nothing else, it still pleased her to spend Sumner's money.

Mr. Thornwell proceeded to escort Mrs. Hemmings to the elegant tea room where they were promptly seated at a table for two by a window.

"I must tell you, Mr. Thornwell, I feel rather scandalous. I have never dined alone with any man except my husband."

"I can reassure you, Mrs. Hemmings, I am entirely safe and a devoted husband. Your husband and my wife have often dined together. Perhaps it's time we follow suit."

"But that was before you married."

"All the more reason it is perfectly safe now. How is your tea cake?"

"It's delicious. I admit this is a welcome reprieve from shopping. Thank you so much."

"Tell me about your house. You're in the process of moving?"

"For the first time, Sumner and I will have our own home. I know it seems unlikely given our long history, but it's true."

"You seem excited. Things are going well?"

"Quite well." Madeleine could not help but be suspicious.

"You see, marrying Ann was a dream come true for me. I pined away for her for years. Although we were friends, by the time I worked up the courage to ask her out, she was seeing Sumner, er, Mr. Hemmings.

"The forget-me-nots on the dishes were a lovely touch. I think Ann needed to know she would not fade into the dustbin of history. She needed to know she made some kind of difference to Sumner, as he did to her. It was an extremely thoughtful gesture, even more so if it was yours. I can't say this to just anyone, but I know Ann married me on the rebound. I'm not a fool. I was willing to take what I could get."

"So, you want to know if Sumner is happily married to put your mind at ease?"

"Please, Mrs. Hemmings, you make me sound extremely calculating. Here I am, sitting across from the most beautiful woman I ever laid eyes on, and you are casting me in a conniving light. Have I said something wrong?"

"No, I enjoyed our conversation until you commented on my looks."

"Is that subject taboo?"

"I can't tell you how tedious it is to be judged by appearance. I would not be exaggerating to admit there are many people who consider me a dimwit simply because they find me attractive. After all, an appealing woman must not have a brain. It's a sore spot given the fact my aunt—I'm sorry. That's irrelevant to our discussion."

"My apologies. I am quite taken with your brain." Prescott received a hesitant smile in return. "If I promise not to mention your unrivaled beauty further, could I discuss something else? You see, there's simply no one who understands my dilemma as do you. It's your dilemma as well."

"What dilemma?"

"Your husband and my wife had a lengthy relationship. Ann did not hesitate to explain her desire to invite Sumner to our wedding. She wished to demonstrate her bond with him was at an end. Instead I saw quite clearly his relationship with her was at an end. His declaration of best wishes for us was extremely sincere, shockingly so to my wife, I'm afraid. Her desire you attend, I believe, was meant to satisfy her own curiosity."

"And was her curiosity satisfied?"

"I imagine so, not especially to her liking. She never believed Sumner's assessment of you, either physically or personally. Your marriage was also on display that day whether or not you realized it. To be honest, I couldn't tell if you seemed happy. Ann couldn't either. If she were honest, she would have to admit her desire to tell Sumner, 'I told you so,' as far as you were concerned."

"There's nothing I can do about any of this except to assure you Sumner is devoted to our marriage. I know our actual time together has been comparatively brief, countable only in months not years. I understand your concern at their long-term relationship, but I don't think you have anything to worry about. Ann is yours to win. There's no one to stand in your way."

"What a tremendous relief."

"It sounds as if you're happy in your marriage?"

"Oh, I should say so, but there are memories I haven't managed to overcome. I'm hoping for a baby soon. Children cement a marriage as little else can, especially for the wife. It's not always the case for a husband, unfortunately, but fatherhood would mean the world to me."

"I wouldn't count on a baby to strengthen your marriage, Mr. Thornwell. It's best you do so on your own. Your wife was a true innocent in all that happened. My return ruined all her plans. I have nothing but sympathy for your situation. I'm certain Sumner wishes you all the best. I'll be sure to tell Sumner Ann has found happiness. I imagine her life with Sumner might not have turned out to be all she hoped even had I not turned up."

"Why do you think so?"

"From things Sumner said, I don't think he ever fell madly in love. He was confident they would have made a good marriage. He did love her. But I don't think it was the kind of love you have for Ann."

"She was completely in love with Sumner. She's been honest. But I believe our marriage is growing stronger all the time."

"I'm glad to hear it. My, what personal

information we're trading here, and we don't even know each other."

"I feel I can trust you. I hope you feel the same," Prescott offered.

"If there's ever anything I can do for you, please feel free to get in touch. I enjoyed our tête-à-tête. I wish you all the best."

"Thank you again for your help. Wherever did you develop such wonderful taste?"

"My aunt was a fine arts dealer. She continually brought home her acquisitions. Of course, they never stayed. Everything, no matter how much she liked or enjoyed it, was subject to sale at the right price. But I imagine the endless parade of objects d'art had some subliminal effect on me. My limited knowledge certainly enables me to spend my husband's money to good effect."

Prescott chuckled. "It has been delightful, but I must excuse myself. Can I escort you anywhere before I go?"

"No. I believe I'll sit here and look over my shopping list before I continue. Thank you again." Madeleine took a sip of tea as Mr. Thornwell walked away. She hadn't given Ann any thought since the wedding. Sumner seemed committed to their marriage. Was she being a fool?

* * *

All too quickly, it was moving day. Sumner went to work planning to return at 11 to escort his wife to their new home and deal with the mass of deliveries Madeleine scheduled for the afternoon. It was their plan to be settled in enough to spend the night.

Madeleine was a bundle of nervous energy as she

placed her last piece of clothing in the steamer trunk. She had few other personal items. Her electric sewing machine was already packed in its case. Sumner took it downstairs before he left. She was surprised when James rapped on her door to announce a visitor, Mrs. Graydon.

Hurrying downstairs, warm smile in place, Madeleine approached the neighbor and offered her hand in greeting. "I'm so happy you came. I need to apologize—"

"No, you don't. I need to apologize. My husband is home today so I've put him to work watching the children. I needed the opportunity to confess. I shouldn't have left so abruptly the other day. After all, you were the only neighbor to be truly friendly. How could I turn my back on you not even bothering to ask why you never told me you lived in my house?"

"You must have heard stories."

"I did. People were only too glad to share gossip when I moved in. Those same people went to great lengths to avoid me and everything to do with my home. Perhaps the stigma of living in my house will never fade. I can only imagine the stigma you have at being Mrs. Argyle's niece. You are her niece, aren't you?"

Madeleine gave a tentative nod. "But that's not why I kept my past a secret. I thought it would be awkward if you knew I lived in your house. You kept so much the same, and I didn't mean to intrude. I was curious about your children never having been around little ones before. When you asked me in at Christmastime, I was completely unprepared. I should have told you then."

"So, the things in the attic, the clothes, shoes,

hats, paintings—those belong to you?"

"You bought the house and contents. Those are yours now."

"But there must be something with sentimental value. I can tell the clothes are beautifully made. Won't you come to the attic and take what you want? I'm serious. I don't feel comfortable keeping your things. You're welcome to anything at all."

"You're extremely generous." Madeleine grinned before sassily replying, "What if I told you the parlor furniture constituted my fondest remembrance of the house?"

Mrs. Graydon laughed. "Well then, we will have our hands full trying to put it all in your husband's Rolls." She linked her arm in Madeleine's. "Won't you come and have a look before you move?"

Madeleine shortly found herself in the attic of her childhood home. Not wanting to tip her hand as to previous exploration, she allowed Mrs. Graydon to direct her to the clothing on the shelves.

"I really only want a few things," Madeleine declared as she pulled out Sumner's favorite red dress, the dress she wore for their first wedding and a few other items. "Fashion has changed since I wore these."

"There's nothing else? What about your watercolors?"

"You're welcome to the paintings. My husband has my favorites. He managed to obtain them before the house went up for sale." Madeleine noted her studies of fall leaves displayed in Sumner's office at the bank. She could only imagine how he pilfered them. "I have new things." Madeleine felt the need to explain at least in part. "I want to be honest."

"You don't owe me any explanations. I know the

gossip about you is untrue. I can't tell you how much your friendship and kindness have meant to me these last few months. I want you to promise when you come back to visit, you'll stop and see us." Mrs. Graydon noted the hesitation on her friend's face. "Oh, I don't get along with my mother-in-law either."

Madeleine laughed. "I'm sure I'll return no matter how much I would like to avoid this street." She looked around the attic with distaste. "This house was just a prison," she muttered to herself.

Uncomfortable at that admission, Mrs. Graydon changed the subject. "Are you sure there's nothing else you'd like to take?"

"Oh, there is something. In my closet, I kept a box with a Dutch oven and a cookbook. You don't happen to know where those might be?"

"I think I do. The oven looked new. I thought it might come in handy as a gift someday. Let me see," Mrs. Graydon mumbled as she walked to the other side of the attic. "Here it is!"

"I can't tell you how much this means to me," Madeleine became fearful this friendly gesture was headed toward an overly emotional parting.

"It must have been hard to abandon all your belongings. I can't believe these few items are all you want."

"These things have to do with my husband. I don't have a desire to remember anything about this house but our times together. It took a while to work out our problems, but we're doing well now. Promise me you'll bring the children to the beach. They'll have such fun. Your friendship has meant so much to me. You're my first real friend."

Mrs. Graydon did not see how that could be true,

but Mrs. Hemmings seemed sincere. "We'd love to! But you must assure me you'll get settled in before you contemplate the idea of company. You need to take care of yourself. Your husband is prepared to do most of the work today, surely?"

"Well he might not know he is," Madeleine admitted as the pair headed for the staircase.

Sumner was surprised when he exited his car to see Maddie and the neighbor woman hugging and bidding each other a dramatic and tearful farewell. He walked toward his wife to take her box.

"What was that all about?"

"I have a girlfriend, Sumner! I'll tell you all about it on the way to the beach. The trunk is all packed. I'll wait here while you tell your mother goodbye."

Sumner hid his half-smile. "You mean you aren't going to help me out here?" He received only a quiet stare in response. Turning on his heel, he faced the unpleasant aspect of his own unavoidably dramatic parting.

Chapter Eighteen

As Mr. and Mrs. Hemmings settled into their new home, they attempted to make the most of each day. They viewed the future as some vague eventuality but for differing reasons. Madeleine dreaded the last months of her confinement, fearing she would fail as before. She tended to fret about her baby's health. The idea Sumner was in trouble with the law or might still be in love with Ann plagued her.

Sumner could not picture himself as a father and despite his wife's expanding girth, pretended the actuality of a baby in their family was some distant problem.

His refusal to discuss anything about the investigation so as not to cause distress was foiled by Lt. Corbett's second visit—at Sumner's new home.

Although Madeleine stayed upstairs out of sight, she managed to hear the officer's examination.

"I have a few additional questions for you, Mr. Hemmings."

"Fine. I'm in rather a hurry today," Sumner replied nervously, hoping to keep all unpleasantness from his wife.

"This is a lovely home. Is it new?"

"Yes, but it's quite modest. Not really the sort most bankers choose."

"I did a little research into Mary Argyle's murder. So many loose ends. I wondered if you might tie a few up for me."

"I'm no expert."

"But you do know some of the players. Dr. Coolidge, for instance."

"I never met the man. Why? Has he been murdered too?" Sumner added, facetiously. "I would much prefer meeting at the bank. Is there some reason you sought me out here, specifically?" If the lieutenant meant to intimidate with his knowledge of Sumner's whereabouts, he failed. Sumner simply didn't wish to upset his wife.

"No reason. But I'm here now, and I'd like to get my information since you're available. Dr. Coolidge was named trustee of Mrs. Argyle's estate, or trustee for your wife, I believe? Your wife, or your ex-wife, would have been the recipient had she not passed on."

"I believe Dr. Coolidge would have served as Madeleine's trustee in either case. He was a suspect in the murder for that reason, but I don't think there was much left. Several business partners put claims against the estate. I remember there were other lawsuits. If greed were his motive, he didn't come out with much actual cash."

"There was the house, the one next door to yours."

"You mean next door to my father's house. I inherited half interest when he passed. Mrs. Argyle's home did not bring much in the way of profit due to its notoriety."

"You weren't well off before your father died."

"I made a good living as a bank officer. I can't complain."

"But when you married Mrs. Argyle's niece, you were living on the generosity of your father?"

"If you're suggesting I married her for her money, I can assure you she was as bereft of funds as me. Her aunt's money was in the trust. Madeleine wouldn't have controlled any of the estate even if she were alive. If you're looking for motives, money doesn't fit your agenda. I believe your questioning has gone far enough. The next time you wish to chat, I'll bring an attorney."

"If you feel it's necessary. I'll have you brought down to the station. But I only need your comment on one other issue. Trace Beggs was your alibi after Mrs. Argyle's death?"

"There were other people, but I was with Trace in San Francisco at the time of the murder."

"Do you remember the identity and addresses of any of the other witnesses?"

"I don't know them well. They were people who corroborated my visit in San Francisco. I'm certain all their information is in your files."

"Mr. Beggs was with you during the war, wasn't he? Didn't you win some award for a rescue when his airplane was disabled?"

Sumner silently fumed, refusing to comment.

"Mr. Beggs apparently owes you his life. I can't help but think it would motivate him to provide an alibi when Mrs. Argyle was murdered."

"I think that's quite enough, Lieutenant. I have no intention of commenting further on any of your ideas. I suggest you refer to your predecessor's work on this case."

"Have no doubt, I've been studying the prior investigation, Mr. Hemmings. Good day then. I'll have you come to the station in the near future. I suggest you hire an attorney in the meantime since you wish to be represented."

No sooner did Lt. Corbett walk out the front door than Evelyn Hemmings approached.

"Who was that dour little man?" she asked as she entered her son's cottage.

"No one. Why have you decided to honor us with your presence this fine spring day?" Sumner asked as he kept an eye on the police officer who climbed into his car and drove away.

"I brought something for the baby," Evelyn enthusiastically replied.

"You realize Madeleine feels it bad luck to prepare in advance?"

"Such a silly idea; so old fashioned. Besides, it's nothing especially babyish. I found this charming braided rug in pastel colors. I thought it would go nicely in the nursery. Where is Madeleine?"

"She's upstairs. Why don't you go show her the rug? I'll be up shortly. I have to make a telephone call."

If Evelyn was unable to ingratiate herself with her daughter-in-law at least there seemed less animosity between them. It was obvious to Evelyn her son was happy in his marriage. Although she was traditionally less than concerned about his happiness, Evelyn determined to put her feelings about Ann aside in an attempt to support her son's new life. She had no idea why Madeleine seemed accepting of her but assumed it was for similar reasons—Sumner's well-being. The fact they were no longer all living under the same roof helped immensely. Madeleine had her own home, and Evelyn was as free to live the way she liked as she had been in New York. Her relationship with Mr. Williamson, the man she met on the train, blossomed as a result.

Normally apathetic toward her daughter-in-law, she was taken aback to find Madeleine sitting despondently in the rocking chair of the soon-to-be nursery, staring out the window with a worried frown. The girl appeared on the verge of tears.

"Is something wrong?"

"You once told me you were worried Sumner might be charged in Aunt Mary's murder."

"True, I was. Surely too much time has passed by now."

"A policeman was here. I listened to the questions he asked. I believe Sumner will soon be charged with homicide."

"Oh, that can't possibly be true."

"I know what I heard, Evelyn. I stood at the top of the stairs and listened to the entire conversation. We have to do something." An unspoken bond formed between the two women who both understood Sumner's part in Mary Argyle's death.

Evelyn tried to quell the panic she felt. "Aside from hiring the best attorney, what can we possibly do?"

"I don't know! I'm trying to think." Madeleine turned to address Evelyn directly. "Aunt Mary took me away and ended my marriage. Now it appears from the grave she will take Sumner from me. I can't let this happen."

Evelyn historically wondered about Madeleine's

competency. Even though her assertion seemed a bit unhinged, Evelyn's doubts were laid to rest. The girl appeared lucid and logical of late, quite the opposite of the quiet, withdrawn woman Sumner retrieved from Ojai.

"I will help any way I can, but I don't know what to do."

"We have to think, Evelyn."

"About what?" commented Sumner as he entered the room.

"Why, about the nursery," Evelyn smiled as she steered the conversation in an acceptable direction.

Sumner looked toward his wife who quickly turned to stare out the window. Whatever topic the women chose certainly upset Madeleine. It seemed to him the two female members of his family recently called a truce, if unofficially. He was disappointed but not surprised it didn't last.

* * *

Once Sumner bade his mother farewell, he turned to find Maddie standing on the staircase, looking distressed.

"I'm sorry you and my mother aren't getting on. I thought things were better." His comment was met with a curious stare. He was surprised as he approached to see a tear fall down Maddie's cheek. "Surely things aren't that bad." He put his arm around her waist. "Come sit down on the davenport and tell me all about it."

But Madeleine did not walk down the stairs. "Why was that man here?"

"I don't want you to be concerned. It's not important."

"It is important, Sumner. For the first time in our lives we are living in our own home, on our own terms. I don't want to lose this."

"We're not going to lose anything. I don't want you to be upset. I know you worry. Explain your concerns."

"My concern right now is for you."

"Why?"

"I heard his questions. Why didn't you tell him I was alive? He's insinuating he has a case against you, even I could tell from what little I heard."

"I'm hiring an attorney. If the Lieutenant even bothers to call me in for further questioning, it will all be taken care of. I don't want you to worry," Sumner repeated in the most even tone he could manage. He felt it his duty to protect Maddie. Not understanding how trite he sounded, he attempted to change the subject, offering platitudes about their new life at the beach. This only served to infuriate his wife.

"How can you pretend nothing is wrong? This is serious, Sumner. You won't put me off so easily. When he finds out I'm alive, this is only going to make you look guiltier than ever."

"Do you think I look guilty?"

"Yes, don't you?"

"I need you to trust me in this, Madeleine. This is not your concern."

"How can you say that? What if they take you away? I can't go through this again! I'm not a child who has to be sheltered from the truth. Don't treat me as if I am some invalid or worse yet, emotionally unstable. I expect something more from you. Or have you always believed I was what Aunt Mary made me out to be?"

"I certainly have not. How can you accuse me of that?"

"Holding me at arm's length about this is not going to help, Sumner."

"Look how upset you are. I want you to calm down," Sumner yelled as his wife ran up the stairs and slammed the bedroom door.

* * *

Madeleine could not free her mind from the idea something horrible was about to occur. The beach house, originally a happy venture, seemed another prison where Maddie awaited her inevitable separation from Sumner. The idea history was repeating itself pounded through her mind.

Dark notions about another tiny grave crept into her thoughts. Sumner's belief everything was fine baffled and aggravated her. Long walks down the beach served as reassurance of her own freedom. Maddie walked as far as she was able, sat in the sand and attempted to figure some way out of their difficulties.

A deep hatred of Mary Argyle grew. The idea Madeleine was turning into the lunatic her aunt always claimed her to be only caused more distress. She refused to think of the woman as her mother. Not even Jem's visits or reassurance did the least to quell her anxiety.

Madeleine also recognized her faith in Sumner was shaken and might never be what it was. On some level, she understood why Sumner ceased to look for her. She could imagine how she would feel if someone turned up at her door and told her Sumner crashed his plane into the ocean. Perhaps her sorrow would have fostered doubts about his death. Perhaps she would have stood on the beach waiting for him to swim ashore and prove everyone wrong. Only after he did not return might she accept his fate. Madeleine had chosen not to come home.

Despite Sumner's assertions he did all he could to find her, the solitary months in the basement caused her to hold back now. She believed in him completely only to be disappointed. Possibly, her prior mindless devotion to Sumner was merely a youthful infatuation. It seemed likely mature adults were not so blinded by their love. This realization caused an obvious reserve on Maddie's part.

Sumner took advice from his mother who claimed expectant women often behaved strangely, although Evelyn understood as well as anyone the root of Madeleine's distress. She attempted to discuss the police investigation to no avail. Either Sumner was extremely good at hiding his concern, or he simply didn't embrace the idea he was in any sort of trouble. His long-ago desire to murder Mrs. Argyle haunted Evelyn's dreams almost nightly.

Although Sumner believed nothing further would come of Lt. Corbett's investigation, he hired an attorney. Determined to keep his initial meeting a secret from his wife, Sumner conversed with the lawyer from his office. But he learned his attempt at secrecy failed when he returned home from work one afternoon. Madeleine met him at the door with serious intent.

"I haven't received a greeting at the door in quite some time. What's the occasion?" he cheerily inquired, although it was obvious from Maddie's frown he was in some sort of trouble.

"Your lawyer called," Maddie replied in a flat tone.

"Really? Did he need me to call him back?"

"No, he said he wanted to meet you 30 minutes early on the day of your appointment. He asked me to let you know."

"Thank you for telling me. What's for dinner?"

Incredulous at her husband's flippant reply, Madeleine screeched, "How can you act like this? I know why you're going. I need to understand, Sumner. Don't shut me out."

Sumner, originally intent on secrecy, sought some way to ease Maddie's concern. "All right. I don't want to answer any more questions without an attorney present. There's no need to worry. I have a good alibi, and Trace will be back in the States before the month is out. He'll be able to put all Lt. Corbett's questions to rest for good and all."

"Because he's being honest or because he owes you his life?"

"What is that supposed to mean? You think he's lying?"

"Has he been?"

"Certainly not. What has gotten into you?"

"I think we were never meant to be together. I think this is all history repeating itself except you are the one being taken away instead of me. I told you before I can't face this again. I want us to leave now, while we still can. I want to go away, far away where no one will ever find us. We can go tonight."

"Maddie, you're not being realistic. First of all, I'd look guilty if we took off. You certainly couldn't travel far. There's no need to leave." He watched helplessly as tears spilled down Maddie's pale cheeks.

She didn't look well. He was becoming truly concerned. "Why don't I take you upstairs? You can lie down, and I have something I want to talk to you about."

"What?"

Sumner put his arm around her shoulders and started for the staircase.

"I've had an offer on the bank. It's a good offer, and I'm going to talk to my mother about taking it."

"Why would you sell the bank now?"

"It's doing well; times have been good. But my father always warned good times don't last forever. Bad times don't either. I think this is an appropriate time to sell."

"What would you do for a living?"

"Why, I believe I'll be content staying home and strolling on the beach."

Madeleine's deepest fears came unbidden to her mind. Sumner was preparing to be put in jail or something worse. He wanted to leave her as well off as possible. He accepted his fate. She turned to look for the truth in his eyes.

"Madeleine?" Her face had gone completely white. "Madeleine?" Afraid his wife was about to faint, Sumner scooped her in his arms and took her upstairs. Laying her on their bed, he warned, "Don't try to get up. Relax here for a while." He unbuckled the straps on her shoes and dropped them on the floor. "Do you want some water?"

"Please. I don't feel well."

"And no wonder."

Sumner hurried off to retrieve a glass of water and a wet rag. Returning, he held Madeleine's head while she took a drink. After setting the glass on the nightstand, he laid the rag across her forehead. Placing his elbows near her shoulders, Sumner gently rubbed his thumbs across her temples.

"Now I have you right where I want you. You have no choice but to listen." His remark drew a scowl. "Maddie, I need you to do something for me."

"What?" she asked suspiciously.

"I will explain. You once accused me of only wanting you because of your looks. I'll be the first to admit if you were some sourpuss sitting alone in your garden that first day, I probably wouldn't have thought a thing about you. I never would have noticed the way you scrunch your mouth to the side when you draw or the way you absent-mindedly push your glasses up the bridge of your nose. I would never have heard your wild giggle or watched your delight when I taught you to dance. But I was a shallow man in those days. The truth is, you are my extraordinary and extravagant gift. I don't know what I did to deserve you, but you can't condemn me for admiring your wrapping.

"I'm no longer a shallow man. I appreciate you in ways I never could have imagined when I met you. I love you more than when we went out together. I love you more than when we first married. I even love you more today than I did yesterday. You've made me a better man, a better provider, a more caring person than I could ever have been without you.

"I know you worry, but everything is going just fine. We're not repeating things from our past. You are already further along than you were before and without any complications. All is as it should be. We have our own house, you are my perfect wife, and I know you will be a wonderful mother. I'm not so certain how I'm going to adapt to fatherhood, but I know you'll be there to encourage me.

"I have everything under control, everything. There's nothing to worry about. What I need is for you to believe in me. I'm not going away. You're stuck with me.

"As far as the bank is concerned, I simply feel this is a good time to sell. The truth is, I never picked my own occupation, and I want a chance to try a few things and see what I like. But if all I ever get to pick is you, it's more than enough. We're well off, even if I do complain about money. After the sale of the bank, we could probably live on what we have for the rest of our lives if we live modestly. I have no ulterior motive in selling. I wasn't looking for a buyer—this opportunity developed on its own.

"Madeleine, you are worrying yourself into a frenzy. This has to stop. I need to know you trust in me to take care of you and believe I'm doing what's best for our family. There's nothing Lt. Corbett can do to me. I want you to calm down before you do yourself some permanent harm. Trust me?"

Tears welled in Madeleine's eyes as she put her arms around Sumner's neck. "I so want to, but I'm afraid."

"Where is your faith? Everything is exactly as God has planned. The tough times are behind us, I know they are." He held her tightly as she sobbed uncontrollably. Somehow her outburst served to relieve the tension. Over the next days, Madeleine seemed happier, more focused and calmer. But it would not last.

* * *

Evelyn kept a watchful eye on her son as they spent the

morning signing paperwork at the bank. If she doubted his motives for the sale, his demeanor only indicated displeasure at the profundity of bookkeeping. Although he seemed anxious to attend to the final matters waiting on his desk, Evelyn grasped his arm and urged, "Could we have a few minutes? I'd like to buy you lunch."

In light of his mother's unusual request, Sumner decided to indulge her. "How can I possibly resist? Just to give you fair warning, I plan to order the most expensive menu item."

Evelyn chuckled, "I think I can afford that." Taking her son's arm when he offered it, the pair strolled across the street to a trendy new café. "I've never been here before. Is it good?"

"Quite good. I think you'll enjoy it." As the maître d' first seated the pair then offered menus, Evelyn waved hers off. "You can order for me," she explained. "I trust your judgment."

"I wish my wife was so trusting."

"Surely Madeleine doesn't mind if you order for her?"

"I shouldn't have said that. She's more than willing to let me order." Sumner needed to watch what he said. The last thing he desired was to give his mother any ammunition.

"She must be happy about the sale of the bank."

"Why would you think so?"

"You'll be home. I thought you two were doing well." Evelyn caught sight of a frown before Sumner replied.

"We are doing well, but Madeleine has a lot of concerns right now. The baby is coming soon, only six more weeks. It will be a big change. Then she wasn't actually pleased about the sale of the bank."

"Why not? You must have explained your desire to investigate a different occupation. I thought she would be thrilled for you."

Sumner ordered when the waiter returned then gave his mother an earnest appraisal. How much could he tell her? "I know you and Madeleine don't get along. All I can say is she's apprehensive about the future, so much so I'm afraid it may be affecting her health. I'm worried about her. Her imagination is running wild and not in good ways."

"Most women are fearful about delivering their first child. It's only normal. I suppose even I had some trepidation about what I would do once you were born."

Sumner never explained Madeleine's ordeals, knowing she would disapprove. "Yes, but then you found out money can buy substitute mothers, and you were off the hook."

"Sumner, that's an unattractive comment."

"Seriously, I am trying my best to make her comfortable and secure."

"I commend you for your efforts."

"So you can tell me I'm too good for Madeleine and missed my opportunity for a happy marriage to Ann?"

"No. You are mistaken. I see how happy Madeleine makes you. I'll be honest and tell you I don't exactly understand why this should be, but I believe you made the right match. I've seen for myself Ann is happily married. She's expecting, did you know? Do you two keep in touch at all?"

"No, but what happy news. Give her my regards when you talk to her again. I'm relieved you made peace with my choices."

"You didn't really make choices regarding your marriage, if we're being honest."

"I did make my choice. I chose Madeleine all those years ago. I always felt married to her, despite what her aunt did."

"Speaking of Mary Argyle, Madeleine told me the police questioned you again."

"Really? I wasn't aware you two shared such intimate conversation." Sumner was becoming suspicious.

"She told me she had concerns about your welfare—another of her worries?"

"Yes, I imagine it is."

Evelyn stared at her son. She knew beyond doubt it was Madeleine's biggest concern. "Have you addressed this issue? Attempted to quell her fears?"

Sighing deeply, Sumner replied, "Yes, but nothing I've done or said comforts her. She's convinced we are on a path toward some apocalyptic event." He could see the conversation made his mother uncomfortable. "Are you worried too?"

"Certainly not. If you say you have the situation in hand, I feel completely confident in you," Evelyn lied. "What does Madeleine suggest you do to ease her concerns?"

"She believes we should flee, immediately and permanently. As much as I believed she would enjoy our home and feel secure there, she paces about like a caged lion. I want her to be happy. I don't know how to help," Sumner realized how much he missed conversing with his mother.

"As I say, I give you credit. I wish I had a brilliant piece of advice for you, but I'm sorry to say, I don't."

Evelyn had her own topic of discussion. "So, tell me, what do you think of Mr. Williamson?"

"I think he is a charming gentleman. I don't understand what he sees in you, however. I have the almost irresistible desire to tell him to take flight each time we meet. No doubt Madeleine would be eager to go along. Do you think I could impress him with the impossibility of a happy marriage if I put my mind to it?"

"Sonny! I'm trying to be serious here. I want to know what you would do if he asked you for my hand in marriage."

"*Me*? Why would he ask me?"

"You are my closest male relative."

"But you're a mature woman, why wouldn't he simply ask you?"

"He's very proper."

"And you believe you will be welcomed into his large and boisterous family?"

"I do, but I believe Mr. Williamson rather likes the quiet home I offer."

"Does he know about the boatload of money you just made?"

"He does not. My finances will remain my finances."

"Doesn't the State of California have something to say about that?"

"Not if I put my money in a joint account with you. I expect any husband of mine to support me not the other way around."

"This sounds extremely serious."

"Yes, doesn't it?" Evelyn asked, a gleam in her eye.

Their discussion continued once the waiter

brought their meals.

"I know you enjoy making fun of me, but I'm attempting to make changes in my old age," Evelyn admitted.

"What kind of changes?"

"Madeleine is the most important person in your life, which is as it should be. I can see my opinions and bluster have served to alienate you both. I've come to appreciate our relationship when we were working so closely together—overcoming all the obstacles presented by your father's illness and our mutual losses—and I miss having you as part of my life."

Sumner quickly took a sip of coffee to hide his grin.

"I see you find this amusing, but you will notice a difference in me. I already made inroads with Madeleine."

"Apparently. I'm stunned to find the two of you have discussed my legal challenges."

"Sumner, I understand you feel as if you never made choices in your life, but that's not the case. You made choices when you decided to comply with other people's plans. You were always content to let others lead, but it *was* your choice. I believe you were willing to go along with anything Ann wanted, and I doubt your compliance would have proven beneficial in the long term.

"Madeleine made a world of difference in you from the start. I find your desire to ensure her happiness quite endearing. You have become a determined and strong-minded man and exemplary husband. You inspire me to take my relationships to more agreeable levels. I'm intent on making Mr. Williamson a fine wife."

"He has discussed marriage then?"

"Not in so many words. We had a mutual need when we met on the train. He missed his wife and wanted someone to accompany him socially. I was busy with your father's ill health for so many years, I forgot what it was to have fun. Our friendship grew from there. I'm certain your warnings to him fall on deaf ears. Actually, I imagine he thinks you're being quite harsh."

"Because you are such a delightful and even-tempered companion?"

"Don't laugh, Sonny. I am, and I want Mr. Williamson to have a favorable opinion of you. I'm hoping to do better all around."

"What noble ambition, Mother. You have my best wishes."

"You doubt I can accomplish this?"

Sumner considered his reply carefully. "I'm certain if you are sincere in your goal, no one could stand in your way."

"How tactful of you."

"Yes, I am ever the tactician of late. I only wish I were more a success as far as Madeleine is concerned. She's led a tragic life. I imagine her anticipation of an imminent return to misfortune is to be expected. I let her down before, and I can't seem to undo that.

"I do love you, Mother. I enjoyed our lunch together. We'll have to do this again soon."

Evelyn was caught off guard at her son's affection, so much so, she discreetly wiped a tear from the corner of her eye.

Chapter Nineteen

Sumner took a deep breath, relieved Maddie's handbag rested on top of the dresser in its usual spot. Although she apparently fled the house, he imagined she took off down the beach—her customary retreat when the house closed in on her.

After grabbing a cookie in the kitchen, he went outside and scanned the coastline. There was no sign of his wife so Sumner walked toward the southern end of the bay—Maddie's normal route.

His wife was difficult to understand. She invited Jem and Mrs. Graydon and her children over on a few occasions and busied herself with cleaning and cooking in preparation for their visits. She would stand teary-eyed at their departure, and this from a woman who essentially had little use for other people and spent years hiding behind a veil.

As it started to drizzle, Sumner spotted Maddie sitting near the water's edge, staring toward the ocean, a shawl pulled over her head. As he approached, Sumner regretted having worn his new suit. The idea of sitting in the sand was not appealing. Instead he tugged on the legs of his slacks and squatted beside his wife.

"What are you doing? It's chilly today." He was not prepared for the overwhelming sympathy he felt when a distraught Maddie looked up at him. It was at odd moments like this he wished his wife actually was an empty-headed beauty, too small-minded to be worried about anything and eager to trust in him completely. He sighed deeply, realizing this would never be the case. Maddie was his bright and able partner in life, and he didn't want it any other way. "What's wrong?"

"I can't get up."

"Why?"

"I don't know. I walked until I couldn't go any further. I can't get up."

"What's in your hand?"

"A letter from Reverend Neelson."

"Did it upset you?"

"No. Why would you think so?"

"Something evidently set you on your retreat."

"He enclosed a Bible verse. 'And seek not ye what ye shall eat, or what ye shall drink, neither be ye of doubtful mind. For all these things do the nations of the world seek after: and your Father knoweth that ye have need of these things. But rather seek ye the kingdom of God; and all these things shall be added unto you.' I don't have enough faith, Sumner. I'm having a hard time."

"Well, as it turns out, I have enough faith for both of us." Sumner surrendered to his desire to sit beside his wife in the sand despite the new suit. He put his arm around her shoulders and continued, "Maddie, look around and tell me what you see."

"I see the way the light shines off the water, the

dark outline of the shorebirds against the clouds as they fly over the ocean and the tan color of the sand in stark contrast to the gray day."

"That's your artist's eye taking in the scenery. Do you know what I see?"

"The same things."

"No, I see my lovely wife filled with anxiety, desperate to escape her melancholia."

Maddie turned toward her husband. "I'm sorry. I thought you wanted me to tell you about the beach. You focused on me."

"You are first in my thoughts. To be honest, you are actually much too focused on me. I'm glad you told me about what you see, and I'm not offended you didn't put me in your field of vision. Have you given up on us, Maddie?" Sumner asked, sincerely.

"No, why would you think so?"

"Because we're missing opportunities here—to be together, to talk, to share our lives and enjoy each other's company as never before. I've thought about this, and I'm pretty sure I'm not the culprit this time. Feel free to correct me if I'm missing something.

"I understand you have a lot of fears, and I may be adding fuel to the fire when I ask you for blind faith. I admit I can't keep bad things from happening. A wave can come along and wash our house away. We could be struck by lightning as we sit here in the sand. One of the unpleasant ideas you can't escape might actually occur. No one can say what the day might bring. When I say things will be all right, it's because I know together, you and I can overcome anything with God's help. We have a lot under our belt already and not nearly enough quiet time together. I can't figure out how to help you enjoy today and leave your concerns behind. I *can* take care of you."

"I don't need you to take care of me. I learned to take care of myself."

"I know you're able, but as your husband, I want you to believe in me. You don't have to take care of yourself, we're in this together—for now and always."

"I can't disregard my real worries about what might happen. Sumner, I never wanted anything in my life. I was content enough to live each day for what it was always understanding I wasn't healthy and wouldn't live long. Everything changed when I met you. I want so much more now." Madeleine considered her husband closely, remembering the unabashed love and trust she had in him when they were first married. Perhaps she would never trust anyone so completely again.

"You don't have to dwell on your concerns. Just for today, can we go back home before it starts to rain and try our best to think about the good things? We have so much to be thankful for. Soon we'll have a baby. You made us a warm and cozy home. We live in an ideal locale. We have financial security. If we can manage a happy day today, who knows? Maybe we can repeat the performance tomorrow, and it might become a habit.

"I love you, Madeleine Hemmings, and I need you. All I'm asking is for you to relax and trust in our future for a few hours. Can we give it a go?"

Madeleine gave a timid smile, "Well, maybe if you bought me an Abba Zaba, it might have a calming effect."

"Abba Zaba again? I used to feel that way about liquor. I think we might be setting a dangerous precedent."

"I thought it was your life's work to make me happy? Surely this is a minor request."

"How about we make a deal. I'll buy you an Abba Zaba bar if you bake me cookies. I ate the last oatmeal cookie when I left the house."

"What kind of cookies?"

"How about the butter cookies you dip in chocolate?"

"I don't know, those are a lot of work. I don't think I'm getting any kind of bargain here."

"Well I am an adept man of business, after all, but I could volunteer to help."

"No, you'd eat all the dough. We wouldn't end up with any cookies. I have my eye on you, Mr. Hemmings."

Sumner grinned as he stood and pulled Maddie to her feet. "Well, what if I buy you an Abba Zaba today, and you make me cookies tomorrow?"

"Do you trust me enough to strike a bargain?"

"We'll shake on it." Sumner turned to face his wife and give her hand a firm shake. It was apparent she was not steady on her feet.

"I love you, Sumner."

"And well you should. I'm determined to be the best husband in the history of the world. It's only a matter of time until you realize how lucky you are to have me."

Madeleine suppressed her sudden notion it would be difficult to be a good husband from jail. Weary of hopelessness, she decided to comply with Sumner's wishes as much as she was able.

The couple made their way toward the street. Sumner planned to minimize the walk home by catching a trolley. He imagined he cajoled his wife out of her sullen mood, if only for a while.

They didn't have to wait long before a streetcar picked them up. Once they were seated, Sumner removed his jacket and draped it over his wife's shoulders. Damp on the outside, at least the jacket provided some warmth.

"I have a thought."

"Oh, no," mumbled Madeleine.

"You'll like this one. Suppose you and I head to Ojai for a few days?" Sumner was amazed at the intense reaction those few words initiated. Madeleine put her arms around her husband and hugged him fervently, burying her face in his shoulder. He would never understand his wife's infatuation with her primitive little house. Perhaps there was some way to get phone service and a hot water heater installed. Those modest improvements would make life more tolerable.

"We signed the papers on the sale this morning. They made me a job offer."

"To do what?"

"They want me to manage the bank. It's a good salary, a steady position without any risk."

"Are you going to take it?"

"No. I planned to stay home for a while. I still intend to."

"So, you're staying here to spy on me?"

Sumner laughed. "What a tempting idea. But no, that was never my motive."

Maddie longed to have a conversation about Aunt Mary's death. She knew the topic would frustrate Sumner, and she was afraid of his answers. She could not decide if knowing the truth would serve to ease her doubts or make her more apprehensive.

"I know you don't want me to think about this, but if we were separated again, it would be as if Aunt Mary came from her grave to ruin our life."

"Madeleine, you must not say that."

"Why?"

"Because it makes you sound crazy."

"All right, but before we begin on our frivolous afternoon, I need you to tell me the truth. Have the police contacted you again?"

Honestly, Sumner answered, "No."

"And you give me your word, you will tell me if they do?"

"I give you my word." But it was a pledge Sumner found difficult to keep. His concern for his wife's well-being seemed more relevant than his off-hand promise on this foggy, dismal day.

* * *

Sumner stood dumbfounded as his normally sedate wife bawled uncontrollably with Teresa Neelson. The women were hugging each other, so emotional neither could form words. Reverend Neelson stood by, apparently unperturbed and accepting of the touching reunion. Sumner could not help the wave of relief he felt when Teresa finally held Madeleine at arm's length to "have a better look" at her.

"You are simply radiant! I'm so glad you came, but the trip must have been difficult."

That was an understatement as far as Sumner was concerned. Maddie's discomfort riding in the car became immediately apparent even close to home where the roads were good. Their frequent stops, which included short walks, rests by the side of the road and brief visits to cafes along the way, meant their journey took the entire day.

"You two simply must stay the night here," Teresa cooed. "We can catch up, and you'll have a chance to rest. I have a roast cooking. There'll be plenty to eat."

"We just ate for about the fourth time since breakfast," Sumner offered. Maddie shot a hostile look his way.

"We would love to join you for supper," Madeleine replied. "I don't know what Sumner is talking about. He's miffed the ride in the car was so time-consuming."

"I can only imagine," gushed Teresa. "I can't believe you undertook such a journey when you're this far along, but I'm certainly glad you did!"

An astonished Sumner watched the two women proceed to the kitchen, heads together, nattering pleasantly. Up until ten minutes ago, Madeleine was intent on independence while nit-picking endlessly about his driving. She even slapped his hand away when he attempted to help her out of the car.

Who was this sweet, emotional girl content to be coddled and cooed over? His confusion must have been evident as Hiram slapped him on the back, interrupting his reverie.

"Women are a mystery, are they not?"

"I must admit, they are. I don't think I even know my wife. She's like a different person since walking through your door. She wouldn't even let me help her out of the car."

"My wife is like a mother to Madeleine. She had no choice but to submit to Teresa's care when she first came. I imagine that set some kind of precedent. Expectant mothers are a challenge, at any rate. It's wonderful you brought her. How do you intend to take her home, or was it your intention to stay here until the baby comes?"

"That was never my intention. If it was Madeleine's, she kept it to herself. We're weeks away from becoming parents," Sumner admitted to soothe himself. "I thought we'd only stay in Ojai a few days. I wanted to get Madeleine away from the house for a while. I had no idea travel in the car would be so difficult."

"Well, the ladies can be a bit devious when they're intent on having their way."

Devious? If this was some grand plan of Madeleine's, he had fallen into her trap, so much so, he believed the whole excursion was his idea. Sumner abruptly felt the need to defend himself from Maddie's wiles. The thought of weeks in the miniscule house in Ojai did not sit well. He nervously stuck his finger in his shirt collar and pulled it away from his throat. His desire to have a private moment with his wife became overwhelming although from the look of things, that moment was not forthcoming.

In fact, the opportunity to chat with his wife was thwarted at Sumner's every overture. Maddie fell instantly asleep once they retired to the room she referred to as "hers." Try as he might, Sumner was unable to rouse her once her head hit the pillow.

Although it would be a tight fit in Sumner's sporty car, it was decided Teresa would accompany them to Ojai in order to set the little house in order while Madeleine rested. The Reverend planned to drive up in the evening for dinner and to gather his wife. This agenda spoiled any hope of privacy.

A Keepsake Love

* * *

Determined not to sleep on the short mattress ever again, Sumner left the cottage to the two ladies and headed into Ojai immediately upon arrival the next morning. He had a market list for the grocer and a list of linens needed to dress whatever bed he chose.

Sumner used the opportunity to investigate the possibility of phone and electrical service and was undaunted when the cost of connecting those utilities proved extreme. He purchased a hot water heater and arranged to have it installed.

For some reason, the idea of an ice cream cone proved irresistible so before picking up the grocery order, Sumner found himself seated at a small table in front of the soda fountain enjoying his treat. He took a careful look at the recently rebuilt town.

The original western-style downtown named Nordhoff burned to the ground in 1917. The glass manufacturer, Edward Libbey, invested heavily in the rebuilding of the town, renamed Ojai. Anti-German sentiment during the war included disdain of any German-sounding locales. Sumner was taken with the contemporary Spanish Colonial Revival architecture.

Another important citizen by the name of J. Krishnamurti, the great Indian mystic, put Ojai on the map when he recently made the town his North American base. Devotees now flocked to the area to enrich their spiritual well-being. During his initial visit, Sumner noticed he was not the only tourist in town.

As he finished his treat, a sign across the street drew his interest. A sudden desire to investigate a building company caused him to add one additional stop before making a reluctant return to Maddie's little house.

* * *

Hiram could not help but laugh at his young companion's plight.

"Don't lose patience," he urged as the two men sat on the porch enjoying the Reverend's home-made dandelion wine. The feminine conversation occurring in the kitchen was barely audible, distant enough to ensure no one could overhear their own discussion. Hiram took a drag on his cigarette and continued, "My wife claimed I smelled when she was expecting. Her complete distaste for my odor caused extreme embarrassment."

"Madeleine was so happy to come here yet she's had nothing but disdain for me since we left home. I don't understand."

"These young mothers are uncomfortable and unsure of themselves. She's probably taking her distress out on you.

"I think your ideas shocked her. She's territorial about her house. I think she'll probably warm up to the bed you purchased. I certainly don't see a thing wrong with it. Your ideas about taking out the wall between the parlor and the bedroom and building an addition might be harder to sell. I can see your enthusiasm for these projects, but I was watching Madeleine's face while you spoke at dinner. It was all I could do to keep from laughing. You were so eager and uncomprehending."

"Well, you might have kicked me under the table to shut me up. I might have rethought my plan if I took time to read the room. But to be honest, Madeleine has more than enough reason to feel disquiet, baby or no."

"I'm sorry. I assumed things were going much better for you two."

"They are. I don't mean to infer our marriage is not on firm ground. But given her history, Madeleine has concerns about giving birth. She occasionally has misgivings about the woman I was going to marry. I assured her in every way possible I love her and am completely happy, but I catch her looking at me in odd ways. I know she still has doubts. Then, there is the investigation into the Thomasons' murders."

"I know something about that. The Santa Paula police chief is a friend of mine. I'm surprised you heard about the murders all the way in Los Angeles. It was certainly big news here. I didn't want to bring it up in front of the ladies."

"Oh, Madeleine knows all about it. A fame-seeking detective in Los Angeles reopened the case of Mary Argyle's death and decided I can answer his questions about all three murders. This is upsetting Madeleine even though I try to reassure her. I'm concerned about her."

"So, Mary Argyle is Madeleine's Aunt Mary? I didn't know her aunt had been murdered."

"Madeleine didn't know either until I told her. She stayed away from Los Angeles because of her aunt, not knowing she was dead all these years. The police are groping around to find anyone who knew all three victims, and I fall into that unfortunate category.

"I tried my best to make Madeleine understand I have her best interests at heart, and I'm taking care of our problems. This only seems to aggravate her. She became independent during the years we were apart. Self-sufficient ladies have become common in these prosperous and wild times."

"Yes, I often find myself praying for guidance. It seems as if the entire world has fallen off a cliff.

Morals have deteriorated at an alarming rate these last years. Mothers who fought long and hard for women's rights are stunned at the wild and inappropriate behavior of their liberated daughters. I don't think anyone saw this coming. But you're surely not implying Madeleine's morals have faltered?"

"No, of course not. But she embraces equality for women and has proven to herself she is competent to make her own way in life. She doesn't need me to support her. I imagine the traditional roles of husband and wife as we knew them are probably gone forever. It's difficult to envision a successful marriage with these new parameters.

"To be honest, I frequently find myself longing for the Madeleine of six years ago. She was sweetly naïve and trusting. I was a young, irresponsible fool. I never should have let her out of my sight. I was offended by her assertion I didn't do all I could to find her. But I've come to realize if I were a more responsible husband, things might have turned out differently. I guess I don't blame her for doubting me."

"I'm certain the two of you will find your way. It's heartening to see the improvement since you remarried. I know your current problems will all be ironed out in time. If there's anything I can do to help, please feel free to ask."

Considering the Reverend's last heart-to-heart chat with Madeleine, Sumner thought it best to handle his own problems. The last thing he needed was for Maddie to be more upset than she already was.

* * *

Sumner put his hands behind his head as he considered the ceiling of Maddie's tiny bedroom, trying to estimate the square footage of the room. Feeling rather proud of his comfortable and spacious purchase, it was all he could do to refrain from gloating as Madeleine crawled in bed next to him. After she extinguished the bedside candle and wiggled around in an effort to find a comfortable sleeping position, she settled next to him. Placing a tentative hand on his chest, Maddie was unsure how receptive her husband might be to her touch. After all, they'd done nothing but argue for two days.

"I suppose this is a comfortable bed."

Smiling in the darkness, Sumner commented, "I liked a sleigh bed more but felt it might be too masculine and heavy. The spindle bed better matches the rest of the furnishings." Regurgitating the salesman's ideas made him sound knowledgeable when in actuality, he never purchased a piece of furniture in his life and couldn't tell the difference between a spindle and a sleigh. Sumner knew what felt good though. His new mattress was the most comfortable in the store.

"Why don't you turn on your side, and I'll rub your back," he suggested.

Always grateful for a back rub, Madeleine complied. Sumner used his strong hands to work out the kinks in her back as he hummed *If You Knew Suzie*. The dandelion wine and his wife's reluctant compliment served to lighten his mood, and he chuckled.

"What's so funny?"

"Do you know the line about Shakespeare writing Suzie is a wow? I think that is hilarious."

"Sumner, how much did you have to drink?"

"I don't know. Hiram kept topping off my glass.

It's been months since I took a drink. Your Reverend does not fit my preconceived ideas of God's representatives."

"What do you mean?"

"He smokes, and drinks and lectures petulant wives about their sexual obligations."

"Men of God are only men, Sumner. They have their faults the same as anyone else. I don't know why you would consider them holy. Isn't that rather naïve of you? And what did Hiram tell you about his visit with me?"

Sumner bit his lip. He had too much to drink and needed to watch what he said. Enjoying the conversation with his unexpectedly mellow wife, he wished to avoid putting his foot in his mouth.

"You're the one who told me about your conversation. He never spoke of it." Moving his hands to Madeleine's shoulders, he inquired, "Feel better?"

"Wonderful. I think I got tense riding up here. Maybe this has been too much for me."

These words caused instant concern. Was it Maddie's plan all along to stay in Ojai? Was the difficult trip back simply a ploy so they would stay? Perhaps he could fish around for an answer to this dilemma if his wine-soaked brain would cooperate for a few minutes.

"I thought we could have the work done on this house once we went home."

"Shouldn't we be here to supervise?"

Red flags went off in Sumner's head. Madeleine was adamantly opposed to his ideas at dinner. Why was she suddenly talking about staying to supervise workmen?

"Does this mean you think my idea has merit?

After all, where will we put all the children when we come up here? They're not going to sleep in my new bed, I'll tell you that."

"Children?"

"Why would we stop with one?" He felt Madeleine's entire body tense at his comment.

"You mean two?"

"Well yes, two. Of course. But I'm talking about how many youngsters this house can hold, and at present, the number would be zero. The new addition would provide us a larger bedroom. You could have a sewing table in our expanded space, and I could put a desk in our front room. We could put two bedrooms upstairs and throw all the boys in one and all the girls in the other. That's more space than a lot of families have in a primary residence."

"What are you planning on doing at your desk?"

"I don't know yet."

"What if you find you like banking? Do you think the new owners will still give you a job?"

"I imagine they'll find someone to take my place in short order. If I decide banking is my true calling, maybe we can start up our own bank. I'm not willing to commit to anything. I've only been out of work for two days.

"What do you say we take our time going home, maybe travel for a few hours a day over three days or so? We can be as leisurely as you like. I can go back into Ojai tomorrow and hire the builder, and I'm certain Hiram wouldn't mind driving up here a few times to check on their progress. Just think, the next time we come here, we'll bring our baby, and we'll have electricity, hot water and a telephone—and a brand-new bedroom where our bed will actually fit."

"I like when you talk like that, Sumner."

"About building?" He truly did not understand his wife. How could something that infuriated her hours ago be cause for comfort now?

"No, when you talk about the future, our future. It soothes me. There are so many obstacles, it's difficult for me to envision our future."

Sumner leaned over and looked at Maddie's face. "There are no obstacles except the ones you imagine."

* * *

Reminded of a morning months ago when he awoke alone in Maddie's bed, Sumner winced at the pain in his head as he swung his feet to the floor and made a feeble attempt to sit up. Even the way the light flooded through the window provided an eerie sense of déjà vu. The previous scenario proved disastrous. Sumner hoped to avoid a similar outcome today. Hiram's dandelion wine proved too much for him. Although it wasn't his head that hurt last time, Sumner dealt with a wave of apprehension along with an unpleasant wave of nausea.

Padding barefoot to the kitchen, Sumner rubbed the stubble on his jaw, deciding his best course of action was to down a cup of coffee. He could smell it brewing on the stove. Walking through the kitchen door, he offered a tentative greeting.

"Good morning."

"Your coffee's on the stove," stated Madeleine, agreeably enough, as she rinsed a dish at the sink.

Sumner walked to the stove and noticed a pan of muffins in front of the burner with the coffee pot. He pushed the pan aside, realizing too late it was just out of the oven.

"Shit!" he yelled as he waved his burnt fingers up and down.

"I will not abide that kind of language in my kitchen. What did you do?"

"The pan was hot. Why didn't you tell me?"

"Things on a stove are usually hot," replied Madeleine who walked over to Sumner and removed the top from the flour tin.

"You're going to bake while I'm suffering?"

"No," Madeleine replied disgustedly. She took his burnt hand and dipped it in the flour.

"What do you think you're doing? Am I some piece of pastry?"

"Sumner, wait a few minutes."

"And what? I'll turn into a doughnut?"

"No. The pain will stop."

"It will not. Do you take me for some imbecile? I need ice."

"You certainly do not. Trust in me. In ten minutes, the pain will be gone." Madeleine almost laughed at Sumner's stricken and incredulous expression. She decided to distract him.

"When Ann married, do you think she was eager to fulfill her wifely duties?"

Sumner at least managed to close his mouth as he considered this shocking change in conversation. Maddie was up to something, and he felt an intense need to carefully consider what he said.

"I wouldn't know. What makes you ask?"

"I never told you this. We were busy moving at the time, but I ran into Ann's husband at The Broadway. I helped him make a purchase, and we had tea."

"How rakish of you."

Madeleine glared. "He was obviously smitten with his wife and wanted nothing so much as to make her happy, but Ann wanted to marry you. She probably expected to give herself to you, not Mr. Thornwell. She was in love with you. Don't you think it would make for a difficult wedding night?"

"You would know better than I would."

"No. I was, as you recall, more than willing to go along with anything you suggested. I was ill-informed about societal preconceptions regarding the marriage bed, and you were gentle and loving. You were my entire world. I didn't know anything else. As you recall, I was not exactly timid."

A broad grin stretched across Sumner's face. "True enough. What would it take for me to be your entire world now?"

"Too much has happened," replied Madeleine. "I will never be so naïve again. That's not such a bad thing. Isn't it better to be an adult and accept you on adult terms?"

"I don't want to be accepted; I want to be adored. Besides, you just asked me to trust in you and I did."

"Do your fingers hurt?"

"Of course, they do."

"Stop and think. Do they hurt?"

Sumner considered his answer. "No, the pain is gone."

"Ten minutes in the flour will do it every time."

"I'll get blisters."

"No, you won't." Madeleine lifted Sumner's hand from the flour canister and wiped it with her dish towel. "See, your skin isn't even red."

"Those boys were wrong."

"What boys?"

"Your cookie eating little chums. They once told me you weren't a witch. I think you are."

"Don't be ridiculous. Using flour to treat minor burns has been around for decades."

"I've never heard of it."

"Now you have. Are you going to shave and dress or can we go ahead and eat?"

"If you have no objections, I think I need to eat," Sumner commented as he sat down. "And have a cup of coffee. But Maddie, I need you to believe in me the way I just believed in you."

Madeleine gave her husband a serious glare. "You didn't want to believe me."

"I need you to know I'm handling our problems, and there is nothing to worry about."

"Why?"

"You made me promise I'd tell you if the police contacted me again."

"And you kept this from me?"

Sumner made out the steely glint of anger in his wife's eyes before he replied, "I am keeping my word. Before we left to come here, Mr. Saunders at the bank called to let me know the police were looking for me there."

"And you knew when you left town? Sumner, this makes you look guilty."

"No, it doesn't. I'm going back."

Madeleine was incredulous. "Why didn't you tell me this before?"

"Because you're already upset enough."

"So why are you telling me now?"

"To keep my word."

Madeleine fumed. Breathing heavily, her shoulders rose and fell dramatically. She pushed away from the table and, untying her apron, threw it on her chair and marched out the back door.

He offered a parting comment, "If we're taking our time going back, I think we should leave tomorrow."

Sumner sipped his coffee and ate breakfast. He intended to keep on track today, hiring the builder and preparing to return home. He kept his word. Only time would prove his theories about the murder investigations were correct. If Madeleine was determined to disregard his ideas in favor of her own, there wasn't much he could do to make it easier on her. Smiling a sly smile, Sumner determined to be as sweet, loving and considerate as could be, which was sure to infuriate Madeleine. Her fury was more welcome than her fear.

Chapter Twenty

Madeleine waited until she heard the sound of Sumner's car speeding away before returning to the house. After warming and eating her breakfast, she did the dishes and considered her options. How did she most want to spend this precious day in her own home before Sumner hauled her away again?

It had been months since Maddie took an interest in her art, but today was a beautiful, warm, spring day. She settled on walking up the canyon to sketch. It was almost lunchtime so she packed a thick slice of homemade bread and a jar of lemonade in a basket, added some art supplies and headed out.

Madeleine's mind became deliciously void of thought in the breathtaking surroundings. A world with no worries, no fears and no tomorrow was entirely invigorating. As the footpath veered closer to the streambed, Madeleine focused on items she could draw.

Her desire to visit her art dealer in Santa Barbara would likely end in frustration. Sumner would have to drive 40 miles out of the way. Maddie never bothered to write down the address of the business, simply offering her art and shaking hands with the dealer. The location in Santa Barbara proved the most financially beneficial outlet for her botanical watercolors. Some if not all of her larger pieces were likely sold by now.

She managed to obtain her profits from the shop in Ojai and wondered what awaited her at the venues in Ventura and Carpinteria. There was a possibility she could talk Sumner into stopping in Ventura before heading home. He knew that store well enough.

Sumner's name vibrated around in her head once she brought him to mind. Sumner was a problem—a curious and ever-present problem. Madeleine took a seat on a rock near the water and thoughtfully munched on her bread.

She knew without doubt she loved him. No one in her life even came close as far as capturing her affection. Beyond question, he was her biggest disappointment although she was willing to concede his intention was never to disappoint her. Words of Reverend Neelson precipitously came to mind.

"Madeleine, do you think anger comes from God?" he bellowed at her one day. Knowing anger could not possibly come from God, she understood its evil origin. If only she never had blind faith in Sumner. If only she hadn't soothed her anxiety with the idea he would come to the rescue. If only she didn't imagine an ending where their daughter was born healthy and happy because Sumner saved them.

Maddie ceased to worry about her husband's feelings for Ann. Sumner seemed much too happy, much too committed to their marriage to be in love with someone else. Madeleine realized, as Sumner asserted, it was her own worries about the future that blanketed their life in despair. Having never considered she had a future all the years she was growing up, Madeleine recognized the irony in her current concerns.

Her fears about the investigation put a wall between them as surely as if Sumner were already in prison. She couldn't commit herself completely to a temporary marriage. No matter how much she loved Sumner, no matter how sincere his apologies, no matter how superficially secure their lives, the next few weeks seemed fraught with danger. Sumner could be arrested at any moment. She could die in childbirth or the most abhorrent of all scenarios could occur. Their baby could be stillborn.

As her baby gave a strong kick, Madeleine clung to the suddenly remembered notion God would not give her more than she could handle, but He had come so very close before.

A subtle breeze blew the grass along the side of the creek bed. Dappled sunlight drew her attention to a colorful patch of purple. It was an Ojai fritillary uncommonly and intensely mottled with purple. She usually found the greenish yellow flowers only slightly mottled. Taking her pencil and paper, she sat down on the grass beside the flower and began to sketch.

Focused on the rare opportunity, Madeleine didn't notice how long the shadows grew as she sat beneath the sycamore tree. The light dimmed as the sun sank below the ridgeline of a nearby mountain. Maddie glimpsed subtle motion out of the corner of her eye.

It would be hard to determine who bore the more startled expression, Madeleine or the huge mountain lion approaching the stream. She couldn't help but admire the beauty of the magnificent cat. Its shiny coat gleamed in the dappled light. The sharp and curious features of its face stood in relief to the greenery framing it. But the danger of the situation became apparent as the cat glared at the small living being across the water.

Madeleine's heart raced. She knew better than to run. Even if she was fit enough to climb a tree, the big cat could easily overtake her. She realized the need to appear threatening but couldn't imagine how as she sat low to the ground. Her only weapon was her pencil, which she gripped firmly like a knife, waiting to see what the cat would do. As the moments dragged on, Madeleine tried her best to remain calm but soon started gasping for air.

* * *

Sumner started to think the irritating project director would never get in his truck and drive away. His meeting with the builder went well, but before an accurate estimate could be drawn up, Mr. Wilkins wanted accurate measurements and a site inspection. Harold was sent on this assignment.

The day went by incredibly fast. Since Mr. Wilkins wasn't expected in his office until after lunch, Sumner grabbed a newspaper and a cup of coffee in a diner while he waited. The wait proved worthwhile. A careful plan was accomplished. Mr. Wilkins was thorough and receptive to Sumner's ideas about the new "wing" of Maddie's modest cottage. All that remained was the inspection and a final draft of the estimate. Mr. Wilkins didn't believe in being paid until his clients were completely happy.

Sumner hurried home, disappointed to find Maddie still absent. He took a surreptitious look through the shed window to confirm the Model T was parked inside. The vehicle hadn't been driven in months and likely wouldn't start. But Madeleine was a resourceful woman, and he knew better than to underestimate her abilities.

The inspection seemed interminable, even though the site was exactly as Sumner indicated. There was not so much as a tree to be removed. Harold, however, proved to be a yapper. When Sumner explained his wife was probably on a walk, the man first warned a mountain lion was spotted in the area in recent days then commenced a recital of every ugly accident occurring in the vicinity over the last 100 years.

His gory and detailed accounts of animal attacks grated on Sumner's nerves. Harold assured there hadn't been a mountain lion attack in many years, but bears were another matter, especially mothers with cubs. His account of a bear partially eating a grown man before he was able to seek refuge in his cabin proved particularly unsettling. A long recital about poisonous snakes ensued before Sumner was able to send the man on his way.

Turning away from the road, Sumner impulsively opened the trunk of his Rolls. When he moved his things to the beach house, he left various items in the trunk, uncertain where they would belong. A box of bullets and a pistol he brought home from the war were stored there so he quickly filled the chamber and tucked the gun in his belt. It was always better to be safe than sorry.

He checked the house to be certain Maddie hadn't returned before heading down the canyon, all the while assuring himself everything was fine. Maddie lived for years on her own. Surely, she understood the dangers of this remote location.

But as the sun set behind the mountain range to the west, an eerie feeling overcame Sumner. He was reminded of flying during the war. He was careful, always so very careful and developed a habit of scanning the sky by quadrants to understand where the greatest danger might lie. His methods served him well. After all, he was still alive. Sumner stood in his tracks and sectioned off the surrounding area, inspecting each quadrant to determine what caused his discomfort. He caught his breath as he looked down the slope toward the stream. Maddie cowered near the water as a large mountain lion stared at her.

Sumner slowly drew the pistol from his belt. He didn't have a clear shot from where he stood. He was unfamiliar with the idiosyncrasies of the gun and had no idea if it would shoot straight or at all. Even if he accomplished a true shot, it would come too close to Madeleine. If she moved, he might hit her. As he watched, the big cat snarled and crouched as if to attack. Sumner was out of time. He had to act now.

A shot rang out. Sumner stared in shock as Madeleine collapsed onto the ground as the mountain lion scampered off through the trees. A frantic Sumner ran toward his wife and knelt beside her, grasping her shoulders and pulling her onto her knees.

"Are you hurt?" he screamed. Sumner almost fell backward, so unexpectedly did Maddie throw herself against his chest. She grabbed onto him for dear life as he wrapped her in his arms. Shaking violently, she began to sob.

"It's all right. I've got you," Sumner assured.

"Sumner—you saved my life. You saved our baby's life," Madeleine managed to utter.

"I don't know about that. You scared me to death

when I fired my shot in the air. Are you all right, Maddie?"

He felt her head nod against his chest.

"What were you doing on the ground?"

"I—I was drawing." Words came tumbling out of her mouth. "When I looked up, the mountain lion was standing there, watching me. I didn't know what to do. But you came and saved us, Sumner."

Sumner pulled slightly away to look into his wife's face. He found an expression he had not seen for years and frankly never thought to see again. It was clear from her adoring mien, Maddie's doubts about him were somehow resolved. He hardly felt the hero, managing simply to show up at the right time. Was that all it took to be back in his wife's good graces?

"I think if you managed to fight back at all, the cat would have run off. He was probably confused by how small you looked on the ground and thought you might make a good dinner. What have you got in your hand? Something's poking me in the back."

"It's my pencil."

"See, you were armed. You didn't need my help at all." Sumner could not help but smile as Maddie laid her head against his chest, unwilling to loosen her grip.

He kept a wary eye out in case the mountain lion was still in the area but wanted nothing so much as to get his wife to the safety of her house before it got too dark to see.

"Madeleine, give me your pencil."

"No. Hold me."

Tired of being poked, Sumner struggled to pry the pencil out of her hand.

"We need to start back, it's almost dark." He stood and pulled Maddie to her feet, then took a short step to see if she would walk beside him.

"Wait, my basket is over there." Sumner walked her toward it. Madeleine's hands shook so badly, she was unable to pack her belongings. Sumner bent down and quickly filled the basket, then started toward the house.

"But my sketchpad is by the water."

Sumner cooperatively walked her back to the creek and retrieved the tablet.

"While you're there, pick one of those purple flowers and drop it in the basket. I need to press it so I can take a careful look at the mottling pattern."

"Anything else I can get you, my queen?" Sumner joked as he finally managed to direct his wife toward home.

* * *

Never having previously given much thought to how a woman's mind worked, Sumner was astounded at his circumstances once he "rescued" his wife. Realistically, he reacted to Harold's frightening litany of terror and carried along his pistol on a whim. All he did was fire a warning shot. Although he cringed at anything harming his wife, he didn't believe he saved her. Nothing he said about this event seemed to make the slightest difference to Madeleine. For the first time as they drove away from Ojai, Sumner had the feeling Maddie would rather be with him than her little home.

When she politely inquired if he would mind heading to Ventura so she could see to her business interests, he didn't hesitate to comply, even if it was out of their way. It was likely far enough for them to travel in a day. They stayed at the Pierpont Inn.

"Did you come here with Ann?" Maddie asked.

"We dined here, but these are the best rooms in the city. We can eat somewhere else."

"I think we should eat at the best possible location. I want us to enjoy our trip home. I'm not jealous of Ann."

Conceding his wife may not be jealous, Sumner found it difficult to hide his guilty conscience whenever Madeleine drug Ann's name into conversation. He had no logical reason to feel guilty, but that did nothing to suspend the unpleasant feeling.

If ever Sumner imagined some ideal marriage from the movies, he seemed to be living it now. Madeleine sought to hold his hand and touch him at every opportunity. She was as eager to please and converse as she was on their dates so many years ago. Maddie appeared the epitome of cooperation and graciousness. Although he didn't expect this to last, Sumner meant to make the most of it.

"What did you eat when you came before?" Madeleine inquired as she perused the menu.

"Steak. It was delicious."

"Sounds a bit heavy to me. What did Ann have?"

At this, Sumner almost fell off his chair. Why did he always feel as if he were walking a tightrope? "I truly can't remember."

"But you must have ordered for her. Did she have steak or something else?"

Sumner suddenly wished he selected less memorable accommodations. "Maddie, I don't remember; I truly don't. There are some restaurants in Los Angeles where we ate several times and ordered favorite foods. I could tell you things Ann ate there, but I have no idea what she had here. Why do you keep bringing her up?"

"Does it make you uncomfortable?" asked Maddie in apparent shock. "She was a part of your life for years, much longer than I have been. I assure you, there's nothing subversive in my request. You must have spoken of me to her, surely."

"But you were dead. I was suffering through a difficult time in my life. I spoke to her as a friend."

"If you shared your loss with her, surely you can share your grief with me as well."

"What grief? I have no grief."

"You lost Ann. I believe we should be able to talk about anything from our past."

"Even your Aunt Mary?" Sumner shot back.

Madeleine placed her menu on the table. "As a matter of fact, we should talk about her."

"You're not angry any longer?"

Maddie considered her reply. "I'm trying to get over my anger. Whatever she did, we landed up here together and happy. Who can say how or why these things come about? If she were a sane person, she wouldn't have kept me imprisoned in her house. I might have met someone much nicer than you and been married by the time you fell out of the tree," Maddie finished with a smirk and a gleam in her eye. "I suppose I'm trying to prove your relationship with Ann doesn't matter to me. I feel secure in our marriage. Unlike poor Mr. Thornwell, I don't anticipate a day when I will wake to find you eloped with your former love."

"Do you think he anticipates that?" Sumner asked.

"Ann is the most innocent of all Aunt Mary's victims, you once mentioned that yourself. Well, perhaps her husband is even more innocent. I wish them all the best. There's actually nothing I wouldn't do to help them."

"Short of surrendering me over to Ann, I hope?"

"Short of that, definitely. Has this served to jar your memory of Ann's meal?"

"Not in the least," admitted Sumner, less ill at ease.

"Then you'll have to order me the crabmeat croquettes. Will you remember *my* order forevermore?"

"I can't promise. And I don't want to make any promises I can't keep. But I will attempt to remember you like crab."

"Fair enough. I like shrimp and lobster too. I love you, Sumner."

"I have to ask, is your love something new? I'm befuddled by you, I must admit."

"You be befuddled. I'm a woman; I don't wish to appear predictable. I have always loved you, but I think I lost my way for a while. I feel content to take you at your word. If you tell me you're able to deal with our problems, I'll accept your assertion on face value, whether you're talking about a leaky roof or impending legal entanglements. I think you're right. I need to take care of myself and our baby and leave the weightier issues to you. I'm content to do so. But I'm also prepared to share any burden with you."

"And if I stumble and fall?"

"Then you're a person the same as me, and I'll help you get up." Madeleine decided to fish around a bit. "Sumner, what about you? Have you forgiven Aunt Mary?"

"To tell you the truth, once the woman was in her grave, it seemed pointless to feel anything about her. I never considered the evil aspects of her personality were what brought us together. If it makes you content about us now, I applaud your ideas. Your happiness is my most important goal."

Sumner stared across the table at his unexpectedly meek and mild partner in life. She looked radiant in her blue cotton frock and summer sweater and wasn't concerned when people stared. Maddie's perfect beauty was enhanced with a glow of happiness the likes of which even Sumner had not seen.

"Does this mean you believe in me now?" he asked.

"I'm trying my best to take today for what it is and trust in our future."

Sumner understood his wife's inability to imagine their future. Her Aunt Mary used imminent death as a way to control Madeleine, which robbed her of the idea of a future. He listened intently as she continued.

"When you were talking about what you envisioned the other day, it gave me hope. I am committed to you completely. I expect the same in return."

"You have my word."

"Now and forever?"

"Certainly. But you did run off to tea with Mr. Thornwell the moment my back was turned," he teased.

"Sumner, we're not the foolish children we were when we first married. We've overcome the inadequacies we thought were important. You're a successful businessman. I learned to cook and keep house. Those things were never as vital as we believed. What matters most is us being together; facing life together. I'm putting all my trepidation behind me, at least I'm attempting to. I simply need to know your commitment to our future is all you proclaim."

Sumner took Maddie's hand across the table. "You know it is. I'll do my best to never disappoint you. I love you, Maddie. You told me I was your world once before. You are mine, for now and always."

"Well, I think we need to seal this deal."

Sumner's eyes twinkled in anticipation until he heard her next words.

"You'll simply have to buy me some Milk Duds."

"Some what?"

"The new candy—Milk Duds. I can't get enough of them."

Sumner laughed. "That wasn't the kind of after dinner activity I was anticipating, but if it's your heart's desire, we'll find you some Milk Duds." Sumner considered himself the luckiest man alive.

* * *

Madeleine gave a weak smile as the police escorted her husband out the door. It had not taken the Lieutenant long to fetch his suspect once the Hemmings couple returned to Los Angeles. Sumner protested when they hand-cuffed him.

"Is this really necessary? I have no objections to going in for questioning. Are you arresting me?"

"It's all right, Sumner. Go and get this over with," urged Madeleine.

"I'll be back shortly," Sumner promised.

Maddie tried her best to leave matters to Sumner and do as he suggested, but this day was proving more than she could manage. The idea Sumner might never come home came unbidden to her thoughts. Madeleine was alone in the house and contemplated ways to occupy her mind.

She jumped when the telephone rang.

"Hello."

"Mrs. Hemmings?"

"Yes."

"My name is Virginia Bowman, and I work at St. Vincent's Hospital. There's been an accident. We have a patient who's asking for you."

"Who is it?" Madeleine asked.

"A Miss Doucette, Jemimah Doucette. Do you know her?"

"I'll be right there."

* * *

Sumner relaxed into his seat in Lt. Corbett's office. He'd been carefully coached by his attorney, Mr. Lamkin, but felt the entire meeting was an exercise in futility and a waste of his time. The most aggravating part of the day was its effect on Maddie, who seemed quite the trooper. He only hoped this issue could be laid to rest for all time.

After introductions, the detective got right to the point.

"I'd like you to explain about your wife, Mr. Hemmings."

"What about her?"

"Records show you are currently married to the former Madeleine Crawford."

"Correct."

"That's also the name of your first wife?"

"Correct."

"Madeleine Crawford is alive and married or I should say, remarried to you?"

"Correct."

"How is it you didn't feel obliged to reveal this

tantalizing piece of information?"

"You never asked. I've been thorough in answering your questions, Detective. Besides, how does my wife's abundant good health play any role in your investigation?"

Lt. Corbett's face was turning an unattractive shade of red.

"Let's start at the beginning."

"Haven't we already been over this?"

Lt. Corbett did, indeed, feel it necessary to rehash many of the questions Sumner already answered, much to his dismay. This would likely prove a long day.

* * *

Madeleine approached the hospital bed with trepidation. The nurse explained Miss Doucette's grave condition. She was the victim of a streetcar crash, a rather common occurrence. Although details had not been confirmed, apparently, the operator was traveling at too high a speed. The car flew off the tracks, tipping on its side. Jem was pinned beneath the wreckage. There was little the medical professionals could do except provide narcotics to ease her pain.

"Jem?"

"Oh, Baby Girl—they found you!"

"You need to be still, Jem. I'll stay here, but you should keep quiet."

"No. I want to—do something for—you. Grab the paper there on the—table. Write this down."

Madeleine did as she was told. It was obvious Jem was determined to stay alive long enough to accomplish whatever was on her mind.

"I, Jemimah Doucette—do hereby confess I murdered Mary Argyle—in her sleep the—night of

December 8, 1920."

"But Jem!"

"Listen to me. I know how—scared you are. I want you to—be happy. Let me do this—for you. Now write. I placed the pillow over—Mrs. Argyle's face and—smothered her. I did this in revenge—for the death of her—niece, my dear—Madeleine Crawford. Now get the nurse—I need a witness."

Madeleine hurried into the hall and frantically called for the nurse to come. She read the note aloud, much to the nurse's horror, and put the pen in Jem's hand so she could sign.

Madeleine addressed the nurse. "You're her witness. Please put your name and address here at the bottom." Maddie didn't know what good this would do, but she was intent on putting Jem's concerns to rest. "It's all done, Jem," she announced as the nurse made a hasty retreat.

"Now, I want you to—take that to the—police, you understand?"

"Yes, Jem. I will, but I don't understand."

"A deathbed—confession will stand—up. I should have done—more for you. I always knew—Mary was crazy—how bad you were treated."

"I wasn't treated so badly, not really. I had you!"

"That weren't—enough. You had a right to—a normal life. Now you—can be sure those police—will leave your husband alone. I have a key—in the bottom—of my jewelry box. You can tell them—it's how I got in—if they need to know."

The idea Jem must know of Sumner's guilt seemed apparent. "Thank you, Jem. I love you."

Jem spent her last remaining energy and couldn't respond. A look of peace fell across her face as she breathed her last. She managed to set her Baby Girl free of the evil Mary Argyle.

* * *

"When did you come to know your wife, your former wife, was alive?"

"Last fall. I went to visit her grave, as I explained to you. I met someone there who knew where she was, quite alive. He had no idea she was supposedly buried in the cemetery."

"You're not making sense."

"I'll agree this is a confusing thing to understand."

"Mr. Hemmings, perhaps we should have a word before you continue," suggested Mr. Lamkin.

"I don't think it's necessary. I went to visit my wife's grave. I came to find out she was alive despite a serious illness when she escaped from The Home. There was a fire nearby. She found her way outside."

"But how could she simply disappear? She's not normal. I reviewed the documentation from the breaking and entering charges that resulted in the annulment of your marriage. People would know there was something wrong with her. She couldn't simply blend in."

"I assure you, she is completely lucid. Her aunt sought to control her and keep others away with her charade about Madeleine's health and mental state. But she was quite ill while she lived in Santa Paula, physically ill."

"Why didn't she return when she recovered?"

"She didn't know her aunt was dead and believed she'd wind up in another facility if she contacted anyone in Los Angeles." Seriously, Sumner admitted,

"She blamed me for not coming to her, even though I tried my best. She began a new life. Despite a bit of a bumpy start, we remarried shortly after I found her."

"This puts a bit of a twist on my investigation," the Lieutenant asserted.

"I don't see how."

"Your wife wasn't dead when Mrs. Argyle was murdered. She's a prime suspect. She had the best motive of anyone if what you say is true. Her aunt literally imprisoned her for no reason. She has the best motive of anyone to date in the murders of the Thomasons. She might have a vendetta against them for the way she was treated. An innocent person would try their best to convince their captors they were sane and needed to be released. It would only be normal for Mrs. Hemmings to blame them for her confinement in their institution."

Sumner was stunned. Having never imagined his wife was capable of anything so cold or violent as murder, he never thought she might be considered a suspect.

"Isn't it true your wife might not return home because she was hiding away, comfortable in the knowledge her supposed death protected her from investigation?"

"No, but—"

"Isn't it true she became familiar with the area around Santa Barbara, which was not far from where she lived?"

"You don't understand—"

"Isn't it true she likely blamed the death of her child on Dr. and Mrs. Thomason, not to mention her aunt?"

The Lieutenant had certainly been doing his job.

Sumner remained still for a moment to gather his wits.

"Despite the fact she's the last person who would do such a thing, my wife is small of stature. She doesn't have the strength to smother anyone. She was ill at the time Mary Argyle was murdered."

"I'm afraid I've found anger—rage—can have an invigorating and strengthening effect on a person. That hardly disqualifies her from suspicion."

"She was staying with a couple in Santa Paula. I'm certain they'll provide an alibi."

"After all these years? I doubt they'd be able to document their guest's every move over the time your wife lived with them or account for every hour of her day. As far as the Thomasons are concerned, she most certainly had opportunity."

Sumner's thoughts raced. If Maddie were distraught over the possibility he would be locked up, what would happen if the police locked her up with a baby on the way? She'd believe their lives were replaying in a disastrous manner. Her life and their child's could be lost. He had to do something, anything, to keep Madeleine from harm.

"I confess. I'm the one who killed Mary Argyle and Dr. and Mrs. Thomason."

"*Mr. Hemmings*! Don't say another word. I insist you refrain from further comment immediately." Never in Mr. Lamkin's 25 years of lawyering did a client stray so completely from his logical and well-prepared interrogation plan.

Lt. Corbett yelled, "I knew it! You're the one who murdered Mrs. Argyle. And you're the one who shot the Thomasons to death in cold blood. Where's the murder weapon?"

"I threw the gun in the ocean off a boat when I

went deep sea fishing months later. You'll never find it."

"Mr. Hemmings, you need to shut up right now!" yelled his attorney.

"How did you get into the Argyle house the night of the murder?"

"The way I always came in, through the upstairs window of my wife's old bedroom."

"Do not say another word!" threatened Mr. Lamkin. "I won't be able to help you."

"There's no need for concern," explained Lt. Corbett. "You can go now, Mr. Hemmings."

"How can I go? I just confessed."

"It's clear from your responses, you aren't the murderer. You can go."

"What about my wife?"

"That's another matter. I'll question her shortly."

"You can't. She's not the murderer. By all that's holy, I can't let you."

"You have nothing whatever to say about it, Mr. Hemmings. Your wife is the best suspect so far. She will be questioned."

Len Corbett watched Sumner Hemmings storm out of his office, followed by his disgruntled attorney. He had to give the man credit. Hemmings seemed willing to forfeit his freedom if not his life to keep his wife from suspicion. He still believed Hemmings to be an arrogant and unfairly privileged man with his fine home on the beach, beautiful wife, and pricey lawyer. Although he felt Hemmings was hiding something, it wasn't his part in the murders of the three victims currently under investigation. Everybody was guilty of something, after all.

Mrs. Hemmings was an enigma. Corbett relished

the idea he would soon be able to solve the puzzle that was Madeleine Crawford.

His real interest in the case stemmed from a desire to make a name for himself. He spent years learning all he could about modern investigative techniques. In the end, it all came down to a cop's ability to follow leads and hunches.

These cases could prove the catalyst for the Lieutenant's ambitious plans for his future. The fact Mary Argyle's murder made such a splash in the papers might serve to launch his lucrative schemes if he could solve it now. He visualized the headlines, "Brutalized Niece Seeks Revenge. Local Constable Solves Years Old Murders."

No sooner had he decided to send someone to the beach to pick up Mrs. Hemmings than he found the woman he'd seen at the bank office standing in his office doorway.

"Lt. Corbett?" she inquired.

Unable to believe his good luck, Corbett replied, "Yes, ma'am. What can I do for you?"

"Is my husband here?"

Corbett briefly considered how he wanted to play this out. Should he imply the man was under arrest to put his wife on edge? Or should he admit Hemmings had been released and was no longer under suspicion in order to rest her concerns and gain her trust?

"Mrs. Hemmings, he's not in the office."

Afraid to ask further questions, Madeleine walked toward the officer with outstretched arm and handed him the precious document she carried.

"This is for you."

"And what is this, exactly?"

"It's a confession. A deathbed confession. Those

are important, correct?"

"Whose confession is this?"

"I need to explain. I'm Madeleine Crawford Hemmings. My aunt was Mary Argyle."

"I thought you were dead."

"Well, I didn't know anyone thought I died until recently."

"What did you think?"

"I didn't think anyone cared where I was. I managed to escape from the place Dr. Thomason ran. I had no intention of going back to my aunt. My husband evidently gave up on me. I made a new life. I know you suspect my husband of these murders. This paper was written by a woman who worked for my aunt. She died earlier today, a victim of a streetcar crash. She was my caretaker all the years I lived with Aunt Mary."

Corbett read the note.

"Who is this woman who signed as witness?"

"She's a nurse at the hospital. I witnessed as well, but it didn't seem appropriate for me to sign. Is this all you need?"

"Actually Mrs. Hemmings, your husband managed to clear his own name today." What a shame, Corbett thought to himself. This would be a footnote in the file, not a splashy solution to a crime.

He observed a look of relief wash over the lovely Mrs. Hemmings' features. Her husband was correct to assume his petite wife would not have been strong enough to smother her aunt even if the woman were deeply asleep when the assault began. She was certainly not intimidating enough to have caused the Thomasons' headlong flight from Santa Paula, which ended in their deaths. Deathbed confessions were taken seriously by the courts. Hemmings obviously didn't murder the Thomasons, who were stabbed to death. The gashes showed on their bony remains. There was no gun for Mr. Hemmings to throw in the ocean as he claimed when he so cavalierly confessed. The physical mutilations served as another impossibility for the small woman standing before him.

Although it had been kept out of the newspapers, the lock on the back door of the Argyle home was picked to allow entrance on the night of the murder. A profusion of footprints in the flowerbed next to the backdoor stoop led to the discovery of a tool used to unlock the door. Evidently lost by the murderer, it was found in the crease where the cement stair met the dirt. Hemmings' confession would have sounded convincing if not for the two important details he had entirely wrong.

Corbett considered even he might be taken in by Madeleine Hemmings' stunning beauty. Surely a jury would be. Appearance mattered. This fragile woman would make a compelling witness on her own behalf. Documenting the cruelty she endured at the hands of her aunt would give jurors ample opportunity to sympathize. Frankly, all she would have to do is smile to have any jury eating out of her hand. Her lovely features were not sophisticated or worldly but rather sweetly innocent. The woman seemed sincere even to him, and Lt. Len Corbett was not a trusting individual. None of that mattered now. The deathbed confession ended his hopes of solving the crimes. He'd have to find fame elsewhere.

"How did you get here?"

"I took a taxi. So, this note from Jem is all you need?"

"Why don't you let me drive you home?" Corbett was intent on getting the answers to a few more questions if only to satisfy his own curiosity.

* * *

Corbett watched Mrs. Hemmings exit the patrol car and approach her husband as he emerged from their house. The reunion would have been appropriate for a moving picture and seemed overdramatic to the Lieutenant.

"Where have you been, Maddie? Did the police pick you up? I was frantic to find you." Then he whispered in her ear, "You were right to want to leave. Are the police watching you?"

"Why would they be watching me?"

"I meant us—they could be watching us."

As the police car drove away, Lt. Corbett gave a thumbs up out his window.

"But the Lieutenant explained you cleared yourself. Why would we need to leave now? Besides, Sumner, Jem was in an accident. She died this morning. She signed a deathbed confession, claiming she was the one who killed Aunt Mary." Tears spilled down Maddie's cheeks as the shock of the day hit her.

"Do you believe she did it?" Sumner was incredulous.

"No. I think she wanted to clear your name. She considered it a gift to me. I took the signed confession to the police station, hoping to find you there."

"Something I said led the Lieutenant to believe in my innocence. For the life of me, I don't know what it was. Let's go inside. I want to hear about Jem." Sumner knew if Corbett questioned Maddie, she didn't catch on. He needed to be careful so nothing he said would cause her any more concern than she was undoubtedly feeling at Jem's sudden death.

Maddie stopped as Sumner held the door. When he tried to guide her through, she stood fast and looked up at him. "Sumner, we are finally free of Aunt Mary." The import of that statement hung between them.

Sumner nodded thoughtfully then took his wife in his arms as she began to sob.

Epilogue

"You're going to wrinkle your tuxedo." Madeleine glanced at her husband in the mirror as she fixed her hair for the New Year's Eve celebration. She recalled Sumner's initial reaction to fatherhood. The moment she first placed Adam in his father's arms was a memory she would always treasure.

"Don't do that, Madeleine."

"You need to be able to hold your son. Relax."

"I'm not kidding. I don't know how."

"I assure you, he's quite sturdy. You aren't going to hurt him in the least."

"He's too small for me to hold."

"I never held a baby before either. You can do this."

"No, Madeleine, I can't. Don't do that! Don't—"

But she placed Adam in his father's arms anyway. She laughed at both their expressions: Sumner's of complete terror, Adam's of what seemed to be curiosity.

"This is your Daddy, Adam. He's acting quite the fool, but you'll have to get used to that." Her next comments were directed at her husband. "See how well you're doing? He isn't even crying."

"I don't think a father needs to be able to hold a baby. It's the mother's duty. I'm only supposed to pay bills."

"And you do that so well," taunted Madeleine. "But you can do this, too. Each time you try, it will get easier. Soon you'll be an expert." And to see the men in her family together now, rough-housing on the bed, no one would ever suspect Sumner's initial trepidation.

Adam giggled as his father tickled him relentlessly. At almost a year-and-a-half, he was a sturdy and healthy baby, the apple of his father's eye.

Tonight marked a rare event in the Hemmings household. For the first time since becoming parents, Sumner and Maddie were going out on the town. The baby's birth marked a much-needed quiet and calm period for the Hemmings family. Life at the beach was incredibly peaceful. They often visited Madeleine's new and improved home in Ojai, but they were always together.

The sale of the bank left Sumner temporarily idle. He quickly took to investing, which was a sideline for him previously. Realizing the good times had been good for a while, he tried to pick stocks he felt would weather any storm.

Madeleine paid little attention to his lengthy explanations regarding business interests, but the names of companies and corporations fascinating to her husband were imprinted on her brain. She could recite facts and figures about Container Corporation of America, Douglas Aircraft and Zenith Radio, among others. Sumner made small investments in local businesses he felt were well-run and could stand the test of time.

If Madeleine was obliged to learn Sumner's business, she felt exonerated in teaching him about their household. Sumner quickly caught on to drying dishes, changing diapers and took an avid interest in their garden.

The fact the couple had spent most of their time apart caused them to appreciate their time together. Adam was accustomed to his parents' constant attention so tonight would be a grand experiment.

If Sumner seemed awkward with babies initially, his mother was no less so. Madeleine wondered at Evelyn's completely clumsy and inept early attempts to interact with Adam. The baby won her heart, however, and as time went by and Adam grew, Evelyn became more competent. She was set to watch her grandson tonight although she would have ample help. Her fiancé, Mr. Williamson, was coming along in support. After months of relentless pursuit, a coy Evelyn agreed to marry the man who was quite an avid grandfather with vast experience.

Sumner thought the whole idea absurd. Maddie slapped his arm each time he commenced a conversation on that topic, assuring his mother would prove a loving wife this time around. Sumner would shake his head in disgust, certain some things in life never changed.

Suddenly solemn, Maddie stared at her own reflection in the mirror as Sumner scooped Adam off the bed and walked behind her.

"Having second thoughts about tonight?" he inquired.

"No. I was thinking about Jem. She would have enjoyed Adam."

"More tickle," urged Adam.

A Keepsake Love

Sumner grabbed his son by the ankles and held him upside down, much to his delight.

"Do you ever wonder what really happened to your Aunt Mary?"

Madeleine viewed her husband curiously. Surely, he must know she understood his part in her death. There was no reason to pretend she didn't. "I think your mother and I figured out what happened years ago."

"You did?" Sumner sounded surprised as he turned Adam right-side-up.

"We always wanted to protect you."

Sumner blurted out, "Protect me? From what?" The meaning of her words registered. "Maddie, whatever makes you think I had anything to do with your aunt's death?"

Maddie rose from her seat and walked toward her husband's nightstand where she pulled the picture of her grandmother out of the drawer, its traditional location. "Where did you get this?"

"Who is that in the picture?"

"It's my grandmother."

"I forgot I had it. I scooped up the contents of my old drawer and shoved them in there."

"How did you get this picture?"

"Jem gave it to me."

Maddie looked doubtfully at her husband. "How can that be?"

"I used to visit her after I thought you were dead. I complained we never took a picture. She fished that out of a basket and gave it to me. She said she didn't know who it was, but you bore such a strong resemblance to the woman, she wanted me to have it. Why do you think this had anything to do with your

Aunt Mary's killer?"

"It was in the box, the box with my things inside. All the contents were evidently burned except this picture. What does that mean, Sumner? Did Jem really kill my aunt? Was her confession real?"

"I don't think so. Maybe the picture wasn't in the box when she found it." Madeleine's reasoning did not lack merit, but he didn't want his wife to believe Jem was the killer. "This isn't important anymore. There's my mother at the door. We're off on a fine adventure tonight. I want to enjoy our evening together." Sumner set his son on his shoulders and raced downstairs.

Madeleine stared at the picture before returning it to Sumner's drawer. Perhaps some things were better left a mystery.

Little Adam was excited to see his grandmother and the man he called grandpa. Having been properly wound up by his father's rough-housing, the baby was not ready for bed by the time his parents left. Fully engaged by his grandparents, Adam didn't notice their exit. Hoping the baby wouldn't be upset once he realized they were gone, a reluctant Madeleine climbed into her husband's new, white Packard.

The couple drove a few blocks in silence when Sumner abruptly pulled to the side of the road and stopped the car.

"What's wrong?"

"Why did you think I murdered your aunt?"

"I thought you weren't going to let it bother you?"

"Well, it does. How could you think that of me?"

"There were things you said, and your mother told me you wanted to kill Aunt Mary when you came back from Santa Paula. Then I found the picture in your drawer."

"What did I say?"

"There were things you started to say, and I thought you caught yourself before revealing something incriminating. I guess, in a way, I didn't mind so much if you did it."

"How can you say that? Do you honestly believe I could murder your aunt and pretend nothing happened? I thought we were honest with each other? Why didn't you ask me about it? No wonder you were so frantic when the police questioned me. You thought they had their man, and it was me!"

"It's not as if you never believed anything bad about me. Don't be so self-righteous."

"I've never believed anything bad about you."

"You're not being honest, Sumner. You believed I was crazy. Sometimes I think you still do."

"Where do you get these ideas?"

"So, you never worried about my competency? Not even in the beginning? Not even the first time we went to Santa Paula and visited the baby's grave?"

"Well, I—"

"It's all right, Sumner. I don't care. I know I'm not crazy or at least not crazier than the average person. And there have been times when I was abundantly happy Aunt Mary was gone. Before Adam was born and I thought they might take you away, I would have considered killing her myself if she wasn't already dead. I may never get over the bad feelings I have toward her, but I'm trying. It's not a good thing, but I thought you more heroic for having killed her. That might be shocking, but it's true."

Sumner was stunned at this admission. "There's something else, Maddie, something you're keeping from me. You said you knew the picture was in the box. How did you know? I thought you never found the box."

Madeleine took a deep breath. She revealed more than she intended. "Why did you think Mary sent me away?"

"She found out we were together so she sent you packing."

"That's not the reason, Sumner. I decided to come to you, do as you asked and leave for Venice. When I went to use one of Aunt Mary's old pieces of luggage, I found the box. She caught me looking through the contents. She couldn't have me knowing what was inside."

"Why, what was there?"

"Newspaper clippings, letters, medical reports she forged through the years, the picture and my birth certificate." At this Madeleine put her hand on Sumner's arm. "I'm ashamed of what was in the box."

"It doesn't matter to me. Nothing you could say would make the slightest difference."

Madeleine took a deep breath. "Mary was not my aunt. She was my mother. She had a youthful affair with an older man, a man of some influence. I was a source of income from him. I was nothing to her, Sumner, only a way to make money. The few advantages I had, education, my art—were all due to Jem."

"Don't you want to contact your father? Is he alive?"

"I believe he is, but he never cared about me. He only wanted to keep me a quiet little secret. He paid Mary handsomely to keep me shut away. Why would I want anything to do with him?

"Sometimes I wonder if I'm an evil person like

my parents. I fear something deep inside me, which I can't control, will become apparent as time goes on. I found the Bible passage from the sermon last week quite distressing. 'For a good tree bringeth not forth corrupt fruit; neither doth a corrupt tree bring forth good fruit.'"

Sumner drew her into his arms. "Maddie, there's not an evil bone in your body. I don't think you have anything to worry about. Why didn't you tell me this before?"

"I'm ashamed, so ashamed. What can I say when Adam asks about my parents, about where his other grandparents are?"

"You can tell him they died when you were small. Those people gave you life, but they were never parents. You won't be lying."

They sat in silence, considering Maddie's revelations.

"I'm glad this is out in the open, aren't you?" Sumner asked. "Isn't it a relief?"

"You don't think less of me for this?"

"It's nothing you can help, Maddie. I'm glad you told me. I need to thank you."

"For what? Believing you murdered Aunt Mary?"

"No. Because from the day I met you, you changed my life completely."

"And that's a good thing?"

"Very good. The best. I feel like the happiest man alive. You redeemed me. But you need to thank me too."

"I do?"

"Yes. Because I rescued you, as well."

"When? Are you talking about the mountain lion?"

"When I first found you in Ojai. I rescued you with mad passionate love."

Madeleine laughed. "Leave it to a man to believe that."

"It's true. If not for our night together, you'd still be dressed in black hiding behind your widow's veil. I changed your life."

Madeleine seriously replied, "You make me happy, Sumner. I feel so fortunate. I can't believe you still love me."

Sumner decided it best to change the subject. "You understand my intention for this evening, don't you?"

"No."

"We went to this event two years ago and were at odds. I contemplated how fun it would be to return and dance the night away while enjoying each other's company. Let's go and have the party we deserve!"

Madeleine looked adoringly into her husband's face. She knew he saw her as a complete person, no longer a pretty façade. They became incredibly close since their move to the beach house—best friends, confidants and lovers. Now Sumner knew her last secret and didn't care. Well, almost her last secret. She planned to surprise him at midnight—there would be a new baby in 1928.

Before starting the engine, Sumner kissed his beautiful wife. They had a date at the Crystal Ballroom he was not about to miss.

* * *

Walter Randall sat in the corner of the New Year's party at the hotel where he was staying. As he nursed his "coffee" along, he contemplated the irony of a man of his prominence finding anonymity amidst the noise and commotion of a raucous band of revelers. He managed to do just that.

Staring at the couple in the midst of the dance floor, he was unable to take his eyes from the beautiful woman in the gold beaded dress who looked exactly like his mother. He would have recognized her anywhere.

Damn Mary Crawford, the lying bitch. Suddenly, Walter chuckled to himself. He should have married that woman. She was the only person he ever met who gave him a run for his money. Instead, he cautiously married the milquetoast Theodora with her fine family connections and Victorian attitudes. The woman failed to provide him an heir and was nothing but a thorn in his side since the day they married. He plotted his revenge against Theodora carefully.

The only thing Mary had to do to ensure the success of his scheme was keep his daughter alive. She failed him in the end. Perhaps he should not have become so enraged when she asked for a final payment, meant to quiet the couple who allowed the girl to die. He never understood how those people discovered he was Madeleine's father, but perhaps it was only a ruse on Mary's part to extract money. That woman would always remain a delightful enigma.

It was too easy to find people to do one's bidding. A little money could buy anything—fine chefs, policemen, executives, politicians, murderers, it was all the same to him. When he learned of Madeleine's death, he was devastated his carefully-planned revenge could no longer be accomplished. His scheme to leave everything to the retarded girl and cut his wife out of his will was not to be once Mary failed him.

Now he could see she lied about the girl's mental capacity. He watched carefully as his daughter put her hand on her husband's neck and whispered in his ear as the band played the first song of 1928. She must have revealed some delightful secret. The man's reaction seemed extreme as he hugged and kissed her—inappropriate for such a public place. He certainly skimped on his wife's wedding ring, a modest gold band. Walter briefly imagined the man was not well off, but the couple's clothing and Madeleine's other jewelry belied this idea.

Most of all, he longed to hear his daughter's voice and assure himself of her intellect. Perhaps it was not too late to construct a new plot against Theodora. He needed time to plan.

Rising from the corner table, Mr. Randall had a word with the concierge, pointing out the woman in the gold dress and slipping him a few bills before exiting the ballroom into the promenade. He was content to let his imagination run wild. It was too long since there was anything worthwhile to dream about.

About the Author

Author Jean Jegel lives with her husband, Carl, in Santa Clarita, a suburb of Los Angeles County. A lifelong Californian dedicated to marriage, raising three children and working for the Man, Jean now enjoys quilting, gardening, sewing, reading and, of course, writing.

California as it used to be serves as Jean's inspiration and the background for her vintage romantic novels. Love of research is the catalyst for the rich details of historical eras she portrays. Visit www.jeanjegel.com for book excerpts, giveaway information, Jean's blog and the latest news. Come home to a simpler time and fall in love.

Works by Jean Jegel

Truer Beauty

By Light of Day

A Keepsake Love

Catching Nettie Gordon

A Home on Carroll Avenue

What Money Can't Buy
　　Book One—The New Saleslady
　　Book Two—Family Ties
　　Book Three—Character
　　Book Four—Brotherhood
　　Book Five—Trust
　　Book Six—Love